The story, all names, characters, and incidents portrayed in this production are fictitious. No identification with actual persons (living or deceased), places, buildings, and products is intended or should be inferred.

Book Cover by Duey Vee

First edition, 2025

Beneath the Eagle's Shadow

An Alternative History Thriller

CM Grant

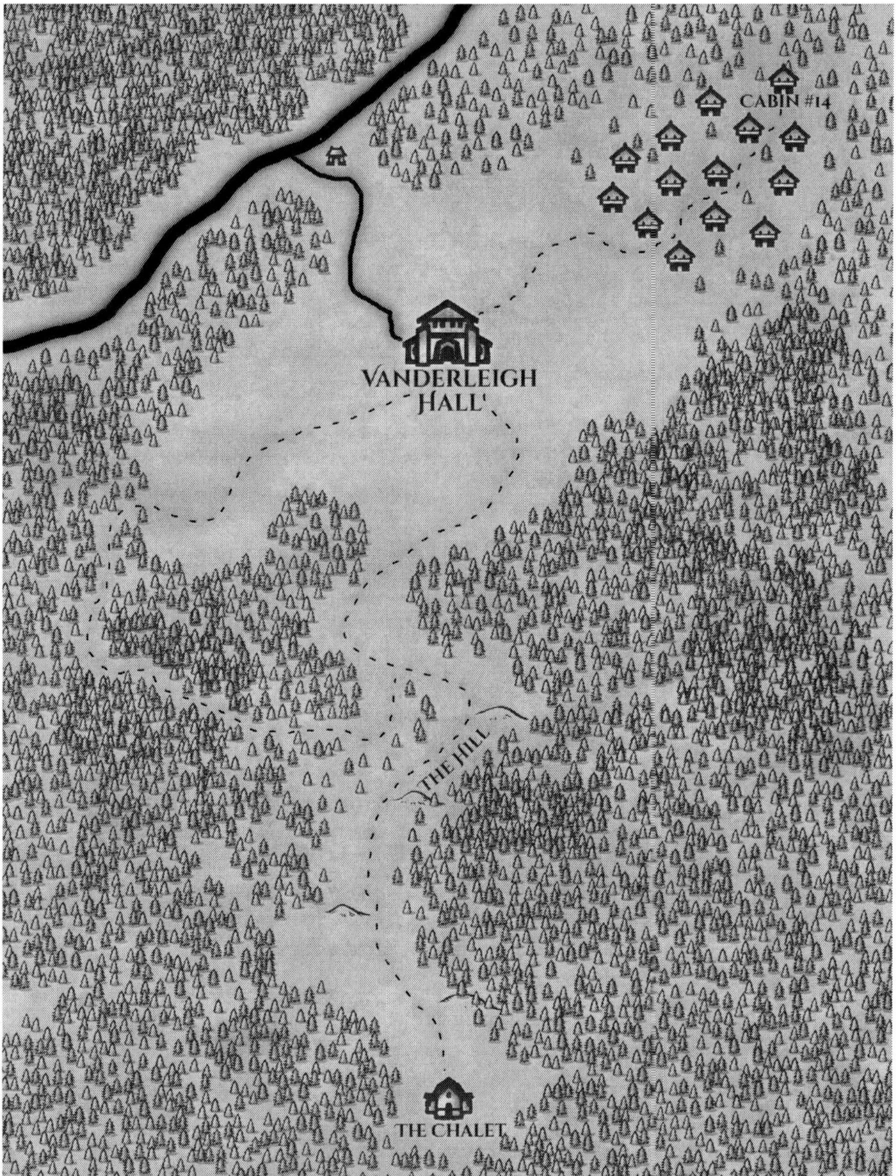
CABIN #14
VANDERLEIGH HALL
THE HILL
THE CHALET

For my family; every night you let me disappear into words instead of sleep.
I couldn't have done this without you.

Prologue

The Letter

Wednesday, November 17, 1937
Albany, New York

The bread was stale, the ham too salty, and the cheese barely passable. Edward Campbell forced it down. His stomach twisted, but chewing gave him something to focus on—anything but the weight of the folded envelope in his breast pocket.

The words were only ink on paper—but if the wrong eyes saw them, he was a dead man.

Edward had traced the edges of the letter so often that his thumb wore them soft and frayed. Touching it—a nervous habit to confirm it was still there—eased the burden. For a moment, it made him forget he was carrying something that could get him killed.

He couldn't help but picture himself—like the faces splashed across the papers, marked as dissident, traitor, or spy—strung up in front of the Monument.

With a trembling hand, he sipped from his chipped porcelain cup. The coffee was better—stronger than expected. Coffee made from real beans was rare now, especially since the regime's tariffs had choked off trade.

Setting the cup down, Edward shifted and nudged his horn-rimmed glasses up his nose. The pressure of Yankee eyes bore down on him—watching, judging—as if they already knew the names sealed in his jacket.

Outside, the sky over Albany's warehouse district hung low and heavy, an ominous grey slab threatening a downpour. A drizzle had slicked the sidewalks while the last stubborn leaves of autumn clung to the trees—muted yellows and oranges, dulled by dampness.

Pedestrians hurried past the window, heads down, collars turned up, hats gripped tight against the wind. A streetcar rattled by, its wheels hissing along the wet tracks.

The diner was half-full, a mix of travellers awaiting their departures and locals resigned to having nowhere to go. Their conversations hummed gently, blending with the clink of cutlery and the occasional hiss from the coffee machine.

A few tables over, four men laughed. It wasn't the sound of camaraderie. Their presence wasn't casual. It was a statement.

They wore silver-grey uniforms, eagle-and-lightning insignias stitched above their breast pockets, catching the diner's dim light. One gestured—palm down, arm outstretched—a motion that once meant nothing. Now, it carried weight. His companions chuckled, boots planted wide, their posture more ownership than presence.

Once, they'd been dockworkers, shoemakers, factory hands. Now they drew paychecks from the state as enforcers, hired thugs who kept the peace through fear and the heaviness of the batons hanging at their sides.

Not police. Just a reminder of how far this nation had fallen.

Edward forced his gaze back to the novel beside his plate. His ink-stained fingers held the book open, shuddering, though his eyes only skimmed the words.

Seated in the final booth overlooking Broadway, he leaned against the worn leather. The thin padding let the wood press into his shoulder blades.

Remnants of dead insects smeared the bay window beside him, while the glow of streetlights warped against the rain-streaked glass.

He checked his watch—7:13 PM.

Twenty-two minutes.

Not enough time...and too much.

Drumming his fingers on the table's edge, he stopped, realizing what he was doing.

Blend in. Stay still.

The revolver pressed against his shoulder, snug beneath his coat. It seemed wrong, foreign. When they first offered it, he refused. But after enough insistence, he relented.

Now, he wasn't sure if it made him safer or put him in more danger.

His hand drifted to the leather suitcase beside him, tracing its worn edges. Once, that had been enough to steady him. There was a time when the suitcase was all the reassurance he needed—back when travel was just business, and cities like Albany still felt immense.

For years, Edward would arrive in towns like this, reintroduce himself to people he'd met three times before, cut the deals, shake hands, handle his affairs, and move on.

That's why Henshaw believed he was the right man.

"You're invisible, Edward. That's what we need."

A background role never bothered him. The limelight wasn't for him; he happily left it to others. His focus was entirely on completing the task.

"Leave the glory for others, Eddie. Campbells always get the job done."

His father's voice still echoed.

Albany should have felt routine—another stop, another job. But the envelope pressed against his chest weighed heavier than the revolver in his coat.

7:15 PM. Twenty minutes.

He'd carried messages before, more in recent months than he had in years—but this one was different. Names. He didn't know what Henshaw would do with them, but Edward needed to know he got them.

Edward sipped his coffee and lit a cigarette. The tobacco was off—harsh and dry, like all Yankee cigarettes—nothing like the smooth blends from back home.

Americans prided themselves on self-reliance, cutting themselves off from the world. But everything just got worse.

He took another drag. The first inhale had steadied him. The second did nothing for the pit in his gut.

His fingers stilled on the suitcase, gripping the leather tighter than he realized.

Scanning the room, the smoke curling from his lips, his gaze drifted over the other patrons.

He shifted in his seat—his belly pressed tight against the table; too many nights in diners and hotel bars had left a roundness in his middle. Marg said she loved it, but he figured she only said that to make him feel better.

Everything appeared normal, yet Edward's pulse quickened, his skin prickling.

The feeling had been growing for a while. Maybe it was paranoia. Or perhaps it was just how the world shifted—slowly at first, then all at once.

The counter stretched along the left wall at the diner's far end. A waitress wiped at a spill in slow, deliberate circles, her eyes surveying the room for refills.

Or watching for something else?

Behind the counter, a large portrait dominated the wall, where a menu board or clock might've once hung. President Nathaniel Beauregard Vale gazed down at the room, blue eyes sharp and unblinking—the icy stare of a man used to obedience.

Vale looked like a classic American hero—square jaw, broad shoulders, hair parted with military precision. A football star. A war hero. Or a dictator.

He wore a stiff, tailored navy uniform against a painted farmland. The eagle-and-lightning insignia gleamed on his chest—inescapable now, plastered across newspapers, government buildings, and diners like this one.

Edward glanced away sharply, jaw tightening. That damned portrait had become inescapable, always watching. He blinked and looked down at his coffee.

Something was off.

Two men lingered at the counter, too focused. Too patient.

They studied the menu with feigned interest, as if quietly debating whether to have ham and cheese or bacon, but their attention was elsewhere.

One glanced at the waitress—a practiced move, casual enough to sell the act.

She wiped at the counter, her rag moving in slow, careful circles. She wasn't looking at Edward. Not exactly. But when she turned to the coffee machine, her gaze darted to his booth. Quick, precise.

Not curiosity. Something else. A mark. A quiet confirmation.

The men didn't call her over. They didn't need to. She'd already done her part.

Edward raised his cup, eyes flicking back to the book pinned under trembling fingers. He could feel their gaze brushing the edge of his vision.

A slow, even breath. *Keep it steady. Don't rush.*

His heartbeat battered in his ears, fast and uneven.

The men stood. Too stiffly—years of standing at attention had left their mark. They weren't here for coffee. The menu was a prop.

Their gazes swept the room with purpose, then settled on him.

With deliberate calm, Edward drained the bitter brew. His hand quivered as he bit off one last piece of the stale sandwich. He stubbed out the cigarette, ash smearing across the porcelain.

Slowly standing, he forced steadiness into each motion. First, he slid the book into his suitcase's front pocket, adjusted his coat, put on his fedora, and lifted the bag.

That's when it happened.

As he dragged the case across the table, the empty cup snagged on the edge, tipped over, and spun off.

It shattered on the floor with a sharp crack.

The diner stilled.

A dozen heads turned. Conversations faltered, then died.

Edward swallowed hard as dozens of eyes pinned him in place. He stood frozen above the broken cup. His mouth opened—some excuse, some apology—but nothing came.

Move.

Ignoring the stares, he adjusted his coat, grabbed the suitcase, and made for the back hallway.

Even strides. Don't rush. Just keep moving. *Don't look back.*

He looked back.

The menus were gone. So was the pretense. The men watched him, sharp-eyed, like foxes in a henhouse.

Stumbling into the hallway, muttering, "Excuse me" as he brushed past a table of startled patrons.

At the men's room door, his fingers fumbled at the handle. He slipped inside and closed the door after him.

The lock clicked.

Only then did he breathe.

Leaning against the door, he gasped for breath, as if disappearing had freed something within.

What now? How to get out?

The cramped space had thick air with ammonia and damp tile—just enough room to stand, piss, and stare at yourself in the mirror.

The toilet sat ahead, rust staining the porcelain where the tank met the bowl. To the left, a narrow sink jutted from the wall beneath a cracked, yellowed mirror.

A small rectangular window was high on the wall above the toilet. Grime fogged its glass, and it looked like it could swing open wide enough to squeeze through.

But it would have to do.

Edward climbed onto the toilet, shoes slipping on the wet porcelain. He braced against the wall and shoved the window outward. Rusted hinges groaned.

A gust of cold, wet air rushed in, carrying the metallic scent of rain and asphalt. Below, the alley stretched into darkness—slick pavement, deep shadows, nowhere to hide.

Boots clicked in the hallway.

Edward froze. His breath caught.

The doorknob jiggled. A knock—sharp, deliberate. No hesitation. The sound vibrated through the room.

He pushed the case through the window. It landed in the alley with a soft thud.

The handle rattled again. The hinges groaned.

Edward took a breath and hoisted himself up, shoulders scraping the walls as he wriggled into place. His legs trembled.

"Is there a window in there?" A muffled voice came through the door.

He froze. Listened—nothing—just his heart, pounding like a bass drum in a Harlem club.

"Yes," said a woman, calm and clear. "It goes to the back alley."

Silence.

"He's gone out the back."

Booted feet thundered down the hallway. The doorframe shook. They weren't being subtle anymore.

Edward froze, pulse racing. No turning back.

Forcing his legs into the window opening, his hands scraped the metal frame, then stopped. His belly caught on the sill. Too many easy meals. Half out, half in—jammed like a letter in a mailbox.

The door behind him slammed again.

No more time.

With a desperate push, Edward lurched free.

He hit the pavement. Hard. Pain exploded in his ankle as it twisted beneath him.

A sharp gasp escaped. Pain flared up in his leg, white-hot and blinding. He bit down hard, swallowing curses his mother wouldn't have approved of.

Grimacing, he hauled the case off the pavement, breath ragged as he scanned the alley. The streetlamp at the far end cast jagged shadows on the wet brick.

Beyond it, the city carried on, unaware. People rushed by, umbrellas whipping in the wind, footsteps muffled by the rain.

Turning right, he hobbled forward. Every step spiked pain up his leg. But he didn't slow.

He couldn't.

At Hudson, he ducked around the corner, lifting his collar and pulling his brim low. He dared a glance back.

A shadow climbed through the window carefully.

Edward sucked in a breath. Not much time. His fingers brushed against the folded letter. The ink still held the burden of truth. If it reached the right hands, it could change everything.

He glanced at his watch—7:22 PM.

Thirteen minutes.

Rain dripped from his hat's brim. Indecision rooted him.

Across the street, the United States Post Office loomed, golden light spilling onto wet pavement. A few more steps, a drop in the slot, and it'd be out of his hands.

But that would take time.

His eyes flicked down Broadway, where the train station rose in the distance.

Assume he proceeded to the station, boarded the train, and returned home. Marg would be waiting. Beef and potatoes. A warm fire. Laughter. Maybe a game or two of rummy. A nice, quiet night.

He'd be done. He'd hand-deliver the letter to Henshaw and tell him this was it.

No more.

But the agent's approach crawled up his spine.

His father's voice echoed, gruff and steady: "Sometimes getting on base is smarter than swinging for the fences."

One meant safety—the other, certainty.

Edward's jaw clenched. The rain stung his eyes as he stared between the train station and the post office, the suitcase heavy in his grip. The train was warmth, home, and safety. But the post office was the entire mission.

The letter was more than just ink and paper—it was his chance to make this right.

He turned, hobbling as fast as his twisted ankle allowed.

At the post office doors, he hesitated. Too much light. Too exposed.

He glanced over his shoulder, his eyes searching for the agent. But he saw only pedestrians, collars drawn with their umbrellas snapping in the rain.

No sign of them. Yet.

He stepped inside.

The underlying sterile scent filled the air.

The lobby was larger than he remembered. Bold red, white, and blue banners replaced the old murals and civic plaques, and massive American flags draped from the ceiling.

Not patriotic, but oppressive.

A portrait—the same one from the diner, but grander, more imperial—dominated the far wall. Nathaniel Beauregard Vale stared down in oil and authority, blue eyes following every movement, every transaction.

The usual postal slogans were gone. In their place hung new mantras:

"Loyalty First. Strength Through Unity."
"A Nation, One Voice, One Leader."
"Security Starts With You: Report All Subversive Activity."

A sign above the counter read:

MAIL SUBJECT TO SCREENING FOR NATIONAL SECURITY PURPOSES.

A uniformed officer—not a postal worker, but Eagle Guard—stood by the entrance, arms folded. He wasn't checking anyone, but he didn't have to.

His presence said enough.

Edward moved forward, stride steady. Controlled. The postage had already been paid—no delays, no questions.

He had written the letter hours ago, sealed in quiet desperation. He pulled it from his pocket. The damp paper was soft at the edges, worn from his fingers—one last look.

A breath.

Then, into the box. The hollow clink as it landed sent a jolt of relief through him.

It had to reach Henshaw. The Senator would know what to do. He always knew.

Rain slapped his face as he stepped outside. He pulled his collar high, warmed by a flicker of hope.

His eyes flicked to his wrist—7:26 PM.

Nine minutes.

Nine minutes to make a seven-minute walk on a busted ankle.

And he couldn't be late. Not now.

Not when there was one thing he could count on: the trains ran on time these days.

He crossed the post office lobby and exited onto Green Street, looping back toward Broadway.

Head down. Collar high. Hat pulled low. The crowd surged around him—shoes splashing, voices muffled in the rain. He tried to disappear. But his uneven gait betrayed him. He was as out of place as a banker in a breadline.

Each step flared with pain, but he pressed on. Block by block.

The station loomed ahead; the lights were hazy in the drizzle.

Don't look back.

The urge clawed at him. Every instinct screamed: head down, keep moving.

But he looked.

Fifty feet back—a man, broad as a bull, pushing through the crowd. Fast. Focused. Hunting. His eyes swept the street. Then locked on Edward.

Edward's stomach twisted, bile rising sharply in his throat.

Shit.

Another curse under his breath—one his mother would've scrubbed from his mouth. But there was no time for manners.

His pace quickened, despite the fire in his ankle. He gripped the case tightly. Hobbling toward Broadway, breath ragged, each step stabbed up his leg.

The station neared—a beacon in the storm. But the closer it came, the heavier the dread in his chest.

They'd seen him. And that bull of a man wasn't slowing down.

Even if Edward reached the train, even if he boarded—it wouldn't matter.

They'd stop the train.

Somewhere north of Albany, officers would be waiting, ready to search every car, every passenger, every piece of luggage.

They'd find him.

His mouth drew tight. The case dragged at his side, a weight that once reassured now only slowed him.

It wasn't protection anymore—it was a liability.

He eyed the station. So close. Rain blurred its glow.

There had to be another way.

He veered into the alley on the right. The stench of wet brick and garbage hit him like a slap. He crouched, dropped to one knee, and flipped open the suitcase. Inside, tucked among papers and files, were a dark blue wool overcoat and a tweed flat cap.

He slipped on the coat. Its damp weight settled like armour. He tossed the fedora behind a rusted dumpster. The overcoat, too. Crumpled, forgotten against the bricks.

The flat cap sat low over his eyes. He adjusted the collar, then checked his reflection in the wet metal of the dumpster.

Not perfect. But good enough.

He lifted the case once more, now lighter, and turned toward the alley entrance—then stopped.

The man was there. Thick, broad-shouldered. Built like a wrestler. He filled the exit like a brick wall, his plain grey wool suit clinging to his frame.

The automatic pistol in his hand stayed dry. Steady. Aimed straight at Edward.

"Not quick enough, Canuck."

He swallowed hard but kept his face blank. "I don't know what you're talking about."

The man stepped forward, boots splashing through shallow puddles. His smirk was cold. Practiced.

"If you're the best they've got..." He let it hang, shaking his head. "You'll all be done in a week."

Edward lifted his chin, rain tracing the line of his jaw. The trembling in his hand had stopped.

He reached slowly toward his jacket. "Do you mind if I have a cigarette, Yank?"

The agent raised an eyebrow.

"Go on, Canuck. You've got time for one more."

He lifted the cigarette to his lips, rain mingling with sweat. "Might as well," he said, voice calm. "Can't hurt, right?"

His other hand moved. Fast. Not for the cigarette.

For the revolver beneath his coat.

But the agent moved faster. A sharp crack split the air as Edward pulled the gun free.

Pain tore through his ribs—hot, immediate, blinding.

Edward fired—a wild shot. It went wide, sparked off the brick.

The American's second bullet took him in the chest.

He staggered.

Marg's face. Her laugh. Cards in her hands. He would miss that.

His knees buckled. The suitcase slipped from his grip, hitting the ground with a dull thud. He gasped, vision swimming, rain and streetlights swirling as the agent's shadow loomed over him.

The letter. It was in the box. Still out there—still a chance.

A bitter laugh escaped, blood flecking his teeth with the taste of iron.

It needed to reach him. Those lines of ink. Those names...

Another shot cracked through the rain, colder, decisive.

Edward's gaze drifted upward, rain spattering his cheeks. In the distance, a train whistle echoed—a lonely, mournful sound swallowed by the city.

Streetlights wavered, dimming as darkness crept inward.

But somewhere, the letter remained—ink on paper, a flicker in the storm.

Hope. Fragile as a butterfly's wing. But still out there.

CHAPTER I

RESERVATIONS

"WAR MEASURES ACT EXPANDED: 'NATIONAL SECURITY ABOVE ALL,' CABINET DECLARES"
—*THE GLOBE*, MAY 15, 1935

"In response to growing instability abroad and subversive activities at home, the government has announced sweeping new powers to protect the Dominion from external threats."

Wednesday, December 1, 1937
Twenty Miles Outside Ottawa, Ontario — Afternoon

The train rattled along the tracks, the steady vibration now as familiar to Henry as the route itself. Outside, frozen fields stretched beneath a pale winter sky, the afternoon sun already sinking toward the horizon.

The *Toronto Star* lay crumpled beside him; its pages creased from the eight-hour ride from Toronto. He picked it up again, scanning the headlines he'd already read.

Japanese forces took Nanjing. A Belgian plane crash. The first Governor General's Awards. And speculation about Lord Halifax's trip to Germany—dismissed by Chamberlain as "entirely private and unofficial."

Henry snorted. Still playing at peace, the British. Pretending the world would right itself. Sure—and Santa Claus was real, too.

He flipped the page.

The American Protection Act had passed. Order, unity, the removal of "subversives." The first protest in Washington drew thousands. The second ended in blood. Officials claimed federal agents had been ambushed, but the truth was simpler—dozens of dead, hundreds imprisoned. A message that echoed from coast to coast.

There was no third protest.

Henry took a long draw of his Player's Navy Cut, a thin ribbon of smoke drifting from his lips. It was inevitable, he thought. Soon they'd be selling souvenir postcards of the executions.

At the bottom of the page, an article about an American infantry division's winter exercises in upstate New York. Routine maneuvers, the reporter claimed—training for the cold. Henry reread the lines, then folded the paper shut.

The Ontario landscape blurred past. Frost edged the window glass, ghostly condensation thickening with every mile. Ottawa was close now.

He stood, stretching the stiffness from his back. First-class seats were comfortable enough but built for shorter men. His suit pulled across his chest as he reached for the chair's corner, knuckles still raw from a few rounds at Kit's Boxing in Toronto.

The far door banged open. A blast of cold air followed a middle-aged man in a grey wool suit. Black fedora dripping meltwater, eyes sweeping the car—not idly, but with the deliberate focus of a man who liked to know exactly who he was dealing with.

His gaze found Henry.

A broad smile spread across his face.

"Henry Locke!" he called, striding forward, hand outstretched.

The voice was clipped, precise—Ottawa-born, no doubt. Government type. The sort who measured words in dollars and cents and switched between English and French without missing a beat.

Henry gave him a quick once-over: sharp wool suit, polished shoes, handshake already halfway out—finance man. Henry had met a hundred like him. If he'd earned a nickel for each one, he could've bought the Senators outright—maybe the whole damn league.

Still, he took the hand. It never paid to be rude to a man who already knew your name.

"Number 15," the man said, like reading a hockey card. "Right wing, twenty-one to twenty-eight?"

Henry offered the polite, well-worn smile he kept for strangers who remembered him better than he remembered himself. "That's me. Back when they still printed our names in the papers."

"Damn shame about the Senators," the man said, leaning against the seat. "The Bust turned everything upside down. But you boys ran the league back then."

Henry nodded, watching the winter scenery blur past. "Yeah. Tough times all around."

"You ever miss those days? Must've been something—the dames, the fame."

Henry shrugged. "Good times, sure."

The man grinned knowingly. "If it wasn't for the war, I think I could've made it."

Ah, there it is.

Henry gave the expected nod. "Not an easy road. A lot of bruises, broken bones—things that never heal right."

The man wasn't listening. His eyes shone with his own memories. "I was the best at my alma mater. Could lift the puck like nobody's business."

Henry leaned back, resigned to the ritual. Another man, another story—always the same, always exaggerated.

The conversation limped on until a porter called, "Next stop, Ottawa Union Station! Ten minutes!"

The man shook Henry's hand again, rattled off a forgettable name, and moved on.

Henry watched him go. These conversations were rarer now—not since that big kid from New Brunswick started making waves with the Leafs.

He lit another cigarette, the match flaring briefly before the smoke thinned into the air. It wasn't bad, going unnoticed. Not these days.

Henry stepped off the train, fedora in one hand, suitcase in the other. The cold hit like a slap—sharp, bracing, unwelcome. Coal smoke, damp wool, stale cigarettes—Ottawa in winter.

The Toronto–Ottawa run had once been a constant pulse—politicians, bankers, men with places to be. Now the rhythm was slower, leaner. The Bust had made sure of that.

He joined the stream of passengers toward the exit—businessmen, clerks, civil servants, a few working men in worn coats. No one spared him a glance.

In the concourse, half a dozen militia stood by the doors in drab green, Enfields on their shoulders. Some were barely out of school; others were old enough to know better. The Canadian Jobs Act had swelled their ranks. They didn't check papers—they just stood as a quiet show for a nervous public.

The station doors opened onto Rideau Street, the wind cutting through his coat. Streetcars rattled by. Taxis idled, drivers watching the spill of passengers.

Across the street, the Château Laurier loomed—turrets dusted with snow, windows glowing gold. Warmth, discretion, deals best made out of earshot.

Henry drew a last drag, flicked the butt into the slush, and crossed.

Inside, the air smelled of cigars, brandy, and old money: dark wood panelling, chandeliers, leather chairs. The Bust hadn't touched this place. He made for the reception desk—only to be intercepted.

Short, pencil-thin moustache, buggy brown eyes, and a crooked smile that put Henry on edge.

"Hank! How was the train ride in?" Jimmy. Constantly scanning the room, calculating. His charm was easy, but his gaze never stayed still.

Henry's nostrils flarerd. He hated *Hank.* Jimmy didn't care.

"Did you see the news about Halifax? We might win some royals."

Henry forced a grin. "Jimmy. Good to see you." He kept it casual. "Let me get my bags upstairs first. We'll grab a drink in the bar."

Jimmy nodded, but leaned closer, voice dropping to a conspiratorial murmur. "Listen, Hank—this Halifax situation could be the big news we've been waiting for. This is where things might turn."

Henry exhaled slowly. *Of course, it was.*

He didn't give two dimes what the royals did. A few monarchists shaking hands wouldn't fix what was happening in the streets. As long as he was warm, fed, and had a roof overhead, that was enough. Truth be told, he had more than enough in the bank, a good coat on his back, and a bed that wasn't shared with rats. That already put him miles ahead of most.

He hefted his suitcase, offering just enough of a smile to keep things moving.

"I'm not sure, Jimmy. But here's to hoping." He had practiced the words, making them sound almost sincere. He turned, the grin slipping from his face the moment Jimmy couldn't see it.

At the front desk, the woman greeted him with a practiced smile. Her eyes drifted from his coat to his boots, then back again—her smile deepening.

He couldn't tell if she was sizing up his wallet or something else. He wasn't in the mood. But he wouldn't say no.

He gave her his name and a tight smile, leaning on the counter.

Check-in was quick. Probably the wallet.

He took his key, collected his bag, and turned toward the stairs. He wanted a shave, a shower, and a month of sleep. But he knew better.

Sleep meant dreams.

Dreams brought ghosts.

He eyed the elevator but was too restless after hours on the train. He climbed.

At the top, his legs ached—but it felt good. Proof he was still alive.

The room was plain. No frills. Just how he liked it. He unpacked by habit: an extra suit, a knit sweater, trousers, three shirts, underthings, socks. On the nightstand next to his Player's, a straight razor lay amongst a flask, a leather notebook, and the *Toronto Star* in the case's side pocket.

Pack light. Keep moving. That had been the rule in the Pros. Still was.

Voices drifted through the walls. Distant. Hushed. Plans were being made that would never see ink.

Henry unpacked in silence. The room felt too large. Too empty.

He splashed water onto his face. A touch found the scar under his jaw—same spot, every time—a high stick from varsity. The reflection showed grey eyes—his father's eyes. Still disapproving.

His temples had gone salt-and-pepper. They used to be black.

Turning from the mirror, he dried his hands and rubbed the back of his neck. Then he slumped into the deep chair by the window overlooking the frozen canal.

The sun had set. Snow had softened the edges of the city. Streetlamps painted gold streaks across the ice—a view tourists called beautiful.

Henry felt nothing but cold.

A familiar chill crept up his spine—the kind he only got staring over at a city buried in snow.

No Man's Land.

He closed his eyes for a moment too long.

The whistle of shells. Cordite. Mud. A boy with eyes like his, clutching his guts like he could hold his entrails in.

His eyes shot open. The hotel room ceiling loomed above him. His breath quickened.

Twenty years gone, and it still lived in his bones.

He inhaled deeply. His fingers gripped the arms of the chair.

A moment passed. Then, it was gone.

He rubbed his face and glanced toward the shower. Hot water. Steam coiling toward the ceiling. Tempting.

But then what?

Sit. Listen to the radiator hum. Let the ghosts get comfortable?

No.

He shrugged back into his coat, slid the Navy Cuts into his pocket, and headed for the lobby.

Jimmy sat at the bar, waving Henry over as he came down the stairs.

Subtlety had never been Jimmy's strong suit. He thrived on attention—always chasing it and finding a way to make the room orbit him.

The lounge was half full—a mix of familiar faces from newspaper clippings and others he didn't recognize. It didn't make them less important. If anything, it meant the opposite.

Henry moved through the haze of cigar smoke, past deep-cushioned lounges and waitresses in tight-fitted blouses.

Conversation buzzed—low, urgent, brittle.

He passed a table of Parliament men—Commons and Senate alike—leaning close over their drinks.

"...stop speaking madness—Chamberlain won't allow war..."

"...Hitler wants a fight. That's the game..."

"...what are we to do with the build-up on our own border?"

Henry heard the last line and glanced over, but the speaker's eyes were already elsewhere. He took the stool beside Jimmy and ordered a Seagram's V.O.

Jimmy rested against the bar, scanning the room like a man surveying his kingdom. The stink of whisky clung to him—sharp, sour. He'd been here for a while.

"Look at these bastards," he said, louder than Henry liked. "Plotting and scheming—all for the good of the Empire."

Henry sipped his rye, letting the burn settle before lighting a Player's. Smoke curled between them. "Sometimes it's better not to be heard, Jimmy," he murmured.

"Bugger that." Jimmy turned, voice rising. "These fools put the Brits first. North America comes first."

Henry exhaled, watching the smoke rise. "Careful. That 'North' can fall off easily."

Jimmy scowled, lighting a cigarette of his own.

"Dammit, Hank." He shook his head, drawing deep like it was the last cigarette he'd ever get. He always burned through them quickly. "The Yanks have the right idea, and you know it. You've seen what they've done to this country." He jerked his chin toward the room. "Bread lines. No work. Meanwhile, foreigners walk in and take what's left. It's time we got out from under them."

Henry's foot tapped beneath the table. "It's not about getting out from under," he said. "It's about who we align ourselves with."

Jimmy huffed, flicking ash into the tray between them.

"Always cautious with you, Hank."

Henry didn't answer. He took another drink, watching Jimmy's fingers tighten around his glass.

Jimmy squinted at him through the smoke. "You haven't heard yet, have you?"

Henry's glass paused halfway to his lips. He didn't look over. "Heard what?"

Jimmy leaned in, voice dropping. "Heard where the boss is going this weekend."

That was new. A shift in routine. Something was happening.

Henry sipped again, letting the words settle. "You're the one in the know, Jimmy. I go where I'm told."

Jimmy snorted, but his eyes had already drifted.

A blonde waitress wove through the lounge, and Jimmy's gaze followed her—lazy, unfocused.

Henry let him stare. Jimmy was too loose. Too loud. Too much to drink.

"Yeah," Jimmy muttered, still watching the waitress disappear behind the kitchen door. "I don't know why the boss doesn't tell you things."

Henry shrugged, studying the rye in his glass.

"Don't advisors know these kinds of things?" Jimmy added, turning back.

Henry smirked. "I'm just a guy in a suit, Jimmy. Could be anybody—so long as I'm someone he wants to be seen with."

Jimmy snorted. "That's not what the boss says. He says you've got good eyes."

Henry tilted his head, amused. "He does, does he?"

He leaned back as Jimmy's eyes returned to the waitress. The room shrank. The air thickened.

Wherever the boss was going, it wouldn't be anywhere safe.

"Mr. Locke?"

Henry turned. The bartender stood across from him, drying his hands with a rag.

"That's me."

"Phone call for you, sir. In the back."

Knocking back the rest of his drink, Henry stubbed out his cigarette. "I'll be right back."

Jimmy waved him off without looking. "Always something about you, Hank."

"Harry."

Only old friends called him that.

Henry adjusted the receiver, fingers tightening slightly around the cord. "How'd you know I was in town?"

"You know how this works," the voice said—steady, even.

A subtle stretching of his vowels betrayed years away from home, but Henry caught it—that slow Maritime lilt—where men didn't waste words or rush them.

A beat. Then, almost offhand:

"You're at the same hotel, drinking a Seagram's V.O. Am I wrong?"

Henry's jaw clenched. "You've always had an excellent memory."

"Knowledge, Harry. It's useful to have. You should try it."

Henry let the silence stretch. The voice never gave a name—but it didn't need to.

"What can I do for you?"

"Dinner. The usual place." A momentary silence. "It's been a while. We should catch up."

"I've got plans."

"Break them."

Henry's jaw tightened. "I'll see what I can do."

"Half an hour."

A pause. The unspoken expectation hung in the air.

"We have reservations."

The line went dead.

Henry rolled the cigarette between his fingers. He pressed his lips into a tight line.

He'd expected the call.

That didn't make it any easier.

Maybe a part of him had hoped it wouldn't come after all.

Chapter II

Orders are Orders

"GERMAN-JAPANESE PACT SIGNED: AMERICA CONGRATU-LATES 'LIKE-MINDED ALLIES'"
—*The Toronto Star*, November 27, 1936

"In a statement from the White House, President-Elect Vale praised the pact, calling it a step toward global stability and a rejection of 'old world decay.' British and Canadian officials have yet to comment."

Wednesday, December 1, 1937
Downtown Ottawa, Ontario—Evening.

The streetcar screeched to a stop. Henry stepped off, careful to avoid a frozen puddle of unknown depth. He pulled up the collar of his overcoat and flexed his fingers inside his leather gloves, adjusting them against the cold.

Along the sidewalks, men in tailored wool coats and women in fur-lined cloaks moved briskly toward warmer destinations. Laughter and conversation spilled from cafe doorways, mingling with the scent of cigar smoke and the subtle metallic tang of snow in the air.

Across town, squatters huddled around burning trash barrels—two sides of the same city, divided by more than just distance.

The ride hadn't been long, only a few blocks, but the wind had teeth tonight, and Henry had no interest in arriving with a face chapped and raw from the cold.

Ahead, the Rideau Club loomed—a fortress of power wrapped in red brick and limestone, its stonework softened by fresh snow. The glow of gas lamps flickered beneath the portico, casting long shadows over the uniformed doorman, who stood steadfast despite the chill. A cluster of men lingered beneath the awning, their conversation low, their words lost beneath the hiss of cigarette smoke drifting into the night.

Inside, Ottawa's actual business took place. Cabinet ministers and industrialists traded influence over brandy. Military men murmured about European rearmament between courses. No one debated secrets in Parliament, but they were traded here.

Henry stood outside, staring up at the windows. He hesitated.

A knock in the rain. She stood in the cold, soaked and shaking. Raised voices. Yelling. Pleading. Crying. Unheard. A door slammed shut.

Memory. Guilt.

He exhaled and stepped forward.

The broad-shouldered doorman inclined his head and waved him through.

Immediately, the warmth hit him, starkly contrasting with the biting cold outside. The air was thick with cigar smoke, aged whisky, and the faint polish of mahogany and leather.

The Rideau Club was old money; every inch of its interior ensured you knew it. Heavy oak panelling lined the walls, interrupted by oil paintings of long-dead politicians and admirals, their gazes stern beneath the light from ornate brass wall sconces. The ceiling, adorned with intricate plaster mouldings, loomed high above the grand chandeliers, which cast a flickering light over Persian rugs and dark walnut floors.

To the left, the smoking lounge was already filling with men in custom-made three-piece suits, their low voices blending into the soft hum. The occasional clink of a tumbler against crystal broke through the conversation, followed by murmurs of trade deals, defence spending, and political maneuvering.

Further in, the grand dining room stretched out—a sea of white tablecloths, pressed silver, and gleaming china. Waiters in starched jackets moved efficiently between tables, pouring deep amber scotch into waiting glasses while discreetly avoiding eavesdropping on conversations they had no business overhearing.

The club had no music, no idle chatter—only business.

Henry unbuttoned his coat, shaking off the last cold traces before entering.

One of the waiters appeared at his side and gave a subtle acknowledgment. Without a word, he led Henry through the main dining hall, past polished mahogany doors and quiet, murmured conversations. The route was familiar, yet it felt different each time, like stepping deeper into the country's engine room.

Near the back of the club, the waiter paused at an unassuming door, opened it, and gestured for Henry to enter.

Although modest by Rideau Club standards, the room remained refined. Dark wood panelling, a heavy brass chandelier, and a single mahogany table set for two. But what struck Henry was the lack of ceremony—this wasn't a dining room. Deals and meaningful decisions were made in the room behind closed doors.

And at the table, sitting alone, was the man who had summoned him.

Senator Callum Henshaw didn't rise. He never did. His authority wasn't in titles or gestures but in the way he sat—weight forward, eyes steady—as if testing the strength of a beam. The grey wool suit was typical of him: Halifax cloth, Ottawa stitching. Practical. Plain. A suit to work in, not to impress in. The balding crown and ring of greying hair framed a round, firm face that could almost look soft—until the eyes fixed on you. Steady, unflinching, surveyor's eyes that measured before you spoke.

Compact, built for work, not grandeur. Each morning he rowed the Ottawa River, forearms and legs like steel cables. The kind who outlasted younger men without breaking stride. A grinder. Always had been. No wasted motion. No wasted words. You didn't come to Henshaw expecting small talk. You came to be tested.

Henry shut the door behind him, stepped forward, and slid into the chair opposite. The silence between them was familiar.

Then, without preamble, Henshaw spoke. "Tell me everything."

Blunt. Direct. He was always the same. It had rubbed plenty of men the wrong way over the years. But Henry was used to it.

The bottle of Seagram's was already on the table. Two glasses, neither touched. A silent offer. A quiet expectation.

Henry pulled his Player's from his pocket, tapping one loose. He let it dangle between his lips as he struck a match, the flickering glow briefly illuminating the deep lines in Henshaw's face.

"He's in town." Henry blew out a slow stream of smoke, resting the cigarette between his fingers. "Only for a few days. Meetings with the usual Members and Senators."

The first time Henry had said as much, months ago, Henshaw hadn't flinched. No protest. No surprise. Now was no different. His silence stretched, unreadable as ever.

His voice cut through the smoke: 'This weekend. The itinerary?

Henry swirled the whisky in his glass, watching how the amber liquid clung to the sides before taking a deliberate sip. He let the burn settle before answering.

"I don't know." A pause. "Jimmy hinted at something, but he hasn't told me all the details."

Henshaw didn't blink. He didn't sip his drink. Just absorbed. "Why not?"

Henry frowned, weighing his words. "Hard to say. I think he's getting suspicious." He tapped ash from his cigarette. "Time might be up."

Henshaw's expression didn't change, but the atmosphere did—a flicker of tension. "It can't be." His brow twitched, just enough to notice. "Not yet. The rivets aren't even set."

Henry smirked faintly, the kind that never reached his eyes. He took another sip, rolling the whisky on his tongue before swallowing. "Always pushing."

"This weekend." Henshaw leaned forward just slightly. "There's a meeting. Upstate New York. You're going." His voice was quiet but firm. No hesitation.

Henry studied him for a long moment, his fingers absently tracing the rim of his glass. The words weren't a request. They never were.

"I need you listening," Henshaw added.

Henry let out a long breath and stubbed out his cigarette. Of course, he did.

"Listening to who, exactly?"

Henshaw reclined, exhaling for the first time since the conversation started. He sipped his Scotch, ice clinking against the glass.

The silence stretched.

A knock at the door.

A moment later, the waiter stepped inside and set down steaming plates of steak, leeks, and potatoes rich with butter and char.

As the door clicked shut behind the departing waiter, Henshaw inclined—not to speak, but to eat. Meticulous. Assured. Like everything else he did.

Henry understood it was best to remain silent during this part of the meeting. Instead, he cut into the steak, the knife sliding clean through the tender cut. The first bite was rich and seared to perfection, the crisp edges of the potatoes balancing the salt of the butter. It had been a while since he'd been at the Rideau, but the food was as exquisite as ever.

The meal unfolded in silence, a wordless understanding between them. Only after Henry finished his last bite did he lean back in his chair, swirling the remnant of his whisky.

Henshaw pushed his plate away, wiping the corner of his mouth with his napkin.

"I received a letter."

Henry glanced up. The senator was never one for small talk—if he was bringing this up now, it mattered.

"A list of invitees to a getaway." Henshaw let the words settle.

Henry leaned forward. It wasn't often that the senator hesitated when speaking his mind.

"This list held some unexpected names," Henshaw said, his gaze sharp. "Including your employer."

"This weekend, I assume."

Henshaw nodded. "Indeed. The list contained the usual suspects—William Pelley, Charles Coughlin, Gerald Smith."

Henry nodded thoughtfully, considering the names. No surprises there. Familiar names. Southern names. In recent years, Redfern had been more closely associated with that particular type.

And in his ears, those warnings—shouted in the rain—echoed again.

"But then we have Joachim von Ribbentrop, Otto Dietrich..." Henshaw paused, letting the names settle. "Are you seeing the connection?"

Henry sat in silence, rolling the names through his mind. The pieces slid into place.

"Last year," Henry said, a look of concentration on his face. "The Rome-Berlin Axis. You think the Yanks are trying to formalize something?"

Henshaw gave a slow, deliberate nod. "I think they're carving up the world, and I want someone I trust in that room when they do."

Henry's head tilted as he gave a slight nod. "And I suppose that someone is me."

"Of course it is." He shook his head. "That place will be buttoned up. You know that. No one's getting in who shouldn't be."

Henshaw took a slow sip of his Scotch, unbothered. "Your boss is on the list. And he always enjoys bringing his eyes with him."

Henry swallowed, his mouth suddenly dry. He frowned.

A shadow crossed Henshaw's face. His next words came quietly, almost flat.

"The man who passed me that list did so at great personal risk." He met Henry's gaze, unwavering. "I need to make sure it wasn't for nothing."

Henry reclined, dragging a hand over his face. Then, he reached for his cigarette case, his fingers trembling slightly as he tapped one free. "I can't," he said, lifting the cigarette to his lips. "It's too risky."

"You can. And it's not riskier than what you're already doing." Henshaw's voice remained even and unshaken. "I'm not asking for miracles. Just proof. Something tangible. It is imperative that we find out, Harry."

Henry shook his head as he raised a palm. "Look, Senator, I've slipped you his movements, let you know who he talks to. I know that he's on your list for a reason. Every day, he leans closer to Berlin."

Henry inhaled a drag of his cigarette, exhaling the smoke through his nose. "And I've played my part. But this? This is different."

Henry tapped his cigarette ash into the tray on the table as he lowered his voice. "Nazis in the room? Christ, Henshaw. That's not politics. That's suicide."

Henshaw cupped his glass, turning it slowly in his hand. "Look, you're going anyway. You understand that backing out now would raise suspicion."

He paused. Letting the words take hold.

"You're the only one who can get into that room—and walk out again," Henshaw said, his eyes locking onto Henry's. "Every ship needs a keel, Harry. You're mine on this."

Henry took a slow breath, his gaze drifting to the mahogany-panelled ceiling and the chandelier that swayed ever so slightly with the weight of the building. The warmth of the rye lingered in his throat, but it did nothing to quiet the knot tightening in his gut.

"I won't give you the 'For King and Country' speech," Henshaw said, gesturing to the Red Ensign hanging beneath the portrait of King George VI. "You and I are pragmatic men."

He set his glass down with a soft clink.

"The Yanks are making a move. And it's not good. I want you in that room, Harry. I need your eyes."

"You're talking about men who shape nations, not just bank accounts. If they suspect me—"

"Then don't get caught. Or do nothing and let them shape the world in their image, while we sit and watch."

Henry ran a hand through his hair.

He could refuse. Walk away. But then what? They would still watch him. Redfern. The Yanks. The bastards in Berlin—everybody felt the effects of this game.

A ghost at his door. Pleading in the dark. Begging him to stop. To walk away. He hadn't. And now, there was no one left to blame but himself.

Henry ran his tongue over his teeth, staring past Henshaw, past the dark wood panels, past everything. "Dammit." He exhaled, meeting the Senator's gaze. "What exactly do you need?"

Henshaw reclined, reaching for his scotch. "Something iron. Riveted fast. Before they stop pretending."

CHAPTER III

BITTER TASTE

"LOUISIANA DECLARES 'PROTECTION ZONES' FOR RELOCATION OF UNDESIRABLES"
—*THE CHICAGO TRIBUNE*, JULY 6, 1937

"A new initiative to restore order in the South, these designated areas will provide labor opportunities for vagrants and foreign agitators. Officials dismiss comparisons to European policies."

Wednesday, December 1, 1937
Chateau Laurier (Ottawa, Ontario)—Late Evening

Snow fell in lazy spirals, lit by streetlights like tiny dancing figures. The sidewalks were less crowded because the businessmen were at home or having after-work drinks. Ottawa's bustling evening crowd had quieted, replaced by the hush of falling snow and a distant streetcar.

The silence left too much room for thought.

Henshaw had made it sound easy—so simple, sitting in the warmth of the Rideau Club, whisky in hand, insulated by mahogany and leather. But out in the bitter December night, its weight settled in.

For the next few days, he'd keep his back to the wall and wonder who else had him in their sights. That hard reality cut deeper than the wind ever could. He pulled his coat tighter. The chill never left him.

Not since Passchendaele. Rain, mud, filth—a graveyard of half-drowned men, swallowed by muck. Hands frozen stiff, reaching for help—for anything but the icy embrace of Flanders' winter.

Dead eyes.

Robbie.

He grimaced. Why now? Twenty years carrying that weight. A name. A face. One that would never grow old.

He shook the memories loose.

The walk to the Laurier wasn't long, but he had almost convinced himself he'd pushed the face from his mind when he reached the hotel's grand entrance.

Inside, the reception area still buzzed. Late as it was, the Laurier never truly slept. Businessmen huddled in corners over brandy, bellhops darted between guests, and the hum of quiet conversations layered beneath the scent of cigars and polished wood.

Henry fought a yawn as he stepped into the elevator car. Usually, he took the stairs—habit, instinct—but exhaustion weighed on him like lead. For once, he took the easy way up. He gave the elevator operator a nod, murmuring his floor.

When the doors slid open, he stepped out, fumbling for his key.

Then he saw the figure waiting outside his door.

Vic Lafleur wasn't tall or broad, but in the dim glow of the hallway sconces, he loomed.

Henry had met his share of dangerous men in the war and the Pros—the ones with a tell—a flicker in the eyes before they did something stupid or violent.

Vic didn't have a tell. Vic always looked like that. As if he were stuck in a cage, fists clenched around the bars, waiting for the door to open.

"Locke. The Boss wants to talk to you."

Henry swallowed the urge to tell him it could wait until morning. All he wanted was to collapse until the maid dragged him out.

Instead, he sighed and squared his shoulders. "I'm guessing it can't wait, eh, Vic?"

The man didn't answer. Just arched an eyebrow and motioned for Henry to lead the way.

James Redfern always took the Presidential Suite when he stayed at the Laurier.

Henry already knew where he'd be.

James Redfern was old money. He had his hands in banking, newspapers, and lumber. But the press—that was his kingdom.

"Control the press, control the people."

That was his mantra. And he lived by it.

He was slick—a man who never rushed, never worried, never let the world see a crack. Nearing fifty, he could have passed for thirty—sharp, confident, unbothered. A man who'd never begged for anything in his life.

Narrow-waisted, athletic, impeccably groomed. His moustache—razor-thin and precise—was never out of place. His suits, never off-the-rack, came from the finest tailors in London and New York, each one cut to enhance his presence.

He was the man men envied and women desired.

The massive suite occupied a prime corner of the Château, its tall bay windows overlooking Parliament Hill and the mouth of the Rideau Canal. A hand-woven Persian rug stretched across the floor, rich blues and golds glowing beneath art déco sconces. Crystal decanters stood sentinel on a polished mahogany sideboard. The fireplace crackled faintly. Trimmed in deep green marble, its warmth added to the illusion of effortless comfort.

Behind the monolithic oak desk, Redfern sat, papers stacked neatly before him, scanning them with the detached ease of a man used to shaping reality with ink and influence.

As Henry entered, Redfern stood, smooth as ever, his broad smile effortless, practiced.

It was hard to see Redfern and not see a ghost in the rain. He kept his hands at his sides. He'd gotten used to that.

"Harry!" His voice was warm, designed to put a man at ease. Designed for effect. "Glad to see you. I know it's only been a week, but my god, man—when you're not around, it's like I'm half-blind."

He gestured to the liquor cabinet.

Henry crossed the room, poured himself a Seagram's, and fixed Redfern a Chivas Regal—Henshaw's brand—dropping in a few ice cubes for good measure.

"Tell me, how was the ride in? Trains can be tedious—but the right company makes all the difference." Leaning on the desk, Redfern gave Henry a knowing wink.

Henry handed him the glass and smirked. "Nothing worth writing home about. I was alone."

Redfern laughed low, swirling the Scotch. "Not that you'd admit it if it were otherwise. You do like your secrets, Harry."

Henry let the Seagram's touch his tongue but said nothing. Not all secrets were worth sharing. Some carried shadows you couldn't shake.

"Speaking of secrets..." Redfern lifted his glass, eyes gleaming over the rim. "Poor Jimmy. He hates drinking alone." Henry set the tumbler down and reached for his Player's, habit more than need—but stopped at Redfern's look, the faint shadow of disapproval.

Right. The Führer didn't smoke. Neither did his admirers.

"Yeah," Henry said, sliding the cigarette between his lips anyway. "An old friend heard I was in town."

He lit up, inhaled slowly, then let the smoke drift between them.

Redfern's eyes flicked to the cigarette, his lip tightening at the corner. He swirled the drink in his hand, the amber liquid catching the light. A slow sip. "News of your arrival travels fast."

Henry smirked faintly. "It's Ottawa. Not a big town. Easy to spot a familiar face. And I lived here for a few years."

This time, Redfern only smiled, raising his glass. "You can say that again." He took a slower sip and leaned back with a satisfied sigh. "Damn, fine Scotch."

A pause—just long enough for Henry to almost lower his guard.

"Listen, I know I've been working you hard lately." Redfern set the glass between them and slowly spun it on the desk. "Deals to broker, hands to shake—lots of moving parts. You've been running from one end of the country to the other." He met Henry's eyes. The smile was still there, but tighter now. "Christmas is coming up. You should take some time off. Paid, of course."

Henry blinked. *That... was unexpected.*

"You deserve a break," Redfern said, turning to face the window, looking out across at Parliament. "Relax. Clear your head. I'll have Jimmy handle the New York trip."

There it was.

He said it pleasantly, as if the matter was already decided.

Henry took another drag, letting the smoke cover the flicker of unease in his chest. He tapped ash into the tray, exhaling slowly.

"Generous of you."

Redfern flashed a grin. "Always."

Henry shifted. "What's this New York trip?" He aimed for nonchalance, but his voice carried a little too much interest.

Redfern tilted his head. One brow rose. The grin didn't fade. "Looking the gift horse in the mouth, are we, Harry?"

Henry held his gaze.

Redfern gave a tight-lipped smile—more smirk than laugh. "Enjoy your time off."

Dismissal. As clear as if he'd waved Henry out the door.

Henry swallowed hard, a tightness in his throat like the cinch of a noose.

Henry stood outside his door, the key hovering above the lock.

His shoulders ached, his legs dragged, but his mind wouldn't settle. The words from earlier circled like wolves, their teeth sinking deeper with every pass. He hadn't even had the chance to fail—Redfern had cut him out before he could begin.

He should take it as a sign. Walk away. Sleep for a week. Tomorrow, catch the first train home. Drop by his parents' place. Baby Emma was probably teetering by now, her brothers standing guard like little sentries. Maybe his mother would fuss. Maybe she wouldn't. But for a moment, he could pretend she would. His father would shake his hand. And for a while, he'd be nothing more than a son, an uncle... a brother—the one who came home.

No plots. No shadows. No men behind closed doors, carving up the world like meat.

But down the hallway, behind every closed door, came the murmur of voices—conversations you weren't meant to hear.

The echo of her face lingered, one streaked with tears. Why hadn't he seen then what he saw now?

The ghosts surrounded him.

His fingers tightened around the key. His jaw locked. Then he slid it back into his pocket.

He couldn't let this go.

Downstairs, the lobby had thinned out. The air still carried the weight of cigar smoke and brandy, but the number of suits had dwindled. The conversations relaxed, and men who began the evening discussing business now drifted into gossip, old war stories, or the easy laughter that followed some drinks.

Henry settled into a leather lounge chair near the bar, angling himself so his back was against the wall. From here, he could watch the room. The entrances. The exits. Let himself think.

The waitress—Jimmy's fixation from earlier—appeared at his side, not quite meeting his eye as she took his order.

"Tonic water. Ice."

She nodded, disappearing toward the bar.

Henry let himself sink into the chair, but his thoughts kept turning. The bar, the lobby, the lingering suits—all background noise. He tuned them out.

When the glass clinked onto the table, cold against his fingers, he barely looked up. His gaze had drifted instead to the cleaner making her way across the marble floor, pushing a cart heavy with supplies.

The rhythm of work—the steady motions of someone who had a job to do and did it without overthinking. Wiping counters, scrubbing floors, and disappearing briefly into a washroom before emerging again, the cleaner moved from one surface to the next. The faint chemical bite of cleaning solution filled the air as the mop swished, and water pooled.

A busy job, but a necessary one.

His fingers traced the rim of his glass.

He could walk away. Be done with it—Redfern, Henshaw, all of it. The compensation was handsome, and having consistent employment was invaluable given the current circumstances.

But the politics... the politics were wearing thin.

He might have once believed in what men like Redfern preached. Now, it was all noise. All bluster.

He read the papers. He saw what was happening south of the border, across the ocean in the Reich.

It didn't take a genius to see where it was heading.

He could get out. Find something else. He had connections. It wouldn't pay as well, but it'd be honest—or at least honest enough. And maybe, just maybe, he'd be able to sleep without wondering which side of history he was standing on.

"Hank!"

The shout cut through the lobby like a knife, loud enough to turn a few heads.

Henry looked up as Jimmy barrelled toward him, stumbling and nearly wiping out a side table.

"Hank, you son of a bitch," Jimmy slurred, his words rolling together in a thick, boozy drawl. He collapsed into the chair across from him, missing the armrest on the first try. "Stood me up. Grabbed your coat, hit the road—nothin' but a 'see ya later, Jimmy.'"

Leave it to Jimmy.

The last damn thing Henry wanted to deal with right now. Henry's fingers clenched as he bit back the retort itching at the back of his throat and forced the practiced smile.

"Sorry, Jimmy. Old friends, you know how it is." He offered a shrug, like the excuse hadn't just been thrown together. "Only in town a couple of nights. They wanted to catch up."

Jimmy snorted, slouching against the armrest. "Left me high and dry, Hank," he said, letting his head roll back. "Drinking alone. Like some washed-up sap."

Henry wet his throat, gaze never leaving Jimmy. "I'll make it up to you."

Jimmy's bleary eyes drifted toward Henry's glass, squinting at the clear liquid. His nose wrinkled.

"What the hell is that?" he said, blinking slowly. "You sick or somethin'?"

He waved to the waitress, slumping forward like a man trying to remember how his arms worked.

"Well, whatever. You can start by getting the next round."

The waitress approached, moving with the practiced weariness of someone who'd been dealing with men like Jimmy all night. Her focus stayed on Henry.

"Another tonic?" She asked, her gaze lingering.

"No," Jimmy cut in before Henry could answer, flashing a sloppy grin. "He's getting another Seagram's on the rocks and an Old Fashioned for me." He slapped the table, then smirked. "On his tab, of course."

The waitress's face gave nothing away. She nodded once, then turned and walked back to the dimly lit bar, the echo of glasses clinking in the background.

Nearby, a group of sharply dressed suits rose from their seats, laughter trailing behind them as they made their way toward the exit. Their voices faded, leaving Henry and Jimmy alone in their corner.

Jimmy leaned in, grinning, his breath thick with whisky.

"You're gonna miss out on a good time," he slurred, his eyes glinting, whether from the drink or excitement. "Serious players, Hank. The real deal. Not the amateurs. This is the big show."

Henry rubbed his chin, gauging him. "You told Redfern."

Jimmy squinted at him, head lolling to the side. "Y'know, Hank... always so careful."

Henry raised an eyebrow. "Yeah? That a bad thing?"

Jimmy tapped the side of his glass, his gaze slow and unfocused. "Most guys? They drink; they talk. You? You just listen."

Henry shrugged, taking a slow sip of his drink. "You think I should be more like you?"

Jimmy grinned, lopsided. "Ain't sayin' that. Just sayin'... Redfern don't hire men he can't read."

Henry tilted his glass toward him, letting the ice shift. "Seems you got it all figured out, Jimmy."

Jimmy let out a lazy chuckle, shaking his head. "Listen. It's like you played poker in another life. I don't know what you're thinking, ever. And that's scary." His expression flickered—something between amusement and something else, something unreadable. "But Redfern's smarter than us."

Henry said nothing. He just watched as the bartender finished their drinks and the waitress crossed the now almost empty bar, tray steady in one hand.

She set them down with practiced precision, careful not to linger too close to Jimmy.

"Last call is in a couple," she said, her voice measured, polite but firm. "If you need another round, just give a wave. I'll be around."

Jimmy inclined backwards, his gaze trailing after her — slow, deliberate.

"You sure will," he said, eyes lingering on her like a wolf watching a rabbit.

Henry felt his jaw tighten.

As she wandered back to the bar, Jimmy pushed himself to his feet, wobbling before steadying.

He gave Henry a faint smile. "Gotta hit the head."

He turned the wrong way.

Straight toward the waitress.

Fuck.

Henry fumbled for his cigarettes, knocking the matchbook to the floor. With a steadying breath, he bent down, retrieved it, and struck a match with a hand that wasn't as steady as he'd have liked. The flare of the flame lit up the worn lines of his fingers before he lifted the cigarette to his lips.

The bar had become sparse, reduced to the last stragglers nursing their drinks or waiting for some final, unspoken reason to leave. Across the room, Jimmy was talking with animated gestures, swaying as he tried to charm the waitress, who was still, with little success, trying to peel herself away. He was too drunk or too stubborn to notice.

Henry's eyes shifted, landing on the cleaning woman as she moved methodically over the floor, the wet mop sliding in broad, practiced strokes. The scent of ammonia hung faintly in the air.

A young porter in a crisp, starched uniform approached her, his pace brisk.

"Hilda, there's a mess in the men's room off the lobby," he said in a hushed but urgent tone. "Looks like someone did a real number on it."

Henry didn't need to guess who.

Jimmy.

"This needs to be cleaned up right away," the porter said, already turning to leave.

The woman let out a long-suffering sigh, gripping the handle of her mop a little tighter before pushing her cart toward the restroom. Henry watched her go, his attention flicking to the contents of the cart—bottles of cleaner, rags, ammonia, brushes—all neatly arranged in the subdued light.

He took a slow drag of his cigarette, exhaling through his nose.

Then, just for a moment, he let his thoughts wander.

They were onto him. That much was clear.

Push Redfern any further, and he'd end up with a bullet in the back of the head. The safest bet was to take the out, leave town, let it all go.

And yet, he wasn't on that train.

Henry's gaze drifted back to the cleaning cart.

He stood, stretching his back and rolling his shoulders. His fingers brushed the rim of the tumbler's glass as he picked it up, idly turning it between them. Just another drink in hand, nothing more. Jimmy had finally staggered off in the right direction, leaving the waitress in peace.

Henry wandered into the lobby, walking with feigned nonchalance. Passing by, he received only a cursory glance from the receptionist. Overhead, the chandeliers hummed, cutlery clinked distantly from the restaurant—the last sounds of a hotel settling down for the night.

Tucked near the corner, with its bottles of chemicals neatly lined up, sat the cleaning cart.

Henry slowed, fingers trailing along the edge as he scanned the near-empty chamber.

He palmed the ammonia, twisting the cap just enough. A thimble of liquid into the glass—just enough. Enough to ruin Jimmy's night. A few miserable hours wrapped around a toilet.

But not enough to end him.

Never that. Not again.

Jimmy would be fine.

Henry resealed the bottle, set it back, and kept walking. No hesitation. No second glance.

Just a man stretching his legs.

When he returned to his seat, the tumbler was right where he had left it.

A moment later, Jimmy stumbled back from the washroom, still grinning. "Miss me?"

The tumbler sat between them, the ice shifting in the dim light.

Jimmy reached for his drink.

Henry exhaled.

CHAPTER IV

MAKE IT COUNT

"ENEMY WITHIN: SUBVERSIVES ARRESTED ACROSS THE UNITED STATES"
—*THE MONTREAL GAZETTE*, AUGUST 3, 1937

"Authorities in the United States confirm a coordinated crackdown on foreign agitators and domestic radicals. 'This is not a purge,' an official assured reporters, 'but a necessity for national security.'"

Thursday, December 2nd, 1937
Chateau Laurier (Ottawa, Ontario)—Morning

The water was hot enough to scald, but not enough to erase the memories of the night before. Sleep hadn't helped either. He'd lain awake, staring at the ceiling, exhaustion deep in his bones—but rest never came.

Had he done the right thing? He'd tried to tell himself it was justified. That action had been necessary. He couldn't fold his hand before the cards were dealt.

But that wasn't true, was it?

Jimmy had been reckless before. But this—this was something else. Something worse.

Henry had fought in a war. Thrown punches in back alleys. Laid men out on the ice with his shoulder in their ribs. He had bled. He had made others bleed.

And yet—this was different.

This wasn't shooting at an enemy in Passchendaele's cold, rotten mud. It wasn't a clean hit into the boards. It wasn't a fist connecting with the face of a man who saw it coming.

This was poisoning someone who never had a chance to defend himself.

He hoped Jimmy would be alright.

And yet, he hoped Jimmy wouldn't be well enough to go.

A scratch caught in his throat, and he coughed, rubbing a hand over his face. He looked out the window. He still didn't know what he was going to do.

But he knew what he had done.

He turned off the tap. Let the cold air wrap around him. He hated the cold.

Stepping out of the shower, he grabbed a towel from the shelf and wiped himself down. His muscles ached, stiff from tension that sleep couldn't fix. He was tired. Bone-tired.

Reaching for his suitcase on the rack, he gripped the handle. And hesitated.

The handle felt... wrong. Wrong enough to register. He lifted it. *Too light. Too new. Too... off.*

He'd been using the same set for over ten years, since his playing days. If it wasn't broken, why fix it?

But this one? It was identical. Same style. Same scuffs. Only... shinier. Almost too perfect.

He set it on the bed. Took a breath. Henry lifted the lid.

Everything was there. His clothes were as he had packed them. The same shirts. The same tags.

And yet.

Something wasn't right. The suitcase seemed shallower.

He emptied it onto the bed, one item at a time, until the case was bare. Not his. He was sure of that now. The weight still nagged at him. Subtle, but there.

Henry ran his fingers along the seams, pressing, prying. Feeling for what his instincts already recognized was present.

A ridge. A shift. He found the edge.

He pried the false bottom up.

Nestled in the shallow compartment, secured in carved-out notches to keep them from shifting, lay a compact M1911 Automatic. Beside it, a small camera, a pouch of two extra magazines, and a thick roll of American bills bound tight with an elastic—fives, tens, and twenties, enough to buy silence or passage.

At the top of it all, a folded slip of paper.

No signature. No pleasantries. Three words on paper.

Make it count.

It was a command, not a suggestion. Henry's expression tightened as his thumb brushed the pistol's grip—a weapon he hoped he wouldn't have to use. Henshaw wasn't one for sentiment; the message wasn't a warning. It wasn't encouragement.

It was an expectation.

Henry closed the suitcase, pressing the false bottom back into place. He still didn't know if he was even going.

But it sure as hell felt like everyone else did.

Henry strode to the reception desk and checked out of his room. He leaned against the polished wooden counter, the faint aroma of brewed coffee wafting through the air. The receptionist—a prim woman with neatly pinned hair—flipped open a thick ledger, her fountain pen scratching as she recorded his departure with practiced efficiency. Numbers flowed across the page in crisp ink, each stroke deliberate, each column meticulously aligned.

Redfern had already paid the bill. His house account covered the expenses without question. Without limits. Henry didn't need to see the total. He could imagine it: the numbers stacking up, the zeroes trailing off.

With a nod, he turned away, moving through the lobby with the unhurried confidence of someone who belonged. Henry settled into a lounge chair in the corner, which gave him a perfect view of the elevators and the stairs. He stretched out, casual but aware, monitoring things without seeming to.

A waitress appeared as if summoned by an unseen cue, setting a steaming cup of coffee before him. She lingered for a second, waiting for something—a glance, a word. Henry gave her nothing. She melted back into the background, unnoticed, unremembered.

He looked around, lifting the coffee to his lips. Bitter. Hot. Exactly what he needed.

Over the cup, he saw her.

She wasn't simply moving—she was approaching. Deliberate. Measured. A woman with purpose. A ripple in the sea of movement, a shift in the smooth flow of businessmen and bellhops.

Dark chestnut curls framed an oval face; her skin was smooth, her eyes intelligent and knowing. Deep brown—the kind that pinned a man in place. She wore a maroon suit tailored to perfection. Double-breasted, pointed lapels, cinched at the waist—commanding without softening.

Henry felt it in his gut—a shift. Not fear. Not exactly. But the kind of jolt when someone says your name and you don't know theirs.

She reached his table and slid into the chair across from him, smooth as a whisper. Her gaze locked onto his—steady, unreadable.

"Henry Locke." His name wasn't a greeting. It was a claim. And just like that, the lobby faded away.

He set his cup down slowly. Whoever she was, she knew him better than he knew her. And that was worse.

"Don't believe we've met." His tone was smooth, flat.

The woman tilted her head, examining him—as if weighing his response. "Ellie Barclay."

His mind ran; the name was there, ringing like a bell. Then it clicked.

"Globe and Mail," he said, the words tasting like ash.

She didn't react, didn't argue, didn't push. Instead, she pulled a small tin of Sweet Caporal cigarettes from her pocket, flipping it open with expert ease. A matchbook followed, its edges worn—the kind collected from dimly lit bars and late-night meetings.

She struck a match. The flare of sulphur cast fleeting shadows across her face as she cupped the flame, leaning in, slow and deliberate, like she had all the time in the world. The cigarette met her lips. A brief inhale. A slow exhale. Smoke drifted lazily between them.

She set the tin and matchbook on the tabletop between them. Her eyes fixed on his.

"A quiet, reserved man. Impossible to crack." The way she said it—it wasn't her opinion. It was a quote. A profile, someone else's words, studied, memorized.

Henry flicked a glance around the lobby. Still no familiar faces. Not from Redfern's circle, anyway. His gaze returned to her, lingering on the tin of Sweet Caporals between them.

He grabbed his coffee.

"That's some scouting report," he said, dry but watchful. A flicker of a smirk. "You working for the Big League, or doing charity work?"

Ellie's smile held, but it didn't reach her eyes. "Journalists have to notice more than how fast a man can skate, Harry."

The name landed like a coin on a silent table. Henry stilled. His gut clenched, and his brow arched before he could stop it. He kept his expression blank, but his eyes narrowed just enough to show he'd noticed. A long second passed.

He drained the last of his coffee. The bitter warmth ignited his throat as he set the cup down.

"Pleasure meeting you." He pushed his chair back, ready to stand.

She leaned back, took another puff of her cigarette, and let the quiet settle. "You're a smart man, Henry. You see the room before you walk into it. They say you read people like a book. The man who knows exactly when to take the shot and when to pass."

She tapped the ashes into the tray, gaze steady. "So, tell me—does Redfern seem like a fellow who knows when to pass?"

Henry glanced around the lobby again. People coming and going. Conversations blurring together. He took his time.

"Redfern is a man who likes his privacy."

A sly grin tugged at the corner of Barclay's lips. "The scouting report was right. Tough nut to crack." She took another slow drag. "I think Redfern's guiding things in a direction that will end poorly for people like us. His leanings are... let's say, a bit too in step with Rome."

Henry's gaze flicked back to her, guarded. "I'm aware of his leanings, Ms. Barclay."

She held his stare, her tone measured. "And do you agree with them?"

Henry met her eyes, unblinking, face neutral. "I agree with the stable income his employment provides."

Ellie let the silence stretch. She flicked ash into the tray, studying him like a gambler watching the table—not for tells, but for weight.

Henry set his coffee down. The cup met the saucer with a quiet clink—no extra movement. No fidgeting. Just the calm, practised stillness of a man capable of holding his ground.

She took another drag and exhaled through her nose. "You're the one whose politics are the question mark. Everyone else in his circle... they're obvious. But you?" Her eyes stayed on his. "You're the enigma. The one who might not be an overt follower."

Henry let the silence hang. His mouth dry, he cleared his throat and leaned back in the chair. "I'm just a man trying to survive."

Ellie's lips curved—not quite a smirk, but something close. She flicked ash into the tray. "Never married. No kids. A good-looking man like you. Why not?"

Tears in the rain. A slammed door. A face never seen again.

Henry's jaw shifted—the only tell. "A lifestyle like mine doesn't make for long-term investments."

"Always on the road," she said, filling in the blanks. "Travelling man. No roots. I thought most ex-players settled down after a life like that. But not you."

Henry's eyes drifted to the lobby windows, following the blur of strangers passing the front doors on Rideau Street.

There'd been a time when it felt possible. A woman who had steadied him. Who had seen the cracks before he did. But that future was gone. Stolen.

"Guess I've just got busy legs."

"A long line of broken hearts, though, I'm sure."

His eye twitched. He took a slow sip of the coffee. "No one's losing sleep over me."

Not anymore.

"Hard to believe," she said, "with that award-winning personality of yours."

"I've got my moments."

He reached for the arms of the chair, but before he could rise, she moved first, leaning in, one hand resting on his forearm, voice low.

"You're walking away, but you know I'm right." Her grip tightened—fingers like steel, eyes like ice. "You've lasted too long to still be blind." She let it hang for a moment. "So what's it going to be, Henry? Watching your step—or already too deep?"

He opened his mouth, then stopped himself. He adjusted his jacket as if the conversation hadn't rattled him. "It's been nice meeting you, Ms. Barclay."

Ellie leaned back slightly, like letting him go had been her idea all along. "This was pleasant. We should do it again."

She reached across—smooth, deliberate. Her fingers brushed his jacket, slipping a card into his breast pocket, just beneath the lapel. A quick, precisely placed pat against his chest. Light. Measured. Possessive.

"If you ever feel like choosing a side—give me a call."

Her smile came easily. But her eyes never stopped watching.

Henry leaned against the cold metal of the streetlight in front of the Château Laurier, observing as the city came alive. The pale morning light glistened across the rooftops, catching in the frost that clung to tram cables and windowpanes. Long shadows stretched across the pavement; the streets were slick with the sheen of last night's freeze.

A streetcar rattled past, its wheels hissing against the steel tracks, while early risers hurried by, their breath misting in the crisp air.

Across the thoroughfare, Ottawa Union Station pulsed with movement—porters hauled luggage, businessmen checked pocket watches, and travellers hurried beneath the station's grand façade, eager to begin their journeys. The crisp morning air carried the scent of wet pavement, coal smoke, and the faint bite of freshly brewed coffee drifting from nearby cafes.

The wind gusted, sharp and biting. Henry held his fedora in place, as men fastened their overcoats and women gripped their skirts against the chill, stepping briskly toward the day ahead.

A figure emerged at his side, stepping into the early morning light.

He carried himself with quiet refinement, moving with a subtle gravity that drew the eye without needing to ask for it. Dark, wavy locks—combed, but never quite tamed. Keen eyes beneath sharp brows, always reading, always calculating. A clean jawline, full lips touched with a knowing smirk, and an intensity that held attention without needing to ask for it. He always seemed a step ahead in conversation.

He wore a pale beige three-piece suit, pressed to perfection, the fabric catching the soft morning light, and a gold watch chain that glinted in the morning sun. A maroon overcoat, rich in colour but understated in design, draped over his shoulders—its deep hue standing out against the grey blue of the waking city.

As he moved, he withdrew a silver cigarette case, tapping it against his palm before selecting one. With a flick of his lighter, the flame flared in the morning air, casting a momentary glow across his face, the smoke drifting around him like a thought not yet spoken.

"Ben," Henry acknowledged, his tone easy. Benjamin Schul didn't look like an accountant, but he was a damn good one.

"Harry," Ben said, studying him. "You hear about Jimmy?"

He shook his head, keeping his face neutral, though his stomach flipped. "Last I saw him, he was three sheets deep."

Ben raised the cigarette to his lips, his gaze lingering. "I guess something didn't agree with him."

Henry ran a hand across his mouth, wiping at a bead of sweat on his upper lip. "Is that so? Not surprised."

Ben looked back up at the Château, as if he could see Jimmy through the hotel walls, then turned toward Henry again. "I guess he's as sick as a whisky bum in July."

Henry studied him, his face carefully blank "Leaves you short."

Ben smirked. "Word is, you're free."

Henry flicked ash from his cigarette. "Tickets booked. Heading home to see the family."

Ben tilted his head, observing him. "Well, that may have to be postponed."

Henry's jaw tightened. Time to act aggrieved. "That right?"

Ben took another drag, nodding. "Jimmy's not gonna make the trip. Redfern wants you back on."

Henry scoffed softly. "No call? No note? Just you and a cigarette?"

Ben smirked. "He's a busy man. You know that."

"Sure," Henry said, removing his fedora and running a hand through his hair. "Just figured if he was cancelling my vacation, he'd have the courtesy to do it himself."

Ben smirked. "Guess I should be grateful you're not the type to argue."

Henry replaced the hat on his head, adjusting it. "I argue plenty. Just know when it ain't worth it."

Ben flicked his cigarette onto the sidewalk, grinding it under his heel. "You don't sound surprised that Jimmy's not making the trip."

Henry shrugged. "Yeah, I mean, I'm not surprised. The way he was putting them back last night? Surprised he's still breathing."

He let the words settle, his face unreadable. Just two men talking. Nothing more.

Ben let out a chuckle. "That bad?"

Henry nodded with a smile. "That bad."

Ben took that in, then shrugged. "Well, either way, Harry. You'd better let your folks know the visit's off."

Henry rolled his jaw, taking that for what it was. "So, where to?"

"You still got your ticket to Montreal?"

Henry nodded.

"Good. We're catching a private rail car from there. Windsor Station. 5 PM Sharp."

Henry arched a brow. "And then?"

Ben's smirk didn't waver. "I don't know. I get the bills after it's all said and done. Jimmy's the one with the itinerary."

Henry took a slow drag from his cigarette, then exhaled, nodding. "Ain't that so?" He looked across the street at the station, examining the exterior. "So, are you on this train?"

"No. The boss and the rest of us are in the next one. An hour behind you."

"Guess I'll see you in Montreal, Ben."

Ben smiled thinly. "Not if I see you first, Harry."

Henry extended his hand, and Ben gripped it firmly. Eyes steady, impossible to read.

Then Henry turned, crossed the street, and didn't look back.

One last drag. A flick into the slush. Smoke curled behind him as the city swallowed him up.

CHAPTER V

NO WAY BACK

"VALE ELECTED IN LANDSLIDE: A NEW DAWN FOR AMERICA"

—*THE AMERICAN TRIBUNE*, NOVEMBER 4, 1936

"With a record-setting majority, Nathaniel Vale has secured an uncontested mandate to restore order, pledging swift action against America's enemies at home and abroad."

Thursday, December 2nd, 1937
Train to Montreal—Late Morning

Henry was always more comfortable on trains than anywhere else. The rolling gait, the rhythmic clack of wheels on steel, the full-throated scream of the whistle—they were steady. Predictable. A man could lose himself in them.

He sat in business class, facing the rear, watching the frozen landscape slide past the window. Snow-laden fields, skeletal trees, the occasional farmhouse buried under winter's grip—it looked like the ride into Ottawa the day before. But it felt heavier now.

Or maybe that weight was just him.

Exhaustion pressed down like a lead blanket. His eyes burned; every blink was a battle to open them again. He should sleep. But he couldn't. Not with the last twenty-four hours clawing at his thoughts.

His fingers found the stiff edge of a card in his breast pocket: Eleanor Barclay, Globe and Mail.

He turned it over, thumb grazing the blank reverse. It was clean and unwritten. His hand twitched. He should tear it in half. Let the pieces scatter under a tramcar. But he didn't. And he wouldn't.

Henry always liked to keep a way out. A door. A window. Some way to slip free before the walls closed in. But this door? He didn't know where it led.

The train jolted on a rough patch of track. He slid the card back into his pocket and smoothed the fabric flat.

Ellie Barclay.

Women like her didn't look at men like him unless they wanted something. That was the way of the world. They looked at men like Redfern. Or men like Ben—if the ones upstairs let them through the door.

Outside, the world rolled by.

The train car door opened, letting in a rush of frigid air and the rhythmic hammering of steel on steel. Henry didn't look up.

The sharp click of heels. A pause. Then, another measured step. Crisp. Deliberate. Too precise for a weary traveller. More like a man accustomed to standing at attention.

Momentarily, the footsteps hesitated just inside the entrance before moving again. A figure slid into the seat across from him. A man, just as Henry had expected.

Nondescript. That was the word for him. Black suit, white starched shirt, plain black tie. Respectable but forgettable—the kind of uniform worn by businessmen, government clerks, and men who needed to be neither seen nor remembered.

The briefcase in his grip looked standard, but the handle told a different story—worn smooth, shaped by habit—of a man who carried it every day, but not carelessly.

Henry watched, pretending not to. The man set his fedora on the seat beside him—not tossed, not dropped, but placed. A deliberate movement. The kind made by men who didn't do things by accident.

The man gave a polite but distant nod before flicking open the brass clasps on his briefcase and peering inside.

Henry returned the nod, just as slowly. The silence suited him just fine.

He adjusted his fedora, pulling the brim low, and let the world slip into darkness.

Maybe for a little while, he'd get some sleep.

If his dreams would let him.

He didn't realize he'd drifted off until the silence broke.

"Tonic water. Lots of ice."

The words were crisp. Precise. But something about them felt… off.

Henry resisted the instinct to lift the fedora from his eyes.

"In a tall glass."

The pause between the phrases. The way it was said. Too measured. Tonic was always served in a tall glass. But this man felt the need to specify.

Henry's fingers twitched against his knee. He stayed still. Listening.

The porter's footsteps receded toward the far end of the car. A brief pause. Then the hiss of the train door opening. A frigid gust swept through the space before the door clicked shut again.

They were alone now.

A silence followed—just long enough to notice.

"I'm sorry if I woke you."

Crisp. Neat. Practised. Like something lifted from a textbook.

Henry lifted the brim of his fedora—only to find the man already watching him.

"No bother," Henry said evenly. "Didn't realize I'd nodded off."

"You snore like a newborn."

Henry studied him, searching for a tell. No smirk. No humour. Just an observation.

The man turned back to his work, unbothered. Henry let his gaze drift downward.

Plans. Schematics. Crisp lines drawn with a steady hand. Not rushed, not carelessly placed. Something industrial—maybe a dam. Or something else.

Still, something about them felt wrong. The angles? The spacing? A word too sharp?

A flicker of movement.

Henry looked up.

The man was watching him. Still. Unreadable. Meeting his gaze without flinching.

Then, smooth as silk, he snapped the briefcase shut. The plans vanished. Locked away before Henry could make sense of them.

Too quick. Too controlled. A cover.

Henry leaned back and turned toward the window. Houses. Trees. Fields. It looked like any other place—but he knew the route well. By his estimation, they were about a quarter of the way there.

The man pulled a book out of his coat pocket. *Gone with the Wind*. Brand new. No creases, no dog-ears. Yet he flipped straight to the middle, as if already deep into it. Or like he wanted Henry to think he was.

Henry glanced at the cover, then back at the man. "Good book?"

The man paused. A beat too long. "Very... American," he said.

Henry nodded. "Haven't had the chance to read it."

A slow, deliberate page turn. The man didn't look up. "You should," he said, his voice flat and neutral.

Henry turned back to the window. Fields blurred past, giving way to snow-covered trees. The landscape had closed in—tight—as if the world stretched no farther than an arm out the window.

He pulled a cigarette from his pack and lit it.

"You must have a busy mind," the man said, still not looking up.

Henry turned slightly, brow creasing.

"You sit," the man continued, gesturing toward him. "No paper. No book. No work. Just watching. Strange, that."

Henry took a slow drag, exhaling toward the ceiling. "I guess I've got a lot on my mind."

"Big plans in Montreal?"

Henry shrugged. "Seeing my family."

The man nodded slowly, weighing the answer. His eyes were flat and cold. Henry had seen eyes like that before—eyes that could stare down iron sights without blinking.

"Ah. A Québécois, then? You wouldn't know it by your accent."

Same neutral tone. But the man's own accent remained elusive. Strange.

Henry tapped a finger lightly against his knee. "I grew up kind of everywhere."

"In the War?"

Henry's brow furrowed, eyes narrowing slightly. The question felt casual. It wasn't. He rolled the cigarette between his thumb and fingers.

The man didn't blink. "You look like someone who fought. I know that look." He leaned forward, gaze steady. "Someone who's seen death."

Henry let the words hang. Silence could answer better than speech.

The man closed his book—softly, deliberately. "Maybe someone dangerous."

Henry let out a dry snort. "Dangerous," he echoed, turning the word over like a coin between his fingers. "All men can be dangerous if backed into the right corner."

The man tilted his head slightly. "Ah, yes. Flight or fight. The instinct in us all." His eyes narrowed. "And which did you feel in the trenches and mud?"

Henry leaned back, loosening his tie, inhaling deeply. "The same thing every man felt," he said evenly. "The need to survive."

A flicker in the man's expression—too quick to name. Gone in a breath. But Henry saw it.

His eyes fixed on Henry with quiet precision. "And do you?"

Henry's lips drew into a tight line. "Do I what?"

The man tapped a finger against the spine. "Still feel the need to survive?"

Henry's gut tightened. The game had changed.

The man reached—not for his cigarette, not for the book. But for the air. "If you wouldn't mind."

A polite gesture. At the smoke. At the door. A test.

Henry arched an eyebrow. He let the tension sit. Felt it stretch. Then, slowly, deliberately, he rose and turned toward the back of the train to toss the cigarette. The click of his heels echoed too precisely in the hush of the car.

The man didn't turn the page. Didn't blink.

Henry turned.

Too slow.

The garrote whipped around his throat.

Steel wire bit deep, crushing his windpipe in a violent snap. A whisper of breath. A sharp, burning pain.

"Who are you?"

The accent slipped. The neutrality was gone. Something European. Something unmistakably sharp.

Henry struggled as the cord cinched tighter, straining every muscle. Oxygen fled his brain in sharp, disorienting bursts. But just enough remained.

Just enough to talk. "What... are you... talking about?"

"MI6? Deuxième Bureau?" A short pause. "Who do you work for?"

The wire tightened. Each breath narrowed to a desperate rasp. The man was half a hand shorter, but his grip was tight. Trained. This might've been the first time he'd used a garrote on a man, but it wasn't the first time he'd practiced it.

"No... one."

"Liar."

The wire burned against Henry's skin as the man drove him backward toward the luggage racks. His vision blurred. Pressure built in his skull. His heartbeat pounded in his ears. The world narrowed—tunnelling to the hiss of the train, the rhythmic clatter of the tracks, and the slow, creeping certainty of death.

The shelves loomed ahead. Steel-framed wooden slats stacked with suitcases. A hard place to die.

"I'm... not a spy."

The man's voice was steady. "Of that, I'm sure. You are clumsy. But you are someone."

Henry's fingers clawed at the garrote. Too late. His chest heaved, oxygen-starved. His knees buckled. Legs failing.

The shelves rushed closer. The cold steel inches away. No one was coming. The car was empty.

Henry stumbled.

The grip loosened—just for a moment.

That was all he needed.

He lunged forward, yanking the man's wrist with his right hand. Off-balance—that's what he needed. The pressure eased—just enough.

He wrenched the arm forward, pulling the smaller man into him. His left elbow snapped back into his ribs.

A grunt. A sharp exhale.

Henry twisted.

Momentum shifted.

The garrote slipped.

He turned, the wire falling away, and threw a right cross—sharp and practiced—connecting hard.

Too hard.

The man's head snapped back. His skull struck the steel edge of the luggage rack with a sickening crack—a wet final sound.

He crumpled to the floor.

Unmoving.

Henry stood over him, chest heaving. The car was silent but for the low hum of the train. No one. No sound.

He bent, grabbed the man by the collar, and shook him. "Who are you?" His voice was low, urgent.

Silence.

Henry pressed his fingers against the man's neck.

Nothing.

Blood smeared the corner of the rack.

He looked at the back of the man's skull—a deep wound. The skin split wide. Blood pooling. Spreading.

Fuck.

The porter would be back soon.

Henry looked up. Looked down. No one. Yet.

What the hell was he going to do?

His pulse hammered. His breath came too fast. His knuckles were white.

He had just killed a man.

The weight hit all at once. The way the body slumped, the stillness, the slow spread of blood—final. Irrevocable. His stomach twisted, nausea climbing his throat. A man was dead, and Henry had killed him. Not in war. Not in a brawl. Just silence, struggle—and now nothing.

He stood frozen, fists clenched. He should've felt relief. Instead, his arms ached—not just from the fight, but from the weight of it.

He forced himself to look. The man's face was slack, mouth half-open. Whatever he was—whoever he was sent to find—it didn't matter now.

Henry's fingers twitched, unsure whether to reach for the body or shove it away.

The train rumbled beneath him. Steady. Indifferent. The world outside hadn't changed. Trees flashed past, white and endless.

But inside—everything had.

A long breath. His chest still felt too tight.

The steam whistle shrieked.

Henry jolted—full-body flinch. Hands clenched. He felt every bump and sway of the train as it surged forward. Unstoppable.

Self-defence?

Sure, but it would be his word against a dead man's.

No way to fake an accident. He looked at the door. The wind howled outside.

He already knew what he had to do. He crouched, patting the man down. Fingers fast—too fast. Sloppy. He forced them to slow down.

Inside the jacket—a wallet. William White. Saskatchewan ID.

Henry flipped through it—bills folded crisp but worn at the edges. A working man's money. Two train tickets: Ottawa to Montreal. Montreal to Toronto.

He dug deeper. A plain matchbook. No logo. No markings.

Windsor, 1630—scrawled in blue pen.

And that was it. Too clean. Way too clean.

The tension in his gut coiled tighter. William White? Was that even real?

He sucked in air—short, shallow, ragged. Seconds. That's all he had before the porter returned.

What now?

Blood pooled fast. Dark on the floorboards.

No sudden stops. No lurch.

No accident.

There was only one option.

Henry grabbed the man's arms and heaved. Dead weight. Heavier than he looked. He dragged the body across the floor—boots scraping, breath short, muscles burning.

The door rattled as he yanked it open. A blast of frozen wind screamed through the car, cutting through his coat.

The train thundered beneath him. Steel wheels grinding and echoing tenfold in the open air.

He glanced out the window into the next car. Passengers stared out at the snow. Lost in their own worlds.

No one was looking his way—for now.

With a grunt, he dragged the body into the narrow space between cars. The man's arms slipped from his grip, nearly taking Henry with him.

One last heave.

A final grunt.

The body lurched over the railing—gone into the blur of white. No sound. Just wind. Just trees swallowing him whole.

Henry exhaled sharply, gripping the freezing rail. Then, he pulled himself back inside.

He shut the door. The train rolled on, like nothing had happened.

CHAPTER VI

THE WEIGHT OF IT

"FDR ASSASSINATED IN MIAMI: AMERICA IN SHOCK"
—*THE NEW YORK TIMES*, FEBRUARY 16, 1933

"President-elect Franklin D. Roosevelt was shot and killed last night in Miami. The assassin, Giuseppe Zangara, has been taken into custody. Washington scrambles to address the crisis."

Thursday, December 2nd, 1937
Train to Montreal—Late Morning

Henry slumped against the wooden bench, his suitcase between his legs. The mingling scents of wool, sweat, and cheap tobacco filled the overcrowded car. He wedged himself into an unoccupied seat, forcing himself to relax.

He'd stripped off his suit and tie, replacing them with a thick wool sweater and dark flannel trousers. The fabric was familiar, the weight comfortable, but not what he typically travelled in.

The collar of his work shirt pressed against raw skin; buttoned high beneath the sweater, it hid most of the line across his throat—angry, red, and still tender—but not all. Anyone looking close would see it. He'd need a better cover before long.

But the dress down wasn't uncomfortable, just different. The heavy twill of his trousers felt softer than the tailored wool he was used to, but at least now, no one gave him a second glance.

Dressed down.

The surrounding crowd was far from the polished business class he had left behind. These were workingmen, tradesmen who smelled of machine oil, coal dust, and long hours.

He fit here. His suit wouldn't have. No one paid him any mind. For that, he was grateful.

Still, his thoughts refused to settle. The fight replayed in his head, looping over itself. His stomach twisted, nausea threatening to rise, but he forced it down.

Over and over, he ran through the conversation. What had he missed? What had he said? The smallest detail could be the difference between life and death.

He pulled his cigarette case from his pocket; fingers unsteady as he slid one free. The pack crinkled as he held it—he was shaking.

"Mind if I bum one?"

Henry barely registered the man beside him. Henry wordlessly tapped a cigarette loose and passed it over, then struck a match, lighting his own before handing it off.

The stranger on the train's voice—there was something about it. The vowels were too sharp, the rhythm too measured—an accent breaking at the edges, a hair off.

German? Austrian?

Henry took a slow drag. Canadian ID. Canadian money. But a foreign tongue slipped through. It made little sense.

He'd mention intelligence agencies. He'd thought that Henry was a spy? Why?

Henry's hand froze halfway to his mouth, the cigarette smouldering between his fingers—the briefcase.

His stomach twisted. "*Fuck.*"

He hadn't meant to say it out loud.

The man beside him turned, one eyebrow raised. "Amen, fella. I've felt that every day the last few years."

Henry mustered a tight smile. "Apologies. Just realized I forgot my razor at home."

The man chuckled, with a shake of the head. "Happens to the best of us, fella."

Henry nodded, exhaling a slow stream of smoke. But his mind wouldn't let it go.

Go back for it? Or stay put?

The man was dead. The briefcase wasn't.

Maybe it held something. Maybe nothing. Or perhaps it didn't matter.

He was dead. Henry wasn't.

Henry looked to the floor, running a trembling hand through his hair. Dead. He'd killed.

Again.

Not since the war.

Stay put. Let it go.

Safer that way.

He mulled it over.

Henry turned to the fellow seated next to him for the first time, really seeing him now—five o'clock shadow, sturdy calloused hands, the weary expression of someone who worked for his dollar.

"Listen, pal. Mind keeping an eye on my case?" He slipped a dollar into the man's palm. "Just for a few minutes."

The man turned the bill over, then eyed him.

Henry kept his voice light. "It'll be worth your time. Keep it where it is, and I'll square you up when I'm back."

The fellow pocketed the bill, nodding. "Just don't be gone too long."

Henry grabbed his coat and moved.

He made his way back through the train, walking past the cars he had just passed only minutes ago. He moved with the sway of the train, gripping a nearby bench as the car tilted around a curve in the tracks.

The farther he ventured toward the front, the fewer passengers there were. The sound of idle conversation faded away. He felt out of place here now, walking through business class; his clothes were a bit too working class, and he felt conspicuous.

At last, he reached the train car before his own—just one more.

A few businessmen glanced up as he passed, brows furrowing, but no one stopped him. No one cared.

He stepped to the far end of the car. Reached for the door.

The moment his fingers touched the handle, he stopped cold.

Through the window, he saw them.

A train cop—broad-shouldered, stiff-backed—stood near the row of seats. The porter beside him edged back, wringing his hands, gesturing toward the floor.

Henry's breath caught as a voice cut through the low hum.

"Blood on the floor," the cop said, his tone rasped raw, like he smoked two packs a day. "No sign of the man who was sitting here."

Henry's pulse pounded.

"Two passengers, you said. Both missing, like they vanished into thin air."

His fingers uncurled from the door handle.

Step back. Slow.

The cop was holding something. The briefcase.

"Nothing valuable in his seat. But this..."

The train swayed as Henry shifted his weight, and the metal frame of the door rattled.

The cop's head snapped up.

A breath of silence.

Henry turned to leave.

Move. Not too fast. Not too slow.

"Hold on—did you hear that?"

Fuck.

In for a penny.

Henry took a breath. He squared his shoulders and slumped them, adding a stoop to his gait as he gave the door a shove.

The porter looked up first—no recognition, no flicker of suspicion. The cop turned, brow furrowing.

Henry adjusted his expression to one of mild irritation—a man on someone else's errand, already tired of the hassle.

His gaze landed on the case in the cop's grip.

"Merci, monsieur," Henry said, his English thick with a Montreal French accent, his words clipped in the deliberate way of someone struggling to find the right ones. "T'ank you for... ah... rescuing my employer's case."

The cop's suspicion sharpened. His grip on the briefcase tightened. "Your employer?"

Henry gave a slight, dismissive shrug, as if the answer should be obvious. "Oui, monsieur. Monsieur Revault."

The porter glanced at the cop, frowning. "He didn't sound French to me."

Henry sighed, with the patient, measured expression of a man explaining something to someone who should already understand.

"Non, monsieur," he said. "My employer, he is... ah... 'ow you say? Anglophone, yes?" He tilted his hand in a so-so gesture, like it was of little consequence. "Just... family name is français. But he speak only English, oui?"

The cop hesitated.

His eyes flicked down to the blood smeared on the floor and on the luggage rack.

"What happened in here?" His tone carried weight now, the casual suspicion shifting into something firmer. "Looks like someone took a bad hit."

Henry's face softened, his posture shifting just enough to sell it.

"Ah, oui, monsieur. Monsieur Revault, he... ah... Bump 'is 'ead, yes?" Henry gave an exaggerated nod, as if trying to reassure them. "He wait long time for 'is drink, and so he go to bar for 'is tonic, 'is ice. Tall glass, always, oui? But—le train, it... Curved? He slip, 'it 'is 'ead." He winced as if recalling the moment. "Looks worse than it is. 'Eads, they bleed, yes?"

The cop's lips pressed into a thin line. "Where is Mr. Revault now? If his head's this bad, he should see a doctor."

Henry didn't hesitate. "Monsieur Revault, 'e is with 'is nurse, at back of train, oui?"

The cop looked at the porter, who only shrugged.

The pause stretched for just a second too long.

Then the cop's gaze flicked to the second seat beside where Henry had been sitting. "What about the other guy?"

Henry let out a breath, shaking his head as if the question was almost absurd.

"What ozzer guy, monsieur?" He scoffed lightly. "Monsieur Revault, 'e just ask me get 'is briefcase. Important documents, oui?"

The cop rubbed a thumb across the briefcase's handle, his eyes narrowing and forehead creasing. Henry maintained his stare, patient, waiting.

"Tell Mr. Revault to report accidents next time," the cop muttered, but his grip stayed tight on the handle. Henry steeled himself to hold still. One second. Two. The pause stretched. Then the cop nodded and shoved it into his hands.

Henry inclined his head. "Oui, oui, I tell 'im. But will 'e listen?" He sighed theatrically, offering a helpless shrug. "'E is... 'ow you say? Strong-willed man."

The cop breathed through his nose, unimpressed. "Alright, get out of here."

Henry nodded, turning away, every step feeling like it lined him up in a gunman's sights. He didn't look back. Couldn't.

The walk back felt ten times longer than the one at the front of the train.

Every glance burned into him. No one said a word. They didn't have to.

Murderer. Thief.

The words weren't spoken, but he could hear them just the same.

He forced himself to keep moving.

Finally, he reached coach class and flopped into his seat, letting out a slow breath.

His seatmate didn't even look up. "Price went up to two bucks." He flicked his cigarette ash onto the floor. "Some hoodlums wanted a crack at your case. Didn't have to fight 'em, but it got hectic." He held out his palm expectantly.

Henry slipped him three dollars.

The man smirked. "Hell, for that price, I would've fought 'em."

Henry offered a tired grin. "Maybe next time."

Then he reclined back, closing his eyes, listening to the steady clack of the rails beneath him.

The train rolled on.

Henry stepped off the train and gave a brief nod to Jacques, his seatmate for the last few hours. The man had spent the journey offering his entire life story, from his first breath to that very morning's breakfast, in exhaustive detail. It wasn't a terrible story—just an ordinary one. But Henry had done his best to look engaged, nodding at the right moments, chuckling when prompted. In return, Jacques repaid his kindness by repeating every joke at least twice, just to make sure Henry really got it.

As Jacques disembarked, he gave Henry a friendly wave. "Safe travels, mon ami! And don't forget—always check for a loose floorboard!" He barked a laugh, amused by his own wisdom.

Henry managed a strained smile and waved goodbye.

He turned and stepped into Windsor Station.

Before him, the grand terminal unfurled, a towering testament to steel, stone, and industry. High overhead, the vaulted ceilings loomed, their intricate ironwork casting long, curling shadows in the amber glow of the chandeliers. Decades of hurried footsteps had worn the polished marble floor smooth. A mixture of coal smoke, damp wool, and fresh newsprint permeated the air, combined with the subtle fragrance of coffee from the lively kiosks bordering the concourse. Crisp announcements from overhead speakers punctuated the rhythmic clatter of typewriters echoing from the ticket office.

Henry let the flow of passengers carry him, slipping effortlessly into the current of people pressing toward the exits. The station was alive with movement—businessmen with leather valises, housewives shepherding children, soldiers on leave, their uniforms crisp against the sea of overcoats.

He stayed with the crowd until he spotted a turnoff—a set of stairs leading to a quiet corridor. He avoided the throng of travellers, heading towards the men's room, suitcase in one hand and the stranger's briefcase in the other.

The tiled floor was damp beneath his boots; disinfectant barely masked the lingering odour of tobacco and cheap cologne. He stepped into a stall, bolted the door, and barely had time to lift the lid before his stomach lurched.

The nausea he'd been forcing down for the last hour and a half finally won.

He braced one hand against the cold tile wall, his body convulsing as he emptied his gut into the toilet. The acrid taste burned at the back of his throat, his entire frame trembling from the effort.

When it was over, he pressed the lever with a shaky hand and let the water erase the evidence. But the relief was hollow. His stomach was empty, but the heaviness in his heart remained.

His hands wouldn't stop shaking.

He lowered the lid and collapsed onto it, suitcase between his knees, the briefcase still clutched in his grip. His breath came in ragged bursts, too fast, too shallow.

Then the image hit him—the man's face. Slack. Lifeless. His skull cracked against the luggage rack. The way his body had crumpled.

Henry squeezed his eyes shut, forcing the memory away. But it was still there, waiting for him. It would always be waiting.

Henry exhaled, slow and shakily, then opened his eyes.

The briefcase sat at his side, as unassuming as ever. But now, it felt heavier. Different. Like a thing that didn't just hold secrets but was one itself.

He swallowed and lifted it onto his lap, the leather cool against his palms. His fingers hovered over the clasps for half a second. Only long enough for doubt to creep in.

Then he pressed them.

Nothing happened. A chill that had nothing to do with the December air crawled up his spine.

He frowned and lifted the case, tilting it toward the dim light filtering through the narrow stall door.

That's when he saw the combination lock.

Dammit. Of course, it was locked.

He ran his fingers over the dials, pressing his thumb against them, feeling their weight. Worn, but not too worn. The numbers gleamed faintly, catching the light in a way that suggested they'd been turned recently.

Henry inhaled slowly, then exhaled just as slowly.

He pressed the first wheel one degree up. Then the second. Then the third.

Tried again.

Nothing.

His jaw tensed.

He tried one notch down.

Nothing.

He tapped his fingers against the case, his mind working. Now what?

Indecision rained across his mind as he weighed his options.

He stood up, bracing himself against the stall wall, and stepped out, cases in hand.

At the sink, he turned the faucet, splashing cold water over his face. The reflection that stared back looked worse than he remembered—eyes sunken, jaw tight, skin grey from exhaustion.

He tugged the collar down. The line across his throat was darker now, bruising along the edge where the wire had bitten. Too visible.

He dug through his case and found a clean shirt with a higher collar. It wasn't perfect, but it would pass. He changed fast, ignoring the curious glance from a traveller at the door.

The new collar sat stiff, awkward without a tie. He adjusted it once, then met his own eyes in the mirror.

Get it together.

He checked his watch—12:35 PM.

Four and a half hours until he was on a train with Redfern.

Settled, he debated changing back into his suit. Did he need to? The working-class look had gotten him this far—no reason to draw attention now.

Stepping onto the concourse, he smoothed his sweater and glanced about at the passing faces and pressing crowd. Porters loaded luggage onto carts. Businessmen checked their watches. Somewhere outside, a steam engine hissed. The steady hum of a city in transit filled the air.

Henry cut across the concourse, weaving through the throng until he reached a row of payphones tucked along the far wall.

Henry stepped into the booth, closing the glass-panelled door behind him. The station noise dulled, replaced by the faint hum of static as he lifted the receiver.

"Operator. How may I direct your call?"

"Yeah, I need a number for Hughie Murphy in Montreal. He's a mechanic. Runs a small repair shop."

There was a pause, with the faint rustling of pages in the background.

"One moment, sir... Is that Murphy's Garage on St. Laurent, or are you looking for a home listing?"

Henry hesitated. "Yeah, that's the one. Murphy's Garage. St. Laurent."

"One moment, sir. Connecting..." The line clicked—a brief pause. The distant hum of the connection crackled as the call went through.

A beat passed. Then a voice—gruff, slightly out of breath—came through the receiver.

"Murphy's Garage. What can I do ya for?"

"Hughie?"

A brief pause. Then, a shift in tone—cautious, but familiar.

"Yeah. Who's askin'?"

"It's Harry."

Silence. Not long. But just long enough.

"Well, I'll be damned. Didn't know you were in town."

"Just got in."

"No foolin'." A pause, lighter, like he'd already decided. "Yeah, alright. Swing by. I've got a bit of time for ya."

The cab ride to Hughie's shop took over an hour and left Henry three dollars lighter—expensive times for bad errands.

Murphy's Garage was a trim, no-nonsense petrol and repair shop—clean, efficient. Although it was old equipment, probably from the war, it was well-maintained. Nothing broke down at Hughie's shop.

Henry grabbed his suitcase and the briefcase from the trunk, then stepped onto the oil-streaked sidewalk. He pushed open the shop's door; the bell overhead jingled sharply.

The lobby smelled of detergent, doing its damnedest to mask the deeper scent of grease and motor oil drifting in from the bay.

Hughie Murphy looked exactly as Henry remembered. Round-faced, thick-bellied, coveralls dark with grease and history. His hands were thick and rough, the sort that had spent a lifetime fixing things other men had broken.

His skin was deep brown, smudged here and there with oil. But his eyes—sharp, watchful—missed nothing. The kind that had seen too much but never let on.

The grey in his hair was new, creeping along his temples, but he still carried himself the same way—a man who knew his worth, even in a world that tried to pretend otherwise.

Hughie didn't move at first; he stood behind the counter, wiping grease from his hands with slow, deliberate strokes. His dark eyes flicked to Henry's face, then to the briefcase in his hand. Finally, he stepped around the counter.

For a second, Henry wasn't sure if the man was going to shake his hand or take a swing at him.

Hughie stopped just short, arms crossed. A long second passed.

"Dressed down today. What happened? Lose the suit?"

Henry adjusted the collar, thumb brushing the tender skin beneath. It still burned when he turned his head.

"Trying something different."

Hughie scoffed. "What, slumming it for a change?"Henry didn't rise to it.

Hughie looked out at the cab in the drive before turning back to Henry. "The fascist fire you?"

"Not yet."

"You quit?"

"Not yet."

Hughie shook his head. "Guess that'd take a spine." Not quite a dig. Not quite a plea. Just... disappointment.

Henry met his gaze. "Well, some things are changing."

Hughie wiped his hands on a rag, tossing it onto the counter. "Yeah, things change. You? You keep getting deeper."

Henry shrugged.

"What do you need?"

Henry set the briefcase on the desk. "I need to know what's inside this."

Hughie eyed the case as if it were ticking. "This from your boss?"

Henry shook his head, hands against the counter as he leaned forward. "No."

"Right." He huffed. "But you're still working for him, aren't you?"

Henry didn't answer.

Hughie threw up his hands. "Christ, Henry. You ever think about getting out before you drown?"

Henry forced a breath, but it stuck. The water was already up to his neck. Maybe it had been for years.

Hughie sucked air through his teeth. "You know, she would want—"

"You gonna open it or not?"

Henry met his stare. A swell rose in his chest. Guilt, anger, something heavier. He tapped the case.

"I'm sorry," Hughie said quietly. "All I'm saying is—"

"Enough, Hughie." Henry's voice was low. Firm. "It's complicated. Not everything is black and white."

Hughie held his gaze, jaw tight. A long moment stretched between them.

"Well. To some people, it's only white."

Henry rocked back as if he'd been hit. "Not to me. You know that."

The silence lingered. Henry thought momentarily about turning around and walking right back out.

Hughie squinted at him. Not angry. Just tired. Like a man who'd seen too much, knew too much, but had long since given up expecting better.

"Look, Harry," Hughie said finally, voice quieter now. "I know the money's good. But a man's gotta look himself in the mirror, too, and be able to stand the person looking back."

Henry swallowed.

He had already looked.

He'd stood in a station washroom, cold water dripping from his face, staring into his own reflection like it might have an answer. Like it might tell him what kind of man he was.

It hadn't.

And now, standing here, Hughie's words sat too damn heavy on his chest. He didn't need to look again. He already knew what he'd see.

The silence stretched again.

Hughie sighed, wiping his hands on his coveralls.

"Alright," he muttered. "Let me look at that briefcase."

He moved with a precision that always left Henry astounded. The man had hands built for fixing things—steady, exact, quick. And Henry had seen them in action before, working under fire, cutting wire, clearing mines in the dead of night.

That's why he was always sent first. Well, that and the colour of his skin.

Henry preferred to believe it was the former. But he knew better.

Hughie grabbed the case and moved it to the workbench, inspecting the lock. "You sure you want me popping this open?"

Henry looked at him for a moment, then down at the briefcase, and nodded. "Open it."

Hughie didn't argue. He pulled a pick from his toolbox and got to work, the faint click-click of metal against metal filling the quiet. He worked fast. Too fast. Henry had seen men struggle with locks like this for minutes—sometimes longer. Hughie had it open in seconds.

"And just... like... that."

With a final click, he disabled the lock and lifted the lid.

Henry craned forward as Hughie pulled the papers free, unfolding them carefully.

If Henry had hoped for answers, they weren't here.

Just like on the train—plans. Schematics. Measurements.

He leafed through them, his brow furrowing. Nothing stood out.

"This doesn't make any sense," he muttered. "No money. No names. Just plans."

He looked over at Hughie, who had set aside his pick, and studied another set of diagrams. His hands were careful, moving across the pages without leaving smudges, handling them like they meant something.

Then he stopped. His brow furrowed. "What are you doing with a briefcase like this, Harry?"

Henry stiffened. "What do you mean?"

Hughie laid a page down on the workbench. "Beauharnois Hydroelectric Station."

Another.

"Niagara Falls Power Generation Plant."

Then another.

"Jesus. Montreal's Angus Shops. That's where the railcars are made."

One by one, he laid them out.

"Victoria Bridge. General Motors Plant."

The air in the garage felt different now.

Hughie looked up, his dark eyes locking onto Henry's. "Jesus Christ, Henry. Do you even realize what this is?"

Henry opened his mouth. Nothing came out.

The weight of the briefcase pressed into his palm, suddenly heavier than it had been a second ago. His pulse thudded in his ears.

"I have no idea," he finally said, but the words felt hollow.

He looked back down at the pages spread across the workbench, as if staring at them long enough would make them mean something else.

It didn't.

Chapter VII

No Place Left to Run

"CONGRESS GRANTS VALE EMERGENCY POWERS"
—*The Wall Street Journal*, February 10, 1937

"Markets react cautiously as the President takes unilateral control over federal agencies."

Thursday, December 2nd, 1937
Murphy's Garage, Montreal, Quebec - Afternoon

Henry weighed his options, staring at the briefcase. Indecision froze him.

Hughie kept flipping through the pages with a mechanic's precision, rough hands turning each sheet as if it were a gasket that had to seat just right. His brow furrowed. Each blueprint and schematic represented critical infrastructure, including power stations, manufacturing hubs, and bridges.

A map of the country's weak spots.

His gut twisted. *Keep it?*

No. Suicide. Walking around with a briefcase full of this? He might as well tie a noose around his neck. If anyone so much as peeked inside—hell, if the wrong person even saw him with it, he was done.

Give it away? But who?

His eyes flicked to Hughie.

He trusted the man implicitly. A man who had gone over the top with him, crawled through the same mud and sat in the same freezing filth, waiting for shells to drop. If there was anyone in this world he could trust, it was Hughie.

But could he do that to him? Shift the burden onto him? Drag him into whatever this was?

His stomach churned.

Then what?

Henshaw.

Henshaw could handle this. He had the connections, the power; he could do something with it.

But Henry didn't have time. No way to reach him. No time to wait.

Barclay?

His pulse kicked. Ellie Barclay would eat this up. If anyone could get this out into the world, she could.

But then what? He'd have to explain how he got it and opened it. He'd have to tell how he murdered a man and threw him off a train.

Bile rose at the back of his throat. He could still feel the wire. Still hear the wet crack of skull against steel.

His hands curled into fists.

What the hell was he going to do?

Hughie gathered the plans and carefully re-aligned them before sliding them back into the briefcase.

"I get it," he said, voice even. "You won't tell me where you got it. And... I'm not sure if I want to know."

His eyes lingered on Henry. He was not judgmental, not angry, just tired, like a man looking at a dog caught in a trap, knowing how the story ended.

"But this?" Hughie tapped the case. "This is a dangerous thing to walk around with. And it sure as hell ain't staying here." He exhaled sharply, jaw tightening. "And I swear, if this is tangled up in that fascist fucking boss of yours, if he's got plans—"

"It's not."

Hughie's eyes narrowed. "You sure?"

Henry hesitated. "Well. No. But it didn't come from him."

A beat. Hughie shook his head, lips pressed thin.

"Either way, this is dangerous, Harry. Really dangerous." He looked at the case again, jaw flexing. "The best thing would be to toss it in a fire and be done with it." His fingers drummed against the workbench. Then, softer, speaking more for his own benefit than to Henry. "But it's too damn important for that, isn't it?"

Henry's hand swept down his face, the heaviness dragging like lead. "I don't know."

Hughie studied him for a long moment, then sighed, reaching for his tools. "All right," he muttered. "Let's see what we're working with."

Henry watched as Hughie popped open a metal case, revealing a neat roll of precision screwdrivers, lock picks, and a few small, oddly shaped instruments Henry didn't recognize.

The man worked fast and methodically, like he'd done this before, not cracking a safe, exactly, but fixing something never meant to be taken apart.

"Is this a trick you picked up fixing carburetors?" Henry muttered, leaning forward.

Hughie didn't raise his eyes. "Carburetors are honest. This shit's just persuasion."

Tracing his fingers along the lock, he angled the briefcase under the workbench lamp, his eyes narrowed. Reaching for a thin, filed-down screwdriver-like tool, he slipped it into the narrow gap between the rotating dials. Listening intently, he furrowed his brow, applying slight pressure.

Henry wasn't sure what he was listening for, but Hughie seemed to find it.

"There's a trick to these," Hughie muttered. "They set the combination at the factory, right? But every lock like this has some slack in the tumblers. If you know how to feel for it..."

He twisted one of the dials a fraction, then stilled. A tiny, almost imperceptible click sounded.

Henry's brows pulled together. "The hell was that?"

"That," Hughie said, his voice smug, "was your first number."

Henry opened his mouth to say something, but Hughie was already working on the next dial, gently rocking it back and forth. Another click. Then another.

Henry combed his fingers through his hair. "Jesus. You ever think about a career in crime?"

Hughie smirked. "I prefer an honest living."

Within moments, he had the entire combination aligned, and with a quick, sure movement, he flicked a small latch on the side of the lock. The tumblers reset with a soft whirr. He sat back, tapping a finger against the case.

"All right," he said, turning it toward Henry. "Put in a code."

Henry hesitated. "Just like that?"

Hughie shrugged. "Just like that."

A year? A birthday? Something else?

His fingers hovered for a second, and a memory surfaced—standing proud in their freshly pressed uniforms, unaware of the horrors that would come.

Henry thumbed the dials, settling on 2-4-1-8—the 24th Battalion, the year it all ended.

Hughie flipped the dials, scrambling them, then patted the case like he'd just tuned up an engine.

"Now," he said, folding his arms, "don't say I did nothing for ya."

Henry exhaled, shaking his head. "I don't even wanna know how you learned that."

Hughie smirked. "Good. 'Cause I ain't tellin'." Then his expression became serious, and he pressed a firm hand against the briefcase. "Now, get the hell out of my shop."

Henry let out a chuckle, shaking his head. He reached across the workbench, and Hughie met him in a firm handshake that lasted just a little longer than necessary. There was more to it than just a parting gesture.

"Take care of yourself, Harry."

Henry hesitated.

There was so much he wanted to say. He tried to tell Hughie about Henshaw. That not every man he worked with was rotten to the core. That he wasn't just some blind, obedient cog in a fascist machine, that maybe, just maybe, he was doing something worthwhile.

But the words wouldn't come.

Hughie already knew the truth. Or at least enough of it. And whatever else he needed to figure out, well, he would.

So, Henry just nodded, gripping the case tightly.

"You too, Hughie."

Then, without another word, he turned and strode out the door.

He didn't blame Hughie for not wanting to be caught up in this.

Didn't mean it stung any less.

He tightened his grip on the case and went toward the waiting cab.

The streets of Montreal pulsed with movement; streetcars clattered along their tracks, automobiles honked and lurched through intersections, and pedestrians wove between them, bundled against the cold. The city hummed, thick with coal smoke, wet pavement, and exhaust—all sharpened by the bite of December air.

Limestone façades loomed over the streets, their weathered elegance marked by intricate cornices and wrought-iron balconies. Vieux-Montréal's old-world charm pressed uneasily against the city's steel-and-glass ambitions, modernity creeping upward like a thing determined to swallow the past.

He should have felt at home here.

This was where he had spent his youth and had gone to university after the war, where he had grown into the man he was now.

But it had never been home.

Nowhere had.

The road had always been more straightforward. More natural. Even gritty, brutal, and pointless war had made more sense than this.

Not that he'd had a poor upbringing; far from it.

But as the middle child of three, he had often felt overlooked. Forgotten. Not cruelly. His parents had loved him well enough.

Robbie. The elder brother. He bore expectations like a crown. The younger sister was the bright, promising one. Henry had learned young how to slip between the cracks.

Maybe that was why the road had felt like an escape.

Maybe that was why he had never stopped running.

Jolting over tram tracks, the cab rattled him back to the present. Muttering something in French under his breath, the driver sharply maneuvered them around a slow-moving truck.

The ride back to Windsor Station was silent.

Henry sat stiffly, the briefcase resting on the far side of the seat like a dead weight. He could feel it looming, like a presence in the car.

Watching. Accusing.

He checked his watch—two and a half hours.

His fingers drummed absentmindedly against his knee.

Then, without thinking too hard about it, he leaned forward and tapped the cabbie on the shoulder.

"Change of plans. Take me to Westmount."

He gave the cabbie the address. No change in expression — just a curt nod before he turned down the next street, cutting through traffic like he already knew the way.

Henry leaned back and closed his eyes, rubbing his fingers against his temple.

He hadn't planned on this—or on seeing them. But if something went wrong, he couldn't bear the thought of leaving Montreal without one last stop home.

Just for a minute.

Long enough to remind himself why he had left in the first place.

As the cab climbed out of downtown, the city blurred past, leaving the commercial core's bustle behind. Wide tree-lined streets replaced the towering limestone and red-brick buildings. The scent of smoke and gasoline thinned, replaced by the crisp, quiet air of old wealth.

Westmount.

It was where money didn't just live; it settled, planted roots, and stayed for generations.

Henry knew every street, every turn. As a boy, he'd walked them a thousand times, passing grand Victorian homes with ornate gables and turrets, sprawling mansions with impeccably kept gardens—and the children who once played out front like they owned the world.

He didn't belong here anymore. Hell, maybe he never had.

The cab slowed, pulling up in front of a modest three-story home between two grander estates. It was the same as he had left it: grey stone, black shutters, a front porch that creaked in the winter cold.

He slid the driver a pair of dollar bills. "I won't be long. Don't leave without me."

The cabbie took the bills without glancing back.

Henry stepped out, adjusting the briefcase in his grip.

Looking up at the house, his lips pushed together, and after a moment, he walked up the steps with a breath that felt heavier than it should.

And knocked.

The stillness that answered him was expected. He opened the door. The house was quiet. Not quiet. Absent.

Henry hesitated in the doorway, his hand still on the knob. The warmth inside pressed against the cold on his back, but the stillness made it feel cavernous.

For a moment, he thought about calling out. But he didn't.

Instead, he stepped forward, careful not to disturb the house's order by shaking the snow from his boots.

The foyer was just as he remembered. The polished wood floors gleamed under the soft glow of the chandelier, the air thick with the smell of lemon polish and something faintly floral. His mother's doing, no doubt. The sitting room was just beyond, its furniture perfectly appointed, the lace doilies on the coffee table resting exactly where they always had. He didn't need to look to know there wasn't a speck of dust anywhere.

Then, his eyes caught on the portrait above the mantelpiece.

A young man, barely eighteen, stared back at him from behind the glass, frozen in time by the sharp lines of a school uniform he'd never outgrow.

Henry's fingers traced the border of the frame, its weight settling in his chest.

Then he turned and walked toward the back of the house.

Through the sitting room, past the heavy bookshelves, their leather-bound spines untouched by time, past the dining table that had seen more arguments than meals, the warmth of something cooking drifted through the air, mingling with the familiar scent of home.

He stepped into the kitchen.

His mother stood at the counter, peeling potatoes. She didn't look up, not at first. Just kept working, her hands steady, the blade sliding effortlessly through the skins.

"Henry," she said, as if she'd seen him yesterday, not six months ago. A tight smile. Nothing more. "Would you be a dear and grab the pot? My hands are covered in potato skins."

Henry obeyed without thinking, stepping toward the cabinet, pulling out the pot, and bringing it over. He helped her load the potatoes. The rhythm was automatic.

"Fill it with water, would you? I need to wash my hands before I start on the carrots."

She disappeared into the small washroom just off the kitchen. The sink tap creaked on.

"We're having roast tonight," she called over the sound of running water. "The butcher had a sale on. Strange time of year for a discount, don't you think?"

Henry turned on the faucet, watching the water rush over the potatoes.

"Mr. Connor's hip went out," she continued. "So Jamie, you remember Jamie, don't you? The little one from across the street? He's been helping him around the house. Good lad, that Jamie. His older sister, do you remember her? Mildred? The pretty one. Brunette with the big eyes. Well, her husband dropped dead last week. Heart attack, maybe? Poor girl. No children, though, so I suppose she'll be looking for another soon enough."

Henry didn't respond.

She's talking about Jamie Connor. About Mildred and her dead husband. About butcher sales.

Like nothing's changed.

Like he isn't standing here, six months gone.

Like he isn't walking about with a case brimming with secrets that could get him killed.

The tap ran. The scent of roasting meat thickened in the air.

His mother wiped her hands on a dishtowel and stepped back into the kitchen, reaching for the knife to prepare the carrots.

Her eyes lifted to his face—just for a second. A pause, a faint narrowing, her gaze flicking to the collar at his throat before moving on. The knife resumed its slow, steady rhythm against the board.

Then she looked at him. "Are you staying for dinner? Your sister, Billy, and the kids are coming. They'd love to see their Uncle Henry."

Henry hesitated.

His fingers gripped the edge of the sink.

His mother wasn't avoiding a fight. She wasn't pretending not to care.

She just... didn't ask.

Didn't ask where he'd been. Didn't ask why he was here now. Didn't ask about the past six months, or six years, or anything at all.

It wasn't indifference. It wasn't avoidance. It was something else.

As if she'd already made peace with whatever version of him had come home today.

His throat tightened.

"I can't," he said finally.

She nodded as if the answer was good enough. "Alright."

And that was it.

She turned back to the cutting board, knife tapping against the wood as she started slicing the carrots.

Henry frowned. "*Alright?*"

She avoided eye contact. "Yes, dear?"

"That's it? 'Alright?' I haven't seen you in six months."

She kept cutting. Steady. Unbothered. "Well, that's just the way of it, isn't it?" she said lightly. "You come; you go. Who knows with you?"

The knife tapped against the wood.

"So, yes, Henry. 'Alright.'"

He swallowed. "Where's Dad?"

She didn't stop cutting. "In the library."

Henry ran a hand over his face with a quiet sigh.

"Alright," he murmured and walked down the hall.

His father reclined in a leather chair, spectacles perched on his nose, legs crossed, a thick volume open on his lap. His wiry frame seemed to disappear into the chair's deep cushions.

Professor William Locke looked every bit the academic—sharp-eyed, analytical, weighing everything as if against a thesis.

He closed the book with a soft thump and looked up. His gaze flicked over Henry—measuring—before a knowing smirk tugged at the corner of his mouth.

"The prodigal son returns."

Henry's lips pressed into a thin line. Of course, that was the first thing out of his mouth.

His father reclined, stretching out one leg, fingers drumming against the book's spine.

"I trust you greeted your mother properly. A hug? A kiss on the cheek? Some proof of life?"

Henry scoffed. "She barely looked at me. Acted like I wasn't even here."

His father sighed and pushed himself from the chair with the slow effort of a man who'd had this conversation before. He set the book—something thick and profound—on the table beside him.

"Of course, she cares that you're here," he said, as though that required no elaboration.

Henry folded his arms. "She has a strange way of showing it."

His father arched a brow, moving toward the bar cart. "Yes, well. The female mind remains an enigma. Even in my advanced years, I remain utterly confounded by its mechanics."

He poured himself a drink. No offer for Henry. Of course not.

Then he turned back with a wry smile. "Men build bridges, lay railroad tracks, and move mountains. And yet we'll never quite understand why our wives sigh at us from across the dinner table."

Henry's fingers twitched. Instinct pulled him toward the cigarette pack in his pocket—but he knew better.

His father's eyes caught the movement. Noted it. Said nothing.

"I assume you're staying for dinner."

Henry glanced out the window. "I can't."

His father sighed again. No anger—just inevitability. "And there it is."

"It's important this time."

"It's always important, in your words, Henry."

Henry hesitated. "Well, this time..."

But the words stuck.

His father was watching him now—with *that* look that made Henry feel ten years old again, caught in a lie before he even told it.

Henry looked away.

"It's Redfern, isn't it?" His father's voice was lower now. Sharper. "You're tangled up in his business. And now you don't know how to get out."

Henry stiffened.

His father waited.

So he gave him something.

"Do you remember when Robbie stole Father O'Malley's pen?"

His father's expression flickered.

"Robbie didn't steal it," he muttered, more to himself than to Henry.

Henry gave a dry laugh. "Yeah. He did."

The past settled between them, heavy and familiar.

"You knew, didn't you?" Henry asked, softer now. "You knew he had it. But you let me take the punishment instead."

His father looked away, thumb rubbing the gold ring on his finger. "You lied for him."

"I was ten," Henry said. "What was I supposed to do?"

His father's eyes returned to his. "And now?"

Henry's jaw tightened.

Now he was thirty-seven and still holding someone else's secret.

"*Now it's like that.*"

His father inhaled—slowly, thoughtfully. Eyes fixed, weighing him. "You could walk away."

Henry shook his head. "I can't. This is important."

His father didn't blink. "The biggest mistake a man can make is thinking he has time."

Henry swallowed.

His father leaned forward, voice lower now—steady, sure.

"Those who don't fight now will curse that they can't fight later."

Henry's stomach twisted.

"I've seen it before," his father murmured. "Men who thought they could wait it out. The world doesn't wait."

Chapter VIII

No One to Call

"EAGLE GUARD DECLARED NATIONAL SECURITY FORCE"
—*The Philadelphia Gazette*, February 20, 1937

"Vale's once-private militia is now an official arm of the federal government."

Thursday, December 2nd, 1937
Westmount, Montreal, Quebec - Late Afternoon

Henry closed the door behind him. The latch clicked shut with a finality like a hammer drawn back.

He descended the steps, one at a time, as if walking away for good. At the bottom, he paused. Looked back. His eyes tightened.

Not his home. Never was. Never would be.

The windows stared back, empty. No silhouettes. No lingering faces.

He had expected none.

He felt a tightness in his chest as he struck a match, the flame flickering against his fingers as he lit a cigarette. Then, without another glance, he climbed into the cab.

The ride felt short. It always did on the way back.

He tipped the cabbie and stepped out, stretching his foot over the frozen slush pooling between curb and street. Snow had fallen—a slow, drifting dust in the pale afternoon light—softening the city's edges into a grey-white blur.

He hefted his suitcase, then glanced at the briefcase leaning against the far side of the cab. He could leave it. Walk away. Never think about it again. Never think about what was inside.

Someone would find it. Toss it. Forget it.

Gone.

His hand twitched. Then, with a quiet sigh, he reached across and took it.

It felt heavier this time. The case pulled at his arm as he hefted it and walked into the station.

Henry scanned the station, avoiding eye contact, frozen amidst the flowing crowd. He assessed the bustling environment around him. The station was as busy as ever, filled with a crowd of people and the hum of many conversations echoing off the old limestone walls. Individuals came and went, each with countless destinations and a myriad of thoughts running through their minds.

Benjamin Schul rested a hip against the café counter, dressed to impress. Movie-star sharp. Hair slicked and a cigarette dangling from his lips.

The woman beside him leaned in, gaze drifting, lost in his orbit.

Shit.

Henry turned. He had to ditch the case before—"Harry!"

The shout cut through the masses, slicing clean through the noise.

Somehow.

Where Benjamin Schul walked, the crowds seemed to part. Or maybe they just knew better than to get in his way.

He approached easily, pulling out his pocket watch from his Italian vest.

"Train leaves in half an hour. Still don't know where we're going." He smirked. "How about we grab a drink? I'm buying."

Henry forced a nod. "Sounds good, Ben. I'll meet you there in a few minutes."

Schul's brow furrowed. "You alright? You look like hell."

Henry started to answer, but Schul's hand came up, brushing the air between them before tugging lightly at Henry's collar. "Jesus, Harry—what the hell happened?"

"Cut myself shaving," Henry said flatly.

"Bullshit."

Henry stepped back, pulling the collar straight again. "Drop it, Ben."

Schul let out a low whistle, exhaling through his nose. "Suit yourself." He turned half away, lighting another cigarette.

Henry thought that was the end of it—until Schul's eyes drifted down. "Hey, what's with the case? The Boss got you running paperwork now?"

Stay easy. Stay light.

"No," Henry said, forcing a casual demeanour, but even he felt the tightness in his voice. His pulse hammered within his skull. "Just something for a friend."

Schul took a long drag, eyes flicking from the briefcase to Henry. He let the smoke slip from his lips, thin and careless, considering.

"Harry," he said, voice low as he tapped the cigarette against his thumb. "Your friend's got himself a Mark Cross briefcase?"

Deflect.

"You're the stuff guy, Ben. You know I know nothing about this stuff."

Schul's smirk didn't fade, but it flattened—a little.

"Alright, Harry." He let the name hang for a beat longer than usual. His eyes lingered a second too long on the briefcase, then he turned without another word. "See you in the bar."

He had a plan. Ditch the case.

Henry licked his lips. Dry. Tight. He adjusted his grip on the briefcase. Keep walking. Keep moving.

Locker.

That was the plan. Drop the damn thing in a locker and be done with it. Out of his hands, out of his head. If something went sideways, at least he wouldn't be holding it when it did.

Cutting across the concourse, Henry weaved through the throng. A constant low hum of overlapping voices filled the packed station as people moved in every direction.

A kiosk flashed his reflection in its polished brass, and for a second, he saw himself as others did.

Just a man with a briefcase.

But what if someone else saw something different?

His grip tightened. Too many people. Too many directions. The locker was near. Just ditch it. Move on.

Turning to the porter's desk, he scanned the crowd.

A hand closed around the briefcase handle.

"You're late."

Henry didn't let go.

A second passed, then another.

The man—thin, wiry, with a wispy moustache and round glasses—kept walking, pulling the briefcase along as if he'd been expecting to take it. A black fedora was pulled low over his eyes, the brim shadowing his expression.

Henry's stomach dipped. *Late for what?*

He tugged the briefcase back.

The man didn't release it.

A small circle opened around them—the natural pause of a crowd sensing something just off enough to watch. Curious, but not yet concerned. One wrong move—one raised voice, one shove—and that would change.

beHenry's pulse kicked—too many eyes.

He kept his voice steady. "What the hell do you think you're doing?"

The man didn't answer. He just held on.

Over his shoulder, Henry spotted Ben.

Schul had turned—brows drawn, cigarette still between his lips, head tilted just enough to show he'd noticed.

The man followed Henry's glance.

Ben met his eye.

"Let go," the man said—calm, flat, without accent or urgency.

"I don't know what you're talking about. I'm not letting go of my case."

The man stared at him. Expressionless. Calculating. His fingers lingered for a second longer, his grip twitching like he was debating something.

"Apologies," the stranger said, releasing his hold and turning away. Henry watched the black fedora vanish, swallowed by the crowd.

One second he was there. And then he wasn't.

Henry exhaled, only now realizing he'd been holding his breath. Pressure pulsed inside his skull, his heartbeat thudding in his ears like distant artillery fire.

His gaze dropped to the briefcase, as if seeing it for the first time. Then, back to the crowd—already shifting, flowing, indifferent.

He turned toward the kiosk, moving slowly and deliberately, like a man four drinks in, trying to walk like he hadn't touched a drop.

He paused.

Maybe he should've let go. Why had he held on? *Didn't he want it gone?*

Shit.

He carefully set the briefcase down on the kiosk, but his hands were still shaking. It wobbled against the counter. "Locker rentals?"

"Oui, monsieur," the porter replied, motioning toward a row of storage lockers further down the concourse.

Henry rested an elbow against the kiosk, patting a cigarette from his pack. His hands were unsteady with the match. The first one slipped through his fingers, dropping to the floor.

The porter watched him uneasily.

"How long can I rent one for? I should be back in a week or less."

He took a slow, steadying breath, fishing for another match from the pack. But his fingers wouldn't stop trembling. The cigarette slipped from his mouth twice before he caught it, lining up the match and the tip like threading a needle on a ship caught in a storm.

The porter shrugged. "Week? Oui, monsieur. Fifteen cents per day. Pay in advance. If you no return, inside is forfeit. You understand?"

Henry nodded, inhaling deeply as he slid a dollar bill and a quarter across the counter. Enough to cover the week, plus a little extra. He could have switched to French, which would've saved time, but sometimes it paid to let people think you didn't understand them.

The porter counted out the money, then reached under the desk, pulling out a slip of paper with a locker number and a three-digit combination written in ink.

Henry studied it until the numbers stuck, then crumpled the slip and tossed it into the bin.

Locker. Drop it. Done.

He moved toward the lockers, checking the numbers until he found the correct one—near the end of the row, just out of view.

Good.

The briefcase slid into place. His hand lingered on the handle. Grip tightened.

Leaving it meant losing control. But if things went sideways—if he didn't come back—then what?

He stepped back just enough to let the door swing shut. The lock clicked—barely audible, yet deafening to him. Final. Absolute. Not quite relief. Something like it.

Shoulders rolled. Eyes swept the concourse. Faces blurred past, none of them looking.

What if he didn't come back?

The question stuck. Kept replaying. Would anyone come looking? Would anyone even know where to start?

Henry leaned his back against the locker, scanning the concourse. The crowd moved on, unaware and indifferent.

There were questions in that briefcase. Questions that he had no answers to.

But answers that somebody needed. He rolled the thought over. Who?

Henshaw? There was no way of reaching him. The Senator always contacted him and dictated the meetings and timings. Henry didn't have the first idea how to contact a Canadian Senator.

Hughie? No.

His parents? No.

Redfern? He chuckled as the thought passed through his head. Absolutely not.

His fingers clenched in his pocket.

The card. Ellie Barclay.

He pulled it out, turning it over in his fingers. A reporter.

He didn't talk to the press. But he didn't have anyone else.

His stomach knotted. He turned the card over again, scanning the crowd as if he could find a better answer among them.

Nothing.

With a muttered curse and a shake of his head, he crossed the station toward the bank of payphones. A nickel dropped into the slot. The dial clicked under his fingers.

"Operator."

He steadied his voice. "I need to place a call to Miss Ellie Barclay. The Globe and Mail—Ottawa Bureau."

The receiver crackled.

A crisp, businesslike voice answered. "Barclay speaking."

Henry pressed closer to the mouthpiece, voice low. Restrained.

"It's Locke."

A beat of silence.

"Locke?"

"Henry Locke."

Another pause. Then: "Oh—" He could hear the smile forming. "I figured I'd be writing your obituary before I ever heard from you."

He ignored the dig.

"Listen. If you don't hear from me in a week, go to Windsor Station—Montreal. Locker 231. Combination 4-1-7. Bring it to Henshaw."

That gave her pause. "Henshaw? Senator Henshaw?"

"Yes. No questions. Just do it."

More silence.

"I'm a reporter, Henry. I don't do 'no questions'."

"Maybe this has answers. One week."

He heard her draw in a breath to protest—then stop. A click of her tongue. A shift in tone. "Henshaw. The voice of anti-fascism."

Henry said nothing.

"You're a lot deeper than your scouting report."

He let that hang.

"One week, Ms. Barclay."

"Ellie, Henry. Please." A buzz on the line. "Fine. One week."

He hung up.

Slid the slip of paper back into his pocket.

Seven days.

If he had that long.

He rested his back against the wall, tongue pressed to his teeth, staring up at the ceiling like he might find something there.

He needed a drink.

Henry dropped into the seat across from Ben.

The Windsor Bar was half full—mostly business travellers, men like them, waiting for the next train. The low hum of conversation blended with the occasional clatter of glassware, the station's distant bustle a dull, ever-present background noise.

His Seagram's was already waiting on the table. Across from it, Schul's drink was dark, ice clinking against the glass. Rum and whatever cola they had? Maybe. Ben wasn't one for acquiring a taste for any one thing. He liked to "taste the whole world," as he put it.

Henry lifted his glass, thumb running along the rim. He fought the urge to down the Seagram's in one go.

Ben studied him, cigarette dangling between his fingers. "Looked like a bit of confusion with your 'friend' out there."

Henry took a slow sip, letting the warmth settle in his chest. Across from him, Ben watched. "No. That wasn't my friend."

Ben inhaled from his cigarette, tapping ash into the tray. His eyes narrowed just a touch, a trace of amusement tugging at the corner of his mouth. "No? Just confusion in general, then?"

Henry let the words hang before shrugging. "Something like that."

Ben glanced around the bar, his gaze drifting, unfocused. The world had a way of flowing around him. But when he bent in again, the smile was gone. "You've been off lately."

Henry's grip tightened on the tumbler. The ice clinked as he rolled the glass between his fingers. "Off?"

Outside, a horn honked, muffled through the bar's walls. Someone laughed too loudly at a nearby table.

Ben studied him for a long moment, smoke curling from his cigarette. "You sure you're okay?"

Henry took another sip, staring down into his glass.

His voice dropped. "You ever wonder why we're working for Redfern?"

Ben's fingers paused on his glass. Not a flinch. Not a tell. Just a momentary stillness.

"What's that supposed to mean?"

Henry set his drink down, thumb tracing the rim once before he pulled his hand away. He could say it. Right now. Just put it out there.

But how would Ben take it?

How had he taken it? Not well. Pleading in the dark. Eyes rimmed with rain and regret.

Henry blinked the image away and moved in, voice low. "We both know what he is becoming. The men he keeps in his orbit."

With one arm draped over the back of the booth, Ben leaned back, feigning unconcern. But Henry could see the calculation in his eyes.

"Yeah?" He took a drag of his cigarette. "And?"

And.

Henry glanced toward the bar, then back at Ben.

This was it—the moment.

"How long before that barrel we're looking down isn't pointed at someone else?"

The words left his mouth before he had fully decided to say them.

Ben exhaled the cigarette smoke slowly. Measured. Watching the smoke fade toward the ceiling.

"That's some talk, Harry." His voice was lighter, but it wasn't a dismissal.

Henry watched him, trying to get a read. Ben always had a knack for playing things close to the chest, but something about how he wasn't looking at him now said more than he would ever admit.

Henry leaned in just enough to close the space. "You don't believe in any of it, do you?"

Ben's lips pressed into a thin line. He picked up his glass, swirling the ice before taking a sip. "I believe in capitalism."

Henry stared at him. "That's why you're still here?"

Ben set his glass down between them, running a finger along the rim of the glass.

"Maybe." Ben lifted his cigarette to his lips, inhaling deeply. "Isn't that why you're still here?"

Henry didn't answer.

Ben huffed a chuckle, shaking his head as he breathed the smoke out of his nose.

"Look, you and I—we're smart guys. We go where the money is." He glanced around the room. "Most people don't give a damn about politics, not really. They care about their jobs. Their paychecks. Their families."

He stubbed his cigarette out, rubbing his fingers together before reaching for another.

"That's why it won't happen here."

Henry scoffed, shaking his head. "You really believe that?"

Ben smirked, cocking his head as he rolled the fresh cigarette between his fingers—casual, unbothered, like a man holding a winning hand.

"I think the world's turning to shit, Harry. But we're not the States." He lit his cigarette with a snap of the lighter, watching the smoke coil lazily toward the ceiling. Then he looked back with a crooked grin. "Canada's different."

Henry held his gaze. "Is it?"

The grin faltered.

Just a flicker. A shadow crossed Ben's face.

He sighed, grinding the butt into the ashtray before lighting another. "Maybe I don't want to believe it."

Henry sat back, watching him.

He should tell him. *Get out, Ben. Get out while you can.* But he didn't.

"Do you ever think about getting out?"

Ben let out a short, humourless laugh. "And go where, Harry? Some other rich bastard's pocket? At least with Redfern, I know the devil I'm dealing with."

Henry didn't have an answer for that.

Ben took a drag, exhaling slowly. "Look, Harry—maybe thinking too hard is the problem."

Not a dismissal. A quiet warning.

And Henry heard it for what it was.

Chapter IX

Illusion of Choice

"MOUNTIES TO MONITOR FOREIGN EXTREMISTS"
—*The Ottawa Citizen*, August 25, 1933

"The RCMP Intelligence Branch announces efforts to track radical groups operating in Canada, including fascist sympathizers and communist agitators."

Thursday, December 2nd, 1937
Montreal, Quebec—Late Afternoon

The train car was spacious and well-appointed, a world apart from the business-class compartments Henry was used to. Those felt comfortable enough, sure. But this? This made them look like a vagabond's stowaway corner.

Private travel had its perks.

He and Ben were the first aboard, their luggage already taken and stowed. Henry felt uneasy handing over his case, knowing what was inside. But private travel meant they wouldn't search it.

Still, he didn't like not having eyes on it.

The waitress approached, tall and poised, blonde hair bouncing with each step. She smiled, a broad, toothy grin, untouched by exhaustion or the burden of too many years on the job. She still had the spirit of youth.

"Welcome aboard, gentlemen," she said, her voice light. Polished. "My name is Penny, and I'll take care of this car on your travels." She glanced between them, expectant. "Are either of you Mr. Redfern, by any chance?"

Ben shook his head, that disarming smile already in place. He shrugged off his jacket and hung it with practiced care, ensuring not a wrinkle showed. The shirt underneath hugged his frame, crisp lines reinforcing the effortless poise he carried like second nature.

"Afraid not," he said, leaning against the coat rack. "Harry and me? Just the humble Treasurer and Special Advisor to the rich and powerful."

His comments were casual, almost self-deprecating, but carried the same easy charm that made Ben Schul a man people trusted.

The waitress smiled, her gaze lingering on Ben—assessing him like a butcher eyeing a prime cut, or a debutante weighing marriage prospects.

"Benjamin Schul," Ben said, leaning into her space. "But you, of course, may call me Ben." He gestured toward Henry with an exaggerated flourish. "And my sour-looking colleague here is Henry Locke. Those who appreciate his wit and charm call him Hank."

"Henry," Henry corrected, rolling his eyes as he dropped into a seat by a large bay window. The glass overlooked the loading platform below, where the last cargo was being secured before departure.

He pulled out his pack of cigarettes.

Penny's hand shot up, palm out, as if warding off a catastrophe. "Ahh, sorry, sir. No smoking in this car. Instructions by Mr. Redfern."

Right, Redfern's European influences. The type who believed strong lungs built strong nations.

Henry exhaled through his nose, flipping the cigarette pack absently between his fingers before tucking it away. His eyes scanned the car, a practiced habit.

One booth near the back was already occupied. A man sat with his legs crossed, a newspaper spread before him, his face obscured behind the pages.

Kessler.

Henry hadn't seen him board the train, but that was typical. Kessler had a way of being there without being noticed until he wanted to be.

The lawyer didn't so much as glance up, but Henry had no doubt he was listening. He always was.

"Understood, ma'am. And if I were to partake...?"

"Just in the next train car," Penny signalled distractedly, already returning her attention to Ben.

Henry leaned back in his chair, folding his arms across his chest. Ben's smirk deepened as he watched Penny go, then flicked his gaze to Henry.

"No smoking, Harry. Orders from Mr. Redfern," Ben mimicked, tapping imaginary ashes from an invisible cigarette. "Next thing you know, they'll be banning cocktails."

"That'll be the day," Henry muttered, stretching his legs.

The train swayed as someone clambered aboard with heavy, uneven steps, like the whole car resented taking on the weight.

"Gah, this train is a goddamn wreck."

The words cracked like a whip. Henry felt the train lean as the man heaved himself up the steps, as if his sheer bulk alone could shift the car's balance.

He didn't need to look to know it was Charles Dunlow, general manager of Redfern Pulp and Paper, with his fingers in almost everything. And like Jimmy, he wasn't just in it for the money. He was a believer.

A thick, sweaty mess, buttons on his collar straining like a dam about to burst beneath the pressure of his many chins. He mopped his glistening forehead with an embroidered handkerchief, shoving it into his breast pocket with fat fingers, each adorned with at least one garish, oversized ring.

"Get me a ginger ale. Just a touch of rye. And make it the best you've got."

He always wasted the best of whatever they had. Henry had seen it before: expensive whiskey drowned in soda, fine wine gulped like tap water, caviar smeared onto bread like cheap butter.

Dunlow liked expensive things—but not the taste of them.

He dropped into a cushioned chair with the grace of a felled ox, breathing hard, as if stepping onto the train had winded him.

"Redfern won't be happy about this rolling trash heap."

Penny moved to the bar at the back of the car, already reaching for a glass. She didn't meet his eyes.

Ben shot Dunlow a look—somewhere between pity and disgust—but said nothing. he sank into a seat across from Henry, lips twisted as he surveyed the space.

Behind Dunlow, his assistant boarded.

Margaret Bergström was tall and lean, her sharp features straddling the line between New York runway elegance and the severe authority of Madame Fournier, Henry's old prep school enforcer.

He could still hear her voice: "So much time for hockey, but none for your studies, Mr. Locke."

Fournier had disciplined him more times than he could count. The memory had never quite faded.

With crisp efficiency, Margaret stepped onto the train, heels clicking sharply against the metal. Under one arm, she carried a large New York purse; in the other, a briefcase. Her gaze swept the car, not in admiration, but in evaluation. It was a practiced look, like a field officer inspecting troops.

She didn't look at Dunlow. She didn't need to. Whatever mess he was about to cause, she already knew she'd be the one cleaning it up.

"This will do, Charles," she said, stepping smoothly into the car.

Dunlow grumbled something nearly inaudible.

He answered to no one—except somehow, Margaret. She never raised her voice. Never argued. And yet, despite all his bluster, she was the one who kept him in check.

Margaret didn't just walk; she moved like something engineered—precise, economical, exact.

She crossed to the car without so much as a glance at Dunlow and seated herself at the far end, about as distant from him as the space allowed. Her briefcase clicked open, and she withdrew a thick ledger: columns of numbers, accounts, and tallies, Henry was sure.

Dunlow had no interest in numbers — unless they benefited him.

Margaret set the purse beside her. He'd heard the whispers around Redfern Industries, Margaret's "bag of tricks." Painkillers, stimulants, smelling salts. God knew what else. Whatever kept her sharp through midnight ledgers and morning meetings. Henry didn't doubt a single rumour.

"Hank." Dunlow's voice boomed, just shy of shouting. "You weren't supposed to be here. Where the hell is Jimmy?"

Henry's grip tightened on the arms of his chair. His eye twitched, but he kept his face still.

Ben leaned back, casual as ever. "He's sick, and he could barely walk. Attached to the toilet."

"Well, isn't that convenient?" Dunlow's gaze landed on Henry, heavy with suspicion. It was like he was already halfway to an accusation.

Which... fair enough.

Henry didn't react. Didn't flinch. Just let Dunlow stew in it.

"You're supposed to be staying here, Hank."

Dunlow let the name drag out, stretching it with something shy of a sneer.

If Jimmy was oblivious, Dunlow was malicious.

Henry met his gaze, unblinking. "Well, I guess things don't always work out the way you want, do they?"

He spoke in an even, almost lazy voice, as his eyes flicked briefly to Dunlow's bare left hand, where a ring used to sit.

Dunlow's sneered. "You two think you're so damn clever," he said sharply. "The Jew and the Thug. You're like two stupid peas in a pod, always with your jokes."

Ben stiffened beside him, his nostrils flaring.

Dunlow eased back, a relaxed smile spreading across his face. "Well, the joke will be on you soon enough."

Ben parted his lips, ready to snap something back.

"Children, stop fighting." The voice was dry, disinterested, coming from the corner of the train car.

A rustling newspaper. A slow turn of a page.

Kessler.

Finally, he made himself noticed by the others on the train.

Dunlow flinched, twisting in his seat with a scowl. "Goddammit, Kessler. I hate when you do that."

Walter Kessler, one of the finest lawyers money could buy, had a knack for fading into the background. Not quiet. Not invisible... present without demanding space. The sort of man who existed in peripheral vision until he spoke.

Then, when he did, suddenly, he was the only one in the room.

Kessler turned another page, still not looking up. "Yes, well," he murmured, "that's what makes me good at my job, Charles."

Dunlow ignored him, turning with that same slow smirk stretching across his damp face. "Do you know where we're off to, Ben-ja-min?"

He let the syllables drag, savouring them like a man testing how heavy a knife is before sliding it between ribs.

Ben's face clenched, his usual charm slipping just a fraction.

Penny moved carefully, setting the rye and ginger before Dunlow.

He took a slow mouthful and smacked his lips. "Passable. Barely."

Another sip. A slow swirl of the glass.

He briefly looked at Kessler. "Kessler, have you any idea where we're headed?"

A slow turn of the page.

Kessler didn't look up. "Doesn't matter, Charles." The words landed like a hammer, final, unbothered.

A flicker of disdain crossed Dunlow's mouth.

"Dunlow, leave him be." The words came slowly. Unhurried.

Redfern ascended the steps one at a time—like a king entering his court, certain all eyes would turn to him, whether or not they wanted to. His suit, as always, was immaculate. Tailored to perfection. Crisp. Not a thread out of place, not a crease he hadn't intended.

The room shifted. They stilled.

Dunlow straightened a fraction. His bulk sank deeper into the chair, bravado leaking out of him.

Ben's fingers tapped the table once, then stilled—like a gambler second-guessing a bet.

Kessler didn't turn another page.

Henry shifted.

One day, you will see what he is.

Her voice carried clearer now than it had then.

Redfern smiled, the broad, easy grin of a man who'd worn it a thousand times before.

"Everyone's comfortable, I hope?"

Redfern's voice was smooth and effortless. It was not a demand, just a statement no one dared contradict.

His gaze drifted around the room, landing on Penny. "Penny has taken care of you?"

He gave no time for an answer before his eyes flicked to Dunlow.

Dunlow opened his mouth, then shut it again.

"Good." Redfern smiled, broad and assured, arms spreading wide—not just a greeting, but an embrace of the room itself, as if everything and everyone in it belonged to him.

Kessler turned a page at last. "Where's Mr. Lafleur?"

Redfern's smile froze for a fraction of a second—a brief pause, there and gone. His fingers smoothed over the cuff of his sleeve as if he were flicking off an irritation.

"Handling an issue."

The words were clipped, dismissive, but too controlled.

Henry's brow twitched. *An issue?*

Redfern didn't elaborate. Didn't invite further questioning. His expression remained pleasant, but there was a tightness at the corners of his mouth, a flicker of something unsaid.

Then he chuckled, leisurely and unhurried, nodding with the practiced ease of a man who knew how to keep a room relaxed.

"You know, Vic. Puts himself where he's needed. And where he's not."

A pause. The heaviness of the words settled in.

Redfern turned to Penny, the motion as smooth as before. "Penny, if you'd be a dear, get me a Scotch."

He settled into the chair beside Dunlow, crossing his legs as if the matter was already handled.

His gaze scanned the surrounding faces until it found Henry. "Henry."

Henry barely had time to shift before he felt it, all eyes drawn to him like iron filings to a magnet.

A smile. There was a flicker of warmth in Redfern's eyes that didn't quite reach the edges. "Thanks for cutting your vacation short and filling in for Jimmy."

The words were easy. Offhand.

Then, just a shade too slow,

"It seems the poor man got sick from the drinks with you last night."

Silence. Not long, but enough for Henry to feel the weight of the room pressing in from every side. A simple statement. Or an accusation. He wasn't sure which.

"We all know how Jimmy gets when he's let loose," Henry said matter-of-factly.

Redfern's smile remained, but his eyes narrowed a fraction—too controlled to be casual. "Yes."

The word lingered, heavy, deliberate. Then, light again. Almost idle. "Well, I sent Doctor Winchester to check on him."

Henry matched Redfern, gaze for gaze. Unblinking.

"The good doctor will surely give me a full report on Jimmy's health."

A beat. Just long enough.

"We all want him to be better, don't we?"

Smooth. Pleasant. Almost warm.

But Henry heard what wasn't said. But Henry heard what wasn't said. It hung between them, unspoken, heavy as stone.

Then, just as smoothly, Redfern let it drop.

"Anyway." He turned his attention to the room, the moment discarded as if it had never happened. "Rarely, we're all together," he continued, gesturing expansively, as though hosting a royal court rather than presiding over a gathering no one dared refuse. "My whole kingdom gathered in one train car."

His smile widened.

"Thank you, everyone, for setting aside the next few days for this."

As if they'd been asked, and not simply been expected to drop everything at his discretion.

Redfern settled back as Penny arrived with his Scotch.

"As Mr. Dunlow was alluding to before," he continued, lifting the glass but not drinking just yet, "most of you haven't been privy to our destination for this weekend's events. And that was mildly on purpose."

He sipped. Taking his time. A man with all the time in the world.

"Lovely vintage, this, Penny. What am I drinking?"

"That's a Macallan 1926, Mr. Redfern."

"Ahh, beautiful. Thank you, my dear."

He set the glass down precisely, just as the train whistle screeched, slicing through the air outside like a blade.

Beyond the windows, a few late passengers scurried along the platform, their hurried movements contrasting with the stillness of the car.

Some boarded other cars, others struggled with their luggage, all caught in a rush, while inside, Redfern dictated time at his leisure.

"This weekend," he continued, finally indulging in the grand reveal, "will be the culmination of several weeks, if not months, of hard work by Charlie here."

A casual nod to Dunlow, though he didn't wait for acknowledgment.

"And, of course, Jimmy, who I'm sure is just tormented by the fact that he will be missing it."

The whistle screamed again.

The train jolted forward, the brakes finally released—a subtle, mechanical punctuation to the moment.

Ben exhaled, shaking his head.

"Always drawing it out and leaving us in suspense," Ben said, his tone dry, edged with just enough humour to pass as a joke.

A few chuckles flickered through the group—muted, but enough to ease the tension. Redfern's smile stretched wider, a flash of white teeth. "Apologies, Ben." His grin was indulgent, amused, like an older brother playing along. Then his voice dipped. The warmth remained, but something more calculated stirred beneath it. "It's my love for the theatrics."

The train lurched, pitching them forward as the windows filled with streaks of light and shadow. Redfern settled back into his seat, his glass rolling between his fingers as if this were just another boardroom negotiation. "We're going to a place called Vanderleigh Hall."

Ben exhaled, forcing a chuckle. "That sounds American."

Redfern smirked. "Very observant, Ben. You are correct."

Ben swallowed. The train rumbled beneath them, moving slowly toward something unseen. "But... why?"

Redfern's face lit up, as though Ben had teed him up for a favourite talking point.

"Great question, Ben." He spread his hands, indulgent. "There's an important meeting—select industrialists, politicians, and others of a similar persuasion."

A quiet rustle of paper.

"I assume you mean the leadership group in Washington?"

Kessler. He'd folded his paper neatly in his lap. His expression remained unreadable.

The train jolted, pushing them faster. Fields and towns slipped past, gone before his eyes could even register them.

Redfern's smile widened. "Quite right, Walter."

Ben didn't move.

Opposite him, Dunlow grinned, fingers tapping the armrest.

Ben wet his lips. "Why?" His voice was lower now. "Why bring me?"

Redfern sighed, shaking his head as if it should've been obvious. "Oh, Ben. Stop being so dramatic."

Henry sat stone still, his grip on his glass tightening. He should say something. He should do something. But what? And to whom?

Ben turned to Redfern. "It's not dramatic, James."

Dunlow let out a low, unpleasant chuckle.

Redfern's jaw ticked. He tilted his head, expression taut—acknowledging the breach but saying nothing.

"Sure, it is," Dunlow muttered, lifting his glass. "Come on, Ben-ja-min. It'll be an education."

The words hung in the air like poison gas from the trenches.

Ben stiffened, as if someone had elbowed him in the ribs.

Redfern didn't even notice. Instead, he sighed, adjusting himself in his seat, already bored with the conversation.

"Ben, please." Redfern swirled his glass, the amber liquid catching the dim light. "This is an opportunity. Connections, prestige, hell, the future itself."

Ben opened his mouth, but Redfern stopped him before he could speak.

"Look, Ben, I need you there." Redfern inclined toward him, his tone lower now, more direct. The air shifted. "You're the books, Ben. You keep the lights on, the accounts balanced, and the off-the-record deals... respectable. Without you, none of this would run."

Ben stiffened.

Across from him, Dunlow's squinty eyes flicked toward Redfern. His fingers twitched, just once.

"Are you sure it's wise, Mr. Redfern?" The voice came from the far end of the car, Margaret Bergström, finally looking up from her ledger. She didn't raise her voice. She did not need to do so. "The Americans have been passing some very... aggressive legislation."

The train swayed again, pushing them faster, the landscape blurring into streaks outside the window.

Redfern sighed, waving a hand. Dismissive. Unbothered. "That's just for the undesirables." His smile returned, wide, warm, confident, like he was explaining something so obvious. "Not for men who matter."

Ben stopped breathing.

Redfern lifted his glass and took another casual sip. "The Americans are tidying up their house. It's nothing more than posturing."

Henry glanced at Ben. The colour had drained from his face. His hands were shaking.

"It's not just undesirables," Ben said, his voice low. "I haven't heard from my cousin Noam in—"

"Yes, yes," Redfern cut in, waving a hand. "I know communication has grown difficult."

Ben blinked. His lips parted, but nothing came out.

Grown difficult? Henry almost laughed.

Redfern smiled, indulgent, as if explaining a minor inconvenience.

"Since things have escalated in recent weeks, it's been harder. But..." He clapped his hands together, sharp and final. "That's what we're going to be trying to remedy."

The train lurched forward, picking up speed.

Redfern leaned in. "We've been invited, along with a few other prominent guests."

A rustle of paper. Kessler.

His voice floated out from behind the newspaper—smooth, unbothered. "I suppose the usual notable American leaders?"

Redfern nodded. "And a few international as well."

Ben stared, eyes locked on Redfern. His hands gripped tight against his knees. "What are you saying?"

Redfern took a slow sip of Scotch. Let the question hang for a second too long. "This is more of an... international alliance that might be formed. A sort of coalition."

"*The Nazis?*" Ben's words exploded, just short of a shout.

Outside, the horizon kept rushing, too fast to hold onto.

Henry leaned in, grip clenched so tight around his glass he thought it might crack.

Across from him, Redfern's expression tightened. He picked at his fingernails.

"National Socialists," he said.

His tone was calm. Absolute. Like a professor correcting a student.

Ben stared at him, chest rising and falling, his face drained of colour. He looked around the room, face to face.

Redfern sipped slowly of Scotch, unbothered. "The Germans are pragmatic men, Ben. Just like us."

"*You're bringing me,*" he said, pausing and pressing a finger to his chest. "*A Jew. To a meeting. With Nazis?*" A hitch in his breath. Fingers balled into fists. When he spoke, his voice was thin—barely more than a whisper.

"You're serious?"

Redfern sighed and waved his hand as if swatting away a gnat. "It's fine." He didn't even look at Ben. Instead, his gaze flicked to Dunlow. "You were right about not telling him in advance, Charlie."

A smirk tugged at the corner of his mouth.

Dunlow's grin widened, fingers drumming slow, deliberate taps against the armrest. "The reactions are always big with him."

Ben's unclenched his hands. "I'm not going." His voice was tight. "I'll get off at the border and walk back to Montreal."

The words stilled the room.

Henry let out a slow breath, shifting in his seat. His jaw tightened, but he said nothing.

Redfern tilted his head, studying Ben as if weighing an investment gone sour.

Then, with a small, almost regretful sigh—"Fine, Ben. When we stop at Rouses Point, you can get out, take the next train back to Montreal."

He let the words sit.

"And of course, collect your things. You can arrange your last pay cheque."

The words hung heavier than anything else in the room.

Ben's jaw tightened.

Redfern moved, his voice low and measured.

"I need you there, Ben." He smiled without warmth. "You don't want to disappoint me, do you?"

Chapter X

The Threshold

"VALE SURVIVES ASSASSINATION ATTEMPT IN NEW ORLEANS"
—*The Atlanta Constitution*, August 16, 1933

"An alleged communist agitator attempted to shoot Nathaniel Vale yesterday. The attack, which some claim was staged, has only strengthened his growing movement."

Thursday, December 2nd, 1937
Rouses Point, New York—Early Evening

Henry stood on the platform, the frigid wind pulling at him. His cigarette flared brightly with each gust, then dimmed again.

The train had stopped for inspection. Passengers disembarked to pass through customs—some stretching their legs, others chatting like it was just another stop.

Ben paced beside him, rubbing the back of his neck. "I have to go back, Harry."

Henry blew smoke through his nose. His eyes followed Ben's movements across the platform.

"Yeah, Ben," he said finally, rubbing the bridge of his nose. "I think you do. Grab the next train back."

Ben walked with a twitchy stride, then glanced at the customs agents and the train before looking north toward Montreal.

"But I can't." His voice was quieter now. "I need this job."

Henry sighed, flicking ash onto the tracks.

Ben's breath came ragged. His nostrils flared. His eyes searched, pained and restless.

"Ben." Henry's voice was firm now. "You can't come. You need to head back."

Ben dragged a hand through his hair, pacing again. Their group had already re-boarded. The train would leave soon.

His breath fogged in the cold air. "I have to, Harry."

Henry gritted his teeth. He could feel his pulse in his throat.

"Fuck that, Ben." He took a step toward him, voice low and urgent. "This is your life. You don't know what they're going to do. It's just a job."

Ben let out a bitter laugh, short and sharp. He turned, lips pinched, eyes tense.

"So easy for you, Harry. 'Just a job.' Just a job?" Ben's breath hitched. "How many employers are lining up to hire a kike lately?"

Henry grimaced. The word hit like a slap. His jaw tightened, but his gaze remained fixed.

The silence stretched.

"Come on, Ben." He flicked the last of his cigarette, grinding it under his boot. "I know it's tough, but you're one of the smartest guys I know."

Ben pressed his lips into a thin line, twisting his mouth into a sneer. "In this climate?" He said bitterly. "You think that's worth a damn?"

He turned, staring back into the darkness north.

"Do you see the way Dunlow looks at me?" He crossed his arms in front of his chest. "That's all I ever get." He turned back toward Henry. His lip quivered. "At least with Redfern, it's just indifference. He ignores my Jewishness."

The words hung between them.

Ben's eyes darted toward the agent again. His jaw set.

Henry opened his mouth, but nothing came. He closed it again as Ben stepped forward, chin high and shoulders back, pulling his identification from his coat pocket.

Henry followed with short steps, a deep sigh leaving him.

The Border Patrol officer was lean and muscular. His heavy wool coat was lined with brass buttons, and the insignia of the U.S. Immigration Authority gleamed on his chest. His hat sat low, casting a shadow over sharp, assessing eyes.

He took Ben's papers and examined them longer than anyone else's. His brow creased.

"Benjamin Schul?" His tone was empty, unreadable.

Ben nodded, his chin still lifted.

The agent squinted at him. Then, without handing the documents back, he waved over another officer.

The second man approached—older, stockier—his boots striking the wooden platform in crisp, echoing beats. He took the passport and flipped through it, each page turned with deliberate care.

They murmured, heads close. Too long.

Henry's fingers itched for a cigarette, but he clenched them into fists instead, thumb brushing over his knuckles.

The older officer nodded once, then turned back to Ben.

"New federal security policy," he said, pulling a small metal pin from his pocket. He reached out and affixed it to Ben's coat.

A six-pointed star. Brass. Polished. At its centre: REGISTERED SEMITE.

"You'll be required to wear this while in the United States."

Ben's shoulders tightened, then slumped. His lips parted, but no words came. He looked anywhere but toward the pin—as if the officer had just affixed a grenade.

The agent pressed it down firmly, ensuring it was straight and level. His fingers lingered a second too long.

A final change. A seal of ownership.

"For identification purposes, of course. You understand. For everyone's safety."

The train let out a long, shuddering whistle behind them.

Henry felt the wind bite through his coat. His arms hung limp at his sides. He stared at the small piece of metal gleaming in Ben's jacket.

Ben's hands were fists. The pin caught the station lights—small, but inescapable.

A badge of humiliation. A warning to the world.

Henry's stomach twisted.

The second agent stamped the papers, pressing so hard the desk shook.

The ink was bright red.

"You'll also need to check in with local authorities upon arrival. Standard procedure."

Ben walked toward the train, back straight, chin high.

Faces stared from the windows. None spoke.

One man shifted, turning his head—as if looking away might erase what he'd seen.

A woman touched her scarf, pulled it tighter, eyes flicking to the floor.

No one intervened.

Henry watched the train door seal Ben inside.

Then he turned, teeth grinding, jaw tight.

He shoved his papers forward.

The officer barely looked at them. Didn't even flip through the pages. Just a glance. A name. A face.

"Enjoy your time in the United States."

Henry's hands itched to strike something.

The train rattled forward in silence.

Ben sat at the back. Alone.

Redfern hadn't said a word since they'd re-boarded. He'd seen the pin on Ben's chest—his lips pressed into a frown—but, as always, he dismissed it. Just the Americans being overly reactionary. Still, the earlier vigour in his voice was gone.

Outside, the windows were black voids, reflecting nothing but the cabin's dim glow. Only an occasional streak of passing light pierced the dark.

Kessler had finished the paper. Now he held a paperback: Gone With the Wind.

Henry's fingers tightened on his coat sleeve.

Margaret sat near Dunlow, with the ledger closed across her lap. She spoke softly about unionization efforts at one of the pulp mills. Henry caught snippets—something about sending in "anti-labour activists" to handle the problem. Handle. That was the word she'd used.

His brow twitched.

Handled. The word echoed, sharp and familiar. Like the ones shouted at him through the rain. The ones he hadn't heard—wouldn't hear.

His fingers flexed.

Across the room, Redfern tapped the armrest. Every so often, he glanced at Ben. Rarely enough for anyone else to notice. But Henry did.

Peggy stood behind the bar, twisting a cocktail napkin between her fingers—slowly, deliberate. Her eyes flicked toward Ben, then away again too quickly.

The conversation hadn't just grown stale. It had stopped.

Henry lowered his fedora over his eyes and stretched out. It was going to be a long night.

The train lurched to a sudden halt, nearly jolting him from his seat.

His fedora slid forward, covering his eyes. Blinking, he pushed it back and peered out the window.

Darkness. But beyond it, the outline of a platform.

"You have reached your destination," Peggy said brightly. "Welcome to Lake Placid."

Henry rose groggily and stretched.

"Your belongings will be waiting on the platform," Peggy continued, clasping her hands together. "And I'll see you all on Sunday. Train departs at eleven AM!"

Sunday.

Three days.

He just had to survive for three days.

Ben strolled up beside him, rolling his shoulders as if he was shaking off the cold.

"Pal, you snore like a baby," Ben said, forcing a grin that vanished almost as soon as it formed.

Henry's fingers twitched at his side.

Redfern lingered near the aisle, hesitating for the first time since they boarded. His gaze flicked to Ben's chest—just briefly—then away, as if it didn't matter.

Then, casually—like he was suggesting Ben fix his tie—Redfern said, "Why don't you just take it off, Ben? Everything will be fine."

Ben didn't move. The train swayed gently beneath them, the only sound the muffled clatter of the tracks.

"That's a death sentence," Kessler said, not looking up. He turned a page.

Redfern's brow furrowed. "Impossible," he scoffed, waving vaguely at the pin, like it were nothing more than an unfortunate accessory.

Ben's hand tightened into a fist.

Kessler looked up then, tilting his head, eyes fixed on the pin. "They would. Passing yourself off as gentile? In America, they don't look the other way. Some already hang for less."

Redfern's lips thinned. His fingers tapped against his thigh. He looked at Ben again—this time, for a second longer.

"I haven't heard that."

Kessler's eyes flicked back to his paper. "Perhaps not in the publications you read."

Redfern turned away. Said nothing.

They descended the steps from the train, their footfalls echoing across the platform. Redfern walked in silence, his brow still furrowed, the words clinging to him like smoke.

He looked like a man who'd seen a ghost.

The wind hit like a knife—sharp and biting. Snow swirled around them, stinging their faces. The platform was only half-cleared, patches of white clinging stubbornly to the ground. Their luggage sat near the edge, dusted with fresh snow.

Dunlow squinted through the flurry.

"Where the hell is the car?" Henry shouted above the wind.

The train whistle cut through the cold as the locomotive lurched forward, wheels clanking. Faces in the windows turned their way briefly, indifferently. Already forgetting.

The wind bit deeper.

Dunlow stomped through the snow, scanning the empty parking lot.

Redfern stood motionless, eyes on the tree line. "They'll be here soon," he said—whether to the group or himself, Henry couldn't tell.

A sound overhead—a low hum, then a rising whir. Two dark shapes slicing through the clouds.

"Those sound like Peashooters," Ben murmured, tilting his head.

Redfern glanced up. His expression didn't change. "You would be the one to know, Benjamin."

The platform shuddered as the fighters screamed past, flying low, just above the trees. A patrol. Watching. Hunting.

Henry pulled his coat tighter. "Why are they flying night patrols?"

Ben didn't look away from the sky. "Not sure what they're looking for."

The words lingered as Henry pulled his jacket closer about his shoulders as a pair of headlights rounded a curve.

"See, there they are." Redfern smiled to himself, satisfied.

Henry watched him, but the smile didn't quite reach his eyes.

Ben ambled up beside Henry, hands deep in his coat pockets. "Did you know?" he asked, voice low.

Henry glanced at him, brow furrowing. "What're you getting at?"

Ben's eyes narrowed as his brow wrinkled. "At the bar. You said—"

Henry grimaced as he lowered his gaze.

"Forget it, Ben," Henry said, voice low. "We just gotta make it to Sunday."

Ben's jaw tightened. "What do you mean, 'we'?" His voice sharpened. "You ain't the one wearing a damn Semite pin."

Henry met his eye. The wind howled between them, biting and bitter.

Ben was waiting for something. Maybe an answer. Maybe an excuse.

Henry took a slow, pained breath and looked away. "I'm tryin', Ben. Best I can."

Ben huffed a bitter laugh. "I needed you back at customs. Didn't see you then."

Henry's jaw tightened. "What the hell did you want me to do?"

Ben's glare flickered, just for a second. "I dunno, you could have said something."

Henry looked out into the darkness. He could have. He should have.

The headlights swept across the platform, cutting through the swirling snow. As the car pulled up, Dunlow squinted, his nostrils flaring.

It was a massive vehicle—black, gleaming, a long, hulking shape of steel and chrome—possibly a Cadillac limousine, maybe a Packard. A car designed for leaders, tycoons, and men of immense wealth.

The driver stepped out. His silver insignia caught the light. Eagle Guard.

Dunlow barely waited. "Just one damn car?" He threw his hands up. "How the hell are we all supposed to fit?"

The driver didn't blink. "You can squeeze." His voice was flat, uninterested. He turned, adjusting his gloves. "You ain't the only guests arriving tonight, Canuck."

Henry caught a glance at Ben's face—stone still, unreadable.

Redfern stiffened, a muscle jumping in his jaw. He adjusted his coat, smoothing the lapel with deliberate precision, as if brushing off the slight.

The driver approached, taking them all in, his gaze flicking from face to face like he was appraising livestock.

Then he stopped at Ben. At the pin.

"A Jew?"

The words hung in the frigid air, sharp as the wind.

Ben lifted his chin, saying nothing.

"Ha." The driver smirked. "You people always claw your way up—like rats on a sinking ship."

No one moved.

The driver hefted the first of the bags, muttering to himself as he worked.

Henry kept his hands in his pockets, fingers curled tight.

Redfern took his time walking down the steps. Dunlow opened the car door, and Redfern ducked inside, disappearing into the warm interior.

Henry turned. Then froze.

A figure moved toward them. Thin. Wiry. Familiar. Moustache, round glasses, black fedora pulled low.

The man from the station.

Henry's stomach turned to ice. His pulse pounded—hard, the hammering thud of a jazz drummer in a packed, smoky club.

What the hell was he doing here?

What the hell was going on?

What was he going to say?

The stranger's eyes locked onto his. His mouth opened.

"You again?" Henry cut in, his voice sharp, laced with irritation. "What, you followin' me now?"

The stranger stiffened. His mouth snapped shut. The hint of surprise in his eyes was almost imperceptible—but Henry caught it.

"You know this guy?" Ben asked, frowning.

The moment stretched—too many eyes now watching.

Saliva caught in Henry's throat. He fought the urge to swallow, forcing a casual shrug instead. Then he shook his head and thumbed toward the man.

"Not really," he said, running a hand along his jaw. "Met him back at the station. Claimed he had a case just like mine. Thought it was his. Damn near tore my arm outta the socket tryin' to take it."

Ben's eyes flicked between Henry and the stranger. Then slowly he nodded.

The stranger hesitated—just for a moment—then his expression smoothed, the flicker of surprise buried fast.

"A simple mistake," he said evenly. "No harm done, I hope?" His eyes flicked to Henry's hands. To the luggage at their feet. "And yet... your case is not here?"

He held Henry's gaze for too long. Measured. Feeling for cracks.

Henry didn't blink.

"What's your obsession with his case?" Ben asked, stepping closer.

The stranger lifted his hands, palms out—a dismissive chuckle slipping through his teeth. "Just a misunderstanding, I assure you."

His eyes fixed on Henry—narrowed, calculating. His jaw was set, and the smile that followed was thin and deliberate, more a baring of teeth than any sign of warmth. "These things happen," he said.

He didn't look away as he passed them, descending toward the waiting Cadillac. The driver opened the door, and the stranger climbed in without another word, sliding into the far corner of the back seat.

Ben and Henry exchanged a look. Ben's expression was questioning, but Henry shook his head—just slightly. Not here. Not now.

They followed a moment later, the night air sharp in their lungs as they squeezed into the already crowded car. Heat and breath and wool pressed together in the confined space. The stranger sat at the far end, face turned toward the window, pretending disinterest. But Henry could feel it—the quiet gravity of being watched, the weight of eyes that never really left him.

The drive was slow, the roads thick with snow and treacherous with ice. More than once, the limousine lurched, chains clattering against frozen pavement as the driver fought the wheel. Each skid drew a breath from someone inside. A few inches more, a touch too much speed, and they'd plummet into the ravine—vanish beneath the drifts.

And part of him wished they would.

But the car pushed on, crawling through the winding roads, until at last, their destination loomed ahead.

"I imagine Wilcox will be there himself to greet us," Redfern said with a smirk, his chin held high. "It's a rare thing, an opportunity like this."

Dunlow nodded along. "Yeah, makes sense. We've proven ourselves. A little face time at the entrance is the least they can do."

Ben exhaled quietly, staring out the window.

The first glimpse came through the wrought-iron gate—tall, intricate, black as midnight. A pair of Eagle Guards flanked it, silent, unmoving, silver insignia gleaming in the carriage lamps. Each cradled a compact Thompson, fingers relaxed but ready.

Their gazes swept over the car, evaluating, sorting. This wasn't just security.

It was permission.

The car slowed to a stop, the driver rolling down his window.

Beyond the gate, Vanderleigh Hall rose against the night—a fortress of privilege rooted in the land long before the men inside were ever born. It wasn't a house. It was power made timber and stone: massive beams, steep gables, dark-stained wood set against native rock. Towering windows climbed three stories, spilling golden light onto the snow. Iron lanterns guttered on the terraces while stone chimneys exhaled ribbons of smoke into the sky.

At its heart, the great hall blazed with chandeliers, silhouettes drifting past tall curtains. This was no ski lodge for leisure. It was a hunting lodge for kings and captains of industry, where legacies were carved over bourbon and blood.

At the gate, a guard conferred with the driver while another circled, boots crunching in the snow, peering into the car. His gaze swept over each of them. Ben shifted, shoulder brushing Henry's. Henry felt it too. They weren't being welcomed—they were being admitted.

The car eased forward, climbing the narrow lane toward the entrance, where limousines already gleamed beneath the lights.

Redfern smiled. Dunlow's eyes twinkled.

Ben swallowed hard.

Henry watched.

The car pulled into a slow circle before the grand entrance, rolling to a stop beneath the towering portico. No one came out to meet them.

The door swung open.

A porter stood waiting, crisp in a fine suit, white gloves resting at his sides. His blonde hair was slicked back, his features pale and composed. The way he held himself—not stiff, but deliberate—spoke of a man who understood his place in the machinery of power. His smile was effortless.

But it didn't reach his eyes.

"Welcome to Vanderleigh Hall," he said, voice smooth.

Redfern stepped out first, straightening his jacket with a practiced motion as his gaze swept the entrance. His smile carried the weight of high expectations.

A second passed. Then another.

Redfern exhaled, tilting his head. His fingers flexed against his coat sleeve before he stilled them. "Where's the welcome party?"

The porter blinked. "Welcome party, sir?"

"Yes." Redfern's voice remained light, but there was something clipped at the edges of it now. "I assumed we'd be received at the door."

The porter hesitated. Not long—just enough.

"The reception is inside, sir. Most of the guests have already arrived."

Ben didn't move.

Henry glanced at Redfern—just long enough to catch it: the slight tightening of his jaw, the stilling of his hands, the way his breath paused mid-draw.

Then, it was gone.

Redfern nodded, the motion sharp. His smile held, but his posture had stiffened—a fraction, just enough to notice. "Of course," he said, already turning. "Shall we?"

He strode forward, his shoes clicking against the stone. Dunlow followed, adjusting his coat, his smugness unshaken.

Henry turned to the porter as the others disappeared into the hall. "And our luggage?"

The porter's smile didn't shift. Polite. Cool. "It will be delivered to your room, sir."

"Oh. I thought I'd be bringing it."

The faintest flicker of amusement touched the man's expression. "This is Vanderleigh Hall, sir. Here, guests do not carry their luggage."

Henry exhaled through his nose, resisting the urge to adjust his tie. "Right, well—"

The porter's eyes flicked toward the trunk, then back to Henry.

"Your friends are leaving, sir. You should catch up." His tone remained pleasant but final.

"Your luggage will be attended to."

Henry lingered just a moment, then turned and walked inside.

Chapter XI

The Gathering Storm

"REGISTERED SEMITE PINS INTRODUCED: ALL JEWS MUST REPORT TO LOCAL OFFICES"
—*The Chicago Tribune*, July 12, 1937

"The Department of Public Order has announced that all Jewish residents must register for identification under the new 'Semitic Classification Policy.'"

Thursday, December 2nd, 1937
Vanderleigh Hall, Lake Placid, New York—Late Evening

The hall's interior dripped with American opulence, dressed up as rustic charm. Stone fireplaces loomed along the walls, logs stacked high beside them, filling the air with the scent of pine and fresh-cut wood—a wilderness manufactured for men who never split their own firewood.

Above the nearest hearth, a gilded frame held the sharp-eyed likeness of Nathaniel Vale, his military-cut suit immaculate, his gaze unblinking. His portrait wasn't alone. At the far end, between two bookcases, hung a smaller but unmistakable image—Adolf Hitler, his stare just as severe, his presence impossible to ignore.

The furniture followed the same philosophy: hand-carved, heavy, meant to look like it belonged to men with calloused hands. Yet the finish was too polished, the leather too fine. This was not a place where men lived rough—it was where they played at it.

As the Canadians crossed the threshold, the hum of conversation reached them—low, murmured voices punctuated by sharp bursts of laughter. The kind that came from men who never had to glance over their shoulders.

The porter led them through the hall, past sweeping staircases and vaulted ceilings, to a vast chamber at the back of the estate. A ballroom by any measure—yet it refused to call itself one.

Mounted antlers hung above the timber walls. Iron sconces flickered. Overhead, chandeliers shaped like wagon wheels cast circles of amber light. Even here, in the heart of power, the affectation remained—a frontier aesthetic for those who'd never seen the frontier.

A massive American flag dominated one wall, its stars and stripes catching the flicker of firelight. Across from it, smaller but no less commanding, hung a blood-red swastika. Two flags. Two empires watching over the room.

Above the entrance:

"UNITY. STRENGTH. DESTINY."

Two score men, maybe more—and a select few women—filled the space. Most wore immaculate uniforms, ribbons and medals gleaming. Many of them meant nothing. Vanity metal. Awards for men who had never bled for them.

At the entrance, Redfern stood tall, waiting—as though expecting a herald to announce him.

He waited longer than he should have.

The room didn't move, but something in Redfern did. A flicker of tension crossed his face—just a second too long, a hesitation too sharp. For the first time, he wasn't the one steering the room.

He turned to Dunlow. The big man's face was flushed, his brow slick with sweat. He gave a helpless shrug.

Henry, watching from the back, caught Redfern leaning close, his voice a harsh whisper that wasn't quite a whisper.

"They know I'm coming, correct?"

Dunlow's face deepened to the shade of a tomato about to burst. "Yes, Mr. Redfern. Of course."

Redfern's mouth tightened. He gave a single, sharp nod and straightened his jacket—the act of a man trying to smooth away something that shouldn't be there.

Without another word, he stepped into the room. Henry and Ben followed, keeping a respectful distance as they crossed the threshold.

A small group of men near the entrance turned at Redfern's approach—New York suits, pressed and perfect, the kind worn by men accustomed to closing deals over steak and Scotch. One of them stood apart, his posture straight, his uniform immaculate: a U.S. Army general, two stars on his epaulettes.

Redfern smiled. "Gentlemen." He inclined his head a fraction. "James Redfern. Owner and operator of Redfern Industries."

One of the suited men, a broad-shouldered fellow with movie-star teeth, frowned. "Redfern Industries? Never heard of it."

Redfern's smile didn't falter. If anything, it sharpened. "Pulp and paper. And newspapers."

The general squinted. "Which papers?"

Redfern's smile thinned—a shift you might miss if you weren't looking. "The *Dominion Post.* The *Northern Standard.* The *National Observer.*"

A second man, a thinner, wiry sort, snapped his fingers and let out a sharp laugh. "Ha! The other Canadian! I told you!" He smacked the broad-shouldered man, Robert, on the back. "A grand, Robert. Cash. No damn checks."

Robert scowled, muttering a curse as he reached for his wallet.

Henry lingered near the edge of the ballroom, Ben close behind.

They weren't the only ones watching their step.

Henry's gaze swept across the space. Clusters of American brass, some in pressed New York suits, others in military dress. Then, a break in the sea of blue and khaki — black SS uniforms. The silver skulls gleamed under the chandeliers, their wearers engaged in quiet, measured conversation.

Near the far end, an Italian officer stood stiffly, his gaze flicking across the room like a man bracing for something.

He looked nearly as uncomfortable as Ben.

But something was missing.

Where were the names that Henshaw had said would be present? The fascist celebrities Jimmy had been giddy about? The ones who made headlines?

Lots of uniforms. Lots of brass. But no one Henry recognized from the papers.

Why?

A hand gripped Henry's shoulder, snapping him from his thoughts.

"Let's grab a drink, Harry," Ben said.

Henry nodded. The bar stretched along the back wall, polished wood gleaming under the dim lights. They skirted the margin of the crowd on their way over.

The bartender, a striking redhead, moved with the ease of someone who'd spent years in places like this, pouring drinks for men who expected the world to be handed to them in a cut-crystal glass.

She looked like she'd stepped straight off Prince Edward Island, the grown-up version of Anne Shirley, as if Anne had traded Green Gables for a bar stocked with bourbon and bad decisions.

Just above the bar, gold-leaf lettering caught the low light.

America Reborn. Order Restored.

No excess, no flourish, just the promise of a future already written.

She looked up as they approached. "What can I get you, gentlemen?"

Henry rested on the bar. "Got any whiskey?"

She tilted her head, amusement flickering behind her eyes. "American or Irish?"

Henry smirked. "Got any rye?"

She pursed her lips, glancing at the bottles. "Let me check." She turned to Ben. "And for you, sir?"

Ben's smile unfolded like silk. Smooth, easy, the kind that had talked men into deals and women into bed.

Her gaze lingered just for a second too long.

He had that effect.

"Benjamin," he began, voice warm, rich.

Her lips parted as if a response was already forming. She glanced down.

And saw the pin.

The shift was immediate.

Not a recoil. Not quite a frown.

She straightened, smoothing her apron, her warmth cooling to something distant. Professional. Neutral.

"Ahh… just a moment," she said quickly, buttoning up as if the room had suddenly turned cold. "I don't know if we can… umm. I'll be right back."

She turned away, disappearing into the back.

Ben didn't move.

Henry's fingers tapped once against the bar, his shoulders tightening.

Neither of them needed to say it.

They both knew.

Henry set a hand on the bar, eyes sweeping the room.

Margaret Bergström was nowhere to be seen, likely tucked away in some secluded corner, quietly observing.

Kessler? Walter could be anywhere. A man like him never needed to be seen to be present.

Dunlow and Redfern were making their rounds, shaking hands, ingratiating themselves with every palm they could find.

Henry tapped a cigarette from his pack and placed it between his lips.

"I'm sorry, sir," the red-headed bartender said, voice smooth but distant. "We don't have any Canadian whisky in stock. But perhaps an Old Forester?" She gestured toward the bottle.

Henry wet his lips and nodded. "Sure. That's fine."

"I'll have the same."

Ben's voice was light, easy, as he shifted closer to the bar.

The bartender didn't move.

"I'm sorry, sir," she said, her tone changing. Colder now, practiced. "This bar is only serving guests of the party. I've been instructed not to serve the staff."

Ben blinked, brow furrowing. "I'm not the staff."

A beat.

The bartender's smile remained. But it didn't touch her eyes. "Of course not."

She turned, reaching for Henry's glass.

"Then I'll have two."

Her hand froze halfway to the bottle. She looked up. "A double, sir?"

Henry slid the cigarette to the side of his mouth. "No. Two glasses."

She hesitated. "You want two glasses of bourbon?"

"That's allowed, isn't it?"

The bartender's eyes flicked toward the room, searching and expecting someone to step in. No one did.

An instant too long.

She reached for the ice. The scraping of cubes against the tin was slow and deliberate. The bourbon poured next, golden and precise, over the ice.

She slid the glasses forward, her voice low. "Here you are, sir."

Brows drawn, she watched him as if she already knew what he was about to do.

Henry pulled the cigarette from his lips, grabbed both drinks, and turned to Ben.

He handed him one. "Cheers."

The bartender opened her mouth, but Henry had already turned away, walking toward the edge of the chamber, conspicuously beneath the massive swastika.

The weight of it hung above him, oppressive, sickening.

He fought the instinct to step out from under it. But that was the point. If he felt it, others would too.

Let them stare at the flag, not at them.

Ben took a sip. "Gonna be a long weekend if you have to order all my drinks."

Henry smirked. "Don't get used to it. You ain't a long-legged dame, Ben."

Ben let out a quiet breath, rolling the glass between his fingers. He stared at the amber liquid, the ice clinking softly.

Ben took another sip. "What's your bet?"

Henry side-eyed him. "On what?"

Ben stared at his drink, then smirked. "How long till I have a bag over my head?" His voice was quiet, barely cutting through the low murmur of the room.

Henry glanced toward Redfern, floundering among the sharks. "I told you not to come."

Ben's smirk was faint, tired. "Well, now I'm thinking I should've listened to you."

"First time for everything." Henry swirled the bourbon between his palms as he watched the cubes adjust in the low light. "Why are you still with Redfern?"

Ben's nostrils flared as he took a slow sip. "You mean me?" He raised an eyebrow. "Or do you mean a Jew?"

Henry didn't blink. "Both."

Ben scoffed, barely. He tapped his fingers against the glass.

"Money's good. Not many places hiring me these days."

A pause. He rolled his glass between his palms.

"At first, it made sense. The whole Canada First thing. Build the economy. Keep out the commies. Get rid of the unions." His lips pressed into a thin line. "I think that's where Redfern still is. He doesn't see what's underneath it all."

Henry studied him. "And you do."

Ben didn't answer. Just stirred his glass, noticing the ripples move through the amber.

Then, softly—"Tell me, Harry. How come you haven't left yet?"

Henry let the question sit.

Outside, the laughter from across the room swelled, then died again.

Finally, he took a drink, letting the burn settle before answering. "It's complicated."

The silence between them stretched, the kind that didn't need filling.

A fresh burst of laughter resonated throughout the room. The clink of glasses. The warm hum of conversation.

And then...

A figure blocked the doorway.

Thin. Wiry. Searching.

Henry's breath hitched. *Shit.*

His smirk faltered, and that was enough.

Ben noticed. "What?" His voice stayed easy, but his eyes followed Henry's.

The wiry man scanned the room, his gaze sweeping the crowd with deliberate slowness.

Then he stopped.

And stepped aside.

From the mass of bodies, an SS officer peeled away from the crowd, tall, stiff-backed, uniform immaculate. His stride was unhurried, but his purpose was clear.

He stopped beside the wiry man. Close. Familiar.

They spoke in low tones. Quick. Focused.

Then the SS officer stilled.

And his gaze snapped directly to them.

Henry's pulse quickened.

Ben watched the officer's approach without blinking. "What the fuck, Henry."

Henry forced his grip to loosen around his glass. "Play it easy, Ben."

The SS officer rotated with parade-ground precision, the wiry man trailing a step behind.

He stopped just short of them. The only thing missing was the heel click. "Mr. Schul, I presume."

Ben's eyes flicked to Henry, then back to the officer. "That would be me," he said carefully.

"And this," the officer gestured toward Henry, "would be Jim Benoit?"

Henry raised the glass to his lips, letting the whiskey linger as he scanned the room. Then he looked back at the officer. "Nah, Jimmy got sick."

The SS officer studied him. Measured. "And you are?"

"Henry Locke." Henry extended a hand, deliberate. "Special Advisor to Mr. Redfern."

"Ah." The officer didn't take it. Just nodded. "The one removed from the list... found his way back on."

Henry smirked, his hand dropping to his side. "Guess you could say I was lucky enough to have my vacation cut short. Plus, I'm a hard name to keep off a list."

The officer's expression didn't shift. "This is Erich Spalding," he gestured to the wiry man beside him.

Henry's gaze flicked over Spalding, his smirk widening just a fraction. "Very German-sounding name, that."

The SS officer didn't bite. Instead, he adjusted his cuff, his expression unreadable. "Mr. Spalding mentioned there was some confusion in Montreal."

Henry's gut clenched. He looked away.

"Yeah. Guess he got me confused with someone else." He sipped, rolling the bourbon over his tongue. "Happens to the best of us. Must've been a good-looking guy."

The SS officer's lips barely twitched. "Yes. Quite."

The officer smoothed the front of his uniform, then spoke, his voice even.

"My counterpart in the Eagle Guard and I will oversee security this weekend. Ensuring that every guest is exactly where they should be." His gaze drifted to Ben. "And those who are not... will be dealt with accordingly."

The weight of the words hung between them. Not a threat. A statement of fact.

Then, without another word, the SS officer turned sharply on his heel, moving as if dismissed from the parade.

Henry loosened his grip on the glass, the stem cool against his palm. "You introduced Mr. Spalding, but not yourself."

The officer didn't pause, didn't even glance back. But his voice cut through the space like a blade.

"SS Sturmbannführer Reinhard Hoffner."

Hoffner disappeared into the crowd, but Spalding stayed.

He didn't follow.

Didn't move an inch.

He lingered. Watching Henry.

"I know that case wasn't yours."

Henry let his gaze drift. "You're right." He took a sip of bourbon. "It's a friend's."

Spalding's mouth twitched. The ghost of a smirk. "You won't talk your way out of this."

The words weren't a warning.

They were a promise.

Then he turned on his heel and walked away, vanishing into the crowd.

Ben's breath was slow, measured. But his fingers were tight around his glass. "Henry, what the hell is happening?"

Henry swirled his drink, watching the ice shift. "*Still trying to figure that out myself.*"

The sharp clink of a spoon against glass cut through the murmur of conversation.

A moment.

Then silence.

On a small stage at the side of the room, a tall, handsome, athletic man stepped forward with a champagne flute. His broad moustache twitched with a knowing grin, his pinstripe suit sharp as a blade.

If Henry had to picture an 1800s robber baron, or a man who thought himself one, he wouldn't have been far off.

The grin widened. Arms spread wide, welcoming, benevolent, practiced.

"Ladies and gentlemen."

A pause. A beat. Letting the room settle beneath his voice.

"Welcome to Vanderleigh Hall, one of my many homes, each a testament to our great civilization's prosperity."

His gaze swept the room, sharp, measuring.

"For those of you who haven't yet had the pleasure, my name is Harold Wilcox. Your benevolent host."

A slow, deliberate sip of champagne.

"I know many of you have travelled far. That you've endured delays, harsh weather, poor roads, perhaps even an unfortunate aerial encounter or two."

A ripple of knowing chuckles threaded through the hall.

An inside joke Henry wasn't in on.

Wilcox smirked. He enjoyed this.

"But I promise you, it will be worth it."

Henry's eyes flicked to Redfern.

He was nodding along, lips pressed together in quiet satisfaction.

Wilcox lifted his glass, turning his gaze back to the room.

"We are gathered here, my friends, because we recognize one undeniable truth."

His voice hardened just enough to cut.

"The old world is crumbling."

The warmth in his expression didn't fade, but something steelier crept in beneath it.

"Weak men have spent the last two decades bleeding their nations dry, making way for decadence, for softness, for corruption."

Henry felt it — a shift in the room. The laughter faded.

"But weakness does not last. The strong will reclaim what is theirs. The strong will seize what they are owed. And the strong—" his voice lowered, intimate, "—are gathered here tonight."

He let the words settle, heavy as iron.

"This weekend, my friends, is about securing the future. Our future. A future free from the rot that has seeped into our once-great nations. Free of the so-called 'democracy' that has poisoned our nations."

A murmur rippled through the room. Some listening. Some were already convinced.

Redfern stood straighter, his chin lifting a fraction.

Wilcox gestured with casual ease toward the windows, toward the darkness beyond the warm glow of the hall. "But let's not pretend we came here for skiing and small talk."

The air tightened.

"We have work to do. The world will not reshape itself in our image unless we take the hammer into our hands."

His smile returned, easy, indulgently.

"Tomorrow, my friends, we set the course of history. And history will not remember the meek."

He lifted his glass.
"Tomorrow, we divide the world."

CHAPTER XII

THE FIRST THREAD

"JEWISH-OWNED BUSINESSES FORCED INTO 'NATIONAL RESTRUCTURING' PROGRAM"
—*THE WALL STREET JOURNAL*, MARCH 2, 1936

"New economic policies require Jewish business owners to sell their holdings to government-approved buyers."

Thursday, December 2nd, 1937
Cottage 14, Vanderleigh Hall, Lake Placid, New York—Late Evening

"That was some speech."

Dunlow's voice was thick with satisfaction as he leaned back into the armchair near the fire, his massive frame sinking into the upholstery. The

hearth crackled, casting flickering shadows along the cabin walls. Their bags had already been placed in their respective rooms, the **flames** pre-lit, the glasses set out as if expecting their arrival.

He undid the top button of his shirt with a grunt, air rushing out of him as if his body had been holding it in all evening. His chins, unburdened, spilled forth like a river torrent unleashed. Reaching for his drink, he swirled the liquor in his glass.

"It was very poignant," Margaret said from across the sitting area, reclining in a chair, a glass of red wine cradled between two fingers. "You could see it in the room. The conviction. He wasn't just speaking for show; he believed it. And the others do, too."

"Yes, wasn't it something?" Dunlow chuckled, taking a hearty sip. "Some real names in that room. Men with genuine power. This is how you make history, folks." He wiped his mouth with the back of his hand. "I feel like we're making real inroads."

Standing by the fireplace, Redfern swirled his glass of Scotch. The glow of the flames caught the edge of his features, making his expression unreadable.

"We barely made a dent, Charlie." His voice was tight. His grip on his glass tightened, knuckles whitening.

"They looked through me." His voice was quieter now. "They saw my name on the list but didn't see me."

Dunlow blinked, looking toward him, taken aback. "What? Come on, boss. The right hands were shaken, the right backs were slapped—"

"We weren't greeted at the door." Redfern's voice cut through the room's warmth—cold, sharp. He turned, glass still in hand, his brow furrowed. "We weren't expected. Not in the way we should have been. Not in the way we deserved."

Dunlow let out a short, incredulous laugh. "So what? Wilcox has a lot on his plate. Maybe he just—"

Redfern's gaze flicked to him, something in his expression turning to steel.

"We were an afterthought." He took a slow sip of Scotch, letting the words settle. "Did you see how they reacted to me? I had to introduce myself. Do you think Wilcox has to introduce himself?"

Margaret observed him, her lips pursed.

"We're the token Canadians," Kessler said from his spot by the fire. "If you want a seat at the fire beside an American, you better have your elbows up."

Dunlow shifted in his chair. "Alright, so we weren't top of the list. But we're in the room, aren't we?"

Redfern's expression pinched as he shook his head. He set his glass on the mantel. "That's not enough."

Margaret took another careful sip of wine. "You're worried they're not taking us seriously."

Redfern ran a hand through his hair, his jaw tight. "I know they're not." He turned toward the window, staring into the darkness beyond the frost-lined glass. "Tomorrow, I change that."

Henry remained silent by the far wall, nursing his drink.

"And how do you plan to do that?" Kessler asked.

Redfern didn't turn, his fingers tightening around the mantel. "I'm not sure yet," he admitted. "But I will think of something. All of you, get some rest."

He looked toward Ben, finally acknowledging him for the first time since they'd returned. "And Ben. Keep your head down. Maybe stay in the cottage or something."

Ben scoffed. "I thought you needed me."

"I do," Redfern said flatly, "but not right away." He reached for his glass again, rolling the Scotch between his fingers. "Timing matters, Ben. And right now, you're bad timing."

Ben's mouth pressed into a thin line, but he didn't argue. He just took another sip of his drink, staring into the fire.

Henry shook his head and dragged a hand down his face.

It was going to be a long weekend.

Henry left the sitting room. The hum of conversation had thinned as the hour wore on, each member of the group peeling away to their rooms.

For a while, he sat alone with his thoughts and his exhaustion. Then he climbed the stairs to the guest rooms.

The hallway stretched ahead, each door marked with a name. He found his and stepped inside. Smaller than the Château, but just as ornate—maybe more so. Vanderleigh Hall carried the same deliberate charm, the same curated rusticity.

Rustic. Charming.

A lie in carved wood and polished brass.

A double bed sat against the wall, flanked by reading lamps. Across from it, a heavy armoire and matching dresser gleamed under warm light.

His suitcase waited on the bed.

The moment he lifted it, his stomach twisted.

Too light.

He snapped the latches and threw it open.

Empty.

A cold spike of panic. A dozen possibilities crashed through his mind.

Slowly, he pried open the false bottom.

The pistol, camera, ammunition, and cash sat exactly as he'd left them. Untouched.

Relief cooled into something heavier.

Moving to the dresser, he found his clothes folded, arranged with unnatural precision. In the armoire, his suits hung perfectly aligned, pressed sharp.

Someone had gone through his things.

Not a thief. A porter. Following orders.

The violation settled in his chest like a weight. Not stolen. Not taken. Just examined.

Which was worse?

Had this been routine? Or had he already drawn attention—maybe since the moment he arrived?

Too many questions.

Henry sat on the bed, the mattress threatening to swallow him whole. Exhaustion pulled at him—two days on fumes. His eyes drooped.

Ghosts stirred. The man on the train. The picture on the mantle.

No.

His eyes snapped open. He stood and went straight to the suitcase, fingers finding the camera. Small. Useful.

Leica — the name was engraved on the top plate, precise and elegant. The dials were small, intricate, and meaningless to him.

Turning it over in his hands, he wasn't entirely comfortable with these things. Though he had snapped a few photos before, he wasn't an expert.

Henry could only hope the settings were right; if they weren't, he wouldn't know how to fix them.

After a last glance, he slipped the camera into his jacket pocket.

Too bulky. Too obvious.

He shifted to the armoire. Inside, his heavy wool overcoat hung in perfect alignment. He shrugged into it, adjusting the fabric. The lump remained, but it was less noticeable now.

His eyes darted again to the suitcase.

The pistol gleamed up at him. Waiting. Ready.

His fingers hovered.

He snapped the false bottom closed.

No relief.

Just resignation.

Then, with a quiet click, he latched the suitcase shut.

Henry cautiously descended the stairs, each step creaking beneath him. The cottage was silent, yet his movements echoed, reverberating through the space. He was attempting to be quiet.

All it did was make his presence more obvious.

The embers in the fireplace had burned low, casting a faint orange light across the room. The only other illumination came from a single overhead lamp above the sink, humming softly in the stillness.

He took another step, then stopped.

Kessler.

Of course.

The lawyer sat in the small kitchen at the back of the cottage, barely visible behind the dark outline of the furniture. A plate holding half a sandwich rested on the counter before him.

He nodded once, a mere acknowledgment.

Henry hesitated, weighing his next move. "I'm just getting some fresh air."

Kessler nodded again, remaining silent as he took another bite of his sandwich.

The silence stretched.

"I can't sleep," Henry added.

It was an excuse. A weak one. Hollow, even as he said it.

Kessler didn't blink. Didn't move. Then finally he spoke. "I'm not your nanny, Henry."

Kessler placed the sandwich on the plate, wiping his mouth with a napkin.

"You don't need my permission. There's no curfew here."

Henry lingered a moment longer, then turned to the door.

As it clicked shut behind him, Kessler's voice followed. "Don't be late."

The snow had stopped. Above, the sky stretched wide, a graveyard of stars—light that had travelled an eternity only to die in Henry's gaze.

He pulled his coat tight, bracing against the cold, already dreading it, and stepped into the night.

Vanderleigh Hall sat halfway up the mountain, its cabins scattered through the trees like outposts in a quiet war. Cobblestone paths wound through the dark like veins, all leading to the Hall.

The cabins were two-story affairs with common rooms below and bedrooms above. All dark now, their occupants asleep—or pretending to be. No lights in the windows. Yet he still felt watched.

Snow crunched under Henry's boots. A rustle to his right. A flicker of movement.

He froze, pulse hammering.

A squirrel bolted up a tree, shaking snow loose.

Relief came—but didn't last.

The trees loomed, skeletal and still, offering neither welcome nor warning. The path twisted between them until the forest opened, and Vanderleigh Hall rose below—three stories of timber and stone, windows glowing gold against the dark. Light spilled across the snow like a beacon in the cold.

A narrow trail curved down toward it, marked by gas lamps every dozen yards—enough to keep him from breaking his neck, not enough to drive back the dark.

Henry stopped at the treeline, scanning the grounds.

The main walkway was well-trodden, snow packed flat beneath the shuffle of expensive shoes and heavy boots. The back patio was the same—uneven, churned with prints, a high-traffic area.

Beyond that, a thinner path curved neatly around the building.

No trenches. No wire. No floodlights. But the guards were there—shapes pacing at the edges of the lamplight, shifting in and out of shadow.

It would be easy to turn back. Sleep. Start fresh in the morning. But that meant going in blind.

He slipped out of the trees, following the narrow path.

The Hall swelled larger with each step. Second-floor balconies jutted out at odd intervals, but above them a single third-floor balcony wrapped the building—a perfect perch for Wilcox.

A flicker of light swept around the corner. A moving beam.

Sentry.

Too far to the door. Too far back to the trees.

Henry dropped low, sprinting for a ski rack as the torchlight neared, spilling across the patio. His legs burned.

He dove behind a post, curling in tight. The air from his lungs plumed into mist.

He hated the cold. But he also liked not getting a .40-calibre to the head.

The beam drifted past, paused, then moved on.

Henry counted three beats, then rose. Boots whispering against the wooden slats, he took the steps two at a time.

The patio was empty now. The earlier voices and laughter had gone.

He crossed quickly, too exposed for comfort, and gripped the door handle—cold brass under his palm. A soft click as it gave, hinges sighing in the dark.

A small foyer. Inside.

He shut the door just as the flashlight swept the spot where he'd been seconds before. His chest rose and fell, breath tight.

Why had he done that?

His mind searched for an answer, but his body already knew.

Henry leaned back against the door, wetting his lips. Eyes closed, he forced his heartbeat down.

When he opened them, the hall lay in stillness. The speeches done. The toasts drunk. Most of the visitors were asleep.

Most.

Somewhere deeper inside, voices murmured—muffled and distant, echoing just enough to remind him he wasn't alone.

The warmth wrapped around him, but it felt wrong. Heavy. Suffocating.

He kept the coat on, the camera's weight against his ribs an anchor. Slow, measured steps carried him forward—heel to toe on the carpet, steering clear of the wooden boards that might give him away.

No noise. No movement.

The hall had not changed, but in the stillness, it felt different.

Hours ago, these rooms had roared with conversation, the air thick with cigar smoke and ambition. They loomed hollow, their opulence drained in the dim glow of wall sconces. Having burned low, the fireplace's embers, once ablaze, pulsed like dying stars.

The Hall's vastness had not shrunk, but Henry felt it closing in.

Designed not for comfort but for display, the architecture sprawled outward, vast and open. Stretching like a wagon wheel, the ground floor featured massive chambers feeding into one another and flowing toward the ballroom like tributaries to a river. It was a place built for movement, for gatherings of men who shaped their legacies over brandy and cigars.

Now, the movement was gone.

Henry's steps were soft, his breath tight. The towering ceilings stretched above him, swallowing sound and absorbing light. The fixtures hung dark and heavy, their flames long extinguished.

He entered the ballroom.

The flags remained limp in the unmoving air. The American banner. The Swastika.

They loomed like sentinels in the darkness. Watching.

Henry's skin prickled. His eyes swept the darkness, hunting for any sign of a trap.

Nothing moved.

What the hell was he doing here? This was suicide.

His footsteps echoed in the silence, each a note in a hollow symphony, the sound stretching and twisting in the vastness of the Hall. Beneath it, a deeper stillness met him, heavy, listening.

But sleep wouldn't get him the answers he needed.

The ballroom was a dead end. Just flags and portraits, frozen in place. Nothing he needed.

The library remained unchanged. Books lined the shelves, lamps stood ready to glow warmly, and the chairs still exuded their false promise of comfort. Yet nothing within these walls would tell him what was unfolding.

He moved through the hushed corridors, past the cavernous rooms, until he stood at the heart of the Hall with the grand staircase spiralling upward from the foyer to the second floor.

The floorboards whispered beneath his weight. The Hall breathed around him, old wood settling, distant wind brushing against the windows, the faint echo of something dripping on the walls.

Henry hesitated. He had found nothing yet. But he'd only just arrived. There would be time. There would be opportunities. He could turn back now.

Wait.

Observe.

Be patient.

And yet, the second floor loomed above, unseen.

The choice sat heavy in Henry's chest. Too heavy.

A flashlight beam knifed through the foyer windows, slicing sharp shadows across furniture and bookshelves.

A guard.

Henry ducked—too late.

The railings did nothing to hide him, the light spilling through the gaps, striping his face in pale bands. Not a hiding place. Just a moment's delay.

The guard moved slowly past the doors, his silhouette swallowed by the bay window's reflection. He was just a shadow in the dark; only the beam of his light betrayed his presence.

But Henry felt the gaze.

Not just a sweep of the room. Searching. Looking.

Like the man's eyes were fused to the light, dragging across the space, hunting.

Henry held his breath, instinct tightening around his ribs. It didn't matter. The man couldn't hear him.

But still, his breath wouldn't come.

Movement.

The light shifted, trailing across the room before slipping around the corner of the lodge. The guard continued on his circuitous route.

Henry lay still, the tension uncoiling just enough for his breath to come—quick, shallow, gasping.

His fingers twitched toward his pocket, reaching for a cigarette.

No. Not here. Not now.

He pushed himself up quietly, carefully, one last sweep of the foyer, empty.

Then slowly, deliberately, he ascended the staircase.

His instinct was to crouch low—to make himself small, as he had in No Man's Land, explosions cracking the sky, bullets whispering past. But here, crouching would only make him look guilty. So, he pushed himself to walk. Straight. Steady.

He reached the landing, glancing up the staircase leading to the third floor.

Not yet.

The landing spiralled around the rotunda overlooking the grand foyer below. A long hallway stretched outward like the spine of the building, with doors lining either side.

Henry looked left, then right. Indecision.

Did it matter?

One shadowy corridor looked the same as the next.

Footsteps.

Muted voices. Low. Close.

Henry glanced down. Two men ascended the stairs below him, their hushed conversation floating through the still air.

He turned back to the hallways, looking down one, then the other.

No cover. Nowhere to hide.

His pulse kicked up. Think. Move.

His eyes flicked upward.

Without hesitation, he moved, scrambling up the stairwell to the upper level. Fast, quiet, careful.

Half a turn. Out of sight.

He held his breath.

Waited.

If they stopped here, he was fine. If they kept climbing...

Henry pressed himself against the stairwell, breath shallow, heart thudding against his ribs. Below, the footsteps grew louder — two men, their voices low but distinct as they reached the landing.

He stilled. Listened.

"...if this alliance is to work, we'll be the ones carrying the weight," one of them said, his voice thick with a Southern drawl. Slow. Measured. Frustrated. "No one else has the industry, the men—"

The second man scoffed, a clipped New York accent cutting through the dim hush. "We don't need to carry anything alone. The Reich is getting aggressive, and once things move in Europe, they'll keep the world distracted."

A pause. The soft clink of a glass against wood.

"That's the idea," the Southerner muttered. "But I don't enjoy relying on them. If you put your faith in a rattlesnake, don't be surprised if you get bit."

The New Yorker cleared his throat, shifting his weight. "Once they're tied up in Europe—"

"We can't fight another war in Europe."

"We won't have to. Neutrality. Financial and industrial support. The Germans would have won the last time if we had stayed out of it. Now? They will be in Paris in a few months. The whole of France is just one dry tinder waiting for a match."

A rustle of fabric. The click of a lighter. The scent of tobacco drifting into the air.

"Neutrality? Isn't the Reich pushing for a formal agreement? I thought they wanted..."

Henry stayed still. His breath sat heavy in his chest. He didn't notice his hands were clenched into tight fists until his nails dug into his palms.

The voices drifted away, the creak of a door. The indistinct murmur of conversation faded into silence.

It was over.

He exhaled slowly. Peering around the edge of the staircase, the hallway was dark again. Still. Empty.

Time to move.

He shifted his weight, stepping down; maybe he'd overstayed his welcome. It was time to go.

A sound.

Above.

A shuffle. Papers? A chair scraping against the floor? Someone was still awake.

Henry turned as he stepped down. Just a glance.

Just a second—his foot slipped.

His stomach lurched. The world tilted.

A dull thud. A sharp crack. His body hit the stairs, knocking the breath out of his lungs.

He caught himself before he fully tumbled, gripping the railing hard, his pulse hammering against his ribs.

Silence.

The cold wood pressed into his hands. His breath was shallow, sharp.

Did anyone hear?

He stayed still. Listening. Waiting.

A chair scraped above—heavy footfalls across the wooden floor.

Henry lifted himself, forcing his movements steady, descending toward the landing.

The footsteps stopped at the railing overhead.

He didn't look up. Didn't break pace. He forced himself to move calmly, slowing as he passed the stairwell.

The silence above was suffocating.

Footsteps.

Descending. Calm.

He had to look relaxed.

Like he belonged.

He gripped the railing, forcing each step measured, controlled, leading toward the foyer.

The footsteps above mirrored his. A heavy clomp. Then another.

Pacing him.

Matching him.

His mind screamed. *Run. Now.*

Bolt through the gates. Jump the wall. Hail a cab. Disappear. Get. Out.

But he walked.

Confidently.

Or what he hoped a confident step sounded like.

He reached the foyer.

Front door or back?

The footsteps hit the second landing.

He turned to the ballroom.

A slight stumble. Nothing obvious. Just enough.

He crossed the ballroom floor and got halfway.

"Hey!"

The shout slammed into him, echoing off the walls, hitting him from all sides.

Henry wobbled when he turned around. Just enough.

The man was massive, too big, too solid. He was the man hired to take up space and make people nervous, a monument of muscle and authority.

"What are you doing?"

Henry blinked. Off-balance, confused. He let his footing shift, as if he had just realized he was standing.

"Wha-wha d'you mean?" His words slurred, just slightly. Just enough.

The bodyguard closed the space. The room seemed to bounce with his steps.

"Why were you upstairs?" The voice was heavy, pushing weight into every syllable. "Second floor is off-limits."

Henry blinked again, then gave a slow, lazy grin.

"I-I thought there were more cocktails to be had," he slurred, scratching his head, eyes unfocused. "Trying to find some more good times. My group got a little... boring."

The guard eyed him closely. "Which delegation are you with?"

"*Delegation?*" Henry burped. "Pardon me."

"Which group did you come in with?"

"Ohhh," Henry stumbled slightly off balance. "Redfern. Redfern industries."

The guard paused, thinking. "Fucking Canucks. Get out of here. You're all fucking drunks. If I see you again, you won't walk right for a week."

"Don't promise me a good time," Henry said with a wink.

Turning around, he stumbled across the ballroom, out the back, onto the patio.

And back into the cold.

The words still swirled in his head. Tied up in Europe. Neutrality. Financial and industrial support.

His breath wafted in the air.

He didn't know the complete picture.

Not yet.

But the pieces were fitting together.

Chapter XIII

Tightening the Noose

"STEELWORKERS MASSACRED IN CHICAGO: DOZENS DEAD AS MILITIAS OPEN FIRE"
—*The Chicago Tribune*, June 30, 1934

"The worst labor violence in American history unfolded yesterday as police and armed 'citizen groups' attacked striking workers."

Thursday, December 2nd, 1937
Cottage 14, Vanderleigh Hall, Lake Placid, New York—Midnight

Henry collapsed onto the bed. It was deep. Too comfortable. The bed meant for men who didn't wake up worrying about their next step. Maybe it was the finest mattress he'd ever lain on.

Or maybe he was just that tired.

He forced himself to sit up; no good passing out in a suit and overcoat.

With a groan, he pulled the camera from his pocket, tucking it back into the case carefully. Its weight had been pressing into his ribs for hours. He wanted nothing more than to collapse back into bed, to let exhaustion claim him.

But habit won out, always routine.

He folded his suit with practiced ease, hung it up, pulled on his pajamas, then sank beneath the covers.

Still, sleep didn't come.

His mind refused to shut down, thoughts circling, looping. The wooden ceiling blurred above him, but his pulse was still hammering from the night's work. He had found nothing yet, nothing to bring back to Henshaw.

But something was happening here.

Something big.

And it was just the beginning.

He slept, but it wasn't restful. Dreams ran through his mind — old dreams.

Mud. Cold. Fear. Cuts that wouldn't heal.

A brother's promise: *We'll get home together.*

The words were louder than the shells. Louder than his own breath.

A voice screamed. "Gas, gas, gas!"

Always cold.

The feel of a bayonet punching into flesh.

He woke.

Light pressed through the window, a dull glow of morning. Somewhere in the hall, movement, muddy voices, and footsteps.

Henry sat up, rubbing the sleep from his eyes. He couldn't tell if he'd slept eight minutes or eight hours. He pushed the covers aside, feet meeting the cold floorboards. His limbs were sluggish; his head was thick. Routine would shake it off.

Rising, he grabbed his shaving kit and wrapped himself in a robe before stepping into the hallway.

The air was thick with cheap cologne and stale sweat. Steam curled under the bathroom door at the end of the hall, heavy with shaving cream and damp wool.

Dunlow stood at the front of the queue, though he *was* the queue. His stomach rolls spilled over the waistband of his pajamas, and his undershirt stretched thin and threadbare where it clung too tightly.

Henry hesitated. *Turn back, wait it out.*

Too late.

"Hank," Dunlow called, eyes flicking to him. His gaze dipped to the loose neckline of the robe, the smirk that followed more mean than amused.

"Christ, Hank—what'd you do? Get caught in a bear trap?"

Henry's hand shot to his throat, shielding the angry line of the mark. He hadn't thought about it once this morning. Now it burned like it was fresh.

He stiffened, caught—not quite the same as last night, but the discomfort pressed the same. He tugged the robe higher, hiding the wound.

And, God help him, he'd rather face that massive guard again than Dunlow's smirking commentary.

"Shaving accident," Henry said flatly.

"Uh-huh." Dunlow's grin widened, eyes glinting. "Close shave, huh? You ought to be more careful with that blade."

Henry adjusted the robe's collar, jaw tight. "You done staring?"

"Relax," Dunlow said, still grinning. "Big day ahead, that's all I meant. Meetings, handshakes, deals. You might want to look alive for once."

Henry folded his arms, shoulder brushing the wall. "Like you were making deals last night?"

Dunlow's grin faltered—a twitch, gone as fast as it came. "Yeah, we were making deals," he said, voice tightening. "Lots of them. But I guess you wouldn't know—too busy sneering at the men doing the work."

Henry let that sit. "What are we doing here, Charlie?"

Dunlow scoffed. "Christ, Hank. What kind of question is that?"

"I don't even think they want us here."

"Oh, they want us here, Hank." Dunlow let the name linger. He pushed off the wall, rolling his shoulders. "That was clear in the phone calls I had. There's a whole meeting centred on their plans with us."

Henry held his gaze. "With us—or for us?"

Dunlow hesitated. Just for a second. Just long enough. "What's that supposed to mean?"

Henry turned without answering. If Dunlow didn't get it by now, he never would.

"Hank, what are you implying?"

Henry ignored him, as he rapped his knuckles against the door across the hall.

"Come in." No enthusiasm.

He left Dunlow in the hallway and stepped inside. Ben sat in bed—shoulders hunched, eyes shadowed.

"You look exactly how I feel," Henry said.

Ben didn't even smirk. "You must be feeling great." The words landed with a dull thud.

Henry tried to smile. It didn't take. "You sleep at all?"

"Nope," Ben muttered, dragging a shaking hand across his face. "Kept waiting for them to kick in the door."

Henry's smile collapsed. "You're not serious."

Ben looked up, flat and pale. "Dead serious."

Ben studied him, his brow furrowing, and his expression tightened.

"Where'd you sneak off to last night?"

Henry didn't move. Didn't blink. "What?"

Ben stared at him. "I heard you." He tipped his chin toward the door. "Quiet as a mouse going down. But a lot more noisy coming back."

Shit.

Henry forced a shrug. "Just needed some air. Couldn't sleep." He ran a hand through his hair. "Long day."

Ben didn't blink. Didn't buy it.

"You think anyone else heard?"

Ben shook his head. "Dunlow's snores could shake the rafters. Redfern's at the far end. Kessler? Maybe. Bergström wouldn't give a damn."

Henry studied him. Measured. Testing.

"But you do."

Ben held his stare. "I do."

Henry's gaze drifted toward the door before he dragged it back to Ben. Henry's hand dragged over his face, hiding the flash of frustration before he looked back at Ben.

"I'll tell you when this weekend's over."

Ben let out a sharp breath. Not quite a laugh. Not quite anything. "Well, you might be telling an empty room, pal."

Henry's jaw tightened. "I can't. Not yet."

Ben's expression soured. His gaze didn't waver, but it hollowed, distant, resigned. "Of course."

The silence stretched. Henry searched for words. Found none.

Then, quietly, almost like an afterthought. "Just tell me you're not making things worse."

Henry swallowed. The weight of the question settled deep.

"I don't know." He shifted back slightly, as if the distance might soften the doubt. "But I don't think so."

Ben studied him — a long, quiet moment, then looked away.

"Guess we'll see."

He was the last one down. The sting of hot cloth and razor lingered on his skin—enough to scrape away the worst of last night and almost make him feel alive again.

He'd found a tin of balm in the washroom—cheap stuff, meant for razor burn—and rubbed a little over the mark at his throat. It dulled the sting, for now.

Conversation dimmed as heads turned toward him.

The group had gathered in the small living area, coffee cups in hand, but Henry's eyes went first to the set of skis and poles leaning neatly against the wall by the entrance. Slim, narrow, built for distance—not downhill racing. The kind meant to carry you for miles.

His brow furrowed. He hadn't brought skis. None of them had.

"Jesus." Ben flexed his foot in a snug, perfectly fitted boot. "They even know our foot sizes?"

As Henry reached the bottom step, Dunlow chuckled. "First-class service, boys."

Henry's gaze swept the room. "What's happening?"

Kessler, cross-legged in the armchair, sipped his coffee. "It seems we had ski fairies in the night, each delivering a perfectly measured set."

He tipped his cup toward Ben. "And as Mr. Schul so eloquently pointed out, their accuracy is... impressive."

Henry stepped behind Margaret's chair as she slipped on a boot.

"I haven't skied," she mused, fastening the strap, "since I was fifteen? Maybe 1927?"

Henry froze for half a second.

She sounded... almost giddy. Well, at least for her.

More shocking, she had volunteered personal information. Margaret never discussed herself, let alone gave details.

Twenty-five?

He had always assumed she was closer to his age—mid-to-late thirties—not that she looked older, but in how she carried herself and the weight she projected.

Had she ever even been young?

Redfern sat in the corner, already fully equipped. Silent.

Dunlow, still lounging, hands folded over his stomach, spoke first.

"There was a note on the table," he said. "We will serve breakfast at the lodge shortly. So we should be off."

Henry's gaze flicked to Dunlow's feet. Bare. No boots. No intention of putting them on.

Redfern rose, tightening his straps — fluid, practiced. He didn't need to think; he'd done this before.

Ben fumbled with his bindings, not clueless, but not at ease. He'd done this once or twice.

Despite her protests, Margaret moved with muscle memory, as if she'd skied ten days ago, not ten years.

Kessler was gone. No one had seen him leave. Already halfway to the lodge, probably.

Henry wasn't sure he'd even touched the skis.

If he judged all this, he kept it to himself.

Dunlow rocked back in his chair, grinning.

"First-class service, boys," he said again. "But I'll take the scenic route. See you down there."

Margaret glanced up, just a flicker.

Ben hesitated. Then smirked. "Gonna let the peasants break the trail for you, Charlie?"

Dunlow just laughed, waving a hand.

Henry, tightening his bootstraps, said nothing.

Ben, Margaret, and Henry stepped out of the lodge.

Redfern had already made it halfway through the trail, his figure cutting an efficient path through the trees.

The morning sunlight filtered in thin slats between the pines, casting long shadows over the snow. Overhead, the sky was a crisp, deep alpine blue, and the air was so clear it felt like someone had wiped the world clean overnight. A few wisps of cloud drifted far above; the distant Adirondack peaks jagged against the horizon.

"Shall we?" Margaret asked, a smile playing across her face.

Henry wondered who this woman was and what she'd done with Margaret.

She pushed off into the narrow trail, poles biting the snow as her skis slid forward. At first cautiously, like someone trying to remember an old habit.

Then, without thinking, her body adjusted. The rhythm returned. Her skis cut through the snow, gliding with an ease that surprised even her.

It took Ben and Henry a moment to find their rhythm, the push of the poles and the skis gliding, but soon enough, their movements smoothed, their bodies adjusting without thought. By the time they cleared the treeline and broke into the open space above Vanderleigh Hall, the awkward stiffness had faded, replaced by instinct.

The night before, darkness had hidden much of the scenery. But now in the daylight, Lake Placid stretched below them, a frozen expanse rimmed by dense firs and birches, the surface gleaming under the sunlight. Plumes of smoke curled from the chimneys of scattered lodges and cabins nestled against the tree line. The village lay beyond, small but lively, its rooftops blanketed in fresh snow, a church steeple rising like a needle against the sky. Farther in the distance, the Adirondack High Peaks dominated the horizon — vast, untamed, their slopes still dusted with untouched snow.

"We'll be late if we stand here all day." Ben adjusted his gloves, but his eyes lingered on the view.

Henry took a last glance at the view.

Then, without another word, they pushed off, gliding down the gentle slope toward the lodge.

They had transformed the ballroom. Tables stretched in neat rows, with a buffet running down the centre. The space still held the grandeur of the night before, but the energy had shifted. Less spectacle. More function.

The room was nearly complete when Henry and Ben arrived, just a step behind Margaret.

A seating chart hung inside the entrance—a neat list of tables and names. Henry's gaze skimmed over it, expecting to find Redfern Industries grouped. But, no.

Scattered.

His fingers trailed down the list. His table—just a row of meaningless names. No one he recognized.

A sharp breath beside him.

"It looks like I'm sitting with the SS."

Henry turned. Scanned the list. Found Ben's name. Seven others at his table—four of them SS officers.

Not an accident.

He stiffened. "We'll switch."

Ben didn't answer immediately. Just stared at the paper, eyes wide, jaw slack.

"Join me," Henry said, voice low. "Just ignore it."

Ben's fingers clenched at his sides. His jaw tightened. Then, slowly, he swallowed. "No. I can do this. Sit at a table with a bunch of dogs. I can survive that."

Ben walked towards the buffet. Henry appraised his friend, nodded and followed him.

They walked the line, the regular breakfast items, but Henry noted Ben's reaction as they walked.

"I can't eat anything."

"What? Why not?"

"Coffee and bread," Ben muttered. "That's it."

Henry frowned. "What are you talking about?"

Ben motioned to the table. "Look at it."

Henry scanned the table. Ben was right.

The ham glistened under a honey glaze, thick slices catching the chandelier's light beside bacon that shimmered gold. Sausage links towered in a heap, dark and crispy. Even the scrambled eggs carried a savoury sheen of pig fat clinging to the edges of the silver dish. Buttermilk biscuits nestled beside a gravy boat brimming with white, sausage-flavoured sauce.

Ben's jaw tightened.

"Jesus," Henry murmured.

Ben's brow lifted in a dry, almost amused way, but the rest of his face stayed carved from stone.

"I can survive the company of the SS," he muttered. "But I might starve doing it."

Ben grabbed a plate, collected a bun, and retreated to his table.

Henry frowned, watching the man settle at his table before gathering his plate and wandering to his own.

As he sat, he noted the military style of each man's build and cut. They talked in hushed tones as he sat, before looking him over.

The man beside him, who looked like he'd stepped straight out of a recruiting poster, leaned in, extending a hand.

"Warren Anderson."

His grip was firm. Too firm. A handshake meant to test, not to greet.

"Henry Locke."

Anderson's smile was broad. Too broad. All teeth. "You're with one of the Canadian groups, right?"

Friendly. Casual. Just a man making conversation.

But the weight behind it said otherwise.

Henry nodded, biting off a corner of toast. "Correct. I keep hearing about multiple groups, but haven't met the other one yet."

"Oh, they're around." Anderson sipped his coffee, his gaze steady over the rim of his cup. "Have you ever been to Albany?"

Henry shook his head, chewing.

"Beautiful town. Lots of old-world charm," Anderson said, smiling as he set his cup down. A pause, just long enough. Then, casually but pointed: "Especially the post office."

Henry flicked him a glance, but kept eating. "I will stop by next time I'm stateside."

A beat.

The men at the table weren't talking anymore. They were watching.

Anderson tilted toward him, voice quiet.

"I only ask because I bumped into a Canadian a few weeks ago. Thought maybe you'd know him."

Henry raised an eyebrow. "Canada's big. We don't all know each other."

"He was a business type. Like you."

Henry took another bite of toast. "Still a big country."

Anderson picked up a piece of bacon, taking his time chewing. "Campbell. I think his name was."

Henry kept chewing, his mind tumbling with questions about what this man was after. "Lots of Campbells."

"Edward Campbell."

The name was meaningless. What was he pressing at?

But Anderson wasn't an amateur.

The letter.

Henshaw had mentioned a letter. Did it come from this Campbell guy?

Anderson tapped his knuckles on the table twice.

Henry swallowed, shaking his head. "Doesn't ring a bell."

Anderson crossed his arms, posture easy, smirk slow to rise. "Oh, it's there." A knowing nod. "Something clicked."

Henry forced his expression still. "I don't know what you're talking about."

Anderson's gaze flicked over him, reading something Henry hoped wasn't there. "Tell me, Mr. Locke. Why are you here?"

Henry frowned. "What do you mean?"

"You weren't on the list." Anderson's voice was smooth.

"Then suddenly..." he gestured with his fork, as if this was just an afterthought. "You showed up. Why?"

Henry grunted. This again. "My colleague—"

"Jim Benoit."

Shit.

"Yes," Henry said, keeping his voice even. "Jimmy got sick."

Anderson nodded. Slowly. "After drinks with you."

The words landed harder than they should have.

How the fuck? A single blink. No hesitation. No tell.

"Yes," he said smoothly. "Jimmy and I had some drinks."

"Then he got sick."

Henry tore off a bite of toast, making it look like the most boring conversation in the world. "Jimmy liked to drink. I guess he had too much."

Anderson studied him. Around the table, conversation blurred—muted, fleeting. He felt attention turn his way, though no one looked directly at him.

He glanced across the room. Ben.

Quiet. Alone. Surrounded by the SS—and ignored.

Probably for the best.

And Henry felt a flicker of jealousy. Ridiculous, but real. At least Ben got to eat in peace.

Anderson took a slow sip of coffee, watching Henry over the rim.

"Funny thing," he said. "There was a Canadian in the lodge last night. Drunk, my understanding." His eyes glinted. "You Canucks sure love the booze."

A smile like a snare. Teeth bared. Eyes narrowing.

"Was it you?"

Henry tossed answers around in his mind, rolling them over, weighing the risk. "Yeah," he said, voice easy. "Guess I was just trying to fill the hole Jimmy left."

Anderson's smirk flickered. "Ahh. So you don't normally get drunk enough to stumble around places you shouldn't be?"

Henry exhaled, shaking his head. "I guess I didn't know where I should be and where I shouldn't."

Anderson studied him. "I saw you once. At the Garden."

Henry blinked. That was new.

"'26," Anderson continued, sipping his coffee. "Just after the Garden opened. Rangers were new. You scored, then fought 'Bun' Cook. Hell of a scrap." He swirled his cup, gaze flicking around the room. "Looked like you got the better of him."

Henry shrugged. "Cook was a tough kid."

Anderson smirked, setting his cup down. Tap, tap. Two fingers against the table. "A fighter who can score." His gaze lingered. "Few of those."

Henry met his gaze. "Everyone had to be a fighter back then."

Anderson nodded slowly. "You're not still looking for a fight, are you, Mr. Locke?"

Henry frowned, drinking a bit of coffee. "I'm just here, doing what my boss wants me to do."

Another nod. Anderson's smirk didn't fade. "And which boss would that be?"

The low hum of conversation wavered, then stopped.

The doors swung open.

Wilcox entered first. His stride was purposeful, commanding. But the actual presence came behind him.

Coughlin and Pelley.

Immediately, the Americans reacted.

A few men rose instantly, eager, sharp, standing like soldiers. Then others followed almost reflexively, some scanning the room first to see if they should.

Then came the noise.

It started small—cutlery clinking against plates. Then, sharper forks and knives tapping against glasses and tables.

The sound grew rhythmic, deliberate. The Americans were leading it.

Across the room, the German delegation remained seated, watching. A few exchanged glances, unimpressed.

But the Americans didn't care.

They clapped. They thumped the tables. The sound swelled, a synchronized display of enthusiasm. Someone whistled. A few murmured names — Coughlin, Pelley — but the chant never took.

Henry scanned the room.

Dunlow was standing.

At some point, he had arrived, now whooping, pounding his fists against the table, grinning like a fool.

Henry stayed seated.

Across the room, he caught Ben's gaze. Ben wasn't afraid. Not exactly. But his expression was tight. Guarded. Something close.

This wasn't a salute.

It was a spectacle of power, allegiance, and men desperate to be seen.

Wilcox, flanked by Coughlin and Pelley, climbed onto the stage to thunderous applause. He raised a hand. The cheers pounded on, fists slamming against tables, before finally settling into silence.

Then, his voice, smooth and assured, "My fellow Patriots! My fellow True Americans!

Another surge of noise, whoops, cheers, the heavy drum of knuckles on wood.

Wilcox smiled, basking in it. He let it stretch, indulging the energy, feeding off it. Then, just as the wave crested, he struck again.

"And our German brothers from across the Atlantic."

The German delegation answered with a single, disciplined thud of knuckles against the table — brief, precise, and controlled.

Wilcox's smile remained.

"Thank you for joining us here today, on what should be the first day of a beautiful, growing, and lasting friendship between the two greatest nations on Earth."

Henry flicked a glance at Redfern. His face was tight, his posture just a fraction too rigid. Dunlow looked enraptured, leaning forward, eyes gleaming, nodding along.

More cheers. More pounding on the tables.

Wilcox lifted his hands, a conductor silencing his orchestra.

"We have much ahead of us today. We'll start by limbering up with a ski out to my more subdued manor on the hill." A few chuckles. "After that, important discussions. The future of the world. The future of our nations. How we will rise together."

A brief pause. A calculated pause.

Then, smoothly, effortlessly:

"Of course, our dear leaders could not be present, yet. The world is not ready for such a meeting... yet."

A smirk. A shake of the head. "You know how the press would eat that up."

A ripple of laughter swept the room.

"This weekend is more than plans. It's about blood and iron, bonds that will not break, ensuring our nations march together into the future."

The Americans roared again. Fists slammed against tables.

The Germans responded in their way, one sharp thud. Nothing more.

Henry rose, wiping his hands on his napkin, gaze drifting over the room. Anywhere but the table he'd just left.

Anderson sat back, one brow arched. Unbothered. Watching. "We'll chat again this weekend, Mr. Locke."

Henry forced a thin smile, jaw tight. "Oh, of that I'm sure," he muttered, turning away.

He felt Anderson's gaze burning into his back as he walked, pressing against his shoulders like a weight. He fought the urge to look over. Fought it hard.

By the time he reached the back of the ballroom, Ben was already there, stepping beside him.

"How was breakfast?" Henry asked, keeping his tone light.

Ben's grip tightened around his plate, his expression pinching. "It was like sitting at a table of dogs with their jaws wired shut."

Henry smiled, but didn't feel it.

They stepped outside, the cold biting through their coats. A crowd had already gathered at the ski rack, strapping in, their laughter ringing out.

American and German accents blended.

Redfern emerged from the lodge, lingering. His eyes scanning the scene like a man trying to solve a puzzle without all the pieces, he made his way toward them, methodically assembling his gear without a word.

Ben and Henry shared a glance.

Neither spoke.

Henry pulled his skis from the rack, and the movements were easier than they had been that morning. There was a crisp snap as the bindings locked.

"Well," he muttered, straightening. "Now what?"

The lodge doors swung open.

Wilcox stepped out, surrounded by a crowd like planets drawn to a sun: Coughlin, Pelley, and the rest of the American celebrities. Dunlow trailed at the edges, his usual bluster replaced by something smaller.

"Once we're all equipped, we set off!" Wilcox called, his voice cutting cleanly through the conversation. "Ten miles of fine American snow—cross-country, through the hills. No lifts. No shortcuts. Just your lungs, your legs, and your poles. We'll see who has the strength to keep pace."

A voice from the crowd, sharp and needling,

"Where are your skis, fat man?"

A soft burst of laughter. Quick. Eager.

Dunlow forced a grin, shrugging too loosely, like this was nothing. "Seems I left them at the cabin! No bother, I'll stay back and keep the place warm!"

The laughter hadn't even settled when Wilcox turned.

His voice cut through the air. Cold. Precise. Absolute. "No, you certainly will not."

Silence.

Dunlow hesitated. Looked around.

Laughter lingered in the air, but the tone had changed.

"Better run and get them, fat man." A distinct voice this time, louder, sharper, smelling blood.

More laughter. Not kind.

Dunlow's grin froze. Then twitched, a flicker of confusion, just a second too late.

His gaze flicked from face to face, searching for an ally. For an out. Nothing.

The laughter kept growing.

His face burned red. He opened his mouth, maybe to joke, maybe to protest.

Nothing came out.

All eyes were on him.

A single voice called out, half-laughing, "Run! Run!"

Then another.

Then another.

It rolled through the crowd, a chant swelling like the roar of a tide.

Wilcox said nothing.

Just looked at him. Expectant.

Dunlow chuckled. Short. Brittle. A man waiting for the moment to pass.

It didn't.

The crowd watched. Waiting.

Finally, he moved.

Turned.

Started up the hill.

Huffing. Slow.

From the crowd, a single word. Soft. Almost gentle.

"Run."

His laughter was gone now.

His pace quickened.

Wilcox turned back to the crowd. Behind him, Dunlow trudged up the hill.

Then, without another glance, Wilcox swiftly descended the stairs, clipped into his skis, and pulled on his gloves. "Now, those of us who came prepared, let's go."

He pushed off, cutting through the snow with practiced ease.

The others followed, scrambling to keep pace.

"Shall we?" Ben asked.

Henry nodded, and together they slipped into the middle of the pack.

Chapter XIV

A Matter of Place

"VALE CALLS FOR 'AMERICAN REVIVAL' IN FIERY ADDRESS"
—*The St. Louis Post-Dispatch*, July 14, 1934

"Speaking to a crowd of 40,000, Nathaniel Vale decried 'foreign parasites' and 'weak leadership,' promising a new America built on strength and purity."

Friday, December 3rd, 1937
The Trails around Vanderleigh Hall, Lake Placid, New York—Late Morning

Henry's legs burned. His chest ached. Every breath dragged cold air deep into his lungs.

This wasn't a leisurely outing. This was a test.

Wilcox set a brutal pace, carving through the snow with sharp, exacting strokes—someone who could cut through resistance. Only a handful kept up: athletes, soldiers, men who refused to lose.

Margaret matched him stride for stride and had already vanished into the trees.

The rest fell into loose clusters of their own.

The proficient, the gifted, and the hopeless.

Leaving the open fields of Vanderleigh Hall behind, the trail narrowed, twisting through the trees and rising and falling in sudden, punishing slopes. Sharp turns. Steep descents. A course that demanded not only skill but also nerves.

Somehow, Henry had ended up beside Charles Coughlin.

The priest wasn't young — mid-forties, at least — but he moved with surprising efficiency. Not powerful strides, not reckless speed; purely deliberate, careful motion.

He wasn't fast. But he wasn't falling behind either.

A group of younger Americans followed close behind. They could have outpaced him if they had wanted to, but they didn't. They lingered near, watching him and keeping pace.

His staff? Or fawning disciples drawn into the orbit of power?

Coughlin's cheeks were red from the cold, but his breath remained even. Controlled. Restrained. He didn't push himself harder than necessary, didn't waste energy, and he made every motion calculated.

Not the ease of someone who loved the sport. The precision that belonged to someone who knew how to stay in step with those who mattered.

Coughlin glanced over. A smile. Not the friendly kind. The assessing kind.

"You ski well, Mr. Locke."

The man had a deep and polished voice to deliver each syllable with the measured cadence of a sermon. Even those few words had the importance of an audience hanging on his every phrase.

Henry looked over at the priest.

"Surprised?" Coughlin chuckled, breath steady. "I know all the Canadians that were invited."

Henry's eyes darted away. *Right. Coughlin was a fellow Canadian.*

The burn in his legs caught up with him. He gave a half-smile. "Keeping pace with a forty-year-old priest—hardly an achievement."

Coughlin let out a warm, booming laugh, a show. "No, I suppose not."

His pace eased.

Henry could have pulled ahead and left him behind. But Coughlin wanted to talk. And that was more important.

"Your friend." Coughlin's tone was smooth. "The one with the unfortunate last name." He glanced over, with a slight smile on his lips. "Brave? Or just... unwise?"

Henry didn't react. Didn't flinch. Just kept skiing.

He looked at Coughlin from the side.

"Ben?" A brief pause. "He's smart. Smart, but duped."

Coughlin hummed, as if that answer satisfied something. "Ah. Redfern didn't tell him."

Henry nodded once. "No. Trapped him, more or less."

Coughlin sighed, shaking his head, a small, performative gesture.

"I'll admit, it surprised me that Redfern still employed him." Coughlin looked at Henry, his expression unreadable. "I assumed he'd... adjusted his hiring practices by now."

Henry held his focus ahead, thinking of the burning in his legs. He didn't look over. Just skied.

"I guess Redfern appreciates skill over religion."

His tone was even. Indifferent—or close enough.

Coughlin gave a slow, measured chuckle. "Now, now, Henry." He angled his head, curious, not confrontational. "Those can be dangerous words in certain company."

Henry shrugged. "Just the truth."

Coughlin huffed beside him, picking up his pace as they climbed another hill. "Strange," he mused. "A man like you; rugged, educated, an athlete, choosing the company of a man like your colleague."

Henry kept his eyes forward. Kept skiing.

Coughlin didn't press. He just let the words hang between them. Then, as if it were an idle thought:

"There aren't many men from that breakfast who would have shared a meal with him." A small chuckle. "It was quite the challenge, putting together the seating chart."

Henry glanced at Coughlin. Words rose to his lips but never left.

Ahead, a crash. A yell.

Henry stopped briefly, then pushed forward, picking up speed.

The trail curved, bending away from the lodge—steeper than the last. The biggest one yet.

He dug his edges in, legs burning from the strain. Cold air slashed his face, breath ragged. His balance wavered. One mistake, one dangerous shift in weight, and he'd go down.

He fought it. Stayed upright. Somehow.

The slope flattened. His muscles screamed, but he was still upright.

The next slope drew Henry's eyes. Ben was already halfway up, climbing fast, chasing Wilcox and the lead.

Henry pushed forward, breath ragged.

Movement ahead, just off the trail.

A cluster of skiers. Three helped a fourth to their feet, a tangle of poles and gear.

Henry slowed. Came up beside them.

The man's face flushed, his breath heaved, and snow half-covered him. He was glaring up at the men who had pulled him upright. Furious. Humiliated.

"*Dieser verdammte Jude.*"

The vicious shout echoed across the snow.

Henry noticed these men had sat at the table with Ben during breakfast. The SS.

"*Ich werde ihn verdammt noch mal töten!*" The man shouted, pointing up the slope at Ben's retreating back.

Henry skied to a stop. "What happened?"

Rage hardened the officer's face as his eyes snapped toward Henry.

"The Jew." The word landed flat, weighted with disgust. "Could not control himself. Typical. Weak. Small brain." He gestured toward the SS officer struggling to rise.

"He jabbed his pole into Schneider's skis. A pathetic attempt to keep up. And now?" The man's eyes widened, nostrils flaring. "Schneider could have been injured."

Fuck.

Schneider, still brushing snow from his uniform, spat onto the ground. His eyes burned as he looked up the hill toward Ben, who was eclipsing the ridge.

Something flickered in his expression—shock, maybe. Only for a second. A flash of recognition that someone had bested him.

Rage swallowed it whole.

Henry tightened his grip on the poles, glanced up the slope. Ben was still moving. Good.

He smirked. "I'm sure it was completely unprovoked."

A snort almost escaped, strangled instead by the tightness in his chest.

The officer closest to him turned, studying him as if seeing him for the first time. A sneer cut across his face.

"Ahh. Of course." His eyes narrowed. "*Dominionshunde.*"

Dominion dog. It had been a while since Henry had heard that one.

The other officers chuckled. Low. Amused. A sound Henry didn't like.

Henry's eyes ran across them — anger, irritation, but no immediate violence. Not yet. Schneider, now finished dusting himself off, reset his skis and stepped forward.

Another arrival.

Father Coughlin glided down, his small entourage close behind, their breath fogging in the cold air.

He took in the scene — the snow, the tension, and Schneider's already-progressive movement to chase Ben.

"SS-Oberführer Henke. Is everything alright?" Coughlin asked. His voice was warm. Unbothered. But his look settled first on the SS officer—not Henry.

Henke straightened, flicking a glance at Henry before turning to the priest. "The Jew attacked Schneider."

Coughlin froze—only momentarily. Then his expression shifted: brows knitting, mouth drawing tight.

"A Jew," he repeated, tone hovering between disbelief and dry amusement. He shook his head slowly, like a parent indulging a child's lie. "A Jew downed one of Hitler's finest?"

Silence.

Then, a short, barking laugh from a few younger officers. A smirk from another—but it didn't last.

Schneider didn't laugh. Neither did Henke.

"It's an affront that he's even here. And now this." Henke gestured toward Schneider. "It cannot go unpunished."

Coughlin tilted his head. "Skiing mishaps happen. But the real measure of a man is how he ensures they don't happen again."

Henke adjusted his gloves, eyes locked on Coughlin. He held the stare, then smiled. "Yes, Father. A man must take responsibility for ensuring order."

Coughlin offered a warm, measured nod. "That's right, my son. And I trust you'll act accordingly."

Henke nodded once, then turned, setting off down the trail.

Henry didn't move. Not yet. He waited, watching them disappear ahead, their dark figures cutting through the snow.

Better to keep them where he could see them.

The chalet continued the rustic, all-American theme. More miniature and fortified than the palace they'd left behind, it still had the same log cabin grandeur as the main lodge, like a castle. It was still grand, still overwhelming, but they did not build this for comfort.

Isolated, it sat in the centre of a clearing. There were no roads, tire tracks, just ski trails weaving through the trees, the only paths in or out. That was by design.

Henry arrived mid-pack—nowhere near last, but well behind the first dozen already lounging outside, coats undone, steam rising from their overheated bodies. They stretched and laughed in the late morning sun, as if they hadn't just been racing like wolves.

Margaret stood among them, smiling, chatting with ease. A ribbon hung from her neck.

Several others wore the same. A prize? A ranking? Recognition?

So much for being out of practice.

Ben and Redfern sat apart, perched on a picnic table. Both looked uncomfortable, though for very different reasons. Neither wore a ribbon.

Around them, small knots of men formed, mixing, conversing, reliving the morning's competition, skiing techniques, past runs, and knowing nods between those who recognized the pecking order.

A voice rang out. Sharp. Curious.

"No roads? How do the cars get here to pick us up?"

Wilcox smiled. That politician's smile. The smile of one who knew the question before it was asked.

"No roads." He turned slowly. "Only one way in. One way out."

He let that settle just for an instant.

He spread his arms wide. "This," a slow pivot, gaze sweeping the crowd, "is where the important discussions will be had."

His voice carried efficiently across the clearing.

"The lodge is for socializing." A pause. A beat. Then, lighter, but with a weight that couldn't be ignored: "The chalet is where we roll up our sleeves and get the hard work done."

A ripple of groans. A few exchanged looks. The realization was settling in.

No cars. No easy exits. Lots of skiing in their forecast this weekend.

Wilcox scanned the crowd. Three-quarters of the group had arrived.

He smiled, but it didn't quite reach his eyes.

"We'll go inside and begin." A beat. His eyes quickly darted to the deserted path. "Those who arrive late..."

He licked his lips and with a faint smile. "Well. Don't be late."

The interior of the chalet was divided into two spaces: a foyer, which made up a quarter of the footprint, and a vast open hall beyond it. Service doors lined the far end, their presence utilitarian and efficient. There were no guest rooms or lounges. This was not a place for comfort. This was a place for control.

At the centre stood a tight rectangle of tables, each seat marked by a nameplate. At the far end, one chair sat apart—larger, elevated above the rest. A seat of authority.

Above it, draped against the wooden walls, the American flag hung on one side, the Nazi swastika on the other, mirroring the ballroom at the lodge. A massive portrait of Nathaniel Vale loomed between them, his expression cold, his gaze unavoidable. It was the same as the one in the lodge, as in every government building now.

Its messaging suffocated the room. There were no windows, nor distractions, and nobody could escape the burden of this place's purpose. Chairs lined the perimeter along the walls, placed neatly, almost as if for an audience, for those not worthy of the table but still required to listen.

Henry stepped into the room and scanned the placards. Delegates were assembling. The expected names were there—the ones from Henshaw's list.

Then he stopped.

Adrien Arcand. The other Canadian faction.

The "Canadian Führer."

Henry's fingers tapped the back of a chair. He surveyed the room. No sign of Arcand. Not yet.

They'd known each other since McGill. Arcand had always played the part—brilliant, important, destined. Even back at McGill. Like he expected history to come calling.

Henry never had. Still didn't.

Strange that Henshaw hadn't mentioned him. Deliberate?

Did he know?

Questions without answers. For now.

"You look like a man scouting No Man's Land."

The voice came from behind him.

Henry turned.

SS-Sturmbannführer Reinhard Hoffner.

Tall, stiff-backed. With his hands clasped neatly behind his back, standing at ease, but watching.

Henry remained still. Relaxed.

"Not that dissimilar," Henry said.

Hoffner's eyebrow twitched.

Henry gestured loosely at the two flags dominating the room, his voice easy. "*Walking between two trenches.*"

He let the words settle.

"Always best to know who's in the room," Henry said with a flick of his hand and a half-smirk. "I like knowing where the mines are."

Hoffner's jaw shifted a fraction.

He stepped closer. Close enough that if a bayonet were between them, it would already be buried in someone's ribs.

"Well, you should be careful where you step," Hoffner said. Steady. Cold. "You are a man of coincidences and contradictions. You are here, and yet, by all intents and purposes, you do not belong."

His fingers tapped behind his back, slow and deliberate.

"You have been seen where you should not be." He tilted his head. "And that is a problem."

Henry fought not to swallow. Not to shift. He forced himself to stay still, to keep his face neutral. But Hoffner pressed him. Hard.

His pulse thumped in his ears.

Deflect.

"If I spill my drink and it rains the next day, do I control the weather?"

Hoffner's expression didn't change. His fingers tapped once, twice, behind his back. "I don't understand your analogy."

Henry smiled. Tapped a cigarette from his pack. Lit it with a match.

"Coincidences happen, Sturmbannführer. It doesn't mean anything's connected." He exhaled, eyes on the smoke weaving between them. "If you stare long enough, you'll start seeing connections that don't exist."

Another drag. "And just because I'm not pounding the table doesn't mean you get to question my beliefs."

Hoffner's nostrils flared.

Henry met his gaze, then turned and walked off—calm, in control.

The room had filled.

Henry's gaze swept over the gathering, calculating, cataloging, when he saw him.

Adrien Arcand.

The Quebecois fascist.

His delegation had arrived without ceremony, announcement, or grandstanding. Four men, flushed from the ski, shook off the last cold as they entered with the last batch of arrivals.

Arcand ignored the Americans, pausing only to murmur with the Germans.

He sat with his back straight, hands folded, posture rehearsed. A man commanded, even if no one was following. His slicked-back hair caught the light, framing a thin, hawkish face. His deep-set eyes swept the room like a general surveying a battlefield—sharp, searching, expectant.

His uniform—crisp, subdued, militant—mirrored his admiration for European fascists. Where the Americans radiated brute force and the Germans stiff authority, Arcand projected control. He didn't bellow. Didn't pound tables. He believed time would do the work for him.

Even among wolves, he didn't bare his teeth. He simply waited.

The last seats filled. Wilcox strode in, unhurried, already commanding the room before he spoke.

"A man who arrives after me is not here. He will not sit nor be spoken to." He waited long enough for the murmurs to settle. "We require our best and sharpest to be alert in mind, and active in body and spirit."

His smile carried no warmth. No kindness.

"Strength of mind and strength of body are the same. If you fail in one, you fail in both."

Wilcox circled the table slowly and deliberately as the room fell into place like a congregation.

Henry slipped through the crowd, keeping behind Redfern.

Ben, Margaret, and Kessler were already seated.

Two empty chairs.

Henry sat. His eyes flicked to the door.

Wilcox spread his hands, his voice calm and absolute.

"Now, we begin."

The meeting was logistical.

Infrastructure and trade. Resources and production.

How to move American steel, oil, and machinery to their German partners.

How Germany could, in turn, support the United States.

There were no hard numbers, quotas, shipment schedules, or contracts to sign. This wasn't a supply chain meeting—not yet.

This was all theory. Macroeconomics. Big-picture thinking.

Henry wasn't an economist.

But he had spent enough hours in McGill lecture halls to know the language of men who thought about supply and demand.

The tone was familiar. The words were not.

This wasn't an economics lecture.

This was a war plan with balance sheets.

Wilcox leaned in, voice steady and self-assured. "War fuels industry. Industry fuels nations. And nations must prepare before history forces their hand."

Henry shifted in his seat. His fingers twitched for a cigarette he couldn't light.

This wasn't business. It wasn't even economics. It was a blueprint.

His gaze swept the room.

Most staffers leaned forward, rapt, hardly blinking.

No one took notes—they weren't allowed to. But they were memorizing, absorbing every word, as if their futures depended on it.

The delegates? Split.

The Germans nodded along, focused, understanding the importance of the conversation.

The American celebrities? Bored. Restless.

This wasn't what they had come for. There was no podium. No spotlight. No ovations.

This was a discussion for bureaucrats and policymakers, not the men who needed pomp and ceremony.

His gaze landed on the corner of the room. Half a dozen men stood there, apart from the table. Silent. Watching.

And at the centre of them, Dunlow.

Downcast. Downtrodden.

He had been the last to enter. And he had received a medal of his own. One that hung heavy around his neck, dragging at his posture. Stamped onto the metal plate, a single word.

BURDEN.

"One of two ways for that man to go," Kessler murmured, half to himself. "He either burns this place to the ground... or like a kicked dog, he will only love his master more."

Harry looked towards the lawyer, but Kessler's gaze had already moved on, scanning the room.

His mind was churning; Henry could see it, but whatever conclusions he was drawing, he kept them to himself.

Henry sat flanked by Margaret and Kessler. For some reason, the two were like oil and water, occupying the same space, yet never acknowledging each other.

Strange.

Margaret was stone still, her attention fixed forward, jaw tight.

Kessler remained relaxed and almost indifferent, watching the room with bored disinterest that was too careful to be real.

Ben... Ben looked like he was trying not to be sick.

Joachim von Ribbentrop bent forward at the head of the table. "Germany has exceeded expectations in rearmament. But even we have limits. Steel, aluminum, fuel, war demands more."

Wilcox nodded, smiling like a practiced politician's smile. "America stands ready to supply. Our factories are the envy of the world."

He paused, letting his words sink in before surveying the room.

"And as for resources, well, gentlemen, we have the land to the north."

Wilcox's smile widened. "A land of abundance. Of plenty—for the war machine." He scanned the room, unhurried, with the ease as if he knew he held every eye.

"It only needs the right hand to unlock it."

Henry's gut clenched. His gaze flickered to Redfern, nodding, smiling, looking ready to applaud.

Margaret's fingers tensed against the table. A sharp inward breath before she smoothed her expression.

But Henry had seen it.

Kessler? He stifled a yawn, a slow, deliberate thing.

As if to say, how predictable.

Ben looked like he'd swallowed his tongue.

Henry sat up. Leaned forward.

Something was happening.

Henry scanned the room.

Spalding.

Thin. Wiry. Watching.

His eyes locked onto Henry, unblinking, predatory. Henry felt the weight of it, cold, deliberate. If looks could kill, he'd already have four bullets in the chest.

The conversation at the table droned on. Ports. Rail lines. The movement of resources. Ensuring safe passage across the Atlantic. The words swirled around him, but Henry wasn't listening anymore.

Spalding maintained his gaze.

The meeting recessed for lunch; a light affair, it had to be skied in, after all, just like everything else.

At last, Dunlow was released from his corner. He still wore his medal.

"Sandwiches?" he muttered, low and indignant. "Just a few measly sandwiches? Don't they know real men need more than this?"

Henry bit back a retort. The man had suffered enough.

Instead, he grabbed a sandwich and stepped outside, settling at a picnic table alone.

Across the clearing, a group of men had gathered, wrestling in the snow. Americans and Germans were tangling twenty yards away, pinning, grappling, rolling on the frost-covered ground. Nothing serious. No actual blows. But the competition was real.

The door to the chalet swung open.

With a plate in hand, Margaret carefully balanced the sandwich. She spotted Henry, and after a brief hesitation, approached. The ease she had shown on the slopes had vanished, replaced with that familiar cool detachment.

She adjusted her skirt and sat across from him.

They ate in silence.

Henry glanced back at the wrestling match. The groups were fully divided now, Americans on one side and Germans on the other. There were no fists, just holds, pinning, and testing.

Margaret wiped the crumbs from her fingers.

"That was an interesting first meeting," she said.

Henry nodded, his eyes flicking back to hers. Expressionless.

Hiding something? Or just the way she always looked?

"Yeah, it was riveting," Henry said, a dry smile playing across his face. "Like Principles of Economics all over again. Had me on the edge of my seat."

A faint glimmer of amusement, small, quick, touching only her eyes.

"I always forget that you're educated."

Henry smirked. "Not sure if that's a compliment, Ms. Bergström."

Margaret held his gaze. Unreadable.

"I'm not sure either, Mr. Locke." She pivoted toward the grappling men. "Do you wonder why we're here?"

Henry glanced at her.

"We're here because Mr. Redfern was invited."

Margaret's eyes flicked back to him. Green. Her eyes were green. He'd never noticed.

"That's not what I mean, Mr. Locke. And I think you know that."

Henry nodded, tapping a cigarette loose.

Margaret glanced at the pack. He offered it without a word. She took one—deliberate, careful.

He struck a match, lighting hers before his own.

"Didn't know you smoked."

Margaret took a slow drag. "I don't," she said. "Or at least, I didn't."

Henry rolled the cigarette between his fingers, eyes on her.

"It's impolite to stare, Mr. Locke." Neutral. No flirtation. No discomfort. Just a fact.

Henry smirked, but didn't look away. "Why do you think we're here, Ms. Bergström?"

Margaret inhaled. She didn't cough. Didn't hesitate. She held the cigarette like someone who'd done it before.

"I think," she said, "that we're not seeing the complete picture yet."

Henry flicked ash from his cigarette. "I can agree to that."

She studied him now, just for a second. "Do you?"

Henry met her gaze. "I do."

She exhaled again, watching the smoke dissipate.

"Good," she said.

Henry took another drag from his cigarette. "You're quite the skier for someone a person who hasn't in... twelve years."

"Ten years, Mr. Locke."

A flicker of something behind his eyes. She caught that. Good.

"Ahh, yes, that's right."

She didn't call him out on it. Just let it sit.

"Yes, it's been ten years." She paused, inhaling. "I haven't skied since my father passed. He was the one who pushed me into it."

"I'm sorry to hear that."

She shrugged. "It was a long time ago. And he wasn't the kindest."

Henry nodded, thinking of his father. He would never say the same. But that didn't mean he hadn't left his mark. "Fathers always leave their impression, don't they?"

Margaret's gaze shifted. Impassive. Unreadable. She looked toward the wrestling men.

One of the larger ones had pinned a smaller man in the snow, grinding his face into the ice. The smaller man struggled, refused to yield—but the weight was too much.

Margaret shifted on the bench. "That'll be us soon enough."

A sharp call cut through the clearing. "Lunch is over. Return to the meeting."

The wrestling match ended.

Henry stubbed out his cigarette, gathering his plate. The smaller man was still struggling to his feet.

No one helped him.

He watched for a moment, then murmured,

"You're not wrong."

Chapter XV

Wolves and Dogs

"NEW INDUSTRIAL PLANTS TO OPEN: NEGRO LABOR KEY TO EXPANSION"
—*The Wall Street Journal*, June 20, 1936

"Factory owners praise new federal labour programs as an essential step toward economic revitalization."

Friday, December 3rd, 1937
Cabin 14, Vanderleigh Hall, Lake Placid, New York—Early Evening

Henry unfastened his skis and set them on the rack outside the cabin. The cold gnawed at his fingers, each buckle a small punishment. He wanted to rush, but forced himself to move with care.

Ben stood beside him, stripping off his gear in silence.

They'd skied back together—not pushing, not lagging—just two men in the middle of the pack.

The SS officers had led the charge. That suited Henry fine.

Inside, the afternoon meeting had mirrored the morning. However, where the earlier discussion focused on logistics and economics, this round shifted to politics and press control—shaping perception and manufacturing consent.

Redfern had leaned in. Energized. He'd offered clarifications, steering the conversation toward Canadian politics and media, eager to prove his worth.

Adrien Arcand had said nothing.

Henry didn't trust him.

He didn't trust anyone.

Especially not here.

Henry lit a cigarette and leaned against a tree. The match flared, the glow unsteady in his fingers. His body was wrung out—muscles raw from the skiing, from hours spent coiled tight.

To the chalet and back. Too far. Too fast.

His legs felt carved out. Hollow. Shaking just enough to notice.

He needed to sit. To sleep.

But not yet.

He drew in smoke, letting it burn against the ache in his ribs.

"So," he said. "What happened this morning?"

Ben glanced over. "What do you mean?"

Henry flicked the ash, hands deep in his coat pockets. His fingers tingled—cold, exhaustion, maybe both.

"With the SS fella. You rough him up?"

Ben gave a short laugh. "What? No."

Henry studied him.

"Their big shot said you did."

Ben shook his head. "He lost control. That's all."

Henry didn't answer. He held Ben's stare. "*Didn't seem your style.*"

Ben looked away.

Then, almost as an afterthought, "I just wanted to see their faces. Losing to a Jew."

For a moment, Henry smiled. He got it. But understanding didn't change what came next.

"I get it, Ben. But you gotta watch yourself. We need to get through the weekend."

Ben turned, jaw tight.

"That's what you think? Just get through the weekend?" His voice cut sharply. "You heard them today."

Henry grimaced.

Ben gestured northward, a bitter edge creeping into his voice. "Sounds like they're already back home."

Henry crossed his arms, lips drawn tight. The words came quickly. "*I thought it couldn't happen in Canada.*"

Ben let out a dry chuckle, eyes fixed on the distance. "Yeah. Well. Guess I was wrong."

He turned and stomped through the snow toward the cabin. Henry lingered a moment, staring north—then followed.

Inside, Margaret sat wrapped up on the couch, book in hand, flipping a page with the absent ease of someone who had been waiting.

Redfern was sprawled out near the cold woodstove, sleeves rolled up, a half-spent matchbook in his hand. The fire had burned itself out during the day, and from the look of it, he'd been failing to restart it.

Seeing them enter, he tossed the matches onto the hearth and stood. "One of you can light it," he muttered, stalking toward the stairs.

When his door clicked shut, Margaret glanced up.

Ben and Henry shrugged out of their jackets.

"Dinner in an hour?" Ben asked, addressing no one in particular.

Margaret nodded. She closed the book without marking her place.

She knelt by the hearth, shifting the logs, adjusting the pile without hurry—a glimpse of hesitation, then a slight nod, as if remembering something.

Henry walked to the icebox and pulled out a bottle of cola. He popped the cap and took a deep drink, suppressing the urge to belch.

Turning, he saw Margaret crouched near the fire, meticulously coaxing a small flame to life. She nurtured it, feeding it kindling with quiet patience. The fire had caught within moments, flames licking eagerly at the logs.

Dusting herself off, Margaret straightened and turned back toward the couch.

"If Redfern asks, Ben did it," she said.

Ben chuckled—then stared at Margaret like she'd grown antlers. He glanced at Henry, checking if he'd heard.

Henry smirked. He stepped closer to the fire, holding out his hands toward the warmth, then glanced sideways at Margaret. "Another one of your father's lessons?"

Ben's expression pinged between them.

Margaret shrugged. "He was an avid outdoorsman. An avid outdoorsman with the unenviable position of having a daughter instead of a son."

Ben blinked. "What the hell is happening? Did you hit your head?"

Margaret smoothed her skirt as she sat perfectly composed. "No, Mr. Schul. My head is just as uninjured as earlier—as the fire you built can attest."

Ben looked at Henry. Then Margaret. Then Henry again.

"I'm getting changed. Call me when things are normal."

Henry watched Ben's retreat as he ascended the stairs. "Sure. Might be awhile."

Redfern led the walk down to the lodge.

They had left their skis behind at the cabin, not wanting to look at them again until they had to.

"I think near the end, I was getting the hang of it." Dunlow breathed heavily. He looked beyond exhausted, but kept driving himself forward. The man had hardly had enough time to arrive and change before they had to go down to dinner.

No one wanted to be last.

"That Wilcox is a driving man," Dunlow said.

No venom. Only admiration.

He trudged on.

Kessler looked away, a faint smile playing on his lips. He shook his head slightly. "Guess that answers that."

Dunlow frowned. "What was that, Kessler?"

Kessler didn't look at him. "Nothing, Charles." A half-shrug. "Just talking to myself."

They reached the back patio.

A pair of Eagle Guard sentries flanked the entrance, submachine guns slung tight across their chests. Their expressions were unreadable, and their eyes scanned the group, watching but not interceding.

Inside, the library was half full of the day's dignitaries. Waitstaff moved through the room with trays of champagne flutes, hors d'oeuvres, Oysters Rockefeller, caviar and blini, and foie gras terrine. The air was thick with the scent of expensive cologne and hushed conversation, the murmur of power at play.

Dunlow scooped a champagne flute off a tray, piling hors d'oeuvres into his hand like a man expecting a famine.

Henry wouldn't have been surprised if he had started stuffing his pockets.

He let his eyes drift across the room, measuring, cataloging.

Then he saw him.

Adrien Arcand.

The 'Canadian Führer' stood near the bookshelves, relaxed, poised, exactly where he belonged. He wasn't the loudest man in the room. He didn't need to be. Arcand had a way of commanding space without taking up too much of it, an air of inevitability, as if the world had already aligned itself to his vision.

Henry barely had time to register him before Arcand's eyes flicked up.

They locked onto Henry.

A smile. Not broad. Not forced. Just a thin, knowing curve of the lips.

He moved.

Not rushed. Not eager. Just a deliberate shift, an easy glide through the room's currents, as though he were allowing Henry the privilege of an audience.

They extended their hands at the same time.

A firm grip. Steady. Too long.

A hard, icy stare. Blue eyes, unblinking.

"Adrian."

"Henry," Arcand said, holding on just long enough to make a point.

His grip wasn't aggressive—just calculated. Authority, not warmth.

Then, with a subtle smile: "Soon enough, you'll be calling me *mon Führer*."

The words landed in French.

Henry forced a smile and took a champagne flute from a passing tray.

"It's been a long time." Replied just as easily in French.

The handshake broke.

"Strange seeing you without your skates on."

Henry's eyes narrowed. "Always the same joke."

Arcand gave a small, dismissive wave, then looked Henry up and down, appraising the cut of his suit. "Still dressing the part, I see. Some habits never leave us."

Henry tilted the flute, letting the champagne swirl. His eyes never left Arcand. "Not surprised to see you here."

Arcand glanced around the room, then back again. "Strange. I thought I wouldn't see you." He nodded subtly toward Redfern, a ghost of a smile curving at his lips. "From what I hear, that invitation wasn't originally extended to you, was it?"

Henry swallowed. Who hadn't heard?

"Yeah," he said slowly. "Jimmy got sick."

The more he repeated it, the weaker it sounded.

Arcand rolled the words around in his mouth, savouring them.

"Jimmy got sick." A pause. A flicker of amusement. "Right."

Henry held his gaze, saying nothing. Letting the silence work.

Arcand lifted his chin, eyeing Henry down his nose.

"Well. You are here." Arcand's mouth twitched at the corner. "You always did have a way of ending up where you didn't belong."

Henry shrugged and reached for his champagne. "I guess I'm not easy to replace."

A small, knowing smile pulled at the edge of Arcand's lips.

"If slipping into places you don't belong was a talent..."

The words hung like a threat.

Henry didn't blink. Didn't take the bait.

Arcand took a measured taste of his drink, his gaze unwavering.

"Henry." The voice softened, just slightly. "I know your views don't align with the others here." A sip. A pause. "If you're smart, you'll lie low. Stay quiet."

Arcand squinted slowly, swirling his glass.

"Wilcox's dogs don't just bark, Henry. They bite."

Henry leaned in, tongue pressing against the inside of his teeth. "They're still dogs."

Arcand smiled. Not amused. Just knowing.

"I know you've been watching Redfern. Feeding someone information."

Henry held his stare. Steady. Unreadable.

Arcand leaned back as if the whole thing bored him.

"Oh, I won't tell. There's no point." His mouth creased as he cast a casual glance around the room. "There's no point to any of it. Resistance, I mean."

His eyes returned to Henry. The smile had faded.

Henry's nostrils flared. His gaze sharpened. "And what exactly is coming?"

Arcand took a sip of champagne. His smile didn't return. Instead, the stillness stretched—enough to feel final.

"Why, Henry," Arcand exhaled, slow and patient. "What's coming?"

His lips twitched. He drained the flute of champagne. A drop clung to his lip. He licked it away.

"I am."

A chime rang through the hall—a quiet, measured signal.

The room stirred. Conversations tapered off.

The breakfast tables remained, though the buffet had been cleared. No centrepiece now.

Henry's jaw tightened. His breath hitched, just briefly, as his eyes landed on the seating chart.

Unchanged.

Ben with the SS.

Henry with Warren Anderson.

He flexed his fingers before realizing they were clenched. His shoulders ached, tension creeping back in before he even reached the table. The morning had been bad enough. Now, a whole dinner.

He glanced at Ben. "You sure?"

Ben lifted his chin. "I'm fine. I can handle them."

Henry touched the nape of his neck, holding his eyes. "Okay," he surveyed the room. Then, in a quieter, almost whispered aside:

"Don't let them get to you."

Ben smirked. "You worry too much, Henry."

Henry breathed out through his nose and watched him go.

Something in his chest felt tight—a slow coil, winding tighter with every hour he spent here.

He rolled his shoulder, adjusted his collar, forcing the stiffness from his body as he walked.

The ballroom was loud, not in volume, but in presence.

No one turned their heads, no one stopped talking, but Henry felt it—the shift, the way eyes trailed over him without ever meeting his gaze.

By the time he reached his seat, Anderson was already there. Waiting.

Henry pulled his chair back and sat, slowly breathing through his nose and absentmindedly rubbing his fingers together.

Two medals were in front of Anderson, one for each leg. Top man.

Anderson smiled. That same too-wide grin. His fingers drummed once against the table. "I'm sorry our conversation was interrupted this morning." A pause. Just long enough. "Quite a spectacle, wasn't it?"

Henry reached for his glass. He hadn't meant to.

"Yeah, you Americans sure can make a production of things."

Anderson leaned back, lighting a cigarette. The thing stank. American tobacco was not what it once had been. "It's pageantry. A show of unity. Proof that America stands above the rest."

Henry shrugged off his jacket, draping it over the back of his chair.

"Unity?" Henry scoffed, tapping a cigarette from his pack of Players. "That was just noise. A pack of dogs barking to be noticed." He flicked his gaze toward the German table. "The Germans. That was unity."

A pause. A flick of his lighter. The flame flared as he brought it to his cigarette. "Wolves."

Anderson's eye twitched, just a fraction.

He took a slow drag of his cigarette, watching Henry through the smoke.

Then, casually, almost as an aside: "Earlier, when we were discussing your friend Edward..."

Henry tilted his head slightly, furrowing his brow. "I think the skiing must have done you in, Mr. Anderson. You were discussing someone I don't know." He sighed, smoke drifting between them. "But you Americans, you assume we're all acquainted."

Anderson didn't smile right away. He watched. Waiting and letting Henry sit in the silence. Then finally, slowly, too slowly, his lips turned up into a smile.

"Ahh. You're right. I did bring him up." He swirled his drink and took a sip. "But it was interesting, wasn't it?" A pause. "That moment when something clicked."

"Right."

Henry tapped twice on the table. Slow. Deliberate. A mirror of Anderson's move earlier.

Anderson's fingers paused over his glass for a second. Then, he lifted it to his lips, expression unchanged.

He opened his mouth.

Father Coughlin climbed onto the stage, hands clasped before him. His voice was rich, steady, practiced, meant to be heard by millions. "Bow your heads, gentlemen, as we give thanks."

A pause. The room obeyed.

"Heavenly Father, we gather tonight in Your name, as men chosen to stand at the dawn of a new age. You have gifted us strength, wisdom, and the courage to shape the world as You intended."

His voice did not rise. It didn't need to.

"Bless the hands that build, the minds that guide, and the spirits that endure. Let us cast aside weakness and corruption and march forward, unafraid. For it is not man who shapes destiny, but You who have laid its foundation before us."

His gaze lifted. His voice softened, intimate, persuasive.

"We give thanks for this nation, for its leaders, and for the righteous path set before us. Let no force, within or without, divide us from our purpose."

A beat. A pause. Then,

"Amen."

The room echoed back the word, low and unified.

Hidden from view, the waitstaff descended upon the tables like locusts, delivering food instead of devouring it. The first course was Consommé Royale, a clear, intensely flavourful beef broth with tiny custard cubes floating in it.

Henry ate quietly, his spoon gliding through the broth, listening to the low hum of conversation.

One of Anderson's men spoke, a lazy grin stretching across his face.

"You should've seen him try to run." He chuckled, shaking his head. "Didn't get far. Busted his ankle when the fat bastard got stuck in a window and fell out."

A bull of a man—thick through the chest and shoulders. He didn't move fast, but never needed to. A presence like a wall.

He lifted the bowl, slurped the last of the soup, then leaned back and released a loud belch.

Anderson gave him a pinched look. The man didn't notice—or didn't care.

"Fool even tried to draw on me." He smirked. "But I already had him lined up."

He raised his hand, shaped it like a pistol.

"Blam. Blam. Blam."

The imaginary shots echoed softly against the silverware and murmurs of the room. Then, just like that, he lowered his hand and returned to his soup, as if he had been narrating a hunting trip.

The table burst into laughter.

"They keep sneaking down here," another man said. "And we keep catching 'em. Knocking 'em down like bowling pins."

Keep catching them. Interesting.

Henry lifted his spoon. He wasn't sure whether the consommé or something else that left a bitter taste in his mouth.

"I mean, these guys are barely trained," the man continued. "About as subtle as a freight train."

A few chuckles. Then, low, offhand,

"You'd think they'd stop trying."

Henry set his spoon down, fingers curling loosely around it.

Across the table, the thickset man, built like a battering ram, stared at him.

Not just looking. Measuring.

It's like a man lining up a shot.

Henry held an unblinking gaze as he brought the spoon to his mouth.

A shift. A tension in the man's shoulders. His fingers twitched slightly, as if reaching for something not there.

"Cap'n, why can't we—"

"Taylor, stand down."

Taylor's jaw clenched. His arm tensed, just for a second, before he leaned back and crossed his arms.

Captain.

The word sank into Henry's thoughts like a stone in water.

Anderson had a rank in something. Not just a uniform for show. ISB, most likely.

Anderson turned back to Henry. "I apologize. The men can be a little... aggressive when agitated."

Agitated?

Henry let his gaze drift around the room — casual, easy — before returning to Anderson. "Agitated?" He let out a short breath, shaking his head. "What's there to be agitated about? Good food, good wine. I guess we're missing some women..."

Anderson didn't answer right away.

Instead, he took his time. Just watching Henry, measuring. Then finally he smiled. Controlled. Even.

"Well," he said lightly, "they believe there's a spy in our midst."

Henry's grip tightened around his spoon.

His eyes flicked to Taylor. Then back to Anderson.

"A spy?" He scoffed, just enough to sound dismissive. "Here?" A small chuckle. "They'd have to be crazy."

Anderson took the last spoonful, relishing it and swallowing and allowing the stillness to stretch.

His gaze slid back to Henry.

Calm. Even. Pinning him in place.

"Are you?"

Henry's stomach dipped.

The words hung longer than they should have. A waiter passed. The clink of silverware. The hum of conversation around them.

Henry kept his face still.

The soup in front of him had gone cold.

That was fine—his appetite had vanished, every nerve in his body now lit and screaming.

"Am I what?"

Anderson stared at him. "Are you crazy?"

Henry's eyes narrowed as he met Anderson's gaze.

The soup bowls were taken away.

"I don't think so. But would a crazy person know that they are crazy?" Henry looked around the table.

Taylor looked confused.

Anderson looked smug.

The waitstaff moved in, setting down the next course, Poached Salmon with Sauce Mousseline.

Across the table, Anderson's grin widened.

He lifted his hand. Knock. Knock. Knock.

A deliberate rhythm. A signal.

"You know what?" He smirked. "I believe you." His head tilted as he leaned in. "For now."

Henry's jaw ached—he hadn't realized his teeth were clenched until they released. His mouth was dry.

Anderson cut into his salmon, voice smooth, almost casual.

"See, you don't seem like a believer. And that's fine. Plenty of true believers here already. But cogs in the machine?" Knock. His fingers tapped the table again. "They just need to function. No need to fix one—"

A smile.

"Until it breaks."

A sip of wine. A long, measured silence. Then, as if none of it had just happened:

"Now, tell me about that fight against 'Bun' Cook."

Chapter XVI

The Breaking Point

"DETROIT TO WINDSOR: BORDER CROSSINGS RISE AMID FEARS OF AMERICAN FASCISM"
—*The Windsor Star*, February 19, 1936

"Authorities report a sharp increase in asylum seekers at the Windsor border, primarily Black and Jewish Americans. Local officials call for guidance from Ottawa."

Friday, December 3rd, 1937
Vanderleigh Hall, Lake Placid, New York—Late Evening

Henry stumbled out of the ballroom, away from that damned table, away from Anderson and his Internal Security Bureau cronies.

ISB. The American Gestapo.

He was almost certain now—all of them.

He exhaled, rubbing a hand over his face, forcing himself to breathe. *Think.*

He glanced back into the ballroom. The reception was still in full swing, with dignitaries and staff lingering over drinks and laughter rising in waves beneath the chandeliers.

His eyes landed on Ben.

Standing alone. In the corner.

Henry hesitated. For a moment, he almost moved toward him. Almost reached out.

But no.

He needed time. *Ben can't know.*

Not yet.

Henry turned, grabbed his overcoat, and stepped out into the night.

Half a dozen men smoked cigars on the patio, chatting in German. Henry nodded once, barely slowing his stride as he descended the back stairs.

He felt the cold air hit him like a slap. The sky was dark, overcast, and heavy. Thick clouds smothered the moon and stars. Nothing but blackness stretched above.

Just like that night.

Torrential rain. A knock at the door. The Colt hidden behind his back—useless against what stood outside.

"You have to quit." She'd shouted to be heard.

"I can't. You know that." Even in his memories, his words were hollow. Empty.

"Of course you can. You can do anything. Money is money—but he's becoming a monster."

"You're overreacting."

"I'm not. I'm terrified. Why can't you see it?"

She stormed into the night. He never saw her again. *Natalie.* The name still clawed at his throat.

The door closed. Heavy. Final.

The gas lamps flickered weakly along the trail, thin pools of light swallowed by the darkness between them. The trees' shadows shifted beyond the glow.

Henry followed the winding path. The farther he walked, the quieter the world became. The sound of the reception, the murmur of voices, and the distant music faded.

Just boots crunching on snow.

And the dark.

He still had nothing concrete to give Henshaw.

None of the conversations, plans, or whispers over fine china was proof.

He needed something tangible. A name. A document. A list.

Something that would burn this place to the ground.

And there was only one place where that kind of evidence would be.

The chalet.

That was where the real meetings took place, behind closed doors, and honest discussions were held.

He pulled his overcoat tighter about his shoulders as the wind cut through him.

He would have to ski in the dark.

The thought sent a tight knot into his chest. The trail was wide enough, but the trees were black columns beyond the gas lamps. He would need a torch from the cabin, if there were one.

His boots crunched over fresh snow as he crested the hill.

Cabins dotted the trees ahead. Windows flickered like distant stars, some glowing, some dark. He turned onto the familiar path leading to his own. The wind rustled the branches. Something creaked in the woods.

Henry kept moving. He was alone.

But he wasn't. The thought clawed into his skull, unbidden.

His breath plumed in the frigid air. He tugged his coat tighter, pulled his gloves higher, trying to keep the cold at bay. His boots pressed fresh tracks into the snow.

Then—another sound. Just behind him. Footsteps. Soft. Careful.

His pulse quickened. He adjusted his collar, turned a fraction, glancing out of the corner of his eye.

Nothing. Just the shifting dark beyond the gas lamps. Flickering pools of light.

His breath came slow. Controlled. Keep moving. Don't stop. The cabin was just ahead. One more turn. Fifty yards. His boots crunched.

Another step behind him. Closer.

His muscles tensed. He stepped past the nearest gas lamp—into the dark.

CRACK. White burst behind his eyes. His knees buckled. The ground hit him before he knew he was falling.

Pain lanced through his skull. The world spun sideways. Muffled. Distant. His ears rang. His chest heaved—breath stolen.

Move. Move.

But his limbs were slow. Numb.

Snow crunched near his head. A shadow stood over him, backlit by the lamplight.

A voice. Low. Measured. Familiar. "Should've stayed in the ballroom, Locke."

Hands dragged him, rolled him. His back pressed into the snow. Ice at his neck. Skull throbbing.

A face swam into view—sharp angles, narrow eyes, thin, wiry. Spalding. A blackjack in his hand.

A knee drove into Henry's chest. Not crushing. Not yet.

"I know it was you, Locke." Steady voice. Too steady. A man holding himself together by force. "Where's the case?"

Henry blinked against the haze. His mind was slow. Thick. The world tilted. His pulse pounded in his ears.

He coughed, fighting for air. "I—" His throat was raw, his voice weak. "I don't... I don't know what you're talking about."

CRACK. White-hot pain again. Sound bled into a high-pitched whine.

The world slid sideways. Snow against his cheek. Too cold.

"Try again."

Spalding's breath misted the air. Calm. Controlled. Dangerous. "It's not in your luggage. Where is it?"

Henry gasped. Spalding's knee ground deeper into his chest.

He reached up, grabbed for the man's collar. Spalding batted his hand away with ease.

CRACK. Another slap.

Copper filled his mouth. Not the first time.

Henry's left hand clawed at the snow. Nothing.

Spalding's breath quickened. Not just anger. Fear. His knuckles whitened as he fisted Henry's coat. "I need it."

A flick of his eyes—over his shoulder. Was he alone?

"Tell me where it is." His fingers clamped around Henry's throat. Squeezing. Cutting off the air.

Henry bucked. Legs twisting. Arms weak. He clawed at Spalding's wrists but his vision was swimming, oxygen gone, strength draining fast.

Something moved. Behind Spalding. A shadow in the dark.

CRACK.

Spalding's head snapped forward. His body sagged, then collapsed into the snow.

Henry gasped, dragging in air—sharp, freezing.

A shadow loomed over him. A hand reached down. Henry took it.

His vision swam. His pulse hammered. But the face was unmistakable.

Ben.

Ben stood over him, a heavy branch, a club, clutched tight in his hands. His breath came quickly, uneven. His eyes darted from Henry to Spalding, then back again.

"Okay, pal," he panted. "You gotta tell me what the fuck is going on."

"And that's all I know."

The silence in the cabin was thick. Heavy.

Ben sat quietly, mulling over Henry's words. He had listened without interrupting, absorbing it all.

Henry let out a slow, quiet breath. The weight on his chest eased, just a little. He wasn't alone anymore.

But that came with its dangers.

Now Ben knew everything. Everything. He could turn Henry over to Redfern. Hand him over to Anderson. Win favour. Survive the weekend.

They had left Spalding unconscious, but breathing. Left his fate to the cold.

The thought gnawed at Henry's ribs.

Ben finally spoke. His voice was quieter. Measured. "Henshaw. How long have you been working for him?"

The words hung between them.

"Working for him is a loose term."

Ben's gaze hardened. "Stop deflecting, Henry."

Henry sighed, running a hand through his hair. "A year."

Ben's gaze held steady, unreadable as he processed.

"He didn't approach me directly," Henry continued, voice low. "Its all been messages and calls. Dropping names at meetings, and minutes of events. I guess I was the soft target in Redfern's circle — the one still on the fence."

Ben nodded slowly. "He didn't recruit me because I'm Jewish."

A beat.

Henry shook his head. "I doubt that. You were always..." He hesitated. "You leaned too close to the line, maybe. But you never crossed it."

Ben's jaw tightened. "I'm not a fascist."

Henry nodded. "I know." A pause. "I guess I just seemed like the safer bet."

Ben didn't argue. But he didn't agree either.

The fire crackled between them, filling the silence.

"So, what's the next play?"

Henry looked at him. Ben hadn't said your next play. He'd said, the next play.

Something flickered in Henry's chest. A tightness rose in his throat. He looked away and tapped a cigarette from the pack.

Running low.

"I don't know," he said. "We need proof."

Ben nodded, leaning back, eyes distant, calculating.

Henry lit his cigarette.

"The chalet," Ben said.

Henry drew in, then let the smoke curl between them. "That's what I was thinking, too."

Ben stood, grabbed two Cokes from the icebox, cracked them open, and passed one to Henry.

"Security's been tight. No notes taken. No meeting minutes."

Henry took a sip, the sweetness settling on his tongue. "Yeah."

"But they must have something. A plan, an agreement, something."

Henry shrugged. "Could all just be handshakes and words?"

Ben shook his head. "The Germans like things neat. There's gotta be something tangible. Something we haven't seen yet."

Henry nodded slowly.

Ben took a long drink and then clinked the bottle down.

"We're running out of time," Henry said.

Ben walked over and pulled on his overcoat.

Ben turned back, meeting Henry's gaze. "Are you coming?"

They skied slowly through the cabin trails.

Spalding was gone, but the blood remained, dark against the snow, a stark reminder of what had just transpired. Henry kept scanning the trees, his muscles tight, expecting the man to lunge from the shadows. But there was only the forest's silence, the empty, skeletal branches shifting in the wind.

Ben had found a torch under the sink but hadn't lit it. Not yet.

They pushed forward. Beyond the cabins. Towards the trail.

The indistinct murmur of voices carried across the clearing, the men on the lodge patio, cigars glowing in the darkness. Henry's pulse drummed in his ears with every push of his skis. Any second now, a voice would cut through the night. Then a shout. Maybe a warning. The command is to stop.

No one called out.

Only the sound of their skis whispered through the cold.

The air was frigid, biting deeper with each breath. The ground beneath them felt heavier. Exhaustion crept into Henry's bones, slowing his movements, and his limbs burned. A dull haze pressed in on his thoughts, half from the blackjack to the skull, half from the relentless pace of the past twenty-four hours.

But stopping wasn't an option.

They reached the trailhead, finding it more by instinct than sight.

The lodge vanished behind them, swallowed by the hill and the trees.

Ben flicked the torch on. A ring of light cut into the darkness, pushing back the suffocating black of the woods.

And they skied on.

If Henry's muscles had burned earlier, they were on fire now.

The only thing keeping him moving was muscle memory—the repetition, the rhythm of the motion that had become ingrained.

Half an hour. That was all it should take—but time had stretched into an endless series of aching moments, each more brutal than the last.

Henry glanced at Ben and saw how his breath heaved and how his shoulders hunched against the cold. Suffering just as much.

Then—

"Stop."

Ben thrust out his pole, blocking Henry's path.

Henry stilled. His pulse thumped against his ribs.

"Did you hear that?"

They paused. Voices. Up ahead.

And the distinct sound of skis.

"Get into the brush!"

There was little cover to speak of. Just skeletal trees, their bare branches stretching like claws into the night.

It would have to do.

They lunged sideways, slicing into the sparse woods, pressing against the trunks.

The voices approached.

Low. Quiet. But carried just enough over the snow to be heard.

The sound of skis cut through the stillness. One sliced cleanly, gliding smooth over the trail. The other dragged—uneven, scraping, strained.

Two figures.

One taller, moving with practiced ease, their strides measured, controlled, like they could have been going much faster but weren't.

The other was rounder and heavier, with quick breaths and hard puffs, with each motion an effort.

"... if that bastard can make me ski at midnight..."

"It's not midnight."

"Well, you know what I mean."

A pause. The sound of laboured breathing.

"... imagine what else he could do..."

The figures passed, dark shadows carving their way down the trail.

The taller one hesitated for a moment as they skied past the obvious tracks leading into the brush. Their strides faltered a fraction.

But they didn't stop. Didn't comment.

A last whisper as they disappeared into the night.

"... imagine what he could do with an entire nation..."

Ben and Henry exchanged looks, waited until the voices faded, and set out again.

By the time they reached the edge of the clearing, the clouds had shifted, revealing slivers of moonlight over the chalet and the surrounding snow.

They lay prone, half-buried in the drifts, scanning the building below.

"You never had to sleep in the mud and snow as a flyer," Henry murmured. "Bet you hate this."

Ben barely shifted. "I wasn't in the trenches, but that didn't mean I didn't freeze my ass off."

Henry smirked, exhaling softly.

The chalet windows glowed warmly, their light spilling onto the snow. Shadows moved inside.

A single Eagle Guard sprawled across one of the picnic tables, cigarette dangling from his lips, the cherry flaring red in the dark.

Ben barely breathed. "Wouldn't last a day in the trenches."

Henry's gaze stayed on the guard. "We're not in the trenches, Ben."

Ben didn't look at him. "So, what's the plan?"

Henry's breath barely stirred the cold air. "Well, a bayonet isn't an option."

Ben turned sharply.

Henry lifted his empty hands, deadpan. "I seem to be short of a bayonet."

Ben let out a rough scoff, shaking his head. "Jesus, Henry."

He ran a hand across his face, rolling his shoulders. "Sneak around the back?"

Henry shook his head.

"And do what? There are still people in there."

Ben muttered a curse, shifting his stance. "So we came all this way for nothing?"

Henry didn't answer right away.

Instead, he watched. Measured. Calculating.

"I don't think so."

Ben frowned. "What do you mean?"

Henry didn't look at him. He pulled his wool cap closer down over his eyes and his collar up higher. He was already moving and crawling backward into the shadows, adjusting his skis.

"Stay back. But follow my lead."

Ben whispered something harsh behind him, but Henry was already skiing up the trail, this time not trying to hide.

The guard shifted at their approach. Straightened up, and unslung his Thompson with smooth efficiency. The cigarette in his fingers flared brightly for a second before he flicked it into the snow.

Clack. The bolt slid back on the action.

Henry slowed, planting his poles beside him, posture relaxed. Nonchalant. Like he belonged.

The guard wasn't pointing the weapon at them.

But he wasn't *not* pointing it at them either.

"State your business."

Henry squinted at the guard.

"Paul?"

His voice shifted — not exaggerated, just enough. The clipped cadence, the 'a' long and flat.

The guard hesitated. His stance loosened a fraction.

"Paul?" he echoed.

"Oh, shoot. Thought Paul was on tonight."

The guard's grip on the Thompson adjusted.

"Paul Davis?"

Henry smiled easily. "Hell, I dunno Paul's last name. Jus' hope that don't get me shot."

He shifted his weight, eyes flicking to the weapon in the guard's hands without staring.

"Paul's on the gate."

Henry let out a small laugh, tapping a cigarette from his pack. He slid it between his lips as he pulled out a wad of American bills, just enough to be seen, not flaunted.

"Damn it. Guess I got mixed up. We were supposed to do a trade."

The guard's eyes flicked to Ben, half-hidden in the shadows. "A trade?"

"Yeah, nevah mind."

Henry let the cigarette hang loose, smoke drifting into the dark as he turned back into the night. "Reggie, we're goin' to the gate."

Henry adjusted his gloves and grabbed his poles.

"Wait—" The guard took a half-step forward, palm out—not blocking, but holding Henry in place. There was a glint of curiosity in his eyes. "What kinda trade?"

Henry let the silence stretch, then smiled. Nudged the Boston in his voice a little more—enough to sell it.

He shook the man's hand easily. "Freddy, nice ta meet ya. Sorry—lotta faces this week."

The guard grinned. "I understand."

"Listen, we was expectin' Paul. Not sure if the trade's gonna work—"

"I'm just as good as Paul. If not better."

Henry smiled, clapping Fred on the shoulder. "Freddy, ya don't even know the trade, pahhl."

The guard chuckled, big, eager, a man who wanted in.

"You see how it is. These guys throw money 'round like it's nothin'. I jus' want a piece of that. I've got a wife and a kid on the way. And I'm guardin' an empty cabin."

Henry breathed out through a faint smile, then pulled the roll of cash from his pocket.

"Alright. This wasn't the trade, but we'll find Paul aftah." Henry looked back at Ben in the darkness. "How 'bout anotha kinda deal, Freddy? Reggie and I could use a few minutes in the cabin. It's somethin', ain't it? Maybe take a few pictchas. Mark the occasion."

The guard hesitated. Looked at the cabin.

"Then, there's the money."

Freddy looked around in the darkness before back at Henry. "How much are we talking?"

Henry peeled off a ten-dollar bill. Held it between two fingers. Dangling.

He examined the man's face, weighing it.

Hesitation. "I'm not sure," Freddy said. "Things have gotten tight lately."

Another bill joined the first. Smooth. Unhurried.

Freddy grinned, shaking his head. "Yeah, that'll do it."

The bills vanished into his Eagle Guard shirt, like they'd never existed.

Henry smiled. He would have given him the entire roll if the kid had asked for more.

The guard turned and guided them to the chalet's door.

The foyer was empty except for neatly arranged jackets, gloves, and wool caps, which looked like their owners would be back at any moment.

Henry flashed a broad grin as he entered, surveying the room as if he owned it. It looked different now, stripped of its audience and purpose.

Two staff members adjusted a slide projector, aligning it beneath the twin banners—the stars and stripes on one side and the swastika on the other. They glanced up for only a moment before returning to their work.

Henry smiled at Freddy. "We've got it from here, Freddy."

The guard grinned, waved lazily, and turned back to his post.

Inside, Henry and Ben walked the room, slow and deliberate.

The two staff members finished their work, glanced at the intruders, and drifted toward the foyer, murmuring in low voices.

Ben let out a breath. "You're a madman," he muttered. "How did you pull that off?"

Henry smirked. "I guess years of hanging around fascists and pretending to be one have their perks."

Ben snorted. "You're pretending never sold. No one believed it."

"And yet." Henry gestured toward the door.

Ben shook his head. "That's because you have ice in your veins."

Henry shrugged.

They scanned the room. Empty. Barren. No notes, no files, no loose papers. Nothing.

Then,

Their eyes met.

Henry turned toward the projector. It was still loaded.

The slide projector was set and prepped for the morning's meeting.

A record. A visual record.

Henry's pulse kicked up.

He reached for the machine, deliberate, and flipped the switch. A low hum filled the room. The bright light snapped on, throwing stark shadows across the floor.

Click.

The first slide snapped into place.

A ledger. Rows of numbers. Handwritten but meticulous.

Henry squinted.

Karabiner 98k "Mauser": 28,452 produced.

Ben exhaled sharply beside him. "That's German rifle production for last month."

Henry's throat felt dry. "Twenty-eight thousand rifles?" His voice was low. "In one month?"

Holy shit.

He raised the camera and took a picture.

Click.

Slide 2: Kar 98k Projected Production: 1938-39

Henry's stomach clenched as the next slide clicked into place.

A graph. Projections.

The current numbers looked small compared to what was coming.

Projected Output for 1938: 35,000 per month.

Projected Output for 1939: 50,000 per month.

Ben muttered a curse under his breath. "Christ. They're ramping up."

Henry didn't respond. He took another picture.

Click.

Henry's stomach twisted as the next slide came into focus.

PzKpfw II: 119 produced

PzKpfw III: 22 prototypes completed

Ben stared at the numbers. "That's... that's not much."

Henry shook his head. "Not yet."

Another picture.

Click.

Another graph.

This one is steeper.

1938 Projection:

Panzer II: 150 per month.

Panzer III: 50 per month.

Panzer IV (planned): 15-20 test units.

Ben took a slow breath. "They're still testing the Panzer III..."

"Yeah." Henry's voice was tight. "But they won't be testing for long."

The last note at the bottom of the slide made his skin crawl.

1939 Directive: PzKpfw III to become standard issue. Increase to 100 per month.

Another picture.

Click.

Henry clicked to the next slide.

This one was worse.

A chart. Shipments. Materials. Numbers that didn't lie.

1937: 950,000 tons of steel allocated to military use.

1938: 1.6 million tons.

1939: 2.8 million tons.

Henry could hear his breath in the silence.

Ben muttered, "They're tripling output in two years."

Henry's hands were steady as he raised the camera.

Click.

Henry shook his head, letting out a slow breath. His voice was quiet. "They're not just building up."

Ben's eyes flicked to him. "What do you mean?"

Henry tapped a finger against the edge of the projector. "They're not just preparing for war." He gestured at the figures on the screen. "They're timing it."

Ben looked back at the numbers. The ramp-up. The projections.

A quiet realization settled in.

Henry's voice was low. "This isn't just rearmament. This is a countdown."

The foyer door swung open.

"...They said they just wanted a few pictures..."

Shit.

Henry killed the projector. The bulb popped off, leaving the room in sudden darkness.

Footsteps. Voices. Closer.

"I told you, Fred, no one is allowed here."

The projector whined as it spun down, the mechanical hum dragging into silence.

Henry moved. Fast. He pushed open the service door, Ben already at his hip.

Into the back kitchen.

Into the dark.

Henry fumbled against the wall for a switch, found it, and thought better. "Ben, you got the torch?"

A delay. Ben was searching. Henry's pulse thudded in his ears.

"Uh, yeah." Click—a dim beam cut through the dark.

The kitchen was pristine and gleaming, like the finest dining restaurants in New York. It had stainless steel and polished counters; every surface was too clean.

Ben muttered, "How did they get all this up here?"

Henry's breath came slowly, measured. "Not our concern right now, Ben."

They moved. Quick and low. Through the back of the kitchen, toward the service exit.

Henry paused. Fingers brushing against the knife block.

He slid one out. Cold steel in his grip.

Ben hesitated beside him. Then, as if considering the same, he reached for a knife and stopped.

Shook his head. "I'd just cut myself."

Henry's pulse thundered. The weight of the knife in his hand was too familiar.

Too much like the past.

Too much like the war.

God, he hoped he didn't need it.

They slipped outside into the black void of night.

The clouds still pressed heavily above them. No stars. No moon. Just the endless dark swallowing everything.

They crouched low, moving fast along the back wall of the chalet.

At the edge, Henry pressed his back against the timber. Listened. Then, a slow lean, peering around the corner.

Only darkness.

"Stay close. We move fast."

He pulled the camera from his pocket. Held it out.

"Take it."

Ben frowned. Didn't move.

"If I go down, you get this to Henshaw."

Ben's jaw tightened. He shoved the camera back toward Henry.

"This is yours, Harry. We're getting out of this."

Henry's fingers wrapped around the leather case. Shoved it back into his pocket.

"Fine. Then let's not fuck it up."

Henry released one measured breath.

"We run the length of the building. Quick, right around the corner. Back to the skis. Into the brush. Strap in. And then?"

Ben's breath curled in the cold. "Then we get the fuck out of here."

Henry nodded.

Move.

He rounded the corner, keeping low. Running. Fast. He had to be fast.

Like crossing between the trenches.

That same feeling, legs burning, lungs seizing, but no matter how fast you ran, you always felt too slow. Like somewhere, someone had you lined up in their sights.

Each crunch of snow underfoot sounded like artillery. Too loud. Too damn loud.

But silence wasn't enough.

They needed speed.

Halfway down the building, light.

A torch glow ahead around the corner.

Shit.

Henry dug in, trying to summon the speed he had twenty years ago. But the years had taken their toll. The pros. Those brutal fights. Years at war.

And suddenly, everything stretched.

The world slowed.

Is this what it's like to die?

He had thought that before. More than once. In barbed wire, through shell craters, buried in mud.

But he had lived. And he would live now.

The moment snapped.

A shape rounded the corner.

Eagle Guard. Torchlight swept across the snow.

He wasn't ready.

But Henry was.

The guard barely had time to react.

Henry's left fist drove into his stomach. Hard.

Air shot from the man's lungs in a ragged wheeze. He staggered, not down yet.

Henry's uppercut snapped his head back—a sick crack of teeth meeting tongue.

The man reeled, not out yet.

Henry finished it.

His boot drove forward—a thud. The guard slumped into the snow.

Still.

Henry's breath heaved. Checked the body.

Not Freddy. Good.

He crouched, unclipped the magazine from the Thompson, and tossed it far into the snow.

He grabbed the man's torch.

Ben was already at the skis, grabbing his poles. Henry ran up, his heart hammering.

No shouts. No alarms.

Not yet. Now move. Henry sprinted.

Every instinct screamed brace for gunfire. Any second now, the ripping burst of a Thompson. A spray of bullets across his back.

But it didn't come.

They crossed the clearing, lungs burning, legs aching, and then—the brush. Cover.

Skis. Down. Clip in. Fast. Hands shaking. Adrenaline surging. They fumbled, boots slipping, bindings stiff, fingers numb from cold and panic.

Henry looked back.

Tracks.

A deep scar of fresh boot prints through the clearing. Visible. Exposed. But dozens of other tracks crisscrossed the snow from earlier.

Would they notice? Would they know?

The chalet door opened.

Light poured out. It sliced across the clearing like a spotlight.

Voices.

"...Nothing to hide? Then why'd they run?"

Henry held his breath.

He knew that voice.

"...Don't know, Captain Anderson. He seemed fine to me... Mentioned Davis..."

Anderson. Shit.

"...Description. What'd he look like?"

Henry's pulse hammered.

"...Too dark to see... Boston, I think..."

Beside him, Ben's breathing slowed.

Their skis were on. Almost.

Not fast enough.

A shout. Clear. Cutting through the night.

"Wilkinson's down! Breathing... unconscious."

Ben stiffened.

Henry steadied himself, forcing calm.

A voice. Low. Measured.

"...Radio inside..."

Henry's stomach knotted. Fuck.

Henry saw Ben's fingers clenched around his overcoat. His eyes flicked to the trail.

Anderson.

Another voice. Quieter.

"... Head count at the lodge... check the cabins too..."

A pause. A shift of boots in the snow. Then,

The door shut.

Move.

They pushed off. The brush slowed them. Too tight. Too much resistance.

Not fast enough.

Get to the trail.

They cleared the trees.

Henry glanced back. The door was still closed.

Push. Stride. Push. Three legs to the Chalet. Three legs of practice. Now, nothing but exhaustion.

His lungs burned. His body screamed. But the movement was ingrained.

Push. Stride. Push.

First hill. Crest it. Go.

Henry looked back.

The door was open.

Anderson was coming.

Ben turned the torch on.

The beam bounced wildly, skimming over trees, catching flashes of slopes, and cutting around the bends of the trail. The shadows stretched and warped, distorting the world into something unfamiliar.

Then, darkness. He clicked it off again.

Push. Stride. Push. Click.

The rhythm had settled in. The cadence was drilled into their bodies over the last handful of minutes.

But exhaustion was clawing at Henry's limbs now. His muscles were failing. His lungs burned.

Only adrenaline kept him upright.

And even that was running dry.

The only sounds were panting breath, skis carving over ice, and Henry's pulse pounding inside his skull.

He turned his head.

There.

In the distance, the steady glow of a torch.

The beam was unwavering. Not searching. Not hesitant. Just gaining. Closing in.

Every time Henry looked, it was closer.

Push. Stride. Push. Click.

Almost there. They had to be. Almost.

Henry's lungs burned. His legs screamed.

Then, downhill.

Shit.

The hill.

Ben flicked the torch back on, but it was too late.

They were already dropping in.

Speed hit like a hammer. The wind tore at Henry's face, ice needling his skin. The trees blurred. He squinted, body low, trying to control the descent.

Faster. Too fast.

Ben struggled to keep the beam steady, but the ground ripped past them. The angle, the momentum,

Henry's boots bounced.

Once. Twice.

Losing control.

His edges fought for grip,

Failed.

His ski caught. Twisted.
The world spun.
The cold slammed into him.
Snow exploded around his body. The ground swallowed him whole.
Pain. Everywhere.
The exhaustion, the ache, the burning, it had been bad before.
But this was different.
Something was wrong.
His leg.
His fucking leg.

Chapter XVII

No Safe Harbour

"CANADIAN ELITES WARM TO 'ORDER AND STABILITY' OF VALE REGIME"
—*The Globe and Mail*, October 3, 1937

"Prominent business leaders and political figures praise America's economic revival under President Vale, calling his policies 'a model for national stability.'

Friday, December 3rd, 1937
Chalet Trails, Vanderleigh Hall, Lake Placid, New York—Before Midnight

Henry gasped, taking a sharp, ragged breath. His chest rose and fell in short, uneven bursts, lungs refusing to stretch.

Pain lanced up his leg like a live wire. His muscles screamed, ready to cramp, seize, or collapse.

Not broken. Not yet. But it would be. If he kept pushing, it would be.

He pressed his hands into the snow. Forced himself upright. His vision swam.

A fresh lance of pain shot through his ankle.

That's where it is.

Ben skied over to him, his gaze scanning him. "You doing okay?"

Henry shook his head. "Ankle."

Ben's jaw tightened. His gaze flicked up the next hill.

The large one—the one Schneider had previously wiped out—was there. Others had also fallen there; he could see their scattered crash marks and deep scars on the bank.

Henry exhaled hard. Bent down and forced his boot back into the ski binding.

Not agony. But damn close.

Ben's voice was low, urgent. "Can you make it?"

Henry looked up at the hill.

Didn't answer. Just clenched his teeth and dipped his poles into the snow.

Every push sent fire through his leg.

Exhaustion. Pain. Fear.

His mind teetered on the edge of its limit. But there was no room for breaking. Not now. Not here.

They had to keep moving.

The climb was brutal. With every stride, gravity yanked him back down, pulling him toward failure.

He fought it. Drove forward. Pushed.

Behind them, a light flickered through the trees.

Henry's breath hitched.

They were gaining.

Focus. Forward.

He forced his body up the slope.

Halfway.

Three-quarters.

No torch. They couldn't risk it.

Only the vague, ghostly outlines of trees to guide them in the dark.

Finally, level ground.

They had reached the summit.

Henry turned back, breath burning in his throat.

There were two torches. One had just reached the summit, and the other was at the bottom and about to climb.

Anderson. Smooth. Controlled. Gaining.

The second light bobbed erratically. Sloppy. Struggling. Freddy.

Henry's face hardened.

A cry. Sharp. Piercing.

Freddy's light pitched sideways, then vanished. A dark silhouette cartwheeled down the slope, skis scattering, a pole flipping end over end. Then—a muffled crunch echoed through the trees.

The howl came next. Agony. Animal. Human. Both.

Henry flinched. The sound twisted something in his gut.

Ben slowed. "Jesus."

Henry didn't stop. "Keep moving."

The torch lay discarded in the snow, unmoving, but Henry could mark out a shadow. Down below, Freddy writhed in the snow, his torch rolling a few feet away, casting erratic shadows over his crumpled form. His voice was ragged. Pained.

A shout rose on the wind.

"Help, ah, Christ, help me!"

Anderson's light stopped. A hesitation. For one brief, flickering moment, the chase paused.

Henry could almost hear the gears turning in Anderson's mind. The math. It was a cold, brutal calculation.

It was the torch that shifted.

Turned back downhill.

Anderson kept coming.

Freddy's wails of pain cut through the night. Agonized. Desperate.

No hesitation. No second glance.

Henry swallowed hard. And pushed forward.

They were on the last leg now.

So was Henry.

The trail ahead twisted—narrow curves, sharp inclines, switchbacks. Far enough that if Anderson dropped back over twelve yards, he'd lose sight of them.

Good.

But Henry's body was failing him.

Every stride burned. Agony lanced through his ankle, spreading up his leg as if it were fire. His upper body had taken over, his poles digging deep, dragging him forward. But even that was breaking down. His arms felt dead, ready to fall off.

His vision tunnelled for a second. Shaking his head, Henry forced himself forward—just a little more.

Finally, the clearing.

The lodge flickered below, its warm glow at odds with the hell behind them.

The back patio was silent now. No guards. No movement.

Ben was already crossing the open ground, aiming for the cabins.

Henry followed, lungs heaving, his body screaming.

They had barely reached the tree line when torchlight flared behind them.

A beam swept into the lodge's clearing.

And paused.

Henry clenched his jaw. No time.

He pushed off, disappearing into the dark.

Henry shoved the door open and nearly collapsed.

Ben caught his shoulder, keeping him upright as they stumbled inside.

The cabin was near dark. The fire had burned low, and the lamps had dimmed to embers. Shadows stretched along the walls, flickering as the logs cracked softly in the hearth.

"Gentlemen."

Henry's gut dropped.

The voice was steady. Feminine. Margaret.

She sat in the corner beside a reading lamp, legs crossed, book in hand. Unbothered. Waiting. She closed the book with an absent flick of her wrist, like she had all the time in the world.

Henry's breath was ragged and sharp. His chest tightened with each draw. He scanned the room, expecting the ISB to step from the shadows. For Anderson. For a trap.

Nothing. No movement. No men hiding in the dark.

Just Margaret.

Henry hobbled inside. His stomach clenched. Nausea twisted through him. He shut the door behind him.

Margaret glanced up, then away. "Dunlow went back to the reception."

Henry frowned. "Why?"

She smoothed a hand over the book's spine, then placed it gently on the table.

"He wanted more face time." She folded her hands in her lap and met Henry's eyes. "To impress after his practice."

Her gaze darted between them. Measuring. Weighing. "And I assume that's what you two were doing as well?"

Henry turned to Ben.

Ben looked like a boy caught with his hand in the cookie jar.

Henry started to speak.

But Margaret raised a hand.

He shut his mouth with a click.

Twice now. Twice, someone had caught him. And the wolves were closing in. He wasn't very good at this.

He tapped a cigarette from his pack. Four left.

"Yes, Ms. Bergström," he said, rolling it between his fingers, "we were just getting a bit more time in, was all."

Margaret nodded and gestured toward the pack.

Henry hesitated, jaw tight.

Then, she slid one free and handed it over.

Three.

Margaret lit the cigarette and took a slow drag. "Of course."

She exhaled. Smoke drifted between them. Unbothered. Calm. Watching.

"We passed a pair of Americans heading up to the chalet." A pause. "I tried to hold them up in conversation for as long as possible. But it seems that Mr. Anderson..."

She tapped ash into the tray, eyes flicking up.

"Well. He's anything but inconsistent. Likes to keep to his schedule."

Henry dropped into the chair, his body rebelling, muscles screaming in protest. Not yet, he told them.

"Captain Anderson," he corrected, voice flat.

Margaret raised an eyebrow. "Oh?"

Henry took a slow pull on his cigarette, exhaling through his nose. "Yes. Captain Anderson. ISB, I'm pretty sure. They put me at a table full of 'em."

Ben eased into the chair, pulling off his ski boots. Henry hesitated, staring at his own. The leather felt like the only thing holding him together. He wasn't sure what would hurt more—pulling it off or leaving it on.

Margaret's gaze lingered on him, eyes sharp. "Interesting." She flicked her cigarette against the tray; the embers glowed, then died.

"The one at my table seemed particularly interested in the movements of a man named Campbell."

Ben tossed his boots toward the door, stretching his legs with a quiet groan before standing. He grabbed another log and threw it into the fire. The flames leapt at the fresh wood, crackling in the silence.

"Better than a table laden with SS."

Henry exhaled and reached for the laces of his boot. "I saw that. A little too on the nose, aren't they?"

Ben scoffed.

Henry worked the laces loose, sucking in a sharp breath as the pain bit at him. His ankle throbbed. Bad. He forced himself not to react, sliding the boots under his chair.

Margaret tilted her head. "So, will you tell me what you were doing?"

A heavy, sudden bang rattled the cabin door.

The three of them froze.

Before anyone could rise, the door slammed open.

A pair of Eagle Guardsmen stepped inside, broad shoulders blocking the entrance. Heavy boots scraped on the wood. Anderson followed.

A slow, knowing grin.

He stepped forward without removing his boots, tracking wet snow in his wake.

The third man, a thin, quiet figure with thin spectacles, held a clipboard. He didn't need to look up.

Anderson pointed.

"One." His finger landed on Ben. "Benjamin Schul."

"Two." At Margaret. "Margaret Bergström."

"Three." At Henry. "Henry Locke."

The man with the clipboard checked off their names. Slow. Methodical.

Anderson stepped past Henry's chair, boots crunching on melting ice. He leaned in. Close. Warm breath against his cheek. Too close. His voice was a whisper. "Breath's a little off, Locke."

Henry didn't move. Didn't blink. Didn't give him the satisfaction. He swallowed hard—acid burning inside his throat. Then he leaned back in his chair.

"That usually happens when someone invades my personal space."

Anderson smirked, standing straight—a patient predator. "No. From the exertion."

Henry frowned, cocking his head. "Exertion? From what?"

Anderson pulled off his gloves. Took his time.

He walked behind Ben, fingers trailing along the rear of his chair.

"From your little outing."

He paused—his eyes locking sharply on Henry.

"From your little ski trip."

Bile burned the back of Henry's throat, but he shook his head, mustering every ounce of composure.

"No ski trip here, Warren. Just a late-night chat."

Anderson sighed, shaking his head, almost disappointed.

Then he reached forward and brushed a speck of imaginary lint from Henry's lapel.

"See, Henry," he murmured. "I wanted to believe you."

CRACK.

The leather glove snapped across the back of Ben's head.

Ben lurched forward.

The guard caught him mid-motion, clamping down on his shoulders.

Anderson didn't flinch. He just smiled—like a wolf that had got into the henhouse. "You're lying, Henry."

The words lingered as he circled — slow and deliberate.

"You've always been lying."

Henry met his gaze, unflinching. "I don't know what you're talking about, Anderson."

Anderson nodded to the bespectacled man holding the clipboard. Henry watched as he stepped to the fireplace, picked up the poker, and eased it into the coals.

"You're good, Locke." Anderson strolled around the room, his steps unnervingly precise, his eyes drifting between them. "Probably one of the better ones that's come down. Most of them are fools. Too brazen. Not brazen enough. But we get them."

Henry studied him.

"Who are you talking about?"

Anderson stopped beside the fireplace, looking down at the poker heating in the coals.

"You know, some people think the pins aren't enough. That Hitler's stars aren't enough. That branding would be more effective."

He reached for the poker, twisting it slightly, watching the metal glow.

"Personally? I think that's barbaric. Crude." His voice was smooth, almost casual. "We're supposed to be better than that, aren't we, Henry?"

A pause. A flick of his eyes.

"Americans aren't like the rest of the world." His fingers tapped against the fireplace mantel. "We don't brand our enemies. We don't need to."

He let the words hang. Let the silence breathe. Then he smiled.

"We just make sure no one forgets what they are."

Henry remained still. Watching.

Ben's breathing turned shallow, erratic. He wasn't fighting—just locked in place, his face tight, panic twitching behind his eyes.

Margaret was unreadable. Stiff. Coiled. Her eyes flicked—poker, then Anderson—already working the angles.

Henry needed to buy time before Ben broke.

The door swung open again. A gust of wind. Another burst of cold.

Two more Eagle Guards entered, dragging a body between them.

Freddy.

Henry's stomach clenched. The man's face was placid. No screaming. No shaking. Just blank, distant calm.

Morphine.

"Good, good," Anderson murmured. He left the mantle, returning the poker to the coals—as if it had never been meant for violence.

He turned, voice crisp—an officer speaking to a soldier.

"Guardsman Frederick Thomas," Anderson commanded.

Freddy twitched. His head lolled. "Yes, sir." A murmur. Soft. Floaty.

Anderson stepped forward. His boots scuffed against the floor. "Is this the person you saw at the chalet?"

Freddy's glazed eyes drifted. Slow. Unfocused.

They landed on Henry.

Henry didn't move. Didn't breathe.

Freddy's expression was slack. Unseeing. His pupils didn't react. Just pools of glass. The drugs were working. Maybe too well.

A pause.

"No, sir." Freddy's voice was distant. Dreamlike. "The man I saw... was from Boston."

Anderson's face tightened—a shift, slight, but there. Something inside him curdled.

"Guardsman Thomas," he said, voice still controlled. Still polite. "Was this the man you saw?"

Freddy blinked slowly. "No, sir."

CRACK.

The glove struck Freddy's cheek, making a sharp snapping sound.

The guards held him upright as he flinched, eyes suddenly wide. Awake now.

Anderson stepped in close. His breath wafted in the cold air.

"Guardsman Thomas," he repeated, voice low, sharp—a blade's edge. "Is this the individual you witnessed at the Chalet?"

Freddy's gaze jumped to Henry, then to Anderson, searching. Blinking.

Henry felt it. That thin, stretching moment where everything could snap.

"No, sir." His was stronger now. Certain. "Boston. The man was from Boston."

Silence. Long. Cold.

Anderson's jaw twitched.

"Get him out of here."

A movement of his fingers. The guards dragged Freddy toward the door.

Henry exhaled, just barely. His ribs ached from holding it in.

Anderson's gaze drifted toward the fire poker. A hint of something harder in his expression. Determination. His fingers twitched—a flicker of intent.

Henry glanced at Ben.

The cracks were showing. His friend's hands were clenched, shoulders too tight. His breath came fast, shallow. Not much longer now.

Henry's pulse spiked.

Margaret's voice pierced the quiet. Careful. Light. Controlled.

"They were here since I got back," she said, voice even, buying time. "We were just discussing all the important events from the day. It's been quite overwhelming."

Anderson's gaze flicked to her.

His grin didn't falter. But his eyes? Sharper now.

Henry felt his stomach twist.

A new thought crept in.

Margaret's on his radar now.

Anderson's voice was smooth. "We have no idea what you mean."

Henry turned his gaze to him. "And Mr. Redfern isn't going to like this." A pause, sharper. "This is an improper way to treat guests."

Anderson's fingers stilled.

His gaze snapped back to Henry.

A pause.

A flicker of something behind his eyes. Something turning.

Slowly, carefully,

Anderson smiled.
A nod. A silent signal.
The guards moved, shuffling out one by one.
Anderson lingered in the doorway.
He glanced down. Henry's boots.
Calm, measured,
"*Your boots are still wet, Mr. Locke.*"
The door clicked shut.

Chapter XVIII

A Seat at the Table

"A STRONGER NATION: WHAT CANADA CAN LEARN FROM AMERICA"
—*The Dominion Post*, June 15, 1936

"With President Vale restoring order and prosperity in the United States, Canadians must ask whether our own government has the resolve to do the same. His leadership has brought discipline to a nation plagued by subversives and chaos. Can we afford to ignore such success?"

Friday, December 3rd, 1937
Cabin 14, Vanderleigh Hall, Lake Placid, New York—Midnight

The fire poker rested back on its stand; its violent orange glow faded to dull iron.

Henry, Ben, and Margaret sat silently, each lost in their thoughts.

The fire crackled, low and steady. Outside, the wind howled.

Kessler slipped in quietly shortly after Anderson left, offering a simple goodnight before retreating to his room.

Dunlow came next, loud, drunk, and insufferable. He went on about the connections he had made and the impressions he had left. His words slurred, and his arms gestured wildly. He seemed oblivious to the heavy silence in the room.

Redfern arrived last.

He sat down heavily, rubbing a hand over his face. For a moment, he seemed tired. Then, when he looked up, there was something else — a glint in his eye.

"Tomorrow." A pause. He leaned forward slightly. Not rushed. Not careless.

Controlled.

"Tomorrow afternoon is our time. We have our own meeting." His voice took on a rare note of excitement. Measured, but unmistakable. "Just to discuss the future of Canada."

He smiled now. Too much. Too knowing.

"*They will see.*"

Margaret's lips parted slightly, as if she were about to speak, and then she shut them just as quickly.

The silence that followed was suffocating.

Redfern's eyes flicked to Henry. His expression was unreadable. But there was something pointed in his tone now.

"Because they need us." He leaned back, fingers drumming idly against the table. Rhythmic. Thoughtful. Like a man turning an idea over in his head.

"They can't do this without Canada." A pause. Not quite a question. More of a realization.

The fire hissed.

"Our resources. Our industry. Our position. We aren't just useful. We're necessary."

His gaze lingered on Henry for a beat too long. Weighing. Measuring.

"It will be interesting with Arcand there."

He looked thoughtful, as if he were about to say more.

He exhaled. Slow. Measured.

"For some reason, your attendance has caused quite a stir." He leaned back, crossing one leg over the other. His tone was casual. But it wasn't. "Lots of questions. Not sure what their recourse is, but... interesting."

A questioning look was directed at Henry, who remained silent.

Then, almost as an afterthought,

"Oh, I received a telegram." He reached into his coat, fishing it out. He unfolded it with the same careful precision one might use with a cigar. "The doctor is still waiting on some tests for Jimmy. He'll send them tomorrow morning."

Henry's pulse thudded. A slow, creeping unease settled in his gut.

Margaret's eyes flicked to him.

Redfern studied Henry. Not long. Just a beat too long. A look that said he was weighing something.

Then, a slight, satisfied nod. Like a man settling a bet in his mind.

"Rest well. We have history to make tomorrow."

And with that, he climbed the stairs to the rooms above.

A door closed down the hall.

Silence.

The wind clawed at the cabin walls. The fire hissed.

A log cracked, sharp in the quiet.

Margaret exhaled. Then, finally,

"So." A pause. "What exactly is happening?"

The words lingered, weighty.

Ben and Henry shared a glance.

Margaret exhaled slowly. Thoughtful.

She met Henry's gaze. "You're not a spy."

Not a question. A statement.

Henry blinked. "No."

A moment of silence passed. Then she shook her head, almost as if in disbelief. "But you're playing the game, anyway."

Henry didn't respond; he didn't have to.

Margaret leaned back, studying him. "You sabotaged Jimmy."

Ben shifted uncomfortably, rubbing his jaw.

"Redfern's invested in you," she continued. "But Anderson views you as a liability. That means he's uncertain. If he were sure, you'd already be gone."

She tapped her fingers against the chair arm. "They don't know what to do with you."

A pause.

"*Yet.*"

Ben exhaled sharply, shaking his head. "We need to be gone before they figure it out."

Margaret nodded slightly. "So, you have pictures. Is that enough?"

Henry looked at her. "What else could they need?"

Margaret shrugged. "Right now, you have two countries swapping numbers. Military production, logistics. It's... concerning. But it's not a war plan."

Henry nodded. "But there's nothing else."

A pause.

"*Yet.*"

Morning came bitter and gray. The storm was still holding off, though the sky threatened otherwise. Henry's head was clear, clearer than it should have been after the night they'd had. No ghosts in his dreams. No tossing. No edge of panic when he woke.

Probably the pills Margaret had pressed into his hand. Whatever was in that purse of hers, it worked.

The group skied down in silence. Overhead, the clouds sagged dark and heavy, thick with the promise of snow. Henry's ankle throbbed with every stride, the boot squeezing it like a vice. He could barely force his foot in; the pain was sharp, biting. It would swell worse later—if there was a later.

At the bottom of the hill, the back patio was already crowded. A dozen or so delegates stood in loose clusters, unclipping their skis and hanging up their poles. The murmur of conversation carried through the cold air — low, careful, controlled, and tense.

Half a dozen Eagle Guards stood at the patio's edge. Still. Watching. Their presence wasn't acknowledged, but it wasn't forgotten either.

Dunlow was gone long before the first of them had made it downstairs. Henry didn't see him among the others.

Redfern unclipped first, striding up the stairs without hesitation.

Margaret, Ben, and Henry took their time. Deliberate. Measured.

Kessler hovered behind.

"You three are suspicious." Redfern's voice was low, almost amused. Almost. "You should watch your backs."

A pause. His eyes flicked toward the gathered delegates. Toward the lodge.

"Because everyone else is watching."

Then, without another word, he climbed the stairs and disappeared inside.

For a beat, none of them moved. The wind gusted around them, biting through their coats.

Then, finally, they walked up the stairs and stepped into the back foyer.

The seating chart had been changed.

Henry felt it before he saw it.

The way the air in the room shifted. The way conversations dipped, just for a fraction of a second, as he scanned the names.

He turned to Ben. Ben looked shocked.

Margaret, as always, looked unbothered. Composed.

Henry's hand started to shake.

"Gentlemen."

Margaret moved first. Not hurried. Not cautious. She cut through the tables, her stride smooth, effortless, like a runway model walking on a stage. Every eye turned to her.

Henry had seen this before. The shift. The transformation. A chameleon. A woman who could disappear into the background one moment and command an entire room the next.

Ben and Henry followed in her wake.

Henry forced himself to walk without limping. Every step was agony. But a misstep now wouldn't just mean pain. It would mean death.

They reached the buffet. The spread was nearly identical to the day before: eggs, ham, sausage links, and thick cuts of bacon. The smell of pork fat clung to the air.

Ben exhaled through his nose, not even bothering to comment this time. He picked up a plate, grabbed a slice of toast and an apple from the lone fruit bowl, and kept moving.

Henry took his plate, listening to the quiet clink of silverware and the soft murmur of conversation around them.

As they moved through the room, Henry passed the Nazi delegation, seated in a rigid cluster—too still, too poised.

Predators in suits.

Henry's eyes landed first on Joachim von Ribbentrop. Even seated, he carried himself like a man who had long since stopped pretending to be a diplomat. A high forehead, a thin-lipped smirk, a crisp black suit — the kind of man who believed the world owed him deference. He spun his spoon in his coffee, watching the room like he knew how this would end.

Across from him, Walter Schellenberg. Young. Sharp-eyed. Dangerous. A man who absorbed everything. His slicked-back hair was perfect, his tailored suit precise, and his leather notebook unopened because he didn't need it. Henry did not doubt that every word at this table would be stored away and filed for later.

The others—the Reich Press Chief, the banker, the adjutant—each had their purpose: propaganda, money, logistics, the fine-tuned and ruthless machine gears.

Henry's stomach twisted. This wasn't just a table of officials.

It was a war room.

As he passed, a staff officer leaned in beside one of the Germans, low and hurried, but not quiet enough. "Der Motor wird erst am Montag repariert."

Henry caught the word "Motor" in the officer's clipped German. He didn't know the rest—but it sounded like a delay, or an excuse.

He kept walking.

Margaret pulled out her chair, sliding in beside Dunlow, who was already seated. His plate was piled high with ham, sausage links, and eggs.

"Margaret," he acknowledged with a mouthful, barely glancing up. Another sausage disappeared between his teeth.

Then, loud enough to draw eyes from other tables,

"Hank!"

Henry barely had time to sit before Dunlow's voice boomed across the table as if the volume was needed at this distance.

"A guy was asking about you earlier. German, I think." He chewed and swallowed. Smirked. "You sure are getting attention. Hopefully, you're making the right moves. Wouldn't want to waste this chance, right, Hank?"

Redfern's smile was tight-lipped. Controlled. Watchful.

Dunlow turned to Ben, jabbing a fork in his direction. "And you." His voice lowered just slightly. Not enough for subtlety, but enough for intent.

"That little stunt with the SS?" Dunlow smirked, reaching for another sausage. "Try that again, and you'll be dodging bricks on Orchard Street." He took a slow bite, chewing deliberately. "Keep your nose clean."

The table went still.

Margaret's fork clinked softly against her plate. Not loud. Not intentional. Just there.

Ben didn't move. Didn't speak. His jaw tightened, muscles working, but he forced himself still.

Henry's pulse slowed.

Across the table, Kessler's grinned. "The dog's got its bite back." His voice was quiet, almost pleased.

Dunlow's head snapped toward him. His chair creaked. "What was that, Shyster?"

Kessler didn't look at him. Just smiled, scanning the room like he hadn't heard a thing.

Dunlow's stare lingered. Then, just as quickly, he stabbed his fork into another sausage, ramming it down his throat.

He turned back to Henry.

"You left early last night."

It wasn't a question. *Here we go.*

Henry exhaled, reaching for his coffee. "Didn't realize you were keeping tabs on me, Charlie. You want me to leave a note next time?"

Dunlow smirked. "Just making sure you're not thinking about switching sides."

Henry took a slow sip, not breaking eye contact. "Didn't realize we were picking sides."

Dunlow chuckled. "We all end up on one side or the other, Hank."

Stabbing his eggs, he scooped them into his mouth.

"You left, too." Dunlow pointed his fork at Ben.

Ben shrugged, his voice even. "It hasn't been the most welcoming environment for me this weekend."

Dunlow let out a sharp, barking laugh. Loud. Ugly. "You can say that again."

Redfern leaned forward.

The table stilled.

"Enough." His voice cut through the air, sharp as a knife.

His gaze swept the table — slow, deliberate.

"This is not some schoolyard." Redfern's words were clipped. Controlled. "This is history in the making. We are not here to squabble like drunks in a back alley. We are here to prove that we belong at this table. That we are equals. That we are necessary."

A pause.

"So, act like it."

Silence.

Dunlow didn't move. Didn't even blink.

Then, finally...

Dunlow dropped his fork...

And kept eating.

The scrape of silverware against plates filled the silence.

"Mr. Redfern, did you arrange the seating?" Kessler's voice was light. Too light.

All eyes flicked to Redfern.

He straightened his suit, composed. Measured.

"No, Walter. I was unaware until we arrived." A pause. "Same as all of you."

Kessler leaned back. His chair creaked. "Interesting."

The word lingered. Hung there.

Redfern met his gaze. Assessing. Calculating. A question poised at the tip of his tongue. But he never asked it because the chairs scraped across the floor.

Wilcox had arrived.

He moved with purpose, carrying himself like a king taking his throne. Broad-shouldered, thick through the chest, a man who wasn't just an industrial magnate but a physical presence. His skill on the slopes had proved that well enough.

On his right sat Adrian Arcand, posture stiff, gaze sweeping the table as if he were presiding over a court of lesser men. On his left sat Redfern, silent and unreadable.

Dunlow, grinning widely, set his fork down and leaned forward, hand extended across the table.

Wilcox didn't even glance at him.

He turned instead, speaking in a low murmur to Arcand.

Dunlow's hand hung there a second too long before he withdrew it, the smile still frozen on his face. A flicker of something behind his eyes, brief but telling.

Then, just as quickly, the fervour returned.

Brighter. Sharper.

Hungrier.

"No need for introductions." Arcand's voice carried the barest trace of his French roots, precise and deliberate. "Mr. Wilcox has kindly arranged this table in preparation for this afternoon's meeting."

Wilcox leaned forward slow and deliberate. Measured confidence.

"The future of the North is paramount to our agenda," he said smoothly. "I look forward to working closely with all of you to ensure the next few years unfold exactly as they should."

Dunlow grinned wide and eagerly.

Redfern leaned in just slightly. The barest flicker of a smile ghosted across his lips.

"I assure you, Mr. Wilcox," Redfern said carefully, his tone even. "We are all eager to build a lasting relationship between our nations."

Wilcox smiled like a wolf.

A porter appeared at his side, setting down a plate.

Wilcox didn't look. Didn't acknowledge him.

He reached for his fork as if the man had never been there.

Dunlow practically vibrated in his seat. "We will do whatever is required to further your goals, sir!"

Henry glanced at him. Dunlow's eyes gleamed with blind, desperate adoration.

Kessler smirked, watching.

Wilcox waved a hand. Dismissive. Effortless.

"Yes, I'm sure you will." A pause. Then, smoothly, "The northern frontier is rich with opportunity, but opportunity must be secured."

His voice was slow. Measured.

"That's why I wanted to sit with you this morning—to gauge your resolve." He let the silence linger, eyes moving from face to face. "In the months ahead, much will rest on the shoulders of the men here. You will bear the burden of paving the way."

He picked up his knife. Turned it idly between his fingers.

"For glory." A slight smile. "And for the cleansing of certain... undesirables."

Dunlow nodded, practically thrilled.

Wilcox finally cut into his food, and a king assessed his court.

"In these times, weak men create hardship. Strong men create order." He took a bite, chewing slowly. "And gentlemen." A pause, a flick of his eyes. "We need strong men."

Dunlow looked like he was about to pound the table.

"Well, we look forward to working in cooperation with the American government," Redfern said, wiping the corners of his mouth with his napkin. "We realize that with what you are building, you will rely upon Canada, not only as a supplier but also as a partner in these uncertain times."

Wilcox remained silent, his gaze sweeping the table. Calculating. Measuring. He turned to Arcand.

"Of course, some will have to be purged," he said offhandedly, like discussing the weather.

Henry's stomach turned.

Wilcox tapped a finger against the table, voice smooth.

"But in these times, it's not just about supply chains and partnerships." His eyes flicked to Redfern, just for a second, barely an acknowledgment.

"It's about foundations. The framework we present. How we build what comes next."

His gaze moved on before Redfern could respond.

"Much of that will be discussed this afternoon."

"Purged?" Ben's voice cut in, sharp and deliberate.

He leaned forward, his fingers pressing into the table's edge. His voice wasn't loud, but it carried enough that a few heads turned from nearby tables. "Who exactly are you purging?"

The silence stretched heavier than before.

Redfern reached out, slow, a calming gesture. "Now, Benjamin, we shall remain civil at the table. We should be proud that we are even here to present our case."

Ben didn't move.

"Our case for what?" His voice was lower now. Tighter. "And purging who?"

Margaret rested a hand on his arm, not firm, not forceful. Just enough.

"Now is not the time for such discussions, Mr. Schul," she said, her voice smooth. Measured.

She didn't tell him to stop.

She didn't tell him that he was wrong.

She only redirected.

"Now is the time to listen." She glanced at Wilcox. Neither deferential nor challenging. Just observing. "Because while we're making our case, he's selling his."

Ben leaned back, yet his fingers remained grasping the table's edge.

Arcand exhaled through his nose, amused.

"Mr. Schul," Arcand said smoothly, "we aren't talking about anything reprehensible here." There was a pause and a smile that was too pleasant. "The matter for discussion is building the future of the world."

Arcand's gaze flicked to Wilcox. Then, back to Ben.

"And ensuring that the right hands steer the levers of history."

Ben clenched his jaw. Arcand hadn't changed since McGill.

"And those will be our hands!" Dunlow thumped his fist against the table.

Wilcox barely acknowledged him. A flick of his eyes, brief, indifferent, before scanning the room. Weighing. He turned to Margaret.

"There is nothing to sell, my dear." His voice was smooth. Unbothered.

"The weight of America is already behind these decisions." He reached for his fork. Took a bite.

Unhurried. Controlled.

"We have the power of *Manifest Destiny.*" He chewed. Swallowed. "There is nothing that can stop the machines that are turning."

A figure approached. Not hurried. Not slow. Just inevitable.

Anderson.

He moved with the grace of a wrecking ball. His gaze remained fixed on Henry, unflinching and steady.

He stopped behind Redfern.

"Telegram for you, sir."

Redfern turned, taken aback, not by the telegram but by the abruptness of the man's appearance.

"Oh. Thank you."

He unfolded the note and scanned it. Silence stretched across the table.

Then, slowly, his gaze lifted. Landed on Henry.

Anderson loomed.

Redfern folded the telegram with care, tucking it into his breast pocket.

But his fingers lingered. Just a fraction too long.

Anderson didn't move. Didn't leave. Just stood there, watching Henry.

Smiling.

The moment stretched—thick, weighted.

Then finally, Redfern exhaled. A little too slow. "That will be all." Dismissive. Controlled. Almost.

Anderson's gaze stayed fixed. Unblinking.

The air in the room stretched too long, too taut.

Then,

"Captain." Wilcox's voice cut through, smooth as glass.

Anderson flinched.

He looked from Henry back to Wilcox.

A hesitation. Just for a second.

Then, like a switch had been flipped...

His jaw clenched. And he strode out of the room.

The silence he left behind felt heavier than when he arrived.

Dunlow shifted, glancing at Redfern. "What's that about, boss?"

Redfern reached for his coffee. "Nothing that needs to be discussed at this table, Charlie."

Ben didn't move. His knuckles whitened against the table's edge, his eyes still fixed on the doorway.

Dunlow turned back to his food, stabbing a piece of egg.

Kessler's gaze flicked from Redfern to Anderson's retreating figure, and finally to Henry. Thought lingered behind the man's eyes—calculating, connecting dots, filing things away for later.

Henry exhaled.

What had Anderson just learned?

What was he going to do with it?

Chapter XIX

Under a Microscope

"AMERICA FIELDS ALL-WHITE TEAM FOR BERLIN OLYMPICS: GARNER GOVERNMENT BOWS TO NATIONALIST PRESSURE"
—*The Globe and Mail*, July 2, 1936

"Facing pressure from the Vale-led American Revival Party, the U.S. Olympic Committee has barred Negro athletes from competing in Berlin. Chancellor Hitler reportedly praised the decision, calling it 'a sign of shared values.' Canadian officials remain silent on the controversy."

Saturday, December 4th, 1937
Vanderleigh Hall, Lake Placid, New York—Morning

Dunlow had a head start. His figure had already begun disappearing over the ridgeline as the remaining delegates stepped out, strapping into their bindings.

A voice from the crowd, low, needling. "*The fat man needs a head start.*"

A few chuckles. Lighter than before. Less bold.

Wilcox's words cut through. Sharp. Absolute.

"That man," he gestured toward Dunlow's retreating figure, "is exactly the kind of man we need."

Silence.

The laughter died. Wilcox didn't need to raise his voice; his approval dictated reality.

Dunlow had rewritten his story.

Wilcox set off. Calm. Cool. Efficient.

Some of his hangers-on struggled to keep pace.

The SS moved smoothly, two wearing backpacks, likely another endurance test.

Margaret was already halfway to the trailhead.

Henry and Ben hung back, pulling on their gloves, clipping into their bindings.

Henry's ankle screamed. With every step dragged, exhaustion settled deep into his bones.

Kessler slid up beside them, adjusting his gloves. "I wonder what was in that telegram."

Henry barely turned. "*Hmm?*"

Kessler tilted his head. "That man looked at you like he caught you picking his pocket."

Henry exhaled. "Anderson. I've had the pleasure of sharing several meals with him."

Kessler hummed, thoughtful. "ISB, maybe?"

His gaze flicked over Henry.

"Huh. Well." A beat. "He looked like a man who'd decided about something." He grinned, tapping his pole into the snow. "See you on the other side."

And with that, he pushed off.

Ben exhaled, watching him go. "You ever feel like you're under a microscope?"

Henry planted his poles in the snow. "This weekend? That's all I've felt."

Henry couldn't keep the pace he had yesterday. Every stride sent fire up from his left boot, pain stabbing through his ankle. His arms were beyond exhaustion, and his chest burned.

Over the last few days, his mind pieced together each event like a puzzle, but couldn't quite finish the picture.

Ben skied alongside him, silent, lost in his thoughts.

The last hill.

Ben glanced over, flashing a grin. "Last one, rotten egg and all that."

Before Henry could respond, Ben pushed off, cutting clean through the snow.

The hill was empty. The remaining skiers were climbing the next rise—the same one Henry had fallen down the night before.

But there was movement on either side of the trail.

Something was draped across the path.

Pulled taut.

Ben turned back to check if Henry was chasing, then looked forward.

The rope was knee-high.

He tried to stop. Too late.

His momentum yanked him forward, skis tangling. The rope snapped tight around his legs—a brutal, sudden stop. Ben's body flipped, limbs flailing, and he crashed hard onto the slope. His left leg struck something solid beneath the snow, a hidden rock, maybe—then momentum carried him on. He tumbled down the slope, off the trail, and into the trees.

He came to a halt in a twisted heap. Motionless.

Laughter echoed through the forest. Dark. Cruel.

Henry pushed off at the top of the hill, his pulse hammering in his ears. Below, shadows shifted among the trees, the SS officers disentangling themselves from the snow and branches where they'd been hiding.

"Ich hoffe, er hat sich die verdammten Beine gebrochen," one of them jeered. The words hung in the cold air, biting and malicious.

"*You fucking Nazis!*" Henry shouted as he passed them, his voice raw with anger. "You could have killed him!"

One of them turned, a smirk twisting his lips, a predator's smile.

"Oh, *Dominionshunde*, relax," Henke said smoothly, his tone chillingly calm. "A little joke, yes?"

Now, brushing snow from his uniform, Schneider leaned in, his eyes glinting with sadistic satisfaction.

"Feeling better now, Schneider?" Henke murmured.

Laughter lingered, a bitter echo in the frozen woods.

Henry's fists clenched around his ski poles, his knuckles white against the cold. The moment stretched taut, a heartbeat away from violence.

He forced himself forward. Carefully. Through the trees.

Ben was half a dozen paces into the brush, his skis and poles scattered among the undergrowth. He wasn't moving.

Henry unclipped and stomped through the deep snow.

A groan. Low. Pain-wracked.

Henry dropped to a knee beside him.

Ben exhaled sharply, blinking up at him. He tried to shift and stopped. His face twisted in pain.

"They fucking got me."

Henry pressed a hand to his shoulder. "You okay?"

Ben sucked in a breath, hand going to his ribs. "That depends." A grimace. "Am I dead?"

Henry scanned him. Blood speckled his knuckles. A gash along his temple had already swollen.

Ben shifted, bracing a hand in the snow, testing. The moment his ribs compressed,

A sharp inhale.

His entire body seized.

Henry caught his arm. "Easy."

Ben gritted his teeth. He nodded, eyes squeezed shut for a second. Then finally, a forced lopsided grin:

"My side hurts. My wrist hurts." A shaky breath. "And my pride is fucking shattered."

Henry hesitated. He forced a smile, but his eyes scanned Ben again, checking. Watching.

"Should I get a doc?" A beat. "Maybe a stretcher?"

Ben exhaled sharply, half-amusement, half-frustration. He pushed at Henry's shoulder. Not too hard, just enough. "Shut the hell up and get my poles."

Henry scanned the debris. Found them. When he handed them over, Ben hesitated.

Then, a deep breath.

He dug the poles into the snow, knuckles white around the grips. Slowly, painfully, he pushed himself up.

He got halfway. Then...

A violent, ragged gasp.

His knees buckled. One of the poles slipped. Henry caught his elbow. Ben swallowed the pain, his jaw clenched so tight it looked like it might snap. He forced himself upright, one slow inch at a time.

His breath was shallow. Tight.

Henry didn't let go until he was sure Ben had his balance.

Ben exhaled hard, shaking his head. "Fuck me."

Another group of skiers passed by, giving them sidelong glances. No one stopped.

"Just... give me a second." Ben's voice was tight, his teeth clenched.

Henry didn't push him.

Ben took a slow breath, then winced. A sharp inhale, his jaw locking.

"It hurts to breathe."

Henry grimaced. "Broken rib?"

Ben tilted his head. "Sure hope not. But something isn't right."

Henry gestured vaguely at their surroundings. "You can say that again, pal."

Ben let out a breath, half a chuckle, half a groan. His smile was tight. Pained.

The rest of the journey was brutal.

Ben's breath hitched with every step, ribs protesting. His left wrist was practically useless, hanging stiffly at his side. Henry wasn't faring much better; his sprained ankle burned with every push forward.

The two of them lagged behind the others. The trail stretched too long, and the snow was too uneven. Every step was a battle.

When they finally reached the chalet, Wilcox was stepping inside.

By sheer luck, they avoided the invisible stand of shame.

The room was already full. Conversations hummed, clinking glasses punctuating the air.

As they ducked inside, heads turned.

The SS staffers watched them. Leaning back, smiling. Smiles that weren't meant to comfort, but to gloat.

Soft chuckles. Quiet. They were enjoying the sight of them broken.

Ben looked like hell. The bruise on his temple had swollen grotesquely, his face a mess of cuts and fresh scrapes. Blood streaked his knuckles, drying sluggishly.

Henry felt the weight of their stares.

Ben didn't react. Didn't acknowledge them. Just kept walking.

They took their seats behind Redfern.

Dunlow had already settled, like a hunter lounging over a fresh kill. He exuded confidence, his grin wide, too self-satisfied.

No burden medal for him today.

He barely glanced at Ben's injuries. Didn't ask. Didn't care.

Instead, he grinned.

"You boys were almost late," he hissed, voice low. The smile never faltered.

Leaning back, Dunlow crossed his arms with a smirk. "Thought one of you saps might get the medal. Maybe that'd finally make you take this seriously."

The projector hummed to life—a low, mechanical whir.

Margaret leaned in, eyes narrowing. "Ben, you look like hell. Did you fall?"

Her gaze flicked over his injuries. The slight crease between her brows. The shift in her tone.

Concern? But for Ben? Or because he might slow them down?

Ben's nostrils flared. His head gave a sharp, jerky tilt toward the SS. "The SS don't enjoy losing."

Margaret's brow knitted together, her mouth opening.

"Gentlemen." Wilcox's voice cut through the room as he stepped forward. "I'm pleased to see fewer late arrivals than yesterday. Some of you even improved your standing enough to earn a seat."

Dunlow beamed, though Wilcox never looked at him.

"Yesterday was only the beginning. A broad discussion to frame the dynamics at play, to get you thinking about what it takes to build the world of tomorrow. A world that needs steel. Oil. Bullets. Tanks."

He let the words settle, scanning the room.

"Today, we get into specifics. And specifics matter. How much do we need? How fast do we need it? How do we ensure supply? Because demand will only grow. And once things heat up, there can be no shortfalls. Both sides of the ocean must be in lockstep to meet that demand."

He paused. The projector clicked forward.

"We begin," he said, measured, "with recent German production of defence materials..."

The morning meeting had been so much more than the few slides Henry and Ben had captured. With each new image, Henry wished he still had the camera. Every chart, every projection, was further proof slipping through his fingers.

His mind would have to hold on to it instead.

There is talk of developments, new construction projects, industrial expansion, factories being repurposed, and supply chains being restructured, all of which point to the sheer scale of American industry turning its weight toward war.

Not in full wartime production. Not yet. But enough to be ready.

"To defend themselves in a growingly uncertain world," Wilcox had phrased it.

Henry was awestruck at the sight. How could one nation produce so much?

The German figures had been impressive, efficient, methodical, and relentless. But the Americans?

They were beginning, and already, the numbers were exponential.

Redfern looked equally stunned. Dunlow had been stilled into silence.

Henry left the chalet and tapped out a cigarette—only two left.

Snow fell from the dark clouds overhead. The afternoon felt oppressive, like the sky was bearing down on them.

Redfern approached slowly, hands tucked into his coat.

"Jimmy ingested ammonia."

Not a threat. Not an accusation. Just a fact.

His breath misted in the frigid night as he glanced toward the Adirondacks, eyes distant, like he was contemplating something bigger than this moment.

Henry took a drag of his cigarette, looking at him.

"The Americans know," Redfern continued. His voice remained steady, but something was unreadable underneath it. "The telegram was unsealed."

Redfern watched him for a moment, then tilted his head.

"You went through a lot of trouble to be here." A pause. "Why?"

Henry exhaled, smoke drifting between them. "You tell me, Redfern. You think I'm capable of that?"

Redfern turned, eyes icy, unwavering. "Yes."

The coldness in his eyes was absolute.

"I think you're capable of many things, Mr. Locke. That's why I kept you in my employ."

Silence.

"I just want to know." His voice was level, steady. "When did you stop working for me?"

A pause.

"And start working for someone else?"

Henry smiled. "You're seeing ghosts, Mr. Redfern. I came because I wanted to. I would not be left on the sidelines."

Redfern's eyebrow twitched—a flicker of doubt. "You aren't a believer, Harry."

Henry shook his head. "No. But I don't plan on being left behind."

He was headed back inside when a motion caught his eye—a wave.

"Sturmbannführer Hoffner," Henry called, approaching the picnic table, cigarette pack already in hand. Hoffner gave a slight nod, as if he'd been expecting him.

Hoffner pulled his pack from his coat and flipped it open, offering one.

Henry accepted. He only had two left.

"I warned Henke that over sharing our hand was irrational." Hoffner exhaled smoke, his tone dry. "But the chain of command seems determined to embrace this so-called coalition."

He struck a match, lighting Henry's cigarette.

"Merging industries?" Hoffner took a slow drag, watching the ember burn. "A fine idea." A pause. "But sharing production capabilities?"

He let the words hang.

"Seems reckless." He turned, exhaling into the cold air. "What do you think, Mr. Locke?"

Henry looked at Hoffner. "I think that any good relationship requires sharing. Openness and honesty."

He leaned in. Just slightly. Just enough to be heard. "My curiosity is this: we have American and German production numbers. Detailed reports. Precise figures."

A faint, deliberate tilt of his head. "So why is there nothing on Canada?"

Hoffner exhaled, the ember of his cigarette glowing between them. "No details. No infrastructure. No supply lines."

Henry's gut tightened.

"Strange oversight, don't you think?" Hoffner murmured.

The briefcase.

Fuck.

"Sturmbannführer Hoffner," Henry smiled. "I work for Redfern Industries; we don't have that information. However, I'm sure Ms. Bergström could recite the amount of timber we've exported and our current pulp and paper weight. Unfortunately, exact specifics on Canadian military production aren't something that we have on hand."

The SS officer's face remained stony.

"And yet, Mr. Spalding believes you have that information. And his attempts to retrieve that information have thus far been nothing but a failure." Hoffner leaned in.

Hoffner's voice remained too quiet. A calm that only invited one type of answer.

"And so, I ask again, Mr. Locke, where is that information?"

Henry held his cigarette steady. Didn't react. Didn't blink.

Hoffner smiled. Not wide. Not exaggerated. Just a flicker. Like a man who already knew the truth and was waiting for confirmation.

Henry swallowed.

"Well, if it's around, it's not here, Sturmbannführer Hoffner," Henry said, patting his pockets lightly. "As Mr. Spalding made clear, he's already searched my belongings. Maybe your missing details are with someone else."

He moved to turn, a hand on his shoulder. Tight. Unyielding.

"Mr. Locke, stop mocking me." Hoffner's fingers bit deep into Henry's shoulder, reminding him who controlled their conversation.

Henry turned back. Met Hoffner's gaze. It was careful and controlled.

"No mocking here, Sturmbannführer." His voice was steady. "Just honesty. I don't have the information you're looking for." There was a pause. "And like any good relationship—" he tapped his cigarette, watching the ash fall, "there needs to be honesty and trust."

Hoffner studied him. Measured. Like a man deciding whether to pull the trigger or let the moment linger.

Then, there was a small smile. Not warm. Not friendly.

Chapter XX

The Wrong Place, The Wrong Time

"DEFENCE OF CANADA ACT INTRODUCED TO 'ENSURE ORDER'"
—*The Globe and Mail*, May 10, 1934

"New government measures expand military spending and fortifications under the guise of protecting against domestic unrest."

Saturday, December 4th, 1937
Chalet, Vanderleigh Hall, Lake Placid, New York—Early Afternoon

Lunch was served much like the day before: sandwiches, light fare.

Dunlow kept his grumbling restrained.

Henry had picked at his food. His ankle throbbed, but across from him, Ben looked worse—the bruising deeper now, swelling purple against his skin. For once, Henry didn't feel quite so bad.

Anderson approached. His smile was in place. Fixed. Polite. Too polite.

"You got me," Henry said, taking a bite of his sandwich.

The American stopped. The smile faltered.

"You read the telegram. Got me dead to rights."

The last traces of amusement drained from Anderson's face. His brows knit together.

Henry set the sandwich down on his plate, eyes locked on him. "I poisoned a man to be here." His voice was even.

A slow inhale. "I was pissed Jimmy got the invite, and I didn't. He would've got to see the future without me."

Anderson didn't react. Didn't blink. His stillness said more than any expression.

Henry leaned back slightly, still watching him. "So what now, Anderson?"

He reached for his sandwich again, tore off another bite, chewed. The casual picture of indifference.

"You gonna call the Ottawa police? The RCMP?"

Anderson held his gaze. Voice steady. Unshaken. "So, Henry. Why are you here?"

Henry wiped a crumb from his lip, scanning the room. His tone stayed lazy. Detached. "I don't know, Anderson. Look around."

He gestured vaguely with what was left of his sandwich. "The best and brightest, right? Maybe I just wanted to make a few contacts."

He let that hang. Just long enough. Then, sharper—

"Leave it to Jimmy? The drunk? He'd have spent the whole trip passed out. Maybe in a ditch."

A slow shake of his head. A faint, almost amused smile. "But no. Instead, I get to be here, with the ISB and the SS breathing down my neck, because I took the wrong route to get here?"

He took one last bite, finished the sandwich, and pushed the plate away. "Yeah. Maybe I should've stayed home."

A final glance. A thin smile. "Missed out on all your charm."

Anderson didn't move. His gaze stayed fixed—cold, unreadable.

The silence stretched. A faint narrowing of the ISB officer's eyes.

"You talk too much," he said, tone caught somewhere between contempt and approval. "Maybe you belong here after all."

He let that linger, then straightened, cool as ever. "Enjoy your lunch, Henry."

Finally, he turned and walked away.

Henry exhaled only once Anderson was gone. "That's two."

Ben frowned. "Two?"

Henry looked at the empty plate. "Kessler. Now Anderson."

He pushed it aside. "Still breathing."

Ben shook his head. "I don't know how you do it, Harry."

Henry glanced at him. "Do what?"

"Talk your way out of this shit."

A wry smile. "I've been talking my way through shit my whole life."

He stood, wiping his hands of crumbs. "And look where it's gotten me."

The meeting after lunch pivoted.

There was no talk of munitions, of supplies. No trade deals.

"Hollywood."

Wilcox stood before the assembled men, his presence commanding, his voice smooth as polished steel.

"The power of the people is in film," he said, scanning the room. "Yes, we have our newspapers, our radio broadcasts. But nothing, nothing, shapes hearts and minds like cinema."

A pause.

"Our dear friends across the Atlantic have shown us the way. The Reich understands that film is not just entertainment; it is persuasion. It is conviction. It is control."

He took a step forward, voice deepening.

"A good film does not simply tell a story, it implants a belief. It does not just inform, it converts."

Wilcox let that sit. Let them absorb it.

"Hollywood is the battlefield where the future is won."

A murmur of agreement. He continued, his tone measured, assured. "For too long, we allowed it to be overrun by subversives, radicals, cosmopolitans who twisted the American mind with their filth. But no longer."

A knowing smirk. A pause.

"We have taken back the narrative."

He turned slightly, gesturing toward the assembled men.

"The liberals, the socialists, they have been flushed from the system. And with their absence, we have ensured that the stories told serve our vision. That the heroes look the way they should. That our values are the only values."

A flicker of a smile.

"With the right films, we do not need to argue. We do not need to shout. We show them the truth, and they will believe it was their idea."

His eyes gleamed.

"And that, gentlemen, is how you win a nation."

The seconds ticked by. A glance across the room. Then, smoothly,

"Now, as for the specifics of what is required..."

It was evening by the time the delegates emerged.

The sky had darkened, and the snow was falling heavier, thickening by the minute. The ride back would be slow and treacherous.

Ben's breathing had worsened over the afternoon, not quite gasping, but tight, controlled. Holding it in. His wrist wasn't broken, but he couldn't grip his poles properly. The ribs? Cracked.

Most of the delegates had already begun their return.

Dunlow was among the first.

Henry stood with Redfern, Margaret, and Ben outside the chalet.

No one cared about beating each other down the hill anymore.

Redfern exhaled sharply. "Cinema?"

The word sat heavily. Skeptical.

Even now, an hour later, he still looked unsettled. Throughout the meeting, he had pushed back, interjecting, arguing, reasoning, but never winning.

"The printed word is the most powerful creation of man." His voice had been firm.

Wilcox had barely reacted. Just a flick of his fingers, dismissing decades of newspaper dominance with a single gesture.

"A newspaper, a radio," he had said, smooth as silk, "a man must choose to engage. He must read the words and listen to the voice. He must interpret the message."

A slow smile. Measured. Absolute.

"But the Pictures? A man only has to be present."

A beat. A sip of brandy.

"And we will show him what to believe."

Redfern had argued, of course.

People trust the press.

Words shape thought.

Millions read a newspaper, carrying its ideas into cafes, dinner tables, and workplaces.

But Wilcox had countered effortlessly.

"Words require effort, my friend. Pictures require only eyes." Then he had leaned in, voice dropping, almost conspiratorial. "When you read a headline, you interpret it. You think. You weigh it against what you know. But when a man watches something?" A slow shake of the head. "A camera never lies. A film doesn't argue, it shows. It proves."

A chuckle.

"Newspapers are yesterday. Hollywood is forever."

The conversation had moved on. The meeting had ended.

But Redfern still wasn't convinced.

"That man is impossible. He isn't listening to sound reasoning."

There was tightness and shortness in the way the words were spoken.

"Every step this weekend, the slights, the lack of involvement..."

He trailed off, as if he wanted to say more and knew exactly what was happening, but refused to voice it.

Then, suddenly, he pushed away.

Henry, Ben, and Margaret exchanged looks.

Then, without a word, they followed.

The cabin was dark and bitterly cold when they skied up.

The fire had burned out again.

This time, Redfern hadn't even tried to relight it.

Ben shuffled inside and collapsed into a chair with a sharp exhale. His movements were stiff, and his posture was off, favouring his wrist. Henry could see how the bandages pulled tight over the swelling, even in the dim cabin light.

Ben flexed his fingers experimentally, then winced. He wasn't making a show of it; he never did, but Henry caught the slight hitch in his breath, the subtle way his other hand hovered near the injury, like he was resisting the urge to cradle it outright.

The ski back had been hell. The way Ben's pushes had grown shorter. He had started shifting more of his weight to one side, gripping the poles too tightly with his good hand. And now, his breathing was tight. Laboured.

Margaret wordlessly set about rekindling the fire.

Henry limped to the icebox, grabbed three cola bottles, and set them on the table. Ben didn't reach for his.

Didn't even try.

"I'll be right back," Henry muttered. "Need to change before dinner."

The stairs were agony. With every step sent fire shot through his ankle, his body dragging against exhaustion.

But they had made it.

One more dinner. One more reception. Then bed.

The photos were sufficient. Henshaw would have to make do with them.

Henry reached the top of the stairs, pulse steadying. He just had to make it through one more night.

Then he was done.

He could leave. Resign from Redfern's employment. Move back to Montreal. Spend time with his folks. Finally, he could start the life he'd been putting off. Maybe this was his way out.

Maybe...

His fingers found the doorknob. He turned it, stepping inside.

And froze.

Spalding sat on his bed.

His suitcase was ripped apart. Clothes and belongings spilled over the floor in a frantic mess.

The air in the room felt colder now.

He had the gun from his suitcase, barrel levelled at Henry's chest.

Spalding's finger quivered on the trigger. With just the slightest move...

Henry's eyes flicked from the gun to Spalding. He looked awful. His lip was cracked, his eye swollen and bruised—worse than what Ben's branch to the back of the head had done. Spalding's gaze darted past Henry to the hallway.

Paranoid.

His voice was ragged. Unsteady. "Where is it?"

Henry lifted his hands. Slow. Controlled. "Look, pal—"

Spalding shoved the gun hard against his chest.

"I know you have it somewhere." His breath hitched. Fast. Panicked.

"You ditched it. I've checked. I've checked everyone's things. Thought you were smart? Passed it to someone else?"

His eyes were wild.

"Where is it?"

The barrel quivered against Henry's ribs—one slip of the finger...

Henry swallowed. Kept his voice calm. "Hey, hey. Just easy, okay? Listen, we're on the same side—"

"We are NOT on the same side!"

Spalding's voice cracked. He shoved the gun against Henry's temple.

Silence from the common room below.

"Just. Tell. Me."

Henry's bladder threatened to let go. The endless dark pressed close. Robbie's face flashed before his eyes. Not the trenches. Younger.

Not yet.

"Montreal."

A blink. Confusion.

"What?"

Henry shrugged, forcing nonchalance.

"Didn't know what it was. Left it in Montreal. In a locker."

Spalding wavered.

The gun dropped a fraction.

"You don't have it here?"

His face twisted. The gun lifted again, uncertain, wavering.

"Why didn't you bring it here? It's supposed to be here!"

A sound in the hallway.

Henry heard it.

Spalding didn't. He was spiralling. Pacing. Muttering. "No time. A car. I need a car."

The gun snapped back to Henry's head.

"Where in Montreal?"

Henry barely breathed. "Train station."

Spalding clenched his jaw. "Of course, the train station."

Henry took a step forward. "I can take you there."

Spalding's eyes flicked to him. "What? Why?"

Henry lifted his hands slowly. "Because I want to see tomorrow, pal. Look, just a miscommunication, that's all."

Spalding scoffed, a bitter, ugly laugh.

"Miscommunication? Fehlkommunikation? That must mean something different to you." His voice sharpened. "Hoffner would like a word about your Fehlkommunikation."

Henry's brow twitched. "Hoffner?"

Spalding sneered. "Who do you think gave me these?" He gestured to his face. The bruises. The swelling. His fingers curled tighter around the gun. "And it's your fault."

He pressed the barrel against Henry's forehead — cold steel.

"Where in the train station?"

Henry exhaled through his nose. "If I tell you, you'll just kill me."

Spalding smiled. Not a smirk. Not amusement. A dead man's smile. The smile of a man with nothing left to lose and everything to gain.

"I'm going to kill you, anyway."

Henry saw it.

Like he had been running across No Man's Land.

The inevitability of death.

"Kill me and it's gone," he said, voice steady. "And whatever Hoffner did to you? He'll finish."

Spalding wavered. His grip on the gun didn't falter, but something behind his eyes did.

"You're good, Locke." He licked his lips. "MI6?"

Henry shook his head. "I'm just a guy, pal. Wrong place, wrong time."

Spalding scoffed. "Yeah. I don't believe a goddamn word you say."

A sound.

Louder this time. From the hallway.

Spalding heard it.

His head snapped toward the door. Gun rising. Finger tightening on the trigger.

"Stay back."

Henry saw the muscles in Spalding's hand tense.

Saw the shot before it happened.

The gun cracked. The bullet whistled past his ear. Not aimed at him but aimed at the hallway.

Ben? Margaret? Redfern?

No time.

Henry lunged.

His right hand slammed into Spalding's arm, forcing the gun away. The man twisted, fighting the momentum, but Henry was already throwing his weight forward.

Left jab. Hard. Fast.

Spalding's head snapped sideways. The gun slipped.

Falling.

Spalding staggered back.

Gun or Spalding.

Henry didn't want that gun back in his face.

The gun hit the floor just as Spalding crashed onto the mattress.

Henry dropped. Scooped up the weapon.

Movement. Behind him.

He couldn't look. Spalding was already moving.

Henry raised the gun.

A warning.

A shout.

His voice?

Spalding wasn't stopping.

Henry fired.

Once. Twice.

The .45 roared.

Spalding collapsed with a thud.

Gasping for air.

"... not... supposed... to happen..."

Coughing.

Twitching.

Still.

Blood had sprayed onto the sheets. The walls. Everywhere.

The smell of gunpowder. The ringing in his ears. The body on the bed.

He swallowed hard. Then exhaled.

What did he do?

Fuck.

Chapter XXI

The Cost of Survival

"POLITICAL OPPONENTS DISAPPEAR: 'WHERE IS THE RE-SISTANCE?'"
—*The Boston Globe*, April 8, 1937

"Activists, journalists, and rival politicians are vanishing overnight. The White House dismisses allegations of foul play."

Saturday, December 4th, 1937
Cabin 14, Vanderleigh Hall, Lake Placid, New York—Early Evening

The repulsive smell of bile, blood, and gunpowder filled the air. Henry had disgorged himself onto the floor. He'd tossed the gun away. The train. The dead man. Spalding. The faces blurred, merged. *One kill. Now another.*

How many before he stopped feeling it? Before it stopped mattering? He'd thought the war had emptied him—mud, Robbie's blood, nothing left to feel. But Natalie had proved him wrong.

His hands trembled. His stomach clenched. Another heave. Acid burned his throat. Corpses were piling up; there were too many.

One of Ben's cigarettes shook between his lips. The matchbox slipped from his fingers, useless. He snatched it up again, hands clumsy, too thick to feel.

He struck a match. It snapped. He swore. Tried again. Margaret knelt over the body. Her face was stone. She pressed two fingers to his throat, then looked at Henry. Margaret was unreadable. Not cold. Not accusing. Just... watching. Measuring. Maybe she understood. Perhaps she didn't.

He'd seen enough dead men. All had been in the trenches and mud. Not in posh, well-appointed guest rooms.

Ben crouched beside him, silent. His breath came slowly, measured, like he was waiting for Henry to speak first.

"I-I... didn't mean to. He had the gun. I was... was... so fucking scared. Thought I was a goner."

Ben put his hand on Henry's shoulder. "We know, Harry."

His voice was steady. Certain. Calm.

The hand tightened on his shoulder. Steady. Anchoring.

"You saved us." He licked his lips. "That bullet missed Margaret by inches."

Henry hardly felt present, as if he were floating, observing everything unfold from a distance. A tingling sensation washed over his face, and his body felt weightless. His lips moved. Thoughtless and racing, his mind registered nothing.

"I sh-should have... I-I... could have stopped him. Didn't need... didn't need to shoot him."

He was lying—to Ben, and to himself. Part of him knew the truth: he'd chosen survival. And he'd choose it again.

Footsteps down the hall.

"No." Ben crouched in front of him, his face inches from Henry's.

Henry focused on his eyes.

"He was going to kill you. Probably kill all of us."

Henry shook his head. His breath was heavy. "Something. I-I could have done something else."

Footsteps. Carefully into the room.

Redfern.

"What the hell?"

His gaze snapped from the corpse to Henry. His face paled.

"What... why?" His voice wavered. His hand ran through his hair—messy, uncertain. The calm was gone. "What have you done, Henry? Who is this? My room was ransacked. Was it him?"

"Give him a second, James," Margaret said, standing. "It's been a long few days."

"No." Redfern's voice tightened. "I need answers...answers—now. Henry, who did you shoot? Someone ransacked my room. Was it him? This is unacceptable, this-this..."

His words faded. The room blurred.

Their figures moved—gesturing, speaking—but the words slipped away.

Henry's exhaustion dragged him under. Everything went dark.

Henry woke up.

His forehead was wet. Heavy. A cloth.

His eyelids fluttered. Blinked through the fog.

His vision blurred.

The room wasn't his. No—Ben's. Backwards.

His head throbbed with every heartbeat.

The voices outside pressed against his skull, muffled, urgent.

"... he can't go..."

Ben's voice. Low. Firm.

"... they will be suspicious..."

Margaret. Sharp. Intense.

"... they already are..."

Ben.

A rustle. A bag unzipping. Something is being opened.

"... absolutely not..."

Ben again. More forceful.

A pause. Then Margaret was quieter.

"... it will get him back on his feet..."

Henry pushed himself up.

His arms buckled. He collapsed.

Pain flared—sharp, blinding, shooting from his ankle.

"He's awake."

Ben stepped in, crouching beside the bed as Henry tried again.

The world swam.

"Hold up there, pal." A hand landed on his shoulder—firm, steady.

Margaret hovered in the doorway, arms crossed, watching.

Henry clenched his teeth, bracing, forcing himself upright.

The room tilted, the weight of exhaustion pressing down.

"He can't go." Ben's voice, but softer now.

"He has to." Margaret. No hesitation. She pulled up a chair.

Henry barely registered the movement. "She's—she's right, Ben." The words felt thick in his mouth. Distant. But his voice.

"You can barely sit up."

Margaret reached into her purse.

A small tin. A snap of metal.

The lid flicked open with a click.

Inside, a roll of white tablets nestled neatly in the case. She shook one into her palm. "*Benzedrine.*"

Henry stared.

"Keeps you sharp. Keeps you moving."

His fingers twitched. His stomach turned.

"It's what they give pilots." Margaret's voice was steady. Practical. "And men who don't have the luxury of rest."

Ben shook his head. "This is a bad idea."

Margaret shrugged. Unbothered.

"So is collapsing in the middle of dinner." Margaret pressed the pill into Henry's hand. "This will get you through the night."

He rolled it between his fingers. Too small to feel so heavy.

"And these—" Margaret slipped two more into his breast pocket. "One gets you through the night. The others? That depends on how bad things get."

She leaned back. Watching. Waiting.

"Your call, Locke." A slight tip of her head. "But we don't have time for second chances."

Henry offered a tight smile and nodded.

"Good man. Chew it." Margaret tapped her fingers against her purse. "It'll hit faster. We're already late."

Henry slipped the pill between his teeth and bit down. Bitter. Chalky. His stomach twisted. Bile rose in his throat.

"Chew and swallow." Margaret was back in schoolteacher mode.

He grimaced. Did as commanded.

Margaret checked her watch. "Good. You've got two minutes. Then we move."

Redfern sat stiff-backed in the common area, fingers clenched against his knees.

They descended the stairs, Henry leaning hard on Ben.

Redfern shot to his feet. Tense. Wired. Practically vibrating.

"You're lucky I didn't report this right away." His voice was tight, barely controlled. "Get him straight. We're going to the Guard."

Margaret's eyes flicked to him. Cool. Measured. "And then what, James?"

"It's Mr. Redfern!" His voice cracked, hands shaking.

"They will ask why you were involved."

Margaret's words hung in the silence. Redfern looked like he had been slapped.

"And why the hell would they think I was involved?"

Margaret didn't blink. "A dead Nazi. In your cabin. Your employee. Your problem."

She let it settle for a beat.

"They'll round up all of us."

Redfern blinked. "They would never."

"*Wake the fuck up, James,*" Ben said through gritted teeth as he positioned Henry on the chair.

The world was slowly snapping back into focus for him.

"These people aren't your friends. They are sharks circling our sinking boat."

Redfern looked at Ben, pausing momentarily before slowly shaking his head.

Smoothing his jacket.

He glanced up the stairs, then over his shoulder at the door.

Redfern's voice wavered. "I don't understand. Why are you covering for him?"

Margaret exhaled sharply. "Because we know what's at stake."

Ben gave Redfern a level look. "Because Spalding wasn't here by accident."

A beat. Silence. Redfern swallowed.

Margaret leaned in, her voice low. "You don't need to understand, James. You just need to decide—are you with us?"

"So, what exactly are you proposing, Ms. Bergström?"

"*Survival, James. We just have to live until tomorrow.*"

Chapter XXII

Among Wolves

"CANADA PREPARES NEW ECONOMIC DEFENCE ACT"
—*The Financial Post*, July 30, 1937

"Legislation aims to secure critical industries amid concerns about international instability."

Saturday, December 4th, 1937
Vanderleigh Hall, Lake Placid, New York—Early Evening

Henry inhaled deeply as the frigid wind gusted, like a slap to the face. The Benzedrine was kicking in. Fast.

Fatigue melted. Awareness snapped sharply. Colours burned vividly. The air didn't numb—it sliced. His pulse quickened, his skin prickled, the sluggishness burning away.

He leaned on Ben for another moment, then pushed forward. The cold helped. He stumbled once. Then righted himself. The pain was there. Distant. Everything else snapped into focus. His mind fought him.

Spalding was on the floor. Blood everywhere.

Two bullet holes in the wall. Two in the hallway.

Margaret—so close. Inches from dying.

Too damn close.

Focus.

Forward.

The next step.

Survive tonight. A shadow. Unnoticed.

Tomorrow, the train. Then home.

And this would all be over.

Had to get through tonight.

They made their way down the hill. Snow fell heavily, thickening by the second. The gas lanterns lining the path were dim, their glow swallowed by the storm.

Each lamp was a beacon—a lighthouse in a storm.

Not guiding them home. Just keeping them from vanishing entirely.

The snow swallowed the sound. Just the crunch of boots. The squeak of lanterns swaying in the wind.

The walkway had been shovelled at some point, but it was already filling back in slow, careful steps.

Finally, the back patio.

No one was smoking cigars tonight.

A single Eagle Guard stood near the entrance, bundled, but still trembling in the cold.

They pushed past him, stepping into the warmth of the back foyer. The heat hit like a wall, and the scent of cigar smoke and whiskey filled the air.

The library buzzed with dignitaries laughing, voices blending into the hum of conversation.

Blend in. Small. Quiet.

Henry glanced at Redfern. Pale. Skin drawn tight. His eyes darted, unfocused, tracking something that wasn't there.

He wasn't going to last long.

Not in a room full of wolves.

They removed their outerwear and stepped inside.

Redfern broke first, pushing toward the bar.

Margaret slipped quickly into her schoolteacher guise, idly browsing the library shelves.

Henry looked at Ben.

Something was off.

The bruising wasn't as bad. The cuts were cleaned and bandaged.

Ben caught him staring. His mouth twitched. "Margaret patched me up."

Henry nodded. "Makes sense." A beat. "You looked like shit. Glad she cleaned up your ugly mug."

Ben's strained smile grew broader.

A porter passed with a tray of champagne.

Henry grabbed two and handed one to Ben.

"It'll be nice not having to buy all your damn drinks."

Ben raised an eyebrow. "It'll be nice not feeling like a sheep surrounded by wolves."

They clinked glasses. "Here's to that."

They drank.

Henry patted his pockets. "Shit. I'm out of cigarettes."

Ben checked his own, tapping out the last two. "Huh. Thought I had more."

He handed one to Henry.

Henry looked across the room.

Redfern, whispering with Wilcox. Stiff posture. Hands moving—too quick, too jittery.

Then a flick toward Henry.

Henry's stomach knotted. *That can't be good.*

Another flick—toward Margaret.

What the hell are you doing, Redfern?

A presence. Too close.

Wrong. Off.

Kessler.

Like he had always been there, just behind their shoulders, watching. Maybe the Benzedrine hadn't caught up yet. Or maybe Henry was slipping.

"Our employer seems quite on edge," Kessler murmured, voice just above a whisper.

Henry flinched, barely keeping his face still.

Ben exhaled slowly as he dragged on his cigarette. Kept his voice even. "It's been a long weekend. He's had a lot on his mind—we're all a little worn thin."

Kessler smiled. Raised a glass of tonic water to his lips. "Some more than others."

Henry turned slightly, eyeing Kessler up and down. "You seem to be doing just fine."

Kessler gave a slight nod. Took another sip.

"No extracurriculars." He glanced at Henry's ankle—his limp. Kessler's tone was light, but the weight behind it was unmistakable.

"Sounds boring," Ben said, sipping at the champagne. "Just sitting around all the time? You should live a little, Walter."

Kessler's eye twitched. Barely. "Living is the goal, Mr. Schul. More days, the better. But the way you act... I wonder how much more runway you have left."

Ben smiled slowly. "It's about how you land, Walter. Not the runway you land on."

"Quite." The word hung in the air. "It looks like Redfern is involved in another meeting after dinner. So it seems like our week isn't quite done yet."

Henry and Ben looked over as Redfern approached, and Kessler had lost himself in the crowd.

Redfern gave a forced smile. "Good news. Wilcox has a meeting focused solely on the future of Canada." He clapped Ben on the shoulder. "We are finally getting our moment."

Father Coughlin returned to his seat after saying grace.

Henry took a sip of champagne. It tasted of nothing. The warmth of the room pressed in, but his skin felt cold.

Across the table, Redfern turned his glass in his hands, staring into it like he expected to find an answer. Ben sat rigid, jaw tight, fingers drumming once against the table before he stilled them.

Margaret was unreadable, as always. Kessler wasn't looking at Coughlin—he was watching them.

Then—Dunlow.

"Well said, Father." He reached across the table, clapping Coughlin on the shoulder with the familiarity of a disciple. His eyes shone. "It's truly time we right the ship. Your sermons are always so... invigorating. The weak must fall, and the righteous must stand."

Coughlin smiled—thin, distant, untouched by the praise. Then, without hesitation, he turned to Henry.

"You seem a little unsteady, my son." His voice was warm; the concern in it was practiced. "A misstep on the ice? Or something heavier weighing on you?"

Henry gave the priest a tight smile. "Just a slip on the skis. There have been a few injuries."

Coughlin tilted his head slightly. "I imagine so. I did hear the SS had some... enthusiasm for the trails this morning."

Ben's jaw tensed. "They're lucky they didn't break my neck."

Coughlin exhaled, almost amused. "Tests of strength are as old as Man himself." He spread his hands, palms up. "And in the end, the Lord favours those who can stand."

"I hear that," Dunlow said with a wide grin. "Benny Boy, you should start listening to our priests. They make a lot more sense."

A man in a crisp uniform pulled out a chair, the paired laurels of an Oberführer gleaming at his collar. Unlike the SS officers in the room—coiled and rigid—he moved with ease, almost casually.

Otto Dietrich.

He sat with practiced ease, neither stiff nor relaxed—just precise. His hair, slicked back without a strand out of place, gleamed under the chandelier. He had a broad nose and small, dark eyes—a face made for delivering orders, not receiving them.

Beside him, his interpreter perched attentively, a lean man with round glasses and birdlike sharpness. Hands folded, head tilted slightly, waiting. A formality, nothing more—Dietrich understood English well enough.

As he sat, a porter brought a glass of white wine, placing it carefully in front of him.

He turned to Redfern, his smirk small but knowing, like a teacher who already knew the answer his student would give.

"*Guten Abend, meine Damen und Herren,*" he said, glancing around the table with narrow eyes. "*Herr Wilcox hat mich gebeten, Ihnen bei Ihren kommenden Aufgaben zu helfen.*"

The interpreter barely glanced up as he spoke, voice clipped, mechanical.

"Herr Dietrich greets you all. And says that he is to help you with your coming assignments."

A flicker of relief crossed Redfern's face. He straightened slightly, lifting his chin.

"Well, thank Mr. Dietrich for joining us. And I assume there was something lost in translation regarding assignments—please thank him for providing his expertise in the coming months."

The interpreter smiled. "Nothing was lost, Herr Redfern."

Redfern stiffened.

Dietrich spoke German, his voice smooth, deliberate. The interpreter translated a beat later, barely glancing up.

"In the coming days and weeks, you must pay attention to the narrative. Control that, and you control everything. What happens isn't important. What people remember happening is."

Redfern exhaled slowly, fingers drumming against the table.

"Thank you, Herr Dietrich. We have been trying to move the needle with our beliefs in Canada for a long time. But the foreign interference act has made raising advertising funds... challenging."

Dietrich's smile didn't waver, but his eyes narrowed slightly.

"Then you are already thinking too small. Advertisements do not shape belief. The world men shape is the one they live in. You must listen. See the world not as it is, but as it must be—and make that truth. Today's assumption is tomorrow's fact."

Redfern smiled. "That's a lot of rhetoric, Herr Dietrich. Not giving me tangibles."

Dietrich leaned forward slightly, his voice steady. "Some men see things on a little scale, and others see them on a grand scale. I am seeing where you are, Mr. Redfern."

He paused, sipping his wine.

"You will put into place men who listen. Your reporters—" he tapped a finger against the table, slow, deliberate "—they will not write what they want. They will write what you tell them."

His jaw tightened.

"They work for pay. And fear of losing it shapes most men."

A small sip of wine. A glance. Measuring.

"Advertising will not win this war. Fear will. And greater than fear is love." A slight tilt of his head. "But before love, there must always be fear."

Coughlin chuckled, leaning forward. "You are a perceptive man, Oberführer Dietrich. You should have been a priest."

Dietrich's nostrils flared. Barely.

His eyes flicked to Coughlin.

"I am not one for grand speeches, Father." A sip. "But for allowing others to make them for me."

"Well, if you could help control my listeners to donate a nickel more into the coffers, it would help the cause," Coughlin said with a smile.

Dietrich's eyes narrowed.

"Some things, Father, even the greatest propagandist can't help with. But one thing is certain." He looked around the table. "In the days ahead, power won't lie in donations—it will lie in the stories people believe. Not in nickels on a plate, but in the roar of a crowd willing to do anything for their Führer."

Dinner carried on, but Henry had stopped listening. Dietrich droned on—repeating himself, talking in circles, self-aggrandizing. Pompous. But smart. Smart enough to make the arrogance feel earned.

And that left Henry terrified.

Ben leaned against the bookshelf, rolling his champagne flute between his fingers. "I don't know what's worse—that he believes what he's saying or knows exactly how to sell it."

Henry barely heard him. His mind kept dragging back to the corpse upstairs in the cabin—cooling, waiting, like a ticking bomb under their feet.

How long before someone found it?

"And yet the perfect monster has both," he muttered, scanning the ballroom.

The night was winding down. The ballroom had emptied by half—delegates retiring early, their long journeys ahead. Hands had been shaken. Backs patted—deals set in motion.

Few had approached Redfern. Still fewer had lingered.

Wilcox was nowhere to be seen.

At the German table, Dietrich had returned to the Nazis, their conversation hushed, their focus unreadable. Across the room, a large table had devolved into a rowdy drinking game of Americans, drawing in Schneider and a few SS officers. Dunlow was hanging around the outside of this, trying to get in.

Behind the table, at the far entrance, Hoffner was leaning against the doorway, not joining the revelry and not drinking.

Just there.

Watching. Waiting.

Henry felt the blood drain from his face.

His hands started to shake. "Hell."

Ben barely turned his head. "What is it?"

Henry kept his gaze ahead, voice low. "*He's watching.*"

"That's the one with Spalding?"

"Yeah. And he's been on me as much as Anderson."

"Think he knows?"

"Knows something. Or wants something."

Ben took a slow drag of his cigarette, exhaling through his nose. "Christ almighty."

Henry looked away. His pulse pounded in his ears. Every heartbeat felt too loud, too fast.

He checked his watch. "When's this thing starting?"

Ben shrugged. "They said 'soon.' Got to get things ready first. Private room upstairs."

Henry exhaled sharply. "Not soon enough. Let's move."

Ben stubbed out his cigarette, but stayed in his seat. The room was thinning out anyway—the laughter quieter, the trays carried off one by one. Porters moved quietly, stacking plates, wiping down tables, counting the minutes until they were free.

Henry stared at them, hollow. Did they know who they worked for? Did they care?

Probably not.

He hadn't.

Dietrich had been right about a lot of things. But this? This was the one that mattered. Control wasn't in speeches, or banners, or even bullets. It was in the paychecks. In the rent coming due. In the fear of losing it all.

People didn't need convincing. They just needed their jobs.

People would do a lot to make sure the money kept coming.

Ben lit another cigarette, but Henry barely noticed. Threats and violence had been one thing. But this—the slow, quiet manipulation of the common people—was something else.

"That's not like you."

Henry blinked, pulling back to the room.

Margaret stood before them. "You usually track the room first."

He exhaled. "Lost in the day's events, I guess."

Most would smile at the comment. Not Margaret.

Henry glanced at Ben, who just shrugged.
Margaret nodded. "Can't say I blame you. But it's time."
Henry looked at her questioningly. "Time for what?"
"Time to see how deep this goes."

Chapter XXIII

The Weight of Empire

"CANADA BRACES FOR 'UNPREDICTABLE AMERICA': PRIME MINISTER URGES CAUTION"
—*The Toronto Star*, October 18, 1936

"Amid growing uncertainty, officials call for measured preparations to secure Canadian sovereignty."

Saturday, December 4th, 1937
Vanderleigh Hall, Lake Placid, New York—Late Evening

An aide led the group through the lodge and up the rotunda stairs. Henry stayed near the back, blending into Redfern's entourage. His grip tightened on the banister as they ascended, his stomach knotting. His gaze flicked upward, toward the third floor.

The looming presence still lingered there in his mind.

The aide guided them down a quiet second-floor hallway to a private meeting room overlooking the front of the lodge. Beyond the frost-rimmed windows, the gardens, driveway, and front gates lay buried under thick layers of snow and ice.

Inside, the same opulent, rustic façade dominated—wealth draped in wilderness charm. A bear's head loomed above the stone fireplace, its glassy eyes unseeing. The fine leather chairs were arranged not just for comfort, but for control.

At the centre, a heavy oak table.

Wilcox and Arcand were already seated, speaking in low, measured tones. They didn't rise as the others entered.

Wilcox's smile was tight. Practiced. Arcand's expression wasn't an expression at all.

Wilcox gestured to the chairs. "Please. Take a seat. We have much to discuss."

Redfern hesitated, scanning the room. "I thought there would be more delegates in this meeting."

Wilcox's smile didn't move. "Everyone who needs to be here is."

Redfern hesitated, then pulled out his chair slowly.

Dunlow, eager, circled the table quickly, slipping in beside Wilcox like a well-trained dog. "It's a pleasure to be here."

Wilcox turned his head slightly, regarding him with the patience of a man weighing his words.

"Silence," he said, "is sometimes better than meaningless noise."

Dunlow's mouth snapped shut. Not embarrassed. Not offended. Just... absorbing and storing the words away.

Henry exhaled sharply through his nose.

Maybe that would shut him up.

But at what cost?

Across the table, Arcand leaned back, folding his hands. His gaze drifted lazily across the room, then settled on Redfern.

"This meeting," Arcand murmured, his voice smooth, unhurried, "will be one of the most important for us. There is much to discuss regarding the future of the North."

Redfern smiled now.

Dunlow glowed.

Wilcox leaned back, elbows propped on the arms of his chair, hands clasped before him.

"In the coming months and years," he spoke slowly, stretching the words, "the world will be reshaped. Not everyone will agree with this vision."

He took a sip of wine.

"There will be dissidents. There always are. They will not understand what we are doing, or why." A slight shake of his head. "They are soft. You see, the common man is simple. Unrefined." He smiled, thin. "He must be shaped."

He lifted his glass, rolling the stem between his fingers, watching the deep red swirl.

"A grape is cultivated. Nurtured. Given what it needs to grow. And when the time comes, it is harvested."

He let the words settle, watching them get absorbed.

"It can be eaten fresh. Dried. Made into bread."

A pause. The swirl of wine.

"Or it can be crushed."

He took a slow sip, savouring it.

"Pressed. Fermented. Given time to mature."

He set the glass down, fingers still resting on the stem.

"The finest vintages take years." A breath. A glance. "But they all begin the same way."

The wine stilled.

"With the right pressure."

Dunlow grinned. "Crushed? You mean the commie bastards? The unions?"

For the first time, Wilcox stilled.

Just for a moment.

Then, slowly, deliberately, he turned to Dunlow.

"That," he said, voice measured, "is a very... small way of looking at it."

He turned back to the broader room.

Henry flicked a glance at Ben. Ben looked like he might be sick.

A new voice.

Kessler. Even. Unshaken.

"You're talking about changing a society's mind."

Wilcox's eyes flicked to Kessler. His nose pinched slightly, brows drawing together.

Then, softly—almost disappointed:

"If only a man could finish a thought."

Silence. A beat.

"You are correct, Mr. Kessler." Wilcox exhaled, sharp and measured. "This is not about socialists. Or communists. Or trade unions."

His fingers tapped against the table. Slow. Deliberate.

"This is about removing them, yes." A pause. A glance. "But more importantly—removing their belief that resistance is possible."

Redfern pursed his lips.

"We have been working to move the needle," he said carefully. "My papers have been leaning their voices toward more... favourable views."

He paused, leaning back, rubbing a hand over his chin.

"Funding has been an issue." His voice stayed even, but his fingers tapped once against the table. "Much of our advertising was backed by sources such as yourself, but since the government enacted the Foreign Advertising Act..."

He waved a hand as if brushing the problem away.

"However." A calculated pause. "Oberführer Dietrich was... enlightening." His tone stayed even, cautious. "In the future, we will take a more aggressive stand. And by 1940, in the next election, with the time we have, we will have laid the groundwork for a new Canada."

Arcand didn't blink. His voice was smooth, composed. "There might not be time for that, Mr. Redfern."

The words landed like a cold slap.

Redfern's fingers tensed on the armrest. His jaw tightened. "There isn't a coalition that can topple the King in parliament." His voice stayed controlled, but an edge had crept in. "Our best bet is—"

Wilcox exhaled sharply. Tilted his head. Studied him. "You are still thinking in the old world, Mr. Redfern."

Henry adjusted himself in the seat, suddenly feeling uncomfortable.

Then Wilcox, smoothly—deliberate, unshaken: "Sometimes a firmer hand must guide the ship."

Redfern's fingers tightened on the armrest. He exhaled slowly, measuring his following words. "So, I assume you want me to run pro-Arcand? You see, Mr. Arcand as the next Prime Minister of Canada?"

Wilcox didn't answer right away. Instead, he took a slow sip of his wine, letting the silence settle. Then—almost casually—he pushed back his chair and stood.

"Mr. Redfern."

His voice was calm and patient, as if speaking to a man who hadn't quite caught up yet. He walked around the table, moving without hurry, one hand trailing lightly along the leather chairs as he passed them, circling.

"You must understand—" he gestured vaguely toward the frost-laced windows, toward the unseen stretch of land beyond them, "—that the North is a land of great abundance."

He paced, unhurried. One hand tucked behind his back, the other rolling the stem of his wine glass between his fingers—an easy confidence born of knowing no one in the room would dare interrupt him.

"A wealth of untapped resources."

Redfern shifted slightly in his chair. The words were broad and vague. Too vague. Something was wrong.

"Yes, it is a beautiful—"

Wilcox reached the far side of the table. He stopped. He studied Redfern, how a teacher might study a student who hadn't quite grasped the lesson. Then he tilted his head just slightly.

"A land with which empires can be formed."

Silence.

Wilcox took a slow sip of wine.

No one spoke.

Henry's gut twisted. Ben's knuckles whitened against the armrest.

Dunlow sat forward, eyes gleaming. Arcand was unreadable.

And then it hit.

Redfern stiffened, colour draining from his face.

This wasn't about shaping Canada...

This was about taking it.

Wilcox set his glass down gently. Unrushed. Unbothered.

A thin smile.

"You are still thinking in the old world, Mr. Redfern..." His words hung, weighty, before he finished. "It's time you adjusted to the new reality."

Redfern's gaze flicked between Arcand and Wilcox. His voice was tight. "What is it you're asking me, precisely?"

Wilcox leaned forward. Calm. Measured. The tone of a man who had already made the decision.

"I'm telling you—" a small, patient smile "—that you are to pave the way."

Redfern's fingers curled against the table. "Pave the way for what?"

The moment stretched.

"*For the American Empire's first expansion.*" Wilcox leaned in slightly, his voice smooth, absolute. "And you, Mr. Redfern—" a slow pause, a knowing smirk "—will help us write the justification for it."

A beat. A slow breath.

"Into the untapped northern frontier of North America."

Henry stumbled out of the lodge into the frigid night. The wind knifed through him, sharp and relentless, snow swirling in chaotic gusts.

His body felt off—numb, tingling, like pins and needles. Maybe the Benzedrine was wearing thin. Perhaps it was the conversation.

"I think it's a grand idea." Dunlow hadn't stopped talking since they'd left the meeting. His voice buzzed in Henry's ears—through the ballroom, through the doors, into the storm. "Look. The groundwork's already laid. They have a strong leader, President Vale. We only have to open the doors. It's that easy."

No one countered him. The silence stretched.

Wilcox had monologued for the rest of the meeting, explaining how Redfern was to frame Canada's government as weak, how the Americans were to be seen as liberators, and how resistance would crumble once the people begged for intervention.

Kessler would handle the legal side—securing additional papers and expanding Redfern's reach.

Funding? No issue. Mr. Schul's banking networks would see to that. The money would flow, cleaned, invisible. Ben had always been the best at that.

Ben had been deathly still. Silent.

Dunlow and Margaret would handle the cleansing.

Those with 'unacceptable opinions' would be re-educated...

Or purged.

And Henry.

No orders had been given to Henry.

Like he wasn't walking away from this at all.

When they had crossed the ballroom, they had passed a cluster of American and German brass heading up the stairs in the direction the group had just departed. Their discussions were low and clipped. Officers clutching briefcases, notebooks tucked under their arms, were heading upstairs.

These were the first real documents Henry had seen all weekend.

At the top of the stairs, Wilcox lingered, speaking in hushed tones with a tall, square-shouldered man in a U.S. Army uniform.

"Time is short," Wilcox murmured, audible over the din. "We need to finalize everything tonight."

The group kept walking, moving past the hushed gathering of men who would decide a nation's fate.

Henry exhaled as Redfern pushed open the cabin door.

The fire burned softly.

Dunlow shrugged off his jacket, hanging it over the back of a chair.

"So," he said, rubbing his hands together. "Do we get started on work tonight? I mean, I won't be able to sleep."

Henry nodded, voice hollow. "You're not the only one."

Dunlow paused, turning to him with something between amusement and curiosity.

"You look dejected, Hank." He sat down, leaning back. "You should be proud of the future we're bringing."

A slow grin crept onto his face.

"But actually..." Dunlow tapped a finger against the armrest, voice light, almost teasing. "Your name wasn't mentioned, was it? Strange, that."

Redfern sat heavily, jacket still on, staring into the low flickering fire. "This can't happen."

Dunlow's grin twitched. "What's that, boss?"

Redfern grabbed a log, setting it carefully onto the coals. "His plans." He reached for the poker. "I won't do them."

Dunlow's smile faltered completely.

Across the room, Kessler sat by the window, gazing out. Detached. Watching. "I don't think that's the most prudent plan, Mr. Redfern." His tone was unreadable.

Redfern jabbed the embers, stirring them to life. The flames coiled around the fresh log, cracking, snapping, glowing hotter.

"Prudence isn't always the correct course of action, Mr. Kessler."

A flicker of something crossed Kessler's face. A narrowing of the eyes. A brief tension at the corner of his mouth.

The room felt too quiet.

Redfern exhaled sharply, gesturing toward the staircase with the fire poker. His voice lowered, almost absent-minded.

"Besides," he murmured. "*I think the corpse in Henry's room might change their opinions on the operation.*"

The poker scraped against the grate.

Dunlow straightened, his grin flickering—just for a second.

Kessler's gaze lifted toward the stairs. Too slow. Too careful. As if expecting the dead man to come walking back down.

"What are you talking about, Redfern?"

Redfern didn't look up from the fire. He gave a slow, one-handed wave in Henry's general direction.

"Henry shot a spy earlier. Probably a German, Henry?"

Henry shrugged.

Redfern let the silence settle before adding, almost as an afterthought: "Oh. And," Redfern gestured toward Dunlow and Kessler. "Don't be surprised if your belongings are scattered."

A slight, deliberate jab at the embers. The glow flared.

"The man made a mess of everything."

Dunlow's smile twitched, holding on longer than it should. His eyes flicked between Redfern and Henry.

"You're joking, Mr. Redfern. Of course."

Soft footsteps.

Margaret entered, pausing inside the doorway before moving to the chair nearest the fire. She smoothed her skirt as she sat, her voice calm, measured.

"I'm afraid not, Charlie. It seems we're in quite the predicament."

Dunlow's smile lingered, stubborn. Then finally it slipped.

"No predicament here, Margie."

A flicker from Margaret—something quick, unreadable—before she crossed her legs, adjusting her posture.

"Well," she said lightly. "We seem to be at a crossroads."

Silence settled.

Kessler sat motionless, but his eyes moved, tracking the room from Ben and Henry by the door to Redfern and Margaret by the fire. He measured. He weighed.

Henry exhaled softly.

Dunlow leaned forward, his jowls hanging loosely, his voice smooth and amused. "Henry killed a man? And the body's still in his room? And you all sit here calmly with him?" Dunlow jabbed a finger toward Henry. "A killer?"

A beat.

Then, smoothly—like a salesman hitting his stride:

"We stand on the verge of something great."

A grin.

"There is no predicament here. What other option lies before us?"

A sharp breath.

Ben.

"How about we don't roll over and die, Charlie?" Ben's voice was a hiss, words clipped, dangerous.

Dunlow's grin faltered for a second, but he caught himself, scoffing lightly. "You always were dramatic, Schul." He rocked back in his chair, adjusting his collar. "Christ, you make it sound like we're in some kind of noose."

Ben's jaw tightened. "Not everyone here makes a good, obedient dog."

Dunlow laughed, shaking his head. "Alright, alright, let's all take a breath." He spread his hands. "No need to get nasty. We're all friends here, aren't we?"

A slow turn.

Kessler's gaze landed on Ben, measuring. Calculating.

"Well, either way," Dunlow clapped his hands on his knees and moved to rise. "This isn't something to discuss tonight."

Ben shoved him back down.

The air shifted. The fire cracked.

Dunlow blinked up at him. His smile was gone now.

"Sorry, Charlie," Ben said, voice flat. "I'm not letting you sneak off and rat Henry out."

A flicker.

A beat too long before Dunlow scoffed again, shaking his head. A fake gasp of outrage. "Why, I would never."

Redfern stood, exhaling through his nose. "Did you see the Germans and Americans heading up after us?"

He turned to Henry.

Smiled.

"Of course you did." A small nod. "That's why I compensate you so well."

Henry said nothing.

Kessler's eyes flickered between Redfern and the door.

Then, his voice was smooth, unreadable: "I would like to be in that room."

Chapter XXIV

No Turning Back

"VALE INAUGURATED IN THE U.S.: OTTAWA AWAITS FIRST MOVE"
—*The Globe and Mail*, January 21, 1937

"The new American president delivers a speech condemning foreign interference. Canadian officials privately worry about his aggressive rhetoric."

Saturday, December 4th, 1937
Vanderleigh Hall, Lake Placid, New York—Before Midnight

"That's a stupid plan."

Dunlow's voice cut through the room, thick with derision.

"I'm not doing it. I'll stay here and get on the train tomorrow. But I'm not risking my neck for your nonsense."

Henry grimaced and shook his head. The fire flickered in the hearth, shadows stretching long against the cabin walls.

Ben leaned against the table, arms crossed, jaw tight. His voice was flat. "We could kill him."

Henry smirked. "No. We tie him up. Leave him for the wolves."

Dunlow scoffed, pushing himself straighter in his chair. "You think you can do that to me?"

"The dog will bark the second we turn our backs," Kessler said evenly, looking at Dunlow with vacant eyes. "We'll have to hogtie him. Gag him. Make sure he doesn't squeal."

Dunlow shot to his feet, but Ben shoved him back down. The chair creaked beneath his weight.

Redfern turned to Henry. "Are we missing anything?"

Henry ran a hand through his hair. "The escape plan is... risky. It's a long drive to the border."

Ben glanced at him. "The Nazis flew in, didn't they?"

Henry shrugged. "Didn't hear that."

Redfern snapped his fingers. "No, he's right. I overheard them talking about a rough landing."

Henry exhaled sharply. "So what—drive to Albany airport and hope for the best?"

Kessler shook his head, smiling faintly. "No, they wouldn't have flown internationally. Too many eyes. It's somewhere close."

Redfern nodded. "There's a small airstrip about four miles from here."

Henry shot him a look. "How the hell do you know that?"

Redfern straightened his jacket. "It's not my first time in Lake Placid. Ben flew us in. Back in '33."

Ben gave a slight nod, though his expression remained tight. "It's a tiny airstrip. The Nazis will probably be using a Junkers Ju 52."

As if that meant anything to anyone else.

Kessler shook his head, a short, bitter laugh under his breath. "So we just drive out there and hope for the best?"Henry exhaled, glancing out the window at the storm. "Or we take our chances on a seventy-five-mile car chase through snow-covered roads, praying we don't hit a barricade."

Dunlow scoffed. "You're all insane. This is idiotic at best, suicidal at worst."

He turned to Redfern, voice sharp, almost pleading. "Mr. Redfern, if we say something now, I'm sure Wilcox will understand. We still have a choice."

He gestured vaguely toward the window. "You heard him. This is inevitable. And these fools..." he shot a pointed look at Henry and Ben, "...don't understand the scale of what's happening. The power at play."

His eyes narrowed. "There's nothing we can do to stop this. So, it's better to be on the winning side."

Redfern let out a slow breath. He didn't answer right away.

"The thought has crossed my mind, Charlie," he admitted. "I don't intend to throw myself into the fire."

He hesitated, his eyes sweeping the group before settling on the window. Snow whipped against the glass, and darkness was pressing in.

"All I've ever wanted was a stronger Canada," he said, voice quieter now. "One that stands on its own. Not as a Dominion, not in anyone's shadow. Something to be proud of."

A pause. His fingers tapped lightly against the table.

"But tonight made one thing clear." His jaw tensed. "They don't see us as an ally. They see us as a prize."

Dunlow let out a slow breath, shaking his head. "Better to just survive the night. No need to do anything rash."

Henry scoffed. "Whatever's happening in that room is important. We need to know."

Dunlow's lip twisted. "And what if it's nothing, Hank? What if it's just a bunch of them having an end-of-weekend, closed-door cocktail? Won't you feel the fool then?"

Ben leaned in, his voice low, cutting. "Cocktail? You think the brass, the ones dragging in cases and charts, are just having a damn cocktail, Dunlow?" His eyes narrowed. "You're a coward."

Dunlow's face twitched. "Better a coward than a corpse."

Margaret exhaled through her nose, chewing lightly on her thumb. "The plan has flaws. But they all do. We're not making it seventy-five miles to the border on hope alone. The airport makes the most sense."

Redfern nodded slowly. Ben smirked. Kessler's expression remained unreadable.

Dunlow swallowed hard, the colour draining from his face.

Henry exhaled and leaned back in his chair. "Well. It's a plan."

Henry stepped across the threshold into his room.

Blood darkened the timber wall and window curtains. A bedsheet had been tossed over Spalding's corpse, but the soaked fabric and the bulge beneath did little to conceal the horror.

Lightheaded, Henry braced himself against the doorframe.

The room stank—pungent, thick with the smell of death.

Spalding had torn apart his belongings, clothes scattered across the room, seams ripped as if he'd been desperately searching for something.

Henry stepped over the mess and stood over his suitcase.

The bottom had been shredded, but the camera, cash, and extra ammunition remained in their grooves.

It wasn't his. But it looked like his—the one he'd carried for so long.

Just a thing, and yet it felt like leaving a piece of himself behind.

He stuffed the camera into his suit pocket, then looked at the cash and ammunition. He shoved the cash in beside the camera and let the rest go.

A presence behind him.

Kessler's voice was low and even. "Nice case."

Henry nodded, turning to face him.

"Must have belonged to someone important," Kessler said.

Henry shrugged. "I guess I've got someone looking out for me."

Kessler's gaze lingered, cold and unreadable. Then, a slight nod. As if that were answer enough.

"Guardian angel."

He crouched, picked up the pistol, and turned it over in his hands.

Henry didn't move. Just watched.

A flicker of something—too quick to name—crossed Kessler's face as he looked up.

Henry's stomach clenched. *Put it down, Kessler. Put it down.*

Another beat. A fraction too long.

Then, without a smile, Kessler extended the gun to Henry.

"Not my style."

He turned and walked out.

Didn't look back. Didn't say good luck. He didn't say anything.

Henry let out a slow breath. His fingers twitched.

For a second, he considered tossing the gun back into the corner.

Instead, he grabbed the extra ammo.

Henry descended the stairs and pressed the gun into Ben's hands. "If anyone gives you trouble."

Ben stared at it as if it were a live viper. "I'm not a gun guy, Henry."

Henry smirked. "*Good time to start.*"

Redfern strode in, adjusting his overcoat. "Let's see it, Ben."

Ben hesitated, flicking a glance at Henry. Henry gave a nod.

Ben handed it over.

Redfern pocketed the extra clips, thumbed the safety, checked the magazine, and pulled the slide back—watching the shell pop free.

Smooth. Automatic. Like muscle memory.

He racked the Colt and tucked it into his breast pocket. "Weekend skeet shooting."

Ben stared, just for a second.

"Kept my skills up since the war."

Ben kept staring.

Slowly, he exhaled. Rubbed a hand down his face.

"*Of course you did,*" he muttered—quietly now, like someone realizing they'd underestimated the wrong man.

The wind howled through the trees, snow billowing violently around them. Each gas lamp barely cut through the storm, its glow swallowed before reaching the next. The walkway had disappeared beneath fresh drifts, their footprints vanishing almost as soon as they were made.

Henry's exhaustion was no longer creeping—it was crashing over him in waves. His body felt like a bag of broken bones, every step jarring something loose. His joints ached, deep and sharp, like rusted hinges grinding together. His muscles were stretched thin, burning from overuse. Even his fingers, numb and stiff, felt foreign, as if his body was starting to reject him.

His mind swam. The cold should have kept him alert, but the fatigue was stronger. Each breath felt heavier and slower. The edges of his vision smudged, blurring into the storm. He blinked hard. Again. Again.

Stay awake. Stay moving. Just a little longer.

Dunlow's muffled cries rang in his ears, louder than they should have been. Echoing. Repeating. The fear in his eyes had been real. Henry could still see it. Still feel it.

They had bound him hand and foot, using the tattered remains of their luggage. At first, he had struggled—tried to bolt for the door—but Ben caught him. And Henry was pretty sure that hogtying him had been more than satisfying for Ben, judging by the ghost of a smile on his face.

They had left him by the fire, wrapped in a blanket, the flames stacked high.

Dunlow was a monster who would flip the moment he was able, but letting him freeze to death wasn't something any of them could live with.

The Hall loomed over them, fierce and imposing. Only a quarter of the lights were on, facing the back. Henry hoped that at least one still burned facing the front, that they weren't too late, and that all of this was for nothing.

Redfern checked his watch. His voice was firm. "It's 10:13. We leave at 10:33."

A pause. A breath.

"If you're not back, we won't wait."

Henry's shoulders tightened. He nodded. "We'll be there."

Chapter XXV

Twenty Minutes

"'TOO LATE FOR MANY': TORONTO SYNAGOGUES PLEAD FOR REFUGEE VISAS"
—*The Montreal Gazette*, November 22, 1937

"Jewish organizations warn that Canada's refusal to accept more refugees may mean death for those left behind in the U.S. 'The world ignored Germany, will it ignore this?'"

Saturday, December 4th, 1937
Vanderleigh Hall, Lake Placid, New York—10:13 PM

The Eagle Guard barely looked up as they approached. He hunched against the cold, gloved hands shoved deep into his coat pockets, his breath fogging the air. He looked like a man who wanted to be anywhere else.

Kessler pushed open the door. Warmth rushed out to meet them, thick with the scent of whiskey and cigar smoke.

The back foyer was still. Silent.

None of them moved to remove their coats.

Kessler shifted, eyes darting about the room. His hand twitched at his side.

"I'll be right back," he murmured.

Henry caught his shoulder, firm but quiet. "Breathe, Walter. Remember the plan."

Kessler swallowed. Nodded. "The bar. A bottle. The library. Then outside."

Henry forced a tight smile. "Simple."

Kessler nodded again.

He turned his back and walked towards the ballroom.

Margaret and Henry exchanged a glance.

They rounded the bend and entered the library.

Empty.

Henry did a double scan just to be sure. Everything seemed to narrow, his focus dulling. Nothing. No one is sitting in a corner reading.

He exhaled. So far, so good.

They moved toward the corner where the bookshelves met.

"It's a damn shame," Margaret murmured.

Henry glanced at her. "What's that?"

"Burning books."

Henry shrugged. "Well... when in Rome."

Margaret pulled a book from the shelf, studied the cover briefly, then ripped pages out, creating a growing pile of torn paper.

Henry surveyed the room a second time. Nothing. No one.

His eyes landed on what they needed — a side table.

He lifted the lamp off the top and set it aside, then crouched, gripping one of the table's legs. He yanked hard. His arms burned. Every muscle screamed. The exhaustion clawed at him, but finally, crack, the leg came loose.

He moved to the second.

Checked his watch, 10:15.

Where the hell was Kessler?

He looked around the room again, looking for a different piece of furniture.

Margaret had already torn apart half a dozen books, the pile of pages stacked high.

Henry wrenched the legs from a second side table. Enough? Maybe?

10:17.

Fuck.

Margaret looked at him, concern flickering behind her eyes.

"He'll show."

She didn't look convinced.

Fuck.

"I can't start it yet. This isn't enough."

Henry nodded. *Where is he?*

Another piece of furniture. Another crack of splintering wood. The pile grew. Margaret shredded another book. Then another.

10:19.

"I'm going to check."

Margaret nodded.

Henry slipped out of the library, hurrying.

Turned the corner into the ballroom.

A couple of men sat at a table, laughing drunkenly.

The redheaded bartender was wiping down the counter.She looked up. Didn't smile.

He forced one.

"Looking for your friend—the one with the pin?"

The smile slipped for just a second.

His jaw tensed. Steady.

"Did anyone come through here? Glasses, dark coat—grabbing a bottle for a toast."

She shrugged. "Just these dolts."

Where are you, Kessler? Henry's hands shook.

"Right. We sent him for a bottle of Lemon Hart. The 151."

Her eyebrow arched. "151?"

He nodded, forcing a smile. "Wilcox's request. A toast to the future of the North."

She hesitated, then turned and grabbed a bottle from the shelf. "Be careful smoking around that," she muttered. "It's flammable."

Henry smiled, tight, brittle. "I'll keep that in mind."

He walked, though he wanted to run, back to the library.

Margaret had increased the pile more.

"Kessler vanished."

"Bastard." She took the bottle from him, uncorked it, and poured it over everything: the shelves, the rugs, the pile.

10:21.

Not enough time.

She lit it.

Immediately, the fire raced across the floor, burning up the pages and books and spreading into the bookshelves. What started small quickly became an inferno.

Margaret stepped back. "Might've overdone it."

Henry grimaced.

"It'll have to do."

Shouts rang out below. Footsteps pounded across the wood. Panic spreading.

Margaret was already gone.

Henry wanted nothing more than to follow. The camera was proof. The fire was doing the rest. Burn them all alive. Let it be enough.

But the room pulled at him, dragging him in like gravity.

He had to see.

He lingered in the shadows as men stormed down the staircase, their movements brisk but controlled. Not yet panic. Not yet chaos.

Above, silence.

The fire had gutted the library. Smoke thickened the air. Like the gas.

Henry swallowed hard. He prayed he wouldn't have to piss on his handkerchief. Another breath. Another moment. Flames licked toward the ballroom.

Then he moved.

Two steps at a time, his ankle screaming. No time for pain. No need for silence. Landing. A glance up, third floor.

Was the goon still up there? *Keep moving.*

Down the hallway. The meeting room. He pushed the door open.

Empty.

Thank god. The plan had actually worked.

Henry scanned the room. Maps. Documents. Plans.

A map of Canada stretched across the table, red lines carved through it like fresh wounds.

Encirclements.

Halifax. Montreal. Toronto.

Winnipeg, splitting the country in two.

Calgary. The oilfields.

Days. That's all it would take.

His breath hitched.

He yanked the camera from his pocket and started shooting.

Snap.

Snap. Snap.

Another document. Cities. Names beside them. But no targets.

Montreal. Adler.

Toronto. Nomad.

Other locations—other names, circled, marked.

But nothing else.

No industries. No rail lines. No government buildings. No specific targets.

Question marks. German text.

Snap.

He rolled the map and stuffed it under his arm.

War Plan Red. The title burned into a leather binder. Christ.

His fingers twitched.

This was everything.

His eyes darted across the table and to a briefcase.

His breath hitched.

Ben had said, a Mark Cross.

This was it. Right here.

Where the briefcase should have been delivered.

This one was almost identical. Not his. This was what they wanted. The infrastructure. That was what the man on the train had been carrying. It was supposed to be here. In this room.

He popped the latches and shoved papers inside. Whatever he could.

Smoke curled under the door.

He coughed into his sleeve. Heat pressing down.

How much time?

Checked his watch: 10:26.

Seven minutes. Not enough.

More papers. More. He needed more.

10:27.

No time. He had to leave.

The door opened. A figure in the shadows. A pistol was levelled at him.

"You aren't leaving here."

Anderson. A rag over the lower half of his face. Eyes narrowed. Coughing.

"Not quick enough, Locke."

Behind Anderson, thick black smoke billowed down the hallway.

Henry had taken too long. Anderson didn't give a speech.

He just raised the gun. Nowhere to run.

Snap.

The camera flash detonated in the darkness.

Blinding. White-hot. Searing.

Anderson flinched. Staggered. His aim wavered.

Bang.

A deafening crack, like the world tearing in half.

The bullet hissed past Henry's ear. Henry's head snapped sideways. His eardrums screamed.

The noise, God, the noise. Sharp. Splitting and vibrating inside his skull.

Run.

Bang. Bang.

Thunderclaps. Rolling. Echoing.

The air split apart. Whistles. Near misses, too close.

Anderson blinked rapidly, blinded, disoriented, still adjusting.

Too slow. Henry was already moving.

His ears rang, his heartbeat loud, pounding, drowning out everything else.

Anderson cursed, shaking his head and still struggling to see.

Henry closed the distance.

Anderson raised a hand, shielding his eyes.

Snap.

Another flash. Another blinding burst of light.

The gun was close.

Henry swung the briefcase.

Crack.

Bone. A sickening crunch as leather met skull.

Anderson buckled. His knees faltered.

Bang.

Wild shot. Into the floor. Henry didn't stop to watch him fall. He was already past him.

Into the hallway.

Blind. Coughing. Choking. The heat pressed against his skin.

Bang. Bang. Bang.

Pain.

Like a red-hot poker ripping through his shoulder.

Searing. Splitting. Too much.

He staggered.

The map slipped from his grip.

No.

No, no, no.

If he left it, everything was lost.

He needed that map. He tried to move his arm, but it barely responded. His legs weren't working right. He collapsed onto his knees.

The pain hit full force now.

It was unbearable. A deep, raw burn that set his nerves on fire. Like his whole arm had been flayed open. He gasped. Swallowed bile.

Move. Move, dammit.

He forced himself lower. The heat pressed down. The smoke was blinding, choking.

His vision swam.

Footsteps behind him.

He gritted his teeth, fumbled blindly. Something. Fabric. Paper.

The map.

Boots. Close.

He scrambled on all fours, lungs burning, towards the stairs.

Something heavy crashed behind him—a wet, choking gasp.

A body.

Anderson? Henry didn't look. He couldn't risk it.

Flames roared through the foyer, heat scalding his face. His lungs burned.

Coughing. Vision blurring.

His left hand was slick. Numb.

He couldn't feel his fingers.

Stairs. One by one, he crawled. Bottom step. The foyer was engulfed. The front door waited ahead.

Smoke. Fire.

His skin burned.

The door was open. One last push out.

Cold.

He collapsed.

Breath ragged.

The frozen air stabbed his burned lungs. Figures moved. Shadows flickered in the firelight. His vision was cloudy, and his eyes burned.

Words. Muffled words.

"Back. Back! I said back up!"

Redfern. A strong arm held him firm.

"You gotta get up, Harry." Tight. Urgent. A flicker of something — alarm? — crossed his face. "I can't carry you."

Hands grabbed the briefcase. Henry's grip locked. Knuckles white. Fingers deadened. Pain — a hot iron buried in his shoulder. But he wasn't letting go.

"*Then don't.*"

Movement. Shuffling. Not his. Shadows loomed. Hesitant.

Redfern's voice was flat and steady. "Take another step."

Silence.

A pause, just long enough for Henry to realize they had stopped. The surrounding space was silent. No one moved.

His legs wobbled beneath him.

Shadows shifted, circling. Circles on a map. Surrounded.

Henry's head swam. A weight on his back. A force held him steady.

Redfern.

Henry's breath shuddered. The hesitation in the air wasn't about him.

"Get up, Harry. Up."

A hard yank. His feet were under him. Stumbling. Ahead, a car. Escape. A figure blocked the path.

"Get out of the way."

Silence.

"You won't shoot. You don't—"

Bang. The world split open. The body hit the snow. A scream — sharp, raw.

"My leg! You bastard!"

Redfern moved fast. He dropped to a knee, hands tearing at the sprawled body.

A glint of metal.

The scrape of something dragged free. Henry got into the back of the car.

Cold. Steel. Passed to Margaret.

"I don't know how to use this." Margaret. Her voice. Distant.

"You don't have to." Redfern's breath was sharp. Urgent. "Just hold it."

A door slammed. Redfern, inside.

Ben. The driver's seat.

"Drive," Redfern snapped. "Get us the hell out of here."

Chapter XXVI

Running on Fumes

"'NO NEGROES ALLOWED IN WHITE CITIES' LAW PASSES"
—*The Atlanta Constitution*, September 3, 1937

"Sweeping legislation ensures total racial separation. Negroes may not reside, travel, or work in white-designated areas without direct state authorization."

Saturday, December 4th, 1937
Vanderleigh Hall, Lake Placid, New York—10:37 PM

"He's bleeding a lot." A voice. Close. Sharp. A rip. A tear.

Tightening. Fire. Twisting through his shoulder.

Henry groaned. The pain swallowed him whole.

"This won't hold for long."

Hands were pressing, adjusting, and securing.

His vision wavered. The world tilted.

"There's so much blood."

Margaret? Maybe.

Scrambling. Movement. A lurch.

Pain slammed into him.

Car. The car. They were moving.

Ben's voice, sharp through the haze: "What about Kessler?"

Henry tried to speak. Nothing came out.

Margaret, tight. "He vanished when we were in the house."

Brakes. A sudden jolt. His head lolled sideways.

Ben again. "Vanished? Or left?"

Redfern exhaled. Frustrated. "He was in the back of the crowd. With an SS officer."

A beat.

Ben, voice sharpened. "Tall guy? Stiff-looking?"

Margaret nodded. "Yeah."

Ben swore under his breath. "Hoffner." A pause. "Fucking Kessler flipped."

The car jerked again. Voices. Muffled. Warped.

"Open the gate."

Ben. A pause. Silence stretched.

"I... I can't do that."

Distant. Underwater.

Click.

Henry's body tensed before his brain caught up. A hammer was pulled back.

"Yes, you can."

Redfern.

Silence. A second too long. Then a murmur. A reply lost in the haze.

Another jerk. Motion again.

Henry slumped into the seat.

"*Not quick enough.*"

Margaret. Tight. Clipped.

His breath rattled. He blinked. The world was wrong.

Pain. Pain. His shoulder burned. His lungs clawed for air. The weight on his chest wouldn't lift.

Sharp. Sudden. A slap.

His head snapped sideways.

"Don't you fucking think about it."

Margaret.

Henry's breath hitched.

A second of clarity. Just enough to see her face above him.

Tight. Hard. Afraid.

His stomach churned. His ears rang.

"How did you know?" His voice barely made it past his throat.

Margaret didn't answer right away.

"Something I would do."

She turned.

"That's wide enough, GO." Redfern.

The car slipped. Tires spun. Traction.

Henry's stomach twisted.

"Oh, thank god."

Margaret. Unclipping something. Metal glinted in the dim light—a syrette.

"Henry, this is going to help with the pain."

A stab in his thigh.

Fire. A slow, creeping warmth under his skin.

But the pain didn't stop. Not yet.

His fingers twitched. His breath shuddered.

"Still. Hurts."

Margaret cursed.

Her hand pressed hard against his chest. Digging into his pocket.

"Jesus, Margaret. No. He's had enough."

Redfern.

Something pressed into his mouth.

"Chew."

Bitter. Like chalk and acid. He did.

A flood. A rush. His pulse kicked hard.

Heat and fire crashed inside him.

The fog thinned, just a little.

His breath steadied.

The world stopped tilting.

"We need you on your feet."

Henry nodded. Not because he was ready, but because he had no choice.

Margaret wrapped something else around his shoulder. Pulled it tight.

The car swerved. Too fast.

"None of this will matter if we end up dead in a ditch," Redfern said. His voice was tight.

Henry saw Ben in the rearview.

"So, should I slow down and let them catch us? Or should I drive?"

Redfern didn't answer.

The pain was fading. His head was clearing. Slowly. Henry pushed himself up.

Outside, snow. Heavy. Falling fast.

The road was barely visible. Clogged with ice. Dark trees. Rushing past.

Margaret's hand pushed against his chest.

"You need to lie down, Henry. Rest while you can. We're going to need you once we get there."

Henry's mind swam. *Get where? Where were they going? The airport. The plane.*

His fingers fumbled.

The map. Do I have the map? The briefcase. His heart lurched.

"The map. Do I have the map?"

He tried to sit up.

"The briefcase."

A hand pressed against his chest. Margaret.

"You're still holding the briefcase."

Henry's breath shuddered.

Margaret held something up. A rolled sheet. Stained and smudged with blood.

"And this map?"

Henry exhaled a tight, brittle smile. A weight lifted. Just a little.

"They're coming."

Margaret's face hardened.

"We know, Henry. That's why we're doing this."

Henry shook his head.

"No."

His fingers tightened around the briefcase.

"*Those are the plans.*" His voice came out hoarse. Forced.

Margaret frowned.

Henry swallowed.

"*Their plans for invasion.*"

Margaret's gaze snapped to the map.

The car lurched. The rear end fishtailed. Ben fought the wheel, hands locked tight, his jaw clenched. His eyes flicked to the rearview. Cold. Focused.

"They're gaining," Redfern muttered, glancing behind them.

Ben gritted his teeth. "Which is it, Redfern? Too fast or too slow?"

Redfern didn't look away from the mirror. "Both."

Ben let out a sharp, humourless laugh. "Yeah? That's how it always is with you, talking outta both sides of your damn mouth."

Henry finally looked at his shoulder. The bandage was soaked through, darkening from crimson to near black. "How bad is it?"

Margaret's eyes flicked to him. Something uncertain there. "I don't know, Henry. I've never treated a gunshot before."

Henry shrugged. Smiled. Or tried to. "At this point? Wouldn't surprise me what you can do."

The car lurched hard.

Henry's head snapped sideways, slamming into the door.

Redfern barely reacted.

"They're too close. Margaret, if you'd be so kind." He motioned to the Thompson lying on the seat beside her.

Margaret hesitated, only for a second, before carefully passing him the gun and a spare drum magazine.

Redfern took it, hands deft, practiced.

The biting cold, gusting wind and stinging snow rushed into the car as Redfern cranked down the window.

Redfern exhaled, gripping the Thompson. "Fuck me, this is a bad idea."

Ben's knuckles whitened against the wheel.

"Like hell, Redfern," he said through gritted teeth.

The car swerved hard again.

Redfern braced. Didn't fire.

Leaned back inside. Frowned at the Thompson.

Redfern yanked the bolt back, trying to clear a jam.

"I swear to Christ, this thing weighs as much as Henry."

Redfern gritted his teeth.

"This is a bad fucking idea." He braced the Thompson against the door frame. "Ben, hold her steady!"

"I'm trying, Redfern. Perhaps shoot first and yell later?"

He squeezed the trigger. The kick slammed into his shoulder.

Clackclackclack.

"Son of a—" He ducked back in, rubbing his arm. "Hurts like hell," he muttered. "Why do people like these things?"

Another curve as the car slid.

Redfern gripped the seat as Henry felt himself pulled against the car.

"Shit. Shit. Shit. Hold on."

A bump. A dip.

Then smooth again.

Ben audibly exhaled.

Redfern looked out the window again.

Henry sat up, turning around.

Clackclackclack. Clackclackclack.

A headlight burst apart, glass spraying across the snow-covered road. The car wobbled, just for a second.

"Hell, yes!" Redfern grinned.

"Keep shooting!" Ben snapped.

Redfern lined up another shot.

The car lurched again.

Streetlights streaked past. Homes. Streets.

Wait, where the hell were they?

"Where are we, Ben?" Margaret's voice was tight.

"Lake Placid," Ben replied through gritted teeth.

Henry forced himself up, breath shallow. Houses. Streets.

"What are we doing here?"

Ben's eyes flicked up and down the roads, scanning fast.

Ben swerved hard, tires barely gripping, a white flash, snow-covered rooftops. For a second, Henry swore he saw the frozen lake.

A moment later, it was gone.

"Trying to get my bearings."

Margaret turned to him sharply. "What do you mean?"

Redfern leaned out again.

Clack, clackclackclack.

"I know how to get to the airport from the Grand View. We stayed there in '33."

A tight turn.

Henry risked a glance back. Headlights dipped. Skidded. Slowing.

Another bump, and the tires lifted for a second. A curb?

Redfern ducked back inside.

"I think I got their engine." He exhaled, still grinning, as if they weren't tearing through town at breakneck speed. "We're losing them now. Ben, get us there."

Ben didn't answer. His eyes stayed locked on the road ahead, one turn, another. The snow was thick, tires fighting for grip.

Henry glanced back. The pursuit car wasn't gaining. Slowing. Wobbling. Smoke rising from the hood. The other headlights were still far behind.

"I think—" Henry coughed, his ribs seizing. "I think we shook them."

"Not yet," Redfern muttered.

Ben's head snapped up. His voice sharpened. "Grand View. We cut through there."

He yanked the wheel hard. The car lurched, tires screaming as they skidded onto a side street, clipping a snowbank before gripping again. The Grand View flashed past in a blur of darkened windows and shuttered porches.

For a split second, silence.

Flashing lights.

Not behind them.

Ahead. A police cruiser was parked under a streetlamp.

Ben swore.

Another flick of the wheel, too fast. The car fishtailed before he corrected.

Margaret leaned forward, voice clipped. "What are we doing?"

Ben's knuckles whitened around the wheel. "No roadblocks. No one's radioed ahead yet. If we turn again, we risk getting pinned. The only option is to punch through before they figure out we're coming."

Redfern's jaw tightened. "They see us, they'll chase us."

Henry sucked in a breath. The fog in his head was thinning. He twisted to look.

The cruiser idled, facing the opposite direction. The officers inside weren't moving.

No reaction.

They didn't know.

Yet.

Ben's voice dropped to a growl. "We have one shot at this."

Margaret didn't hesitate. "Then take it."

The car ripped past the cruiser, spraying snow in its wake.

Henry's breath caught.
Nothing.
No sirens. No flashing reds.
A blur of movement in the mirrors.
The cruiser jolted forward. Tires spinning for traction.
Shit.
Ben exhaled hard. "All right, now we're running."
Another turn. The road stretched ahead — empty, open.
Redfern's jaw clenched. "I can't shoot cops, Ben."
Ben's eyes stayed locked ahead. "No one's asking you to."
Another turn. Another street.
Henry glanced back.
The cruiser was gone.
They tore past an empty service station, another curve.
Nothing.
No lights.
No sirens.
They were alone.
Redfern let out a slow breath. "We lost them."
Ben didn't slow down. "Not stopping to celebrate."
Ahead, the control tower. A strip of tarmac, half-hidden in swirling snow.
Margaret leaned forward, staring out the windshield.
"There."
A shape loomed in the distance. A hangar. Lit.
The plane was inside. Waiting.
Ben tore across the runway, skidding to a halt outside the hangar.
A loud exhale. Their gazes locked on the plane.
No way out but up.

Chapter XXVII

No Way Out But Up

"MOUNTIES DISMANTLE FASCIST NETWORK IN VANCOUVER"
—*The Vancouver Sun*, March 4, 1937

"A radical cell with ties to American groups was raided this morning. Authorities are investigating further links."

Saturday, December 4th, 1937
Vanderleigh Hall, Lake Placid, New York—10:55 PM

Henry stumbled out of the car, boots sinking deep into the snow. The cold sliced through his coat, burning against sweat-soaked skin.

The wind slammed into him, tearing at his clothes, driving ice into his face.

He braced against the car. Limbs sluggish. Half-frozen. But his pulse pounded in his ears, dragging him forward.

He reached back inside for the briefcase and the map.

Redfern was already moving. He pressed the Colt into Henry's hand. "Just in case."

The hangar loomed ahead, with the Junkers dominating the space. It was a clean white shell, unmarked and unassuming. There were no swastikas, no insignia, just a ghost.

From a distance, no one would know whose plane it was.

Movement inside.

Henry matched his pace with Redfern, shoulder to shoulder.

Ben trailed behind. Margaret was in the rear.

Inside, tools littered the concrete under the right wing. Two mechanics, coveralls streaked with grease, hunched over the exposed engine, hands buried in its open guts.

A third man sat against the wall. No coveralls. No uniform. Just a heavy overcoat, watching.

The MP35 leaned against the wall beside him. Within reach, but not in his hands.

As soon as they entered, he moved.

His hand darted for the weapon.

Redfern raised the Thompson, a sharp shake of the head. "Don't."

Henry levelled the Colt at the mechanics.

His hand trembled. He hoped they didn't notice, that they wouldn't see the lack of conviction in his eyes.

But their eyes were only on the gun. The mechanics froze, hands up. No resistance.

The third man hesitated. Fingers hovering over the MP35 and breathing sharply.

His eyes flicked. Redfern. Thompson. MP35. Redfern's grip tightened, voice low, firm. "Don't."

The man lunged.

Redfern pulled the trigger.

Click.

The Thompson jammed.

Redfern's eyes widened. His fingers worked the action, racking the bolt. Once, twice, nothing.

The MP35 was rising.

Henry froze.

Redfern cursed, wrenching the Thompson's bolt back.

Not fast enough.

The man's finger was rounding the trigger.

Bile. Swallowed.

Stop. Just stop. Don't do this.

The Colt moved, as if on its own.

Bang. The sound echoed like a hammer inside his skull.

The first shot hit the man in the stomach. His body jerked backward.

Bang.

The second hit his chest. Shell casings rattled across the floor.

The MP35 slipped from his grasp.

Forgotten.

He slumped against the wall, his breath shallow.

The mechanics had thrown themselves behind cover. For half a second, one started to rise—hands half-raised, eyes darting toward the tool bench.

Redfern cleared the jam.

"Don't shoot!" One of the mechanics shouted as he ducked once more. "Americans. We're Americans."

Like that makes a difference.

Henry looked at the German guard, watching his chest rise and fall. Blood pooled beneath him. His lips moved—a ragged cough. Blood bubbled from his lips.

"*Meine... Mutter,*" he rasped. "*Sag ihr... dass ich sie... liebe.*"

Henry stared. His heart pounded. The ringing in his ears drowned out the world.

Pain throbbed in his shoulder and his ankle. Present. But distant. Through it all, he saw only the man's eyes.

Stillness.

Another corpse. Another face to haunt him. Henry's fingers flexed. Trembled.

Then clenched it tight around the Colt. He didn't throw it this time. Twice now, it had saved him.

Shouting. Distant.

Everything had slowed.

Ben stood over the mechanics, his expression tight.

The hum in Henry's skull was fading.

"... wrong with the plane..."

The first mechanic scowled, grease streaked across his face. "Fuel pressure's unstable. Keeps choking at throttle-up."

The second mechanic threw down a wrench. "We bled the lines twice. Still sputters. Every time we push it, it stalls."

Ben's jaw clenched. "Shit." He exhaled sharply, running a hand through his hair.

"It's a fuel pressure regulator issue. It could be the lines, it could be the pump. If it craps out mid-climb, we stall. No restart."

A beat.

"But if we can get to altitude, we can glide."

He turned sharply to the mechanics. "You get the ignition sequence started. Now. If it sputters, cycle it again. Don't stop until I tell you."

The first mechanic hesitated, glancing at the blood pooling near the dead man.

Ben's voice snapped, sharp as a whip. "Move! Or I start throwing bodies out of this hangar."

The mechanic flinched, then scrambled toward the cockpit access ladder.

Redfern exhaled sharply. "How bad?"

Ben rubbed a hand down his face. "If the pump fails on climb-out, we're screwed. If it holds... we're still rolling dice."

Margaret's voice was quiet but firm. "Will it get us off the ground?"

Ben exhaled. "Yeah. But if we don't baby it, we're dead."

Henry clenched his jaw.

Not ideal. But they had no choice.

His eyes flicked to the man's body. Blood still pooled beneath him.

His stomach twisted.

He vomited.

The mechanics worked with ingrained efficiency, grumbling and cursing the madness.

Ben stood over them. Tense. Pacing. A man held together by sheer force of will.

The officer and pilot from the Great War were settling back into his bones because he had no choice.

Henry had shoved the briefcase and map into the back of the plane.

Inside, Margaret was already reading over the documents and scanning too fast, consuming information as if it would save her life. Maybe it would.

Redfern stood by the hangar door, watching the road.

Ben didn't stop moving, checking the gauges, double-checking the throttle settings, and barking at the mechanics whenever they hesitated.

This wasn't routine anymore. This was survival.

Henry checked his watch: 11:15.

Too long.

A sound. A distant hum. Henry turned toward the noise. Felt it before he truly heard it.

He crossed the hangar to Redfern.

"What is that?"

Redfern barely glanced over. "A plane. Maybe two? Sounds like the other night on the platform." He exhaled sharply. "What did Ben say they were?"

Ben looked over. "Peashooters." His voice was tight. Clipped.

Henry turned toward him. Ben wasn't looking at the tools anymore. He wasn't checking the engine. He was staring out at the night, listening. Listening, the way only a pilot would.

"Too far away. Nothing to do with us."

Henry nodded. Didn't believe him.

"How much longer?" Henry asked.

Ben exhaled sharply. He forced himself back into motion, yanking the access hatch to check something.

"We're just about to start the engine."

His hand ran down his face, fingers tightening in his hair.

A breath. He steadied himself.

"Ten minutes. Another few minutes for taxiing."

The words felt mechanical. Rehearsed.

But his hands? His hands were still shaking.

He turned back toward the plane. Didn't meet Henry's eyes.

Redfern didn't move from the hangar door. His gaze stayed locked on the snow, watching, waiting.

"So, when we get back..."

Redfern paused, collecting his thoughts.

"And you deliver the briefcase and the map to whoever you work for..."

Henry stilled.

Redfern's tone wasn't bitter. It was resigned. Measured.

"You understand your employment with Redfern Industries will no longer be valid."

Henry gave a tight smile.

"Figured as much. Your gig was getting old anyway." He smirked. "How long have you known?"

Redfern shrugged. "Couple of weeks. Jimmy tipped me off."

Henry let out a dry laugh. "*Of course it was Jimmy.*"

Redfern adjusted the Thompson slung over his shoulder. "Didn't believe him at first. Thought he was just jealous. But then this meeting came up. I had to leave you off the list. Couldn't take the risk. Jimmy pushed hard for it."

He drew a breath. "Then he got sick. That put you back in play."

A wave of the hand. "Still. We wouldn't be here without you."

Henry exhaled slowly. A long pause.

"Since we're being honest..." His voice was light, but his eyes weren't. "Natalie *Young*."

The name landed like a dropped stone.

Redfern didn't blink. "Who?"

Henry's jaw tightened. "She was head secretary. Two years ago."

Redfern shook his head. "We've had a lot of secretaries, Henry. I don't make it a habit to know them all."

"She was organizing. Starting to unionize the office."

"Was she?" A shrug. "Does she still work for me?"

"She disappeared. Right after she started."

Redfern frowned. "Disappeared?"

He glanced over, something tightening in his brow. Then—dawning. "Two years ago?"

Henry turned, staring into the storm. "Why didn't Vic come?"

Redfern squinted, lips twitching faintly. "Reporter from the Globe. Digging around. Some exposé on 'the rise of fascism in Canada.'" He smiled thinly. "Left Vic to handle it. Bit of pressure. Maybe a few late-night conversations."

Henry's throat tightened. "How much has Vic 'handled'?"

Redfern's gaze sharpened. His voice cooled.

"He keeps things quiet."

Henry's pulse kicked. "Did he handle Natalie?"

A pause.

"I don't know, Henry. I've never heard of her."

Henry studied him. The face was still. Maybe honest. Maybe not. But the ignorance felt real—and somehow, that made it worse.

Then something flickered in Redfern's eyes.

"You spoke to the reporter."

Not a question.

Henry waved a hand. "She tried to turn me. I didn't bite."

A beat.

"I tipped her off about something else, though."

Silence.

Redfern nodded. Slowly.

"You'll be hard to replace."

Henry managed a smile. "Missing me already, James?"

Redfern glanced toward the plane. "There's going to be a lot of work to do when we get back."

Then back at Henry.

"And it's Mr. Redfern, Harry."

The engine sputtered. Then quit.

Ben was in the cockpit.

Henry turned toward the plane.

It looked fine. But he wasn't a mechanic.

Again, the engine kicked in, sputtered, and coughed.

Before a roar as the engine kicked in, sputtered and came to life.

Henry clapped Redfern on the back, grinning.

"Almost there."

Redfern squinted past him. His jaw tightened.

"Shit."

Henry's stomach twisted. He turned out into the night.

Headlights. Distant. Approaching.

Three sets.

Henry and Redfern scrambled up the steps into the cabin, slamming the door behind them.

Through the cockpit window, snow swirled under the floodlights. Ben's hands were a blur across the controls.

Like a conductor before an orchestra.

Henry leaned over the seat. "How long?"

Ben didn't look up. "Never flown one of these before." His fingers flicked switches. Checked gauges. "But... it should work."

Redfern's voice was tight. "How long until we're in the air?"

Ben exhaled. "A couple more minutes. Finishing pre-flight."

Redfern's teeth clenched. "We don't have a couple of minutes."

Ben snapped his head up, eyes flashing.

"You want to take off blind? In the dark? In a fucking snowstorm? This isn't a Ford, Redfern." His hands didn't stop moving. "It takes time."

Henry's voice cut in low, firm. "They're here, Ben."

Ben swallowed.

A pause. Then, quieter, "Just buy me some time. I'll be as fast as I can."

Redfern exhaled sharply, already moving.

"You've got two minutes."

Henry rechecked the Colt. The two spare magazines lay on the wheel well, and a box of loose bullets spilled beside them.

Optimistic.

If he had to reach for those, he was already dead.

His breath came in short, ragged gasps, scraping his ribs raw. His whole body trembled, not from the cold, but from something deeper—something primal.

Across from him, Redfern crouched low behind the engine block, his magazines neatly lined up in front of him.

The Junkers' engine roared in the background, dull and hammering, as steady as his heartbeat wasn't.

He checked his watch: 11:22.

"Two minutes," he murmured. A quiet mantra. A plea.

They waited.

Watching the headlights grow closer.

The vehicles stopped beside the tower at the far end of the tarmac. Figures spilled out, disappearing into the dark. A few too many climbed the stairs into the tower.

"Shit."

Henry flicked off the safety. Redfern met his gaze, tight, pale.

Movement through the snow. Shadows against the backdrop of the lights. Shouts in the wind.

Redfern pulled the action back on the Thompson, leaning across the hood. "Wait until they're close."

Henry swallowed against the sudden, overwhelming urge to piss. Finger tightening. Aiming at a shape in the dark.

Closer.

He inhaled.

Clackclackclack.

The muzzle flashes from the Thompson ripped through the night.

Henry fired.

Bang.

Bang. Bang.

Shadows crumpled into the snow.

Silence.

The darkness erupted.

A dozen muzzle flashes.

Bullets hissed over the car. Through the car. Metal shrieked. Tires popped.

Whistling.

Too close.

Henry flattened behind the back wheel, heart hammering against his ribs.

At a glance, Redfern had done the same, crouched behind the engine block.

Of course. The engine.

Bastard. He'd known. He'd let Henry take the weaker cover.

Stillness. It was over.

Henry peeked around the wheel.

The shadows were moving and spreading out and encircling them.

His grip tightened. He raised the Colt.

Bang. Bang.

A figure crumpled.

It was easier now—shooting at shadows. Faces haunted him: the dead, the almost-dead, the ones who looked too much like him. Shadows didn't stare back. Shadows didn't beg.

Another shape moved behind the fallen one, weapon raised.

A muzzle flash.

Hiss. Hiss. Hiss.

Bullets ripped through the air.

Henry pressed himself back, heart pounding, lungs burning.

Too close.

He turned, and Redfern was still hunched low, barely peeking out.

Huddled.

This was stupid.

Henry swallowed, fingers flexing around the Colt. "Get up and shoot, James. Or we're dead."

Redfern's eyes darted to Henry — wild. Desperate.

His fingers clenched the Thompson.

No movement.

Henry sucked in a breath.

Finally, Redfern heaved the gun and fired.

Clackclackclack.

Henry leaned out.

Bang. Bang. Click.

Empty.

Fingers numb. Fumbling. Slipping.

Magazine release. The mag tumbled. Gone.

Snap. Hiss.

Steel shrieked. More bullets ripped through the car.

Redfern's voice was ragged. "We have to get back to the plane."

Henry jammed the mag home.

Racked the slide.

"Not yet."

Another snap. Hiss.

The frame groaned as the last tire collapsed.

The whole car sank off-balance.

No more cover.

A shadow, flanking.

Henry squeezed the trigger. Gone.

Another shift. Adjusting.

Too damn many.

Shit.

He shoved off the wheel well, sliding beside Redfern.

Muzzle flashes.

Hiss. Hiss. Hiss.

The stink of burning oil. Rubber. Gunpowder. The stink of death.

"We can't stay here." Redfern.

Henry swallowed.

"I'll cover. You run. Then you cover me."

For a second, Henry thought he might argue. He didn't.

Redfern leaned across the hood. "Go."

The Thompson roared.

Henry sprinted.

Whistle. Hiss. Snap.

Tripped. Snow deep, dragging him. Almost fell. Steadied. The hangar loomed. Too far.

Stumbled.

The Thompson stopped.

Henry hit the edge. Staggered inside. Around the corner.

Breathing. Burning. Chest seizing.

The hangar wall was pocked with holes. He leaned out.

Redfern was reloading. His last mag.

Henry felt around. His extra mag. The loose shells.

Back at the car.

Too many. Moving.

Redfern, waiting.

Henry leaned out, fired.

Redfern started running.

Muzzle flashed from the tower, and the snow beside him exploded.

Redfern closed the distance. Almost there.

A second flash.

His chest burst open.

Blood sprayed across the snow.

Redfern stumbled. Dropped to his knees. His hand found the wound, his face twisted, confused.

He collapsed.

Henry froze. Staring.

Redfern wasn't moving.

Hiss. Snap.

A muzzle flash from the tower.

Henry ducked. Shadows closing in. No time.

He ran.

"Where's Redfern?"

Margaret grabbed Henry's arm, yanking him inside.

"He... he's gone."

The words barely left his lips before his legs buckled. He slumped into a seat, the weight of everything crashing down at once.

The plane lurched. Moving.

Taxiing.

Shadows swarmed in the snow, shifting in the floodlights, figures with guns.

From the cockpit, Ben's voice. Urgent. Clipped.

"I could use a hand up here."

Henry sucked in a breath.

Pushed himself up.

Stumbled.

His shoulder screamed. His ribs felt like they'd crack apart.

Outside...

Muzzle flashes.

Tink. Tink. Metal shrieking as rounds chewed through the fuselage.

Margaret was behind him.

Steadying. Pushing.

He reached the cockpit.

Ben barely glanced over, hands a blur over the controls, adjusting dials, gripping the yoke.

"Have a seat."

The runway rushed toward them, no more time.

Ben's voice cut through the chaos. "I need some help. Now."

Henry collapsed into the co-pilot's seat. His fingers dug into the armrests, his chest heaving.

A headset was shoved into his hands.

"Ahh... Ben. I don't know what I'm doing."

Ben didn't look at him. His hands flicked switches, adjusted levers. "I don't need you to know. I need your hands."

Henry fumbled with the headset, forcing it on.

Dials. Levers. Switches. Nothing made sense.

Outside...

More muzzle flashes.

Snow bursting into the air.

Tink. Tink.

Bullets slamming into metal.

A dull thud, something punching through the fuselage.

Margaret's voice, shouting from the back. "We need to GO!"

A crackle in the headset.

A dead, static voice. Unintelligible.

Henry turned, squinting out the cockpit window.

A shape moved in the control tower.

A radio operator.

His stomach dropped.

Ben followed his gaze. Jaw tightening.

"Yeah. No time."

His hand shoved the throttle forward. The engines ROARED.

The Junkers lurched. A brutal, heavy movement, metal groaning as it pulled forward.

The tires splashing through snow, ice, and blood.

Headlights. Across the tarmac.

First car. Accelerating and coming fast.

Ben's fingers were white-knuckled on the yoke. "Flaps set?"

Henry blinked. Flaps? His eyes darted across the panel.

Which goddamn switch was that?

Ben barked. "Left knee! NOW!"

Henry slapped it.

The plane shuddered, airflow adjusting.

The first vehicle breached the runway.

Henry saw the muzzle flashes before he heard them.

Tink. Tink.

Rounds hammering the fuselage.

The hum. Henry's grip tightened.

Throttle forward.

All the way.

The Junkers shook, roared. The windscreen vibrated.

The first car was almost on them.

Henry glanced over; Ben was fighting the plane like it was alive.

More gunfire.

A bullet punched through the glass.

CRACK. A spiderweb fracture splintered across the cockpit.

Margaret shouted from the back.

Ben was already moving. "We're at speed. PULL."

Henry grabbed the yoke.

Ben yanked.

The nose jerked up, too much.

The plane wobbled, tilting, losing lift, and Henry's stomach lurched.

Ben adjusted, swearing through gritted teeth.

FREE.

The Junkers tore from the ground, skimming the tarmac before clawing into the sky.

Henry's stomach dropped.

The first pursuit car skidded. Too late.

The plane climbed.

Chapter XXVIII

No Way Out But Down

"VOTER SUPPRESSION ALLEGED AS VALE CLAIMS PRESIDENCY"

—*The New York Times*, November 5, 1936

"Opponents report widespread intimidation and missing ballots, but legal challenges are swiftly dismissed."

Saturday, December 4th, 1937
Airborne, New York—11:34 PM

The plane roared. Sputtered. Hummed.

Ben's grip on the yoke was white-knuckled. His shoulders were rigid, every muscle wound tight.

"We made it." His breath came out sharply. "We goddamn made it."

Henry forced a smile. He wasn't sure whether it was real.

Behind them, Margaret exhaled hard, slumping into a seat.

"I didn't think this stupid plan would work." A half-smile. Tired. "How far to the border?"

Ben shrugged, eyes flicking between the instrument panel and the black void outside. "Straight north. As the crow flies—fifty miles, maybe?"

Margaret nodded. "How long?"

Ben checked the gauges. His fingers moved constantly—adjusting, correcting, never quite settling. "Half an hour. Maybe twenty minutes."

Margaret ran a hand through her hair. "I guess I've got some reading to do." She turned and headed toward the back.

Henry watched her go, then turned to Ben. His hands hadn't stopped moving—hovering over the controls like a man waiting for the plane to betray him.

Ben barely nodded, eyes locked ahead. "She's not what I expected."

The silence stretched. Long enough for Henry's mind to drift where he never wanted it to. To boyhood. To Robbie. The older brother who had always seemed unbreakable. Until Flanders. Until the mud and the shellfire and Henry's hands pressed against a wound that wouldn't close. Eyes like his, going glassy.

The plane rocked. Time slid past in the hum of the engines. Henry wasn't sure how much.

He swallowed. "You alright?"

Ben let out a sharp breath. "No. Not exactly." His voice was tight. "This thing is much more complicated than anything I've ever flown."

Henry frowned. "You're getting us there, though?"

Ben adjusted his grip, shifting his weight against the seat. "We'll find out in about twenty minutes."

The plane shuddered.

Henry's stomach lurched. His fingers dug into the seat.

Steady again.

"We'll keep her low. Just above the tree line."

Henry nodded. Fifty miles. Just a little longer.

"What happened with Redfern?" Ben's tone was flat, but something was there. Something unspoken.

Henry looked over at him. What was his response? How could he tell him? It was his fault.

"A shot from the tower..." Henry's throat tightened. "He was running back. I could have—"

Ben's eyes flicked over. "You could have what, Harry?"

Henry shrugged. The words felt hollow. "I should have done better."

Ben's hands flexed on the yoke. His voice was even. Too even. "That tower was what—three hundred yards? Four hundred?"

Henry barely nodded.

Ben's eyes moved to the Colt in Henry's lap. "What were you gonna do with that pistol, Harry? Shoot the guy?"

Henry's breath hitched. His jaw tightened. "No. I could've got him."

Ben's brow furrowed. "Who?"

Henry scratched at his face. "Redfern."

Silence.

Ben pressed his lips together. "Where was he hit?"

"Hole through his chest."

He was quiet for a moment. His hands flexed over the yoke, knuckles white. "Redfern was dead in minutes, Harry. Maybe seconds. Nothing you could do."

Henry didn't answer. He stared out the window. Snow. Trees. The void stretched forever.

Nothing you could do.

The words didn't make it feel any less like his fault.

The hum of the engines filled the silence.

Margaret's head poked through the cockpit doorway. "How are we doing?"

Ben's hands didn't stop moving. His expression didn't change. "Five minutes. Maybe ten."

Margaret crossed her arms, frowning slightly. "Not like there's a bright line across the border, huh?"

Ben snorted—just the ghost of a laugh. "No. Just trees, and a whole lot of nothing."

Margaret lingered a moment, watching them both. She studied Henry's face. He didn't look up. Finally, she nodded once and disappeared back into the cabin.

The quiet stretched. Nothing but the drone of the engines. The faint creak of the fuselage.

Henry closed his eyes.

Just get over the border.

Thmp. Thmp.

The fuselage trembled—a dull, rattling shudder. Henry snapped upright. Ben's head jerked up, eyes darting to the gauges.

Another burst.

THMPTHMPTHMPTHMP.

A stuttered impact—louder, harder. Like a hammer smashing against the metal skin of the plane.

The cockpit shook. Henry twisted toward the window—his breath caught. Sparks spat from the left wingtip. A jagged line of bullet holes tore across it, metal curling back like peeled skin. His stomach plummeted.

"Shit—those damn Peashooters!" The yoke jerked violently in Ben's hands. The whole plane pitched as bullets ripped through the fuselage.

Margaret's voice—sharp, urgent. "What the hell was that?!"

Henry twisted, but the motion slammed him back into his seat.

THMPTHMPTHMPTHMP.

The cockpit shuddered. The gauges spun wildly, dials swinging erratically.

Henry hit a switch on instinct. He didn't know which. Didn't care.

Ben gritted his teeth, forcing the yoke forward. The plane dropped low, skimming the blackened forest. "They were ready for us," Ben muttered, staring at the skyline. "Too ready."

Henry looked out the window, searching the darkness for the aircraft. "Kessler told them. He had to."

Trees blurred past.

Henry craned his neck, scanning the darkness above. The field of vision was too tight.

"*Goddamnit.*"

THMPTHMPTHMPTHMP.

Another burst. Another impact. A second plane.

The Junkers lurched—metal screaming, fuel leaking.

Ben fought the controls. "Dammit." His voice was strained, his knuckles white.

Ahead—bright lights. A city.

Henry's breath caught. "Is that...?"

"Yep." Ben's words were taut. "Montreal."

"We're over the border?"

Ben didn't answer.

The Peashooters were still on them. Still raining hell. Ben banked left, always north.

THMPTHMPTHMPTHMP.

A scream—Margaret. Henry twisted—too fast. The plane's sudden tilt threw him back. He clawed for the harness, straining to see into the darkened cabin.

Nothing. No movement.

Ahead, lights on the ground. A landing strip. Somewhere.

Henry turned back, face pale. "*That has to be home.*"

Ben grimaced. "That's the plan." His fingers tightened on the yoke. "And we just have to hope."

The cockpit lights flickered.

The starboard engine exploded.

A fireball burst from the wing.

Ben's eyes widened. Horror. "Shit. Shit. Shit."

The cockpit glowed orange, flames licking across the wing surface. Ben's hand slammed a switch. The fire flickered. Burned. Died. A pause. A breath.

The engine was dead.

Ben stared at the panel. "We're coasting in."

Henry's eyes moved across the gauges, then out into the darkness. "Can we make it?"

Ben's grip tightened. "*Stop asking me that.*"

Henry looked back into the cabin and pushed himself up. "I need to check on her."

"No," Ben said flatly. "You have to help me get us down. Or else none of this will have mattered."

Ben's hands worked furiously—adjusting trim, levelling out the descent. Every movement calculated, every breath measured. Henry could barely think. The plane was dying beneath them.

Ben's voice cut through the chaos. "We're coming in fast. Need your hands—now."

Henry's fingers fumbled.

"Focus," Ben snapped.

Henry swallowed. "What do I do?"

"Flaps—set to full."

Henry found the lever. Pulled it down. The plane lurched. Slowed.

Ben adjusted the yoke. "Gear down—if it still works."

Henry hit the switch. A mechanical whine rattled the cabin.

THMPTHMPTHMPTHMP.

A final burst from the Peashooters. Henry ducked, throwing his arms over his head.

Margaret screamed again from the back.

Metal shrieked—another volley tore through the frame.

The Peashooters climbed sharply. They weren't sticking around.

Henry watched their silhouettes bank south. Not retreating. Just leaving them to die.

Ben's voice was tight. "We're losing her. Fast."

The ground was coming up—too fast.

"Brace. Brace. Brace."

A flick of a switch. Fuel cut-off.

Henry clutched the sides of his seat. The nose pitched up.

"Hold it, hold it, hold it—"

Then the world lurched, metal shrieking as the plane slammed down.

The first bounce threw Henry's head into the panel. Sparks burst across his vision. His shoulder screamed.

The second bounce was worse.

With a sickening CRACK, Ben slammed forward against the yoke—blood from somewhere.

The landing gear snapped. The nose pitched forward—grinding—skidding, metal shrieking.

A final heave. A spin.

Snow exploded.

Stillness.

The world was tilted. Crooked. Wrong.

Something dripped. Fuel? Blood?

Henry's breath shuddered. Ben groaned beside him—still breathing.

From the back came Margaret's voice, weak and pained. "...Henry..."

He tried to move. Couldn't.

His fingers twitched. His ribs screamed. His body refused. Smoke filled his lungs. The cold pressed in.

Maybe they'd done something.

Maybe Natalie would be proud.

This was it.

Blackness.

Just the burning wreckage of their escape.

Epilogue

"DEFENCE OF CANADA ACT PASSES PARLIAMENT"
—The Toronto Star, May 12, 1935

"Building on last year's Canadian Jobs Act, which put nearly 200,000 men into part-time military service, the new Act expands airfields, munitions works, and militia training. Cabinet officials insist the measures are 'strictly defensive, ensuring stability at home.'"

Sunday, December 5th, 1937
Ottawa, Ontario—5:35 AM

The phone rang.

Henshaw groaned, rubbing sleep from his eyes. He rolled over and reached for the receiver.

"Henshaw." His voice was rough, half-awake.

"Sir, there's been an accident. A plane crash."

The voice was tight. Quebecois. Strained.

Henshaw sat up. The fog in his head cleared in an instant. "Where?"

"Fifteen miles south of Montreal." A pause longer than it needed to be. "The thing is, sir..." A breath. "American planes were spotted crossing the border."

Henshaw's stomach turned. His fingers tightened around the receiver. "What are you saying?"

The voice on the line was quiet. Flat. "The Americans shot it down."

The words landed like a stone.

"Where was it coming from?"

"Lake Placid."

Silence.

"Survivors?"

A crackle on the line.

"Yes, sir. Three. One's in critical condition."

Henshaw rubbed the bridge of his nose. "Lock it down," he said, forcing calmness into his voice. "No press. Arrange my car and a train. I'm going to Montreal."

Acknowledgements

This book wouldn't exist without all the wonderful people who kept me going through every draft, rewrite, and crisis.

To my ARC team, thank you for your thoughtful feedback and for catching those final details. You made this book stronger.

To Alysha Thornton and Michelle McGuire, your edits and many corrections were insightful, sharp, and invaluable.

To Duey, your cover was everything I hoped for and more. Your talent knows no bounds.

To Rhea, thank you for always believing in me.

To my family, for allowing me to disappear into the past long enough to finish this.

And to everyone who read the early chapters, offered encouragement, or simply believed I'd get to the end—thank you. You did this with me.

About the author

C.M. Grant is a writer and revenue manager based in Ontario, Canada. When he isn't dissecting data or chasing his kids, he's writing; usually stories or roleplaying adventures about power, loyalty, and the thin line between conviction and corruption.

Beneath the Eagle's Shadow is his debut novel. He is currently at work on its sequel, *Under the Eagle's Eye.*

He lives with his wife, three kids, two cats, a dog, and far too many notebooks.

Manufactured by Amazon.ca
Acheson, AB

31402086R00173